KT-477-883

THE MARRIAGE
HE DEMANDS

BRENDA JACKSON

BLUE COLLAR
BILLIONAIRE

KAREN BOOTH

MILLS & BOON

First Published in Great Britain 2021
by Mills & Boon, an imprint of HarperCollins*Publishers* Ltd
1 London Bridge Street, London, SE1 9GF

www.harpercollins.co.uk

HarperCollins*Publishers*
1st Floor, Watermarque Building,
Ringsend Road, Dublin 4, Ireland

The Marriage He Demands © 2021 Brenda Streater Jackson
Blue Collar Billionaire © 2021 Harlequin Books S.A.

Special thanks and acknowledgement are given to Karen Booth for her contribution to the *Texas Cattleman's Club: Heir Apparent* series.

ISBN: 978-0-263-28286-3

0321

MIX
Paper from
responsible sources
FSC™ C007454

THE MARRIAGE
HE DEMANDS

BRENDA JACKSON

To the man who will always and forever be the love of
my life, Gerald Jackson Sr.

Therefore shall a man leave his father and his mother,
and shall cleave unto his wife: and they shall be
one flesh.
—Genesis 2:24

One

"What's wrong, Cash?"

Cashen Outlaw eased down into the chair in front of his brother Garth's desk. He then said the words he'd never thought about saying. "Bart just called. He got word that Ellen has died."

Garth Outlaw leaned forward in his chair as he studied his brother. "I'm sorry to hear that, Cash."

Cash nodded, at the moment not able to reply. Their father, Bart, had been married five times. Each of his sons had a different mother. Ellen had been Bart's third wife, and Cash's mother. Like the two wives before her and the two after, Bart had managed to divorce Ellen and get full custody of any child born to their union.

Cash didn't really recall his mother. He still had a picture of her tucked away that had yellowed with age. She was the only one of the five wives who'd called Bart's bluff and took him to court for custody of their son. She lost the battle and was never heard from again. Over the years, Cash hadn't received even a telephone call, birthday card or holiday greeting. It was as if she'd dropped off the face of the earth.

He had often thought about finding her, but didn't want to risk the pain of rejection like Garth had felt when he'd found his mother. Over the years Cash had decided that if his mother ever wanted to see him, she knew where he was. He and his family still lived in Fairbanks, Alaska, where their multimillion-dollar company, Outlaw Freight Lines, was located.

"When is the funeral, so the four of us can be there for you? I'll let Sloan, Maverick and Jess know. Charm won't be returning from Australia until next month."

Twenty-five-year-old Charm was their only sister and the youngest of all Bart's offspring. To this day, Charm's mother, Claudia, was the only woman Bart had ever loved, and she'd been the only one Bart had not married...but not for lack of trying.

"No need. Ellen didn't want a memorial service, and there won't be a funeral either. According to the information Bart received, Ellen wanted her body donated to science. Her attorney wants me there for the reading of the will on Friday. I'm surprised I was named in it."

"And where are you headed?" Garth asked his brother.

"A place called Black Crow, Wyoming."

"Do you need Regan to fly you there in the company plane? I can go along for support if you need it." Regan was the company pilot and Garth's wife. They had been married for nearly ten months.

"Black Crow is right outside of Laramie. I plan to gas up my plane and fly myself since it's less than a five-hour trip from here."

Cash and all his siblings had their pilot licenses. Due to Alaska's very limited road system, one of the most common ways of getting around was by aircraft. Locals liked to say that more Alaskans owned personal planes than cars.

"Okay, but if you change your mind, let me know."

"I will."

Two days later, Cash flew his Cessna to the Laramie Regional Airport. He'd ordered a rental car to be there when he arrived, and it was. Shifting his cell phone to the other ear, he tossed his overnight bag in the back seat as he continued his conversation with his sister, Charm. She was calling from Australia with her condolences.

Charm had tagged along with Garth's best friend, Walker Rafferty, and his wife, Bailey, on a trip to visit Bailey's sister, Gemma, who lived in Australia.

"Thanks, Charm, but you know the real deal with this. It's not like me and Ellen had a close relationship. Like I told Garth, I'm surprised she remembered I existed long enough to put me in a will."

Cash glanced at his watch before starting the car and switching the phone call to the vehicle's speaker system. He would get a good night's sleep, and be at the meeting with the attorney in the morning at eleven. Then he would leave, head back to the airport and fly home to Fairbanks.

"I need to end the call, Charm, so I can concentrate on following the directions to Black Crow. I'll talk to you later, kid."

As Cash headed for the interstate, he thought about the conversation he'd had with his father before leaving. Bart was typical Bart. Even with six adult offspring, their old man still assumed it was his God-given right to stick his nose into their business when it didn't concern him.

Cash had put Bart in his place just that morning when he'd tried telling Cash to make sure he got everything his mother owned because it was rightly due him. Cash had made it clear to Bart that he didn't want a single thing. He'd even seriously thought about not showing up for the reading of the will. As far as he was concerned, it was too late for Ellen to make up for the years she had been absent from his life. The only reason he had decided to come was for closure.

The drive from Laramie to Black Crow took less than an hour. He couldn't help wondering when his mother had moved to Wyoming. According to Bart, when she left Fairbanks thirty-four years ago, she had moved to New York.

Cash saw the marker denoting the entrance into Black Crow's city limits, and recalled all he'd learned from doing an internet search last night before going to bed. It had first been inhabited by the Black Crow Indian tribe, from which the town derived its name. The present population was less than two thousand people, and most fought to retain an old-town feel, which was evident by the architecture of the buildings. He'd read that if any of the inhabitants thought Black Crow wasn't progressive enough for them, they were quickly invited to leave. But few people left and most had lived in the area for years. It was a close-knit place.

He came to a traffic light and watched numerous people walking around, going into the various shops. As he sat there, tapping his hand on the steering wheel, his gaze homed in on a woman who was walking out of an ice-cream shop. She was strikingly beautiful. He couldn't help noticing how she worked her mouth on her ice-cream cone, and he could just imagine her working her mouth on him the same way.

Cash drew in a deep breath as he shifted in the seat. She looked pretty damn good in her pullover sweater and a pair of jeans. If she was a sampling of what Black Crow had to offer, then maybe he needed to hang around for another day or two and not be so quick to leave town tomorrow.

He chuckled, thinking it would take more than a beautiful face and a gorgeous body to keep him in this town. Besides, he doubted that even if he stayed he'd be able to find her. He had more to do with his time than chase down a woman. Chances were, she was wearing some guy's ring. There was no way a woman who looked like her was not spoken for.

The driver behind him beeped his horn to let Cash know the traffic light had changed and it was time to move on.

Not able to resist temptation, he glanced back for one final look at the woman and saw she was gone.

Just as well.

Brianna Banks entered the attorney's office the next morning. "Good morning, Lois."

The older woman glanced up at Brianna and smiled. "Good morning, Brianna. You're early."

"Is Mr. Cavanaugh in?"

"Yes, he's here, and since you and Mr. Outlaw are the only two needed for the reading of the will, we can get started as soon as he arrives." Lois Inglese then leaned over the desk and said in a low voice, "I didn't know Ellen had a son. Did you?"

Brianna drew in a deep breath. She liked Lois. Had known the fifty-something-year-old woman all her life. The one thing she also knew was that Lois had a penchant for gossip. More than once, Lois had gotten in hot water with Mr. Cavanaugh for discussing things that should be confidential.

"I'd rather not say, Lois." Brianna checked her watch. "If you don't mind, I'll take a seat over there and wait."

Lois's smile faded when she realized Brianna would not divulge any information.

Brianna crossed the room to take a chair by the window that overlooked Eagle Bend River. Although she had known about Ellen's son, Lois was the last person Brianna would admit anything to. She'd also known of their strained relationship, which was the main reason Brianna was prepared to not like him. Besides, there was a chance he might not show up today.

She picked up a magazine, deciding that whether the man showed up was not her concern. Brianna was thankful that Ellen had thought enough of her to include her in the will. She would appreciate whatever Ellen left for her.

Everything Brianna had done for Ellen in her final days had been because Brianna had wanted to do so. Ellen had been there for her when she'd been a kid who lived on the Blazing Frontier Dude Ranch. Brianna's mother had managed the ranch and her father had been head foreman.

Brianna glanced up when the door opened and a tall, handsome man walked in. She recognized him immediately. She had seen a picture of him once, when he'd been ten years or so younger. She'd thought he was a hottie then. However, the man she saw now was so strikingly handsome, she could say she had never seen a man who looked that gorgeous before in her life.

The man was none other than Ms. Ellen's son, Cashen Outlaw.

From where Brianna was sitting, on the other side of the huge potted plant, he couldn't see her, which gave her the perfect opportunity to ogle him. He was dressed to the nines in a dark business suit. Very few men in Black Crow wore business suits; they probably didn't even own one. That included the attorneys and politicians. This was strictly a jeans and Western shirt town. Heck, they didn't even dress up for church.

The only time she saw a man in a suit these days was at funerals or when she drove into Laramie. Even Jackson, which was considered the top city in Wyoming when it came to education, jobs and other amenities, still had a very casual dress code. But she had no problem looking at this man, especially when the suit appeared tailor-made just for him.

She figured his height was every bit of six-two or three, and all she saw was his profile. That was enough to send sensations she hadn't felt in months—even years—flowing through her. She couldn't hear exactly what he was saying to Lois, but it was obvious the older woman was hanging on his every word. That proved a woman was never too old to appreciate a nice-looking man.

She really couldn't blame Lois. Cashen Outlaw had a commanding presence. A prime example of raw male power and self-confidence.

At that moment Henry Cavanaugh's office door opened and the older man, who'd been practicing law in Black Crow before Brianna was born, stepped out wearing jeans and a crisply starched chambray shirt.

Mr. Cavanaugh smiled at her and said, "Hello, Brianna." He shook her hand before moving toward the other man, introducing himself.

That is when Cashen glanced over at her, seeing her for the first time. The moment their gazes connected she felt weak in the knees. Lordy, he had beautiful almond-colored skin, a striking pair of dark eyes and hair that was neatly trimmed. He had a square-cut jaw and a wide, firm mouth with full lips that was perfect for his face. What really had her heart racing was a sexy pair of dimples that came into full display when he smiled.

He moved to stand beside Mr. Cavanaugh, and she saw how well his suit accentuated his solid frame. She had a feeling he would look absolutely male in anything he wore. And he smelled good. She was certain the arousing scent was him and not Mr. Cavanaugh.

"Let me introduce the two of you," Mr. Cavanaugh was saying, breaking into her thoughts. "Cashen Outlaw, this is Brianna Banks. She is the other person named in your mother's will."

If Mr. Cavanaugh's revelation surprised him, the man didn't show it. He merely extended his hand out to her. "Nice meeting you, Brianna."

"Same here, Cashen."

His smiled widened a fraction when he said, "Please, just Cash."

"Cash," she repeated, not able to tear her gaze from his. He was still holding her hand and his touch felt downright overwhelming.

"The two of you can step into my office."

With Mr. Cavanaugh's statement, Cash released her hand and said, "After you, Brianna."

"Thank you."

She followed Mr. Cavanaugh, and Cash brought up the rear. She did not have to glance over at Lois to know the older woman's eyes had watched their every move. At the moment Brianna didn't care. Her main concern was how she would share the same space with Cash Outlaw and keep herself from drooling.

Two

It's her.

Brianna Banks was the woman Cash had seen yesterday licking that ice-cream cone. The woman whose mouth he had fantasized about ever since. And she had known Ellen? In what capacity? Since she was here for the reading of the will, he hoped like hell she wasn't a sister he hadn't known about. He would soon find out.

They were sitting in front of Henry Cavanaugh's desk. The man had opened a folder and was flipping through papers. Brianna was staring straight ahead, and Cash was staring at her. At that moment he couldn't stop even if he wanted to.

And she isn't wearing a ring.

He thought the same thing now that he had thought when he'd seen her yesterday. She was simply gorgeous. Everything about her was a heart-stopper. Whether it was the dark curly hair on her head that seemed to lie perfectly around her shoulders, or her striking features or her long, regal neck.

As if she sensed him staring, she glanced over at him and their gazes met. She had a gorgeous pair of dark eyes, a delicately shaped nose and glossy lips, beautifully shaped, succulent and sexy. They were perfect for her face. Perfect for her ice cream. Perfect for his—

"Okay, Cash and Brianna, I am ready to begin."

Mr. Cavanaugh's words had him snatching his gaze from hers.

"'I, Ellen Cashen Embelin, hereby bequeath all my possessions to the following. To my son, Cashen Outlaw, I am leaving you the Blazing Frontier Dude Ranch and the acres it sits on. This will include the barns, detached cottages and contents. Cashen, I am also leaving you all the animals, inventory, merchandise and vehicles. Furthermore, I am leaving you all the proceeds from my insurance policies with Mission Care Mutual and one half of whatever funds I have in my checking and savings accounts, my stocks, bonds and investment portfolio. The other half goes to Brianna Banks.'"

Mr. Cavanaugh paused a minute as he flipped over the sheet of paper. "'To Brianna Banks. In addition to those things named earlier, I am leaving you the foreman house that your parents lived in, that you are now living in, all its contents and the fifty acres it sits upon. I am also leaving you the additional fifty acres that connect to the Blazing Frontier Dude Ranch and back into the Keystone River. I am asking that both you and Cashen, together, go through my personal things, including the boxes in the attic, and jointly decide how the items will be disposed of. This is not a stipulation but a request.'"

Mr. Cavanaugh released a deep sigh and then said, "That's the end of it and should cover everything. I am giving both of you copies of the will." He handed them packets. "Also included is a land surveyor diagram of the one hundred acres that were a part of the Blazing Frontier properties that you now own, Brianna. Are there any questions?"

Cash had one. He still did not know what relationship Brianna had with Ellen. While Cavanaugh had been reciting the will, Cash had seen the tears falling down her cheeks. Curiosity got the best of him.

"Yes, I have one," he said.

"And what is your question, Cash?" Mr. Cavanaugh asked, looking at him intently while leaning back in his chair.

"My question is for Brianna," he said, switching his gaze from Mr. Cavanaugh to her. "What was your relationship to my mother?"

Brianna was so touched by what Ellen had left her in the will that she was too overwhelmed to speak. It took her a moment to pull herself together before she could answer Cash.

"My parents worked at the Blazing Frontier Dude Ranch. My father worked as foreman even before it was a dude ranch, for over forty years, and my mother, close to thirty as ranch manager. As part of Dad's employment, they got to live in the foreman's house. That's the house I was raised in, and the house Ms. Ellen just left for me in her will. Mom died five years ago while I was in college. After college I returned home and replaced her as ranch manager."

"What about your father? Is he still foreman?"

"No. My father died last year."

"I'm sorry to hear that."

"Thanks."

Brianna wondered if he'd asked her because he intended to contest the will. What Ellen had left her—half of her financial assets, the house and one hundred acres of land— had been way too generous.

Cash then turned his attention back to Mr. Cavanaugh. "I have no other questions, but it would help if you could recommend a good real estate agent in the area."

The older man lifted a brow. "Real estate agent?"

"Yes, I would like to put the ranch up for sale as soon as possible."

"But you haven't seen it," Brianna said, even though she didn't have a right to question him.

Cash evidently thought the same thing when he switched his gaze to her. The smile was no longer in his eyes. "I don't need to see it, Brianna. I have no desire to own a dude ranch. Is it still even operational?"

"Not at the moment," Brianna said, trying to hide her disappointment, but knowing she should not be surprised he didn't want the ranch. "It was closed down when Ellen's health began failing. But it can be operational again. When it was open, we operated at full capacity and always had a waiting list."

She was certain Cash heard the excitement in her voice, but he merely nodded and said, "All of that is interesting, but I still plan to sell it."

"I hate to scurry you two off, but I have another appointment in a few minutes," Henry Cavanaugh said, breaking into their conversation, as he glanced at his watch. "You are welcome to use one of my conference rooms if you'd like to continue the conversation."

Brianna could see Cash's mind was made up. She was about to say there was no reason for them to continue their conversation when Cash spoke.

"Continuing the conversation is a great idea, but I prefer not to use one of your conference rooms." He then turned to Brianna Banks. "Would you join me for lunch?"

"Is there a place you suggest, Brianna?" Cash asked as they stepped out of Mr. Cavanaugh's office.

"There is a café if you like hamburgers. Monroe's. And they have the best fries."

He smiled. "I love hamburgers and fries."

"We won't have to move our cars since it's in walking distance. Right on the corner."

"Okay."

When they were leaving, Lois smiled at them before saying, "I hope the two of you have a good day."

"You as well, Lois," Brianna said when Cash opened the door for her. She had a feeling news about Cash would be all over town by evening.

"Is it always this windy here?" he asked, tightening his jacket as they walked.

Brianna tightened hers as well. "Yes, and the wind today is rather mild. There is a scientific reason for all the wind."

He glanced over at her. "Is there?"

"Yes. The town is located right between the mountains. Instead of blocking the wind, the mountains make it move faster. Then the high air pressure across the Great Basin and lower pressure in the Plains make it stronger. This is mild. The worst of it is during the winter. Can you imagine all that wind combined with snow?"

He chuckled. "I can but I'd rather not. Alaska has its own weather issues."

"Yet you like living there?"

"I love it. It's home for me, and I'm used to the harsh weather. I can't imagine living anywhere else. Though I did live in Massachusetts while getting my master's degree from Harvard."

"In what field?" she asked him.

"Engineering." He looked over at her. "What college did you attend and what was your field of study?"

"I have a bachelor's degree in business administration from Clark Atlanta University," she said when they reached the corner. They paused for the traffic light to change before crossing the street.

"How did you like living in Atlanta?"

"It was quite an experience. I had never been anywhere other than Wyoming. I even thought of staying and getting a job there. But then Mom died in my senior year and it seemed to take me forever to fly back home for Dad. After her funeral, I returned to school just long enough to graduate. Then I returned to Black Crow and haven't left since."

They reached the café. "We're here."

He positioned his body next to her to block the wind and opened the door. She would admit the warmth from the huge fireplace felt inviting today. "We can grab that table over there, Cash," she said and led him toward it.

Brianna didn't miss the interest they were generating as they crossed the room. Most of the people knew her, but they didn't know him. Not yet anyway. Lois would make sure they did before nightfall.

"Nice view," he said, glancing out the window. "This town sure has a lot of lakes."

She smiled. "Yes, we do. There are six in all, not counting the ones on the outskirts of town where most of the ranching is. Then there is the Keystone River. Most people who come here for the first time say Black Crow is definitely one of Wyoming's best-kept secrets."

After their waitress brought their drinks and took their order, Brianna glanced up from sipping her tea to find Cash staring at her. The dark eyes holding hers were mysterious and breathtaking—hypnotic. She broke eye contact with him to get her bearings.

"So," he said, returning to their previous conversation, "you've never felt adventurous? Wanted to go other places? Visit other states? See the world?"

She shrugged.

There was no need to tell him there had been a time when she thought she would get that opportunity. That's when she and Alan Dawkins had been together. They had dated all through high school and he had graduated the year before her. Their goal had been for him to join the army after high school and then return to Black Crow when she graduated the following year. They would marry and she would be an army wife, the mother of his children, and travel the world with him.

Things didn't quite work out that way. While stationed

in Germany, Alan met someone. He had returned home
the year she had graduated like he had promised, but he'd
brought his German wife with him. At least he'd had the
decency to write to tell her beforehand. Everyone in town
had pitied her and had considered Alan's betrayal unfor-
giveable. That's why her parents had encouraged her to
put as much distance between her and Black Crow as she
could for college. They figured Atlanta, Georgia, would
be far enough.

"Maybe at one time I did," she finally answered, "but
I got over it."

It was then that the waitress delivered their lunch.

Three

Cash enjoyed the delicious hamburger and fries, but found he was enjoying Brianna's company even more. He loved the sound of her voice and definitely liked looking at her. And if he thought her mouth was incredible, then her eyes followed closely. Whenever she looked at him, they exuded a sensuality that she probably didn't even know she had. If she did, she wouldn't look at him the way he'd caught her doing.

It had gotten quiet between them but now that their meal was almost over, he got down to the real reason he had invited her to lunch. He wanted to know more about her.

But before he could ask her a question, she said, "I guess you want me to tell you all about Ms. Ellen."

He took a sip of his water. He could certainly see how she assumed that, but she was wrong. There was nothing he wanted to know about the woman who had deserted him thirty-four years ago. He'd rather she told him more about herself, but he had time, so he would let her tell him about Ellen first.

"What do you want to tell me? It's been thirty-four years since I last saw her."

"Not since you were a baby, right?"

He lifted a brow, wondering how much she knew. "You've known Ellen for your whole life, for twenty-three years, right?"

"Close to twenty-eight. I have a birthday coming up this summer."

She was twenty-seven? She definitely looked a lot younger. Her copper-colored skin was smooth, soft, ageless and flawless.

"How long were she and Van Embelin married?"

"Ten years before he died. Mr. Van was older than Ms. Ellen by seventeen years, but they were very dedicated to each other. My parents said she made him feel young again. Restored his vitality. Made him smile."

Cash lifted a brow. "He had stopped smiling?"

"Yes. When his wife died of cancer, he became a recluse for close to five years. Ms. Ellen brought him out of it."

Cash paused and then asked, "Did Ellen tell you how long it'd been since she'd seen me?" He convinced himself that he was only asking out of curiosity.

"I understand she took your father to court for custody of you and lost."

"Yes, that's true." Cash decided not to go into how Bart managed to do that during a time when most courts sympathized with the mother. Cash and his brothers were well aware that in Bart's world, their father had had the money and the means to do whatever the hell he wanted to do and usually did. However, that did not excuse Ellen not reaching out to him at some point over the past thirty-four years. She had known where he was. Someone definitely knew how to contact Bart when she passed away.

"Was the Blazing Frontier always a dude ranch?" he asked, to take the subject off him.

Brianna's smile brightened. "No. Turning it into a dude ranch was Ellen's idea. At first the town balked at the idea, knowing that meant a lot of tourists in town, and they weren't sure they would like it. But Ellen somehow convinced them it would be good for the economy and to give it a try for a year. After that time, if the dude ranch had a negative effect on the town, then they would go back to regular ranching."

Cash took a sip of his lemonade. "I take it things went well."

"Better than anyone expected. Even the naysayers had to concede having the dude ranch on the outskirts of town was a great idea. It attracted people who appreciated the Old West and wanted to recapture those times. Those tourists often came into town and spent money. Lots of it." She paused. "The economy took a hit when the ranch shut down. The people of Black Crow would love for it to reopen."

Cash knew what Brianna was hinting at. Evidently, he hadn't made himself clear in Henry Cavanaugh's office. Hopefully he would this time. "Then I'm hoping whoever buys it will make it back into a dude ranch. Let's just hope there is an interested buyer."

Brianna frowned. "Oh, trust me, there will definitely be an interested buyer."

Under other circumstances he would be glad to hear that, but from her tone he had a feeling the person Brianna suspected would want to buy it was someone she'd rather not own it. Cash didn't say anything, refusing to get involved in small-town drama. It didn't matter to him who bought the ranch as long as the sale was quick.

When the waitress returned to remove their plates, he said, "Mr. Cavanaugh never did mention the name of a real estate agent. Possibly you can."

Her frown deepened. "Are you really going to sell the Blazing Frontier without even taking the time to look at it? It's a beautiful place."

"I'm sure it is, but I have no need of a ranch, dude or otherwise."

"I think you're making a mistake, Cash."

Cash lifted a brow. Normally, he didn't care what any

person, man or woman, thought about any decision he made, but for some reason what she thought mattered.

It shouldn't.

What he should do was thank her for joining him for lunch, and tell her not to walk back to Cavanaugh's office with him, although he knew both their cars were parked there. In other words, he should put as much distance between them as possible.

I can't.

Maybe it was the way her luscious mouth tightened when she was not happy about something. He'd picked up on it twice now. Lord help him but he didn't want to see it a third time. He'd rather see her smile, lick an ice-cream cone or...lick him.

He quickly forced the last image from his mind but not before a hum of lust shot through his veins. There had to be a reason he was so attracted to her. Maybe he could blame it on the Biggins deal Garth had closed just months before he'd gotten engaged to Regan. That had taken working endless days and nights, and for the past year Cash's social life had been practically nonexistent.

On the other hand, even without the Biggins deal as an excuse, there was strong sexual chemistry radiating between them. He felt it, but honestly wasn't sure that even at twenty-seven she recognized it for what it was.

That was intriguing, to the point that he was tempted to hang around Black Crow another day. Besides, he was a businessman, and no businessman would sell or buy anything without checking it out first. He was letting his personal emotions around Brianna cloud what was usually a very sound business mind.

"You are right, Brianna. I would be making a mistake if I didn't at least see the ranch before selling it. Is now a good time?"

The huge smile that spread across her face was priceless...

and mesmerizing. When was the last time a woman, any woman, had this kind of effect on him? When he felt spell-bound? He concluded that never had a woman captivated him like Brianna Banks was doing.

"Not sure if today would be okay with you dressed as you are now. Unless you brought a pair of jeans with you."

He chuckled, knowing she had a point. "I didn't, but I'm sure there's a store in town where I can purchase more clothes."

"Of course. Roy's Circle O is only two doors down and has a good selection of items."

Cash nodded. When he returned to Alaska, he would have no reason to ever return here. No reason to ever see her again. So, the way he saw it, he could definitely wait another couple days to leave. "How about if we get together tomorrow morning around ten? Will you be available to show me around the ranch then?"

If he had thought her smile could not get any more enchanting, he'd been wrong. With that kind of smile, he would give her practically anything just to see it on those sensuous lips.

"Yes, I'll be available, and it's best to see it by horse-back. Can you ride a horse?"

He could not help but return her smile. "Yes, I can ride and I look forward to seeing you again in the morning, Brianna."

Brianna was in a good mood when she got home an hour or so later. Ms. Ellen had certainly made her day with what she had left Brianna in the will. Now she was look-ing forward to showing Cash Outlaw around the Blazing Frontier tomorrow. She hoped that once he saw the ranch for himself he would want to keep it.

There was no doubt in her mind that once Hal Sutherland heard the ranch was for sale, he would jump at the chance to buy it. Hal was Mr. Van Embelin's nephew—his first wife's brother's son. Hal had never wanted Mr. Van to re-marry, hoping that would make him Mr. Van's heir. Then the Blazing Frontier would one day be his. Hal's property bordered the Blazing Frontier.

Needless to say, Hal hadn't been happy when Mr. Van had married Ms. Ellen. When Mr. Van died, Hal offered to buy the ranch. He didn't think Ms. Ellen had the grit to operate a working ranch. Ms. Ellen, with Brianna's parents' help, along with all the ranch hands who'd become loyal to her, proved Hal wrong. He hadn't liked that either and tried causing problems.

When Ms. Ellen became ill, Hal again figured he would be her heir. After all, it had been his family's land origi-nally. Hal had begun boasting about what he planned to do with the Blazing Frontier even before Ellen had taken her last breath.

Brianna figured he would know by now—thanks to Lois—that the reading of Ms. Ellen's will had occurred today and since he hadn't been summoned to the reading, he was not in the will. Hal probably also would discover, at the same time most of the townspeople did, that Ellen had left mostly everything, including the Blazing Frontier, to her son. A son only very few people knew about.

Now it seemed Hal might get the land anyway, although he would have to pay for it. He wouldn't like the fact that Ms. Ellen had left those fifty acres on the Keystone River to Brianna. Ellen had to have known those fifty acres and the waterway were vital if anyone ever turned the dude ranch back into a working ranch for cattle. Without water access, the cows would die of thirst unless the owners came up with another alternative to provide adequate water to their herds.

If Cash sold the ranch to Hal, she anticipated nothing but endless drama for her. Hal was a mean rascal who was used to getting what he wanted—except from his fearless adversary, Ms. Ellen, who refused to let him bully her.

After leaving the café, she and Cash had walked back to their cars. Instead of leaving right away as he'd done, she had sat in her car and reread the papers Mr. Cavanaugh had given to her. Everything was legal and final. This house that her parents had never owned was now hers.

Brianna had known about Cash because Ms. Ellen had confided in her years ago. Brianna had begged Ellen to let her contact Cash when her illness got worse, but Ellen had refused. Before she died, Ellen had given Brianna power of attorney to handle her affairs until the reading of the will, and Brianna had honored Ellen's wishes and hadn't contacted Cash.

Going into the kitchen, she poured a cup of coffee, then grabbed the mail. She frowned when she saw one letter that didn't have a return address.

Brianna was about to toss it aside when something about the writing of her name gave her pause, made her heartbeat kick up a notch. She quickly tore open the letter. There was not a date to indicate when it had been written. Her gaze focused on the words scrawled in bold handwriting…

Remember your promise,
Dad

Brianna's breath caught and she fought back tears. Without a shadow of a doubt she knew her father had indeed written to her. But who had he entrusted to send her the reminder? Brian Banks had always been a likable person. Over the years while foreman her father had met a lot of people who'd made coming to the ranch every year a ritual. He could have reached out to one of them to send the letter to her.

It didn't really matter who her father had entrusted to send her the reminder. The message was clear.

Going into her living room, she slid down on the sofa, leaned back and closed her eyes to stop the tears. Sadness was overshadowing what had been a happy day for her.

It was here in this very room, while sitting on this same sofa beside her father and holding his frail hand, when she'd made him that promise. The night before he had passed away while watching his favorite Westerns on television. He had refused the chemo the doctors had advised him to get. Instead, he had chosen quality of life over quantity of life.

Although she had wished things were different, she had accepted his decision and had gone out of her way to make his last days as special and meaningful as possible.

Knowing his life was about to end, Brian Banks had been worried about his only child. He was concerned about what her life would be without him. More than anything he had wanted her to be happy. He asked her to promise him that by her thirtieth birthday she would not be alone.

Her father had known, more than anyone, about her dreams of forever with Alan, and he had known the one thing his daughter wanted more than anything was to one day become a mother.

While sitting on this sofa that night—his last one on earth—he had made her promise him that she would have the baby she wanted, with or without a husband, by her thirtieth birthday. Given how she felt about trusting her heart to another man, he'd known if she did have a child, it would be without the benefit of a husband. He had been fine with that and had given her his blessing. He had let her know that whatever it took to make her happy, he would support her, even in death.

Brianna wiped away her tears. Thanks to Ms. Ellen she now had a home to call her own and was in a better financial position to fulfill her promise and make her dream come true.

She would contact the fertility center's sperm bank to begin whatever paperwork was needed. She was going to have her baby.

Four

"**D**id you say a dude ranch?"

Cash switched his cell phone to the other ear while pulling the rawhide belt through the loops of the jeans he'd purchased yesterday. He had walked out of the store with a couple pairs of jeans and several Western shirts because Roy Dawkins, the owner of the shop, was a born salesman.

"Yeah, Garth, a dude ranch. I decided to stay a couple days longer to check out it before selling it."

"I would hope so. I can't believe you would even think of doing it any other way."

"I know, but…"

"But you want to unload anything Ellen left you. Keeping it will make it seem as if her not staying in touch was okay when you feel it wasn't."

Cash drew in a deep breath. There were times when he thought Garth knew him better than he knew himself. "Yes, that's it. How did you know?"

"I've been there. Remember how my mother rejected me a few years ago when I decided to go see her? At least Ellen thought enough of you to leave you something. Jess's mother didn't leave him a single thing when she passed away four years ago, other than an elaborate New Orleans funeral to pay for. And I definitely can't see Sloan's or Maverick's mothers being generous either."

"I know, but a part of me wants to just leave here, Garth.

The sooner the better. Even at the store yesterday, all I heard was what a kindhearted woman Ellen was. It took everything I had to let them know that as far as I was concerned, she was far from kindhearted."

"Well, the Ellen I remember was kind as well, Cash. Of all Bart's wives, I thought Ellen was the most decent. Definitely way too decent for Bart. She was always kind to me and Jess. Treated us like her own. I can't say the same about Sloan's and Maverick's mothers."

Not wanting to talk about the woman who'd given birth to him, Cash checked his watch. "Look, Garth, I'm supposed to meet someone at the ranch to take a tour of the place. I just wanted to let you know that I won't be returning home until tomorrow."

"Okay, Cash. Take care."

"I will."

After ending the call, Cash walked over to the window. It seemed like today would be a pretty nice Saturday, mostly because he would be seeing Brianna Banks again. He had thought of her a lot since they had parted ways. More than he should have.

Like he'd told Garth, he would check out the land and then return home tomorrow. The last thing he would do was let anyone, especially a woman with a pretty face, weaken his resolve.

No matter what, the Blazing Frontier Dude Ranch would be sold.

Brianna was sitting in the porch swing when she saw the rental car coming up the long driveway. If Cash hadn't been impressed by the mile-long scenic drive he'd taken at the turnoff to Blazing Frontier, then he definitely would be once he saw the ranch house with the Rocky Mountains as a backdrop.

The huge three-story structure had been built years ago

and renovated twice. The last time had been by Ms. Ellen. The purpose had been to house the guests who preferred staying at the main house instead of in one of the sixty cabins scattered around the property.

Due to Mr. Van's lingering leg injury from being thrown from a horse in his younger days, they'd resided on the first floor in their own wing. The other wing was where the check-in desk, dining room, kitchen and storage rooms were located.

Brianna stood when the car came to a stop. She had thought about Cash Outlaw a lot last night, convincing herself she'd only done so for worry of what he would think of the Blazing Frontier and if perhaps he would change his mind about selling it.

"Welcome to the Blazing Frontier," she said, smiling when he got out of the car.

It took everything she had not to weaken in the knees. She'd thought Cash looked good yesterday in a business suit, but the Cash dressed in jeans, a Western shirt, cowboy boots and a Stetson was almost too much for her cardiovascular system. She was certain more blood than needed was rushing through her veins. That had to be the reason she suddenly felt light-headed.

He had been transformed from an Alaskan businessman to a Wyoming cowboy. It was quite obvious his outfit had cost a pretty penny. When he made it up to the top step, her gazed roamed over him from head to toe. "It appears that Roy laid his salesmanship on thick."

Tilting his hat back, Cash grinned down at her. "Yes, you can definitely say that."

Brianna tucked her hands into the pockets of her jeans. She couldn't wait to hear his first impression. "So, what do you think so far?"

"I'll admit I was taken aback. I hadn't expected it to be so large."

She nodded, thinking he hadn't seen anything yet. She couldn't wait until they covered the area on horseback. "Let me show you the house."

The tour inside lasted well over an hour. For someone who hadn't been interested in even seeing the ranch, he was checking out every single detail. That could be a bad thing if he was noticing the needed repairs. She hoped his intense scrutiny was a good thing and that he thought the ranch was a smart investment regardless of any needed repairs.

While giving him a tour, she had shared the history of the ranch, including details of the last major renovations that had been done, and answered his questions. He had commented on the beautiful mountain view that was practically out of every window. She took that as a good sign.

They even went out back to the game center with pool tables, a place to play cards, a theater room and a library. "A number of people bring their kids here to introduce them to the Wild West at an early age," Brianna said. "A fun way to learn history. Usually those kids grow up and return with their kids. Most of the people who come here are regulars. For the past three years we weren't accepting any newcomers unless they were recommended by our regular guests."

The building next to the game center featured an old-fashioned saloon. On the opposite side of the house was a screen-enclosed swimming pool.

Cash admitted he had not expected to see that. "Another amenity for the kids?"

She smiled. "You would be surprised how many adults love to go swimming as a way to relax after riding the range."

When they made it back to the front porch, she said, "We can walk over to the barn and have one of the guys saddle up horses for us."

"There are still men working here?" he asked as he walked beside her.

"Only five. Ted Dennis is the man who took my dad's place as foreman and has worked here for fifteen years. He agreed to stay on until the ranch's fate was decided."

"And the other four men?"

"They are guys who have also worked here for years. They are hoping you or the new owner will hire them on."

"I'd think it would be to the owner's advantage to do that. They would be getting experienced men who know the land."

Brianna didn't say anything. Evidently, he hadn't been impressed enough to keep it if he was still thinking of selling.

All five men were in the barn working and she introduced Cash to all of them. In no time at all, Ted had the horses saddled and ready for them to use.

They started out at a trot and Brianna had to inwardly admit she was impressed with Cash's horsemanship. She had to believe that once they got out on the range, if nothing else had impressed him so far, it would.

He was impressed.

Cash honestly didn't know what to say as he rode beside Brianna, so he didn't say anything at all. Instead, he took it all in. He hadn't known. Hadn't had a clue about the size of the spread Ellen had left him. It wasn't just the size—it was the sheer beauty of the surroundings.

He recalled the first time he had visited Westmoreland Country with his brothers. Westmoreland Country was the section on the outskirts of Denver where his cousins the Westmorelands lived, and it encompassed eighteen hundred acres. This property here was larger than that. Nearly double.

And it was the most beautiful land he had ever seen. Numerous streams, several apple orchards, several caverns, rich valleys, glassy plains and an abundance of mountains.

Then there was the Keystone River, at least a small section of it. He could see why the Blazing Frontier Dude Ranch had been so popular. It was a Westerner's paradise.

They had dismounted to walk to the lake. He tossed a pebble across the waters and watched it skip across the surface. He glanced over at Brianna. She was an accomplished rider. He'd watched how she'd jumped the small streams with the ease. "Where does this river lead to?" Cash asked her.

She had put on her own hat before they had headed out on horseback, and several strands of hair peeked out haphazardly around her face. He wondered if she knew just how beautiful she was. Even with a hat, she looked jaw-droppingly sexy. There was nothing serene or quiet about her looks.

He thought now what he'd thought that day he had seen her coming out of the ice-cream shop. There was no way a woman with her looks wasn't attached, regardless of the fact she wasn't wearing a ring.

The one thing he did know was that she'd once been Roy's cousin's girlfriend. He'd gotten that much from the man while shopping. Roy had said the two were supposed to get married right out of high school, but things hadn't worked out. Cash wondered why.

The reason wasn't really any of his business.

"This waterway leads to the bigger part of the Keystone River."

"Is that part of the Blazing Frontier property as well?" he asked.

She glanced over at him. "It used to be. That's the section of land Ellen bequeathed to me." She turned and pointed east. "Although you can't see it, my house is over there, behind those huge oak trees."

He nodded. Ellen had definitely been generous to her, and after what she'd told him yesterday, he was glad. Her parents had worked for years for the Blazing Frontier. It seemed fitting that she reap some of the benefits.

Brianna explained there was another section to show him. They rode awhile. Then suddenly he brought his horse to a stop and she did the same. The view, for as far as his eyes could see, was magnificent. Spellbinding. Simply breathtaking.

He didn't say anything for a long moment. He just sat there and took it all in. Moments passed before she finally spoke.

"So, Cash. What do you think?"

He looked at her. First of all, he thought Brianna was the most desirable woman he'd ever met. Of course, she wasn't asking what he thought of *her*, but he couldn't let that private thought slip by. Cash knew what she was really asking, but still, he would not tell her anything definite. "I admit I'm impressed, Brianna. I honestly did not expect to see all of this. It's beautiful."

He paused. "Do you know Hal Sutherland?" The tensing of her shoulders and the way her lips tightened were telling. Obviously, Hal Sutherland was someone she didn't too much care for. An old boyfriend, perhaps?

"Yes, I know him. Why?"

"He called me at the hotel last night, ready to make an offer. Told me to name my price."

"I'm sure he did. He's been trying to get his hands on the Blazing Frontier for years."

Cash nodded. "I see."

"Now I have a question for you, Cash."

"Which is?"

"What about Ms. Ellen's request that the two of us go through her personal belongings and decide what to do with them?"

"I honestly don't want to be involved in that. Whatever

you decide to do with Ellen's things is fine with me." Then, barely missing a beat, he said, "It's time to head back."

"I am so happy Ms. Ellen looked out for you in her will, Brie. What she did was so thoughtful and kind. Did you have any idea she was going to do that?"

Brianna took a sip of her lemonade while talking to her best friend, Miesha James. It was a beautiful Sunday afternoon after the downpour late yesterday evening.

"Yes, that was kind and thoughtful of her, and no, I had no idea she would do that."

"Tell me about Cashen Outlaw, now that you've seen him in the flesh. Was he worth the crush you had on him years ago?"

Brianna rolled her eyes. Only Miesha would remember that. Brianna had finished her first year of college, hurt and humiliated after Alan's betrayal. In the summer she had returned home and she'd rarely left the ranch, wanting to retreat from a world filled with pain and self-pity. One day after volunteering to organize Ms. Ellen's attic, she'd come across a private investigator's report that had included a photograph of Cash. It was his graduation picture from college. She had gotten hooked by his huge smile, and on that day he had become her fantasy boyfriend. Daydreaming about Cash all that summer had helped her get over the pain Alan had caused.

Brianna smiled. "Yes. I can sum up Cashen Outlaw in one word. *Hot.*"

"Now you got my bones shivering in lust, girl. Was he really that hot?"

"Yes. Everything about him. His features, his body, his clothes, the way he carried himself. Even the way he rode his horse. However, that picture I saw of him when he was in his early twenties is nothing like the thirtysomething hunk he's aged into. Like I said, he is hot."

"Um…maybe I need to come pay you a visit."

Brianna chuckled. "Too late. He left this morning to return to Alaska and there is no reason for him to come back. In fact, I got the distinct impression that he won't ever return."

"Didn't you say Ms. Ellen left him the ranch?"

"Yes, but he doesn't want it. He'd made up his mind to sell it before even seeing it. After giving him a tour yesterday, I could tell he was impressed, but I doubt he was impressed enough to keep it." She paused, then added, "He did say Hal Sutherland had already contacted him and made an offer."

"Hal Sutherland! Did you tell him what a douchebag that man is?"

"No, and I don't intend to. I will not influence Cash in any way…not that I think I could. Cash is a businessman. For him it will be all about business."

"I think you should tell him."

"I disagree. Can we change the subject?"

"One more question. Did Cashen Outlaw say why he never reached out to his mom over the years? Why he never answered her letters?"

"No, and I didn't ask him. I did just what I promised Ms. Ellen I would do if our paths ever crossed and that was to not bring it up to him and not pass judgment on him because of it. The latter was hard."

"I'm sure it was."

"I want to believe, like Ms. Ellen did, that the letters never reached him. That his father made sure of it."

"That's why you should mention the letters to him, Brie."

"I promised Ms. Ellen I wouldn't."

"You and your promises."

"I know. I know. And speaking of promises, I have some news to share with you," Brianna said, refilling her glass with lemonade.

"What?"

"Now that I know I have a roof over my head for keeps, I'm moving ahead with plans to have a baby. Dad sent me a reminder of that promise on Friday."

"Your dad?"

"Yes." Brianna told Miesha about the letter.

"Wow, Brie. You don't know who sent it?"

"No, and really that doesn't matter because it could be anyone. Dad had a lot of friends who would do whatever he asked. It's good knowing he supports my decision. Now what I want to know is—since you had the procedure six years ago, are there any regrets?"

There was a pause before Miesha said, "Darrett is my world and I won't ever regret giving birth to him. But…"

"But what?"

"If I had to do it over again, I would go about it differently."

Brianna lifted a brow. "In what way?"

"I wouldn't use a sperm bank."

Brianna frowned. She recalled Miesha telling her how easy using a sperm bank had been. She'd filled out the questionnaire indicating the specific traits she wanted her child to have, even down to the eye color. Then they'd selected a donor based on her preference. "Why?"

"Because Darrett is getting older, and now that he's in the first grade and other kids have fathers, he wants to know about his. I wish I had a picture of a real person I could show him instead of a photo of a test tube." Brianna heard the sorrow in her friend's voice when she added, "If I had it to do all over again, Brianna, I would use a human being and go through the process of procreation the traditional way."

"Yes, but that way can get messy," Brianna said. "Very few men would voluntarily get a woman pregnant, Miesha. They would envision eighteen years of child support."

"Yes, but I'd take my time and find a guy who would go along with my plan. There are guys out there who want to be fathers without the benefit of a wife, just like there are women who want to be mothers without the benefit of a husband. The key is to find the right man."

Miesha paused and then said, "And if you find a man who's willing to meet you halfway, one who will sign papers agreeing that you won't ever hit him up for child support or the like, then I'd consider going that route as well." She chuckled and tacked on, "And if the sex is good, then that will be a bonus."

Later that night, as Brianna got ready for bed, she thought about what Miesha had told her. Her friend had definitely given her food for thought, although Brianna had completed the paperwork with the fertility clinic online last night. She had decided on the one in Jackson. The one in Laramie was too close for comfort since a lot of people living in Black Crow commuted to Laramie for work. The last thing she needed was anyone getting into her business.

Brianna drew in a deep breath. She didn't have long to make whatever decisions she was going to make. She would be twenty-eight in a few months and there was no guarantee she would get pregnant right away. Waiting too long would be pushing things too close to her thirtieth birthday for comfort.

When Brianna settled in bed, she knew there was not anyone living in these parts that she would want to father her child. Most of the guys she'd dated over the past couple years she considered nothing more than friends. And she didn't want to fall in love. One heartbreak was enough.

As she drifted off to sleep, the vision of a particular man floated through her mind. Cash Outlaw. She hoped he'd made it back home safely.

Five

"You really inherited a dude ranch, Cash, and are honestly thinking about selling it?"

Cash glanced over at his brother Maverick, but noticed Sloan and Garth seemed as interested in what his youngest brother had asked. They had just finished their weekly Monday midday meeting at Outlaw Freight Lines in one of the conference rooms.

Usually, as soon as the meeting ended, they would quickly scatter to their own respective offices to continue to tackle whatever had been on their agenda for that day. However, it seemed his brothers were more interested in hearing what he had to say than doing their own work. Even Garth, who knew a little more about the situation than the others.

Cash had spoken with Garth before he toured the ranch on Saturday, so Cash figured Garth was only wondering if his decision had changed since then.

"Blazing Frontier is definitely a nice spread, and it's even more enormous than I'd assumed. I admit that I've never seen so much beautiful land anywhere."

Sloan lifted a brow. "Even compared to Westmoreland Country?"

"Yes, but in a different way. The Blazing Frontier is twice the size, so there is more open land, with the Rockies in the background. It's wilderness and frontier."

"You inherited that much property?" Sloan asked in amazement.

"Yes. However, Ellen did bequeath a house and the one hundred acres it sits on to a woman by the name of Brianna Banks. Her parents worked on the Blazing Frontier for years. Brianna even worked there after college while it was a dude ranch. Ellen had a close relationship with Brianna and her parents."

"Are her parents still alive?" Sloan asked.

"No. They passed away."

"How old is this Brianna Banks?"

Cash glanced over at Maverick. He wasn't surprised this particular brother had asked. Maverick was a known womanizer. "She's twenty-seven."

"Is she pretty?" Maverick also wanted to know.

Cash held his brother's gaze. "Why?"

Maverick shrugged. "Just asking out of curiosity."

Cash didn't say anything for a minute. "Yes, Brianna Banks is pretty. In fact, she is *very* pretty."

"Did you hit on her?"

Cash rolled his eyes. "Not everybody is like you, Maverick."

A grin spread across Maverick's face. "And that's a good thing. Less competition means more women for me to enjoy.

"So, tell me more about this woman," Maverick said.

Cash glared at his brother. "Don't even think it, Maverick."

"Do I detect a little possessiveness in your tone?" Maverick asked, trying to get a rise out of Cash.

"No."

"Sounds like it."

Garth, who was known to bring peace whenever there was friction between the brothers, spoke up. "Have you decided if you're going to keep the property, Cash?"

Before Cash could answer, Sloan said, "Of course he's going to keep it."

Cash glanced over at his brother. "I am?"

Sloan countered with, "Why wouldn't you?"

Cash shrugged. "Although I can tell it was a nice dude ranch at one time, it's been shut down a little over a year. I noticed a number of repairs that need to be made to bring it back up to par. Not sure I want to put any money into doing all that needs to be done."

Maverick nodded. "Even if you decide not to reopen the dude ranch, just think of other things you can do with it. The Westmoreland cousins are always looking for more land for their horses. You can turn it into a horse ranch."

Cash knew this was true and had even given it some thought on his flight back home on Sunday. Several of his Westmoreland cousins had partnered to operate a horse training and breeding company, and it was doing great financially. A number of the horses they'd trained had won several derbies over the years.

"I agree with Maverick. If I were you, I'd talk to the cousins," Sloan suggested. "And why limit yourself? With that much land it can be a dude ranch again, too. Heck, I'd even consider coming on as an investor."

Cash was surprised. "You would?"

"In a heartbeat."

"So would I," Maverick said, leaning back in his chair. "I spent time with a woman at a dude ranch in Texas a few years ago and really enjoyed the experience. Both in and out of the bedroom. You wouldn't believe how many Wild West enthusiasts there are. I think it would be a good investment."

"You could count me in as well," Garth said. "I'm sure something like that would interest Jess, too."

Cash was silent as he stared at his brothers. Some people found it amazing that the six Outlaw siblings were as close as they were, considering each one of them had a different mother. But that's the way it had always been, even when, collectively, they'd had to take on Bart. It had taken the six of them to convince Bart to retire as CEO of Outlaw Freight Lines after the board had threatened to oust him.

"You guys are serious, aren't you?" Cash asked his brothers.

"Yes," Garth said, nodding. "Granted, we haven't seen the place. We're going by what you're telling us. You might be sitting on a gold mine and not know it, Cash. I agree with Sloan. If you want to turn it into a horse ranch, you'll have the Westmoreland cousins who will probably be interested. And if you decide to turn it back into a dude ranch, you'll have your brothers as investors."

"I want to see this place, Cash," Sloan said, rubbing his hands together excitedly.

"I think we all should," Garth added. "What about this weekend, Cash? I can call Jess to join us if he doesn't have any plans."

"This weekend will be great," Cash said. "We can all stay at the ranch house," he suggested, thrilled at the idea of going back to the ranch when he thought of a certain woman he would love seeing again…

"There's plenty of room. I'll call Brianna and have her hire someone to come in to make sure the place is ready for us. And I'll call the Westmoreland cousins to see if they'd like to join us. Then they can give me their expert opinions," Cash added.

Moments later they all left the conference room to head back to their respective offices. Cash was glad he had gotten Brianna's telephone number from her before they parted ways on Saturday. He would go so far as admitting that he had been thinking about her more than he wanted to, and had tried blocking any thoughts of her from his mind since returning to Alaska. So far nothing had worked.

Sitting down at his desk, he knew there had to be a reason for his acute attraction to her. An attraction that had him looking forward to this weekend. An attraction that had his fingers itching just to dial the phone so he could hear her voice.

When it came to women, he'd never considered anything remotely close to a serious relationship. It hadn't surprised Cash when Garth had settled down and married. Being the oldest, Garth had wanted to marry. As far as Cash was concerned, his oldest brother had hit the jackpot when he'd realized he loved Regan and took the initiative to do something about it. Now Garth was a happy man.

Their father had not set a good example when it came to love, marriage and happiness. Cash was glad Garth had not let that influence him. However, that didn't mean what worked for Garth would work for Cash, Jess, Sloan, Maverick or even Charm. They would have to find their own way when it came to settling down and having a future with someone or remaining single.

No matter how intense his attraction to Brianna, Cash didn't have the time or inclination to get involved in a serious relationship. But then, how serious could it get when she lived in Wyoming and he lived in Alaska?

Satisfied this attraction to Brianna Banks would eventually fizzle out, he reached for the phone to give her a call.

Brianna ended the call with Cash. She had been surprised to hear from him and even more surprised to hear that he would be returning to Black Crow this weekend with his brothers and cousins. He said there would be as many as fifteen of them in all. Did that mean he might be thinking about keeping the place?

He didn't say and she hadn't asked. The only thing he'd done was request that she hire someone to prepare the ranch house for their visit. He'd also asked that Ted have additional horses available. She would call Hattie, who'd been over housekeeping at the ranch for years.

Cash had said he would be arriving early Friday and the others would arrive sometime Friday evening. Everyone would be staying until Sunday. That meant it would be an all-weekend affair. Fifteen men could consume a lot of food. She would call Dano, who'd been the ranch's chef, to make sure the refrigerators were stocked. Should she suggest that Dano be available to cook meals, too?

No, she had to slow down. Otherwise, she would be calling the entire Blazing Frontier staff. It wouldn't be fair to give them false hope when she had no idea of Cash's intentions. He might merely have planned a weekend with his brothers and cousins as a guys' getaway before he officially sold it.

However, what if he was still deciding? The more impressed he was, the better, and when it came to good cooking, Dano definitely knew how to impress.

A few hours later, all the calls had been made. Long ago, with her parents' help, Brianna had understood the meaning of teamwork when it came to the Blazing Frontier. She'd also come to understand the meaning of dedication and loyalty. That's why everyone she'd called had been eager to come back and do what they could to make Cash Outlaw's weekend at the ranch one he wouldn't forget.

Standing, she grabbed the pail to pick some fresh apples when her phone rang. The number wasn't one she recognized, but she answered anyway.

"Hello?"

"May I speak with Brianna Banks, please?" the feminine voice said on the other end.

"This is Brianna. Banks."

"Ms. Banks, this is Sally Harper at the fertility clinic in Jackson. We got your paperwork and are in the process of reviewing it now."

Brianna smiled. "Yes, Ms. Harper. Is there anything else I need to do?"

"No. We will start looking through our database to see if there's a donor who fits the profile you've requested."

She told Ms. Harper she wanted to move quickly, and the woman suggested they set up an appointment for Brianna's physical for next Thursday. Less than ten minutes later, she ended her call with Sally Harper, telling herself that although she'd taken into account everything Miesha had said, she wasn't sure she wanted to know the identity of her baby's father.

Picking up the pail on the table, she headed outside. Today had certainly been a day for good news. Her application for a sperm donor was being processed and she had talked to Cash again. Of course the only reason she was excited about the latter was that there was a chance he might keep the ranch.

But still, she couldn't ignore the feeling of excitement coursing through her at the thought of seeing him again.

Six

Cash kept telling himself the reason he was excited to be returning to Black Crow had nothing to do with Brianna Banks, and that showing up on Thursday evening instead of Friday morning had nothing to do with the pang of longing he felt whenever he thought about her.

The longing to sample those full, moist lips that had captured him from the first. Or wishing to touch her face, to feel the softness of her skin beneath his fingers. Or wanting the chance to bury his face at the center of her chest to breathe in her scent. He tightened his hands on the steering wheel of the rental car when he saw the marker proclaiming Black Crow's city limits were only ten miles away.

He frowned when his phone rang and he recognized the caller was Maverick. Using the connector on the steering wheel, Cash answered. "What do you want, Maverick?"

"Where are you? I went into your office a few minutes ago and it looked like no-man's-land. Crissy said you checked out for a week."

He'd actually checked out for two weeks, but he figured Maverick would find that out soon enough. "You needed me for something?"

"No, I just wanted to make sure this weekend was still on. I got back to the States last night."

Maverick had jumped at the chance to accompany Sloan to Paris. Sloan was in charge of Outlaw Freight Lines' international sales. Each one of Bart's offspring had a position at the company. Even Jess had been the company's corporate attorney until he'd entered politics to become a senator.

Cash was Garth's right-hand man in the Alaska office, and Maverick's job was overseeing the company's expansion into states like Texas, Florida and the Carolinas. As for Charm… Cash would have to scratch his chin on that one since he and his brothers were still trying to figure out exactly what their sister's duties were. At the moment they'd given her a job mainly to keep her out of their hair.

"How was the trip to Paris?" he asked Maverick.

"What can I say? I love the women there, so what does that tell you?"

Cash shook his head. "I guess you enjoyed yourself."

"Yes, I most certainly did. So now that you've gotten all into my business, answer my question. Where are you?"

"I am on my way to Black Crow to prepare for the weekend." Okay, that would explain why he'd hightailed it out of Fairbanks a day early, but it wouldn't explain why he'd taken two weeks off. There was no way he would admit to Maverick that he'd been so smitten with Brianna that he wanted two weeks with her to figure out why.

"So, the weekend is still on?"

Hadn't he just said that? Um…did that mean he wasn't the only Outlaw who had allowed some woman to mess with his mind? "Yes, Maverick, but that's something you could have easily asked Sloan."

"I'm not speaking to Sloan."

"Why?"

"Because of his rush to get back to Alaska, I had to cut my time short with Phire."

"Who?"

"You don't know her. I suspect some woman in Fairbanks has caught Sloan's eye. Just like I suspect that woman in Black Crow has caught yours."

Cash decided this was where he changed the subject. "Have you seen or talked to Bart?"

He heard Maverick's chuckle, which meant his youngest brother was fully aware Cash was ready to talk about something else. "Yeah, I saw the old man. He asked where everybody was going this weekend and I told him I wasn't sure. It wasn't a lie since at the time he asked, I wasn't certain if this weekend was still on. Besides, I figure the less Bart knows about your business the better."

"True."

But that hadn't stopped their father from summoning Cash to the Outlaw Estates when he'd returned after the reading of Ellen's will. He had told Bart just enough to satisfy his nosiness. Mainly that Ellen had left him a ranch and the land it was on—all but a hundred acres, which she'd left to a longtime employee. Cash had intentionally mentioned that part because Bart didn't feel any allegiance to employees, longtime or otherwise.

Bart even had the nerve to suggest that Cash contest the will on the grounds that Ellen probably was not in her right mind when it was drawn up, and the woman took advantage of her. Bart felt that as Ellen's son, Cash should have gotten everything.

Cash did not agree with Bart's way of thinking. As nicely and as respectfully as he could, he had told his father to mind his own business.

"At least we don't have to worry about Bart finding out and making a surprise visit," Maverick said.

"And why don't we have to worry about it?" Cash asked, coming to a marker that said Black Crow was only five miles away.

"Because he mentioned Claudia was coming to town this weekend. You know what that means."

Yes, he did. Charm's mother, Claudia, was the one true love of Bart's life. She was also the one woman who had refused to let Bart treat her like the others before her. Bart hadn't known Claudia was pregnant with Charm when their six-month romantic fling had ended, and she had taken off for parts unknown with her daughter.

Fifteen years later, Claudia reappeared with Charm in tow, telling Bart she couldn't handle the sassiness of the daughter he hadn't known he had. She'd given custody to Bart and told him he could deal with it now.

"I assume you'll still be coming, Maverick. If so, I will see you tomorrow."

"Hell, yeah, I'm still coming. I want to check out the woman who has gotten you all in a tizzy."

Cash frowned. "No woman has gotten me in a tizzy."

"If you say so. See you tomorrow, Brother Number Three."

The click sounded loudly in Cash's ear.

Everything looked beautiful, including the fresh flowers in the vases, although Brianna wasn't sure if the men would appreciate the flowers. She was pleased with how things looked and had told Hattie so before she left.

Brianna had walked through every room on both floors. The entire house had a scent that was neither male nor female. It was a robust citrus with hints of lime, oranges, tangelo, lemon and pomelo. It was pleasing.

Going back up the stairs, she rechecked all the bathrooms. She smiled when she saw each had a sufficient number of towels and a basket of toiletries on every vanity that included small canisters of shaving cream and a packet of razors, just in case the men forgot to pack theirs.

She had specifically selected each bedroom so Cash's guests would have a gorgeous view of the mountainous terrain outside their windows.

Although Cash had not given her the time of his arrival tomorrow, she figured it would be before noon. He had said the others would be coming later that evening and he intended to arrive hours before they did. She figured he was coming early to check whether the place was decent. All he had asked her to do was make sure it was suitable to stay for the weekend. She had gone even further and hoped he didn't think she had gone overboard.

Brianna was about to head back downstairs when she caught her reflection in the full-length mirror on the bathroom door. There was no way she could lie and say the reason she had gotten her hair styled and her nails done had anything to do with giving Mrs. Chester, the local hair stylist, her long overdue business. Nor did it have anything to do with Brianna deciding to treat herself. The reason she had pampered herself on a Thursday morning was because of Cash. Although, since she had given him keys to the ranch when she'd given him that tour on Saturday, chances were she wouldn't even see him this weekend. But she wanted to look her best on the slight chance she did.

Heck, for all she knew, he might be bringing his girlfriend, even though he had presented this to her as an all-guys trip. She couldn't see a man who looked like him not being in a serious relationship with someone. If he was, then she wished him the best.

Brianna's ears perked up when she heard a car pull up. Checking her watch, she saw it was five in the afternoon. Had Dano gone grocery shopping today instead of tomorrow? If so, when was he going to let her know? He no longer had a key to the place.

She had taken only a couple steps down the stairs when the front door swung open. A surprised gasp erupted from her throat when her gaze connected with that of Cash Outlaw.

It took Cash a moment to not only get his bearings but also reclaim his senses. All five of them. Doing so wasn't easy while his gaze was locked on the one woman he had constantly thought about since he'd seen her last. The woman who was the prime reason he had hightailed it out of Fairbanks on a Thursday instead of a Friday. The woman who even from a distance of at least twenty feet could make every single muscle in his body tighten with desire.

"Cash, this is a surprise. I wasn't expecting you until sometime tomorrow," Brianna said, breaking into the passionate haze that seemed to cloud his mind.

Drawing in a deep breath, he responded, "I decided to come up a day early to check on things."

To check on you.

He had seen her car parked outside, and immediately his body had leaped in joy at the thought of seeing her again. He'd honestly thought he would have to come up with some excuse to see her today. Hell, on the way here he'd been trying to come up with one.

"Well, welcome back to the Blazing Frontier."

"Thanks."

Forcing himself to break eye contact with her, he looked around, taking in the changes. The furniture was the same, but the place looked like it had been spruced up a bit. He even noticed the curtains were no longer drawn but were wide open to take full advantage of the sun and the mountain view.

He smiled when he saw the flowers. That was a nice gesture, even if none of the men would truly appreciate them.

Cash then inhaled the citrus scent. It was nice. He switched his gaze back to Brianna and saw she had come down the stairs and now stood only a few feet away. "Everything looks nice, Brianna."

"Thanks. Hattie would be glad to know you are pleased."

"Hattie?"

"Yes, she was over housekeeping here for years. I asked

her to come back to get things ready as you requested. And Hattie being Hattie, she couldn't help but go all in."

"I'm glad. It looks nice. I'm sure everyone will appreciate it."

Unable to stop himself, he let his gaze roam over her. Gone was the mane of curls from the last time. Now her hair tumbled in loose waves down her shoulders and he liked it. She looked good in her jeans and peasant blouse.

What hadn't changed was the fact that she was just as captivating as before. He shoved his hands into the pockets of his slacks, figuring that would be the best place for them at the moment. Otherwise, he would be tempted to pull her into his arms and give her the kiss he'd dreamed of since first laying eyes on her.

"*You* look nice, Brianna," he said, giving her the compliment she deserved.

"Thank you, Cash." She paused. "I figured you would prefer using the main bedroom suite. Hattie has made sure it has everything you'll need."

"Thanks."

"And so you won't be surprised when he arrives with the groceries in the morning, Dano, who used to be the head chef, has agreed to be your cook for the weekend."

"That's great."

"I paid both for Hattie's and Dano's services, as well as the rental cost for the additional horses this weekend out of the ranch's contingency fund. I will give you a documented breakdown of everything before you leave on Sunday."

Cash figured now would be a good time to tell her that he wouldn't be leaving on Sunday, that he would be staying for two weeks. Garth had been getting on him for months to take time off. His older brother had reminded Cash that he hadn't taken a real vacation in years.

He had not been able to put up much of an argument because it was the same one he'd given Garth a year or so ago when it seemed his brother was determined to work nonstop, all year round. Now Garth used that same argument against him. He could tell Brianna later about his extended stay, when he saw her again, because he definitely intended to see her again before Sunday.

"I will be leaving to let you get settled," she said, interrupting his thoughts.

She had turned to head for the door when he said, "Have dinner with me, Brianna."

She glanced back at him. "Dinner?"

"Yes, I passed this restaurant on the way here. O'Shea's. It seems like a nice place and I would love if you would join me for dinner. However, if you already have plans, I understand."

Brianna shook her head. "No, I don't have plans. But…"

She was nibbling on her bottom lip in a nervous gesture. He wondered why. "But what?"

"Black Crow is a relatively small town and most people know me. They heard about us sharing a meal before. To do so again would cause speculation."

He lifted a brow. "Is it speculation you prefer not to have for fear your boyfriend might get the wrong idea?"

She rolled her eyes. "Trust me, that's not it because most people know I haven't had a steady boyfriend since…"

"Since what?"

Her chin tightened. "Since I broke up with my last boyfriend."

Now she had him curious. "How long ago was that?"

Surprisingly, Brianna chuckled. "Would you believe since my senior year in high school?"

He definitely found that hard to believe. Was that the same guy who was Roy Dawkins's cousin? She hadn't had a steady boyfriend since high school. Over dinner he intended to find out what was up with that. "I'm not worried about any speculation if you aren't."

"No, I'm not worried. And just so you know, a lot of people are curious about you. You're Ellen's son. A son they didn't know she had."

It was on the tip of his tongue to say, no biggie. Ellen had conveniently forgotten about him anyway. "I can handle their curiosity, Brianna."

She nodded. "I just wanted to give you fair warning."

"Fair warning taken. Will seven o'clock be okay?"

"Yes, seven will be fine."

"How do I get to your house from here to pick you up?"

"Step out on the porch and I'll show you."

He followed her and recalled she had pointed out where her house was the day they had gone riding together. "It's through those trees there," she said, pointing east.

He had come to stand beside her. Her scent was so alluring he had to breathe in a few times to retain his composure. That really didn't do any good since all he was doing was drawing her scent through his nostrils even more.

"When you turned off the main road, you probably didn't notice the first driveway you came to. Well, it leads to my home. That's one thing I'm going to have to do when you officially sell the place."

"What?"

"Make another entrance to my property so I won't have to drive on Blazing Frontier land to get home."

"I wouldn't worry about it. I'm sure the new owner will be accommodating."

"Maybe they will and maybe they won't." She turned and, as if realizing how close they stood to each other, she took a step back. "You won't miss my house, Cash. It's the only one there. I'll see you at seven."

He watched her move toward the car. She definitely looked good, no matter what she wore.

She turned and said, "I forgot to tell you that I went through some of Ms. Ellen's items in the attic. There was a packet I thought you might want to see, so I placed it in the top drawer of your nightstand."

He was about to tell her she could have thrown it all out as far as he was concerned. Instead he said, "Sure. Thanks."

"You are welcome, Cash."

He loved it when she said his name. There was such a sexy sound to it. Unable to move, he leaned against the wooden post and watched her get into her car to leave.

It was only after she was no longer in sight that he moved to go into the house, where her scent still lingered. Once inside he remembered he needed to get his luggage.

Maverick was right. Brianna did have him in a tizzy.

Seven

Brianna's heart began pounding when she heard a car pull up outside. Glancing out her bedroom window, she saw it was Cash. She leaned against the bedroom door as she tried to regain her composure. She took a deep breath. No matter how drawn she was to him, she couldn't let her attraction get out of hand. Not tonight. Not ever.

One of the first things she needed to master tonight was the ability not to come unglued around him. He had such an overpowering presence that seemed to captivate her every time she was within a few feet of him. She wished he didn't look so handsome or have such a mesmerizing smile.

Brianna had yet to see his frown. It would probably be quite fetching as well. She would have to say the one thing he seemed to have inherited from Ms. Ellen was her pleasing personality.

While getting dressed, she had convinced herself that the only reason she had accepted his invitation to dinner was that she hoped he would share any news regarding the fate of Blazing Frontier.

Giving herself one final check when he knocked, she left her bedroom and moved toward the door. The dress she was wearing was one she had purchased last year when she had gone shopping in Laramie. The saleswoman had convinced her that it flattered her figure. Now, as she looked at herself in it, she would have to agree.

"Who is it?"

"Cash."

She wished he did not have such a sexy-sounding voice. But then, it complemented the rest of his features, she thought, opening the door. He wore a pair of chocolate-brown slacks and a long-sleeve button-up maple-colored shirt. The combination of colors seemed to enhance his appeal.

"Come in. I just need to grab my purse."

She stepped aside and recalled the last man who'd come to visit. Hal Sutherland. But he hadn't made it inside her house. She had talked to him on the porch. That's when he'd told her that after Ms. Ellen died, he would be taking ownership of her home and was giving her notice that she needed to find someplace else to stay. He'd been so certain that he would inherit everything. She was certain he had heard by now that thanks to Ms. Ellen, this house was now hers. He couldn't be happy about that.

Brianna watched Cash glance around when she went to grab her purse off the dining room table. "Nice place," he said.

"Thanks."

"And you look pretty."

"Thanks again, and I'm ready to leave." The sooner they got out of her house the better. He was no taller than her dad had been, yet Cash's presence seemed to make the house shrink in size.

"I hope you're hungry because I definitely am. I could eat a horse," he said when they walked to the car.

Brianna glanced over at him and smiled. She had noticed that day at lunch that he had a healthy appetite. Very few people could eat two of Monroe's hamburgers, but he had.

"I'm hungry but I won't be eating a horse, Cash. Neither will you. O'Shea's has the juiciest steaks in southeast Wyoming and the most delicious sides to go along with them. You get to select three instead of two."

"Sounds like my kind of place. What about desserts?"

She glanced at him when he opened the car door for her. "If you like peaches then you'd love their cobbler. Their butter pound cake isn't bad either. The reason O'Shea's is so popular is that it has a great atmosphere and the food is wonderful."

A short while later, when she and Cash entered the restaurant, it seemed everyone was focused on them. She was glad they were shown to a table that overlooked the river. The waitress gave them a minute to look at the menus.

"What river is that?" he asked, gesturing to the window. It hadn't gotten dark yet and boaters were still out.

"That's the Keystone River."

"The same one on our properties?"

Our properties.

She knew he hadn't meant it the way he'd said it, but yes, it was the same one on *their* properties since they now shared a part of Keystone River.

"Yes. The Keystone River is enormous and is somewhat in the shape of a huge S. The curve encompasses our properties and Hal Sutherland's land. The tip at the top feeds into the Arrowhead River in Cheyenne."

The waitress returned to take their order and bring their drinks. Cash had ordered a bottle of wine for the table, one she had suggested. She watched as he took his first sip and when he licked his lips, she felt a stirring in her midsection.

"Well, what do you think, Cash?"

He glanced over at her and smiled. "I like it."

She was glad. "Are you ready for this weekend?" she asked, hoping if she got him talking about it, he would give her a clue as to his plans for the ranch.

"Yes. It's always a grand time when my brothers, cousins and I get together. Now I have a question for you."

She lifted a brow. "What question is that?"

He met her gaze and asked, "Why haven't you had a steady guy in your life since high school?"

From Brianna's expression, Cash knew she was surprised by his question. Of course, she had every right to tell him it wasn't any of his business, but since she'd been the one to let it slip earlier, he was merely appeasing his curiosity.

She held his gaze, and for a quick moment he saw a flash of pain in the depths of her eyes. Seeing it should have extinguished his curiosity, but instead it made him want to know that much more. What had happened to her in high school that still affected her now?

"Alan Dawkins and I dated all through high school."

"Dawkins? Is he related to Roy? The guy who owns the clothing store?" he asked, wanting to confirm what the man had told him.

"Yes, Roy is Alan's cousin. Anyway, Alan graduated from high school a year ahead of me. Our plans were for him to go into the army, and then we would marry the next year when I graduated."

"What happened to him?" Cash asked. Did the man lose his life while in the military? That's what had happened to Garth's fiancée Karen. It had taken years before his brother had gotten over losing her. Everyone was glad when Garth had fallen in love with Regan.

"Germany happened. While stationed over there, he met someone, fell in love and married her. End of story."

Not quite, he quickly decided. He was certain the decent thing to do was to let it go, but for some reason, he could not. "He came home married to someone else?"

She hesitated and then said, "Yes."

Cash took another sip of his wine. He could just imagine a younger Brianna, excited about finishing high school while planning a wedding, only to find out the man she loved, a man she thought loved her, had committed his life to someone else.

"I'm sorry that happened to you, Brianna," he said in a quiet tone, truly meaning it.

"Thanks." She took a sip of her own wine. "That was years ago. Close to ten, in fact, and I've gotten over it."

He leaned back in his chair. "If that's true, then why aren't you in a serious relationship now?"

She shrugged. "I only have one heart. It's been broken once, and it took me a while to repair it. I don't want it broken again."

He nodded. "You don't ever plan to give love another chance?"

"I can't see it happening."

He didn't say anything for a moment. "I think that's really sad, Brianna. In the short time I've gotten to know you, I think you're a nice woman who has a lot to offer someone."

It was kind of Cash to say that. "Thank you."

Thinking it was fair to change the subject to what *she* wanted to know, she said, "Now it's my time to ask you a question."

They paused when the waitress came with their food. It smelled delicious and she hoped Cash thought it tasted delicious as well. "What question is that?" he asked after the waitress had left and he was reaching for the steak sauce.

She watched as he poured sauce on his meat. "Is there a reason for this weekend?"

He lifted his head and looked at her. "If you're asking if inviting my family and friends means I'm no longer thinking about selling the ranch, then the answer is no. That still remains an option I am considering."

"Oh."

"However, I will say that my brothers think selling the ranch might be a mistake."

"They do?" She couldn't keep the excitement out of her voice.

He smiled. "Yes. That's the reason they want to come check it out. They also suggested it could become a horse ranch, which is why my cousins are coming. They are in the horse breeding and training business. And then there are a few in my family who believe I can have horses and a dude ranch."

Brianna nodded. She could definitely see any of those options working. In fact, the horse business could benefit the dude ranch. "I think having both a dude ranch and a horse ranch would be wonderful. It would certainly boost the economy around here again."

"We'll see."

Brianna decided not to push the issue. She just hoped whatever plan he came up with would be one in which he would retain control of the ranch and not sell it. Ellen would have wanted that. It made her wonder—had he gone through the packet she had left in the drawer in his bedroom? Obviously not, since he hadn't mentioned it.

Before she could ask him about it, a deep male voice spoke. It was a voice she recognized, and it made her cringe. "Cashen Outlaw, right?"

Cash glanced up at the man who had approached their table. He stood when the man extended his hand. "Yes, I'm Cashen Outlaw."

"I'm Hal Sutherland," the man said, smiling broadly. "I spoke with you last week about buying the Blazing Frontier."

"Yes, I recall that you did." Cash looked at Brianna and then back at Hal. "I'm sure you know Brianna Banks, right?"

Hal barely gave her a cursory nod. "Brianna."

"Hal." Brianna knew he would have ignored her if Cash had not forced him to acknowledge her presence.

Hal glanced back at Cash. "So, when can we meet to talk business?"

"I haven't made any decisions about what I plan to do."

Brianna could tell from the look on Hal's face that he found Cash's words surprising as well as disappointing.

"Why would you want to keep it?" Hal asked as if he had every right to know.

Cash smiled. "For a number of reasons. Now, if you don't mind, Brianna and I want to finish our meal before it gets cold." He sat back down.

"Oh. Okay. Sure." Hal then walked off.

Brianna glanced over at Cash. "That doesn't happen often," she said.

"What?" Cash asked while cutting into his steak.

"Hal getting dismissed by anyone."

Cash shrugged. "There's a first time for everything."

"Thanks for joining me for dinner, Brianna. And you were right. The food was delicious," Cash said when they walked up the steps to her home.

"Thanks for inviting me. I'm glad you enjoyed everything."

"It's a beautiful night," he said, looking up into the sky while leaning against a porch post.

Brianna followed his gaze. "Yes, it is. We don't have the northern lights like Alaska, but I think a Wyoming sky is simply beautiful."

Cash looked over at her. She was beautiful, too. It had been a wonderful night and he had enjoyed sharing it with her. "Speaking of tonight, as nice as it was, there is one thing that I didn't appreciate."

She glanced over at him. "Oh? What?"

"Hal Sutherland interrupting our dinner." He paused.

"I picked up on tension between the two of you. Is there something I should know?"

He watched her nibble on her bottom lip, something that happened whenever he crossed unpleasant waters with her. His protective instincts went up. It bothered him that anything or anyone could upset her.

"Hal was Mr. Van's nephew, and Blazing Frontier was part of their family spread. Mr. Van and his first wife never had children, and everyone, including Hal, assumed if anything ever happened to Mr. Van, the ranch would belong to Hal as his heir."

"Um, let me guess," Cash said. "Mr. Van married Ellen and changed the dynamics."

"Yes. And while Mr. Van was alive, Hal pretty much behaved himself. The minute Mr. Van died, Hal approached Ellen and made her an offer to buy the property, assuming she would sell and move back east. She surprised him when she turned him down. He didn't like it much and caused problems, trying to force her to sell. She didn't." She paused. "He figured you had no reason to want to keep the land and would be glad to accept his offer."

Why did Cash have a feeling there was more? "And what else, Brianna?"

Brianna glanced down at the porch's floor and didn't say anything for a long moment before looking back up at him. "There's nothing else, Cash. At least, not anymore. Hal made it known that if he ever became the owner of the Blazing Frontier, one of the first things he would do would be to evict me from my home."

Cash raised a brow. "Why?"

"Hal is a man who holds grudges. He believes my parents are the reason Ms. Ellen didn't sell the ranch to him when Mr. Van died. Since my parents are no longer alive, he has extended his grudge to me."

"That's crazy."

She shrugged. "It doesn't matter now. Even if you were to sell the ranch to him, thanks to Ms. Ellen, this house and the acres it sits on are mine, and there is nothing he can do about it."

Hearing the strong emotion in her words made Cash glad that Ellen had done that for her. With a life of their own, his hands reached out and gently caressed her face. "I'm glad, Brianna."

Their gazes held and then he felt it—what he felt whenever he was around her. Sexual chemistry. It was stronger than ever tonight. He watched as she slowly drew in a deep breath, and as if they were a magnet, his lips were drawn closer.

His mouth unerringly went to hers. Tasting her was what he needed. This was what he had been thinking of doing since the day he had seen her licking that ice-cream cone. Now he was licking her, and he almost felt weak in the knees when she began licking him back.

Cash hadn't counted on the rush of heated desire that invaded his loins the moment their tongues connected. Nor had he counted on bone-melting fire spreading right into his soul. He began devouring her mouth in a way that should have been outlawed. It was as deep as you could take a kiss, his tongue boldly dueling with hers.

He tasted the pure sweetness of her mouth, and when he deepened the kiss, he couldn't help the moan forced from his throat. She leaned into him, her soft body pressing against his hard one. The sexual chemistry between them was out of control, at a level he had never encountered or expected. His testosterone level had never been revved up this much. But it had reached its boiling point, just for her.

The ringing of his cell phone had him dragging his mouth away from Brianna's. He recognized the ringtone. Charm. He would call her back later. For now, he wanted to pull Brianna back into his arms and kiss her again. He reached out for her, but she took a step back.

"I better get inside now," she said in a rush. "I hope you and your family enjoy your weekend. Good night, Cash." She turned to open the door.

"Wait. There's something I need to ask you."

She turned back around. "What?"

Cash studied her wet and swollen lips and felt a sense of gratification that he had done that. "Would you come to the ranch house tomorrow for dinner? I met Dano when he delivered the groceries today instead of waiting until tomorrow, and he says he's preparing a feast. I expect everyone to have arrived by four, and dinner will be served at seven. I'd like my family to meet you."

She raised a surprised brow. "Why would you want that?"

He really couldn't tell her why. All he knew was that he wanted to see her again and wanted his family to meet her. He decided to come up with a plausible reason. "Because you obviously meant a lot to Ellen. And I'm hoping if you're free on Saturday, you'll agree to be our tour guide. I know it's short notice, and if you have other plans I understand. You know every inch of Blazing Frontier and would do a better job showing everyone around than I could."

She didn't say anything as she studied the porch's floor again. Finally, she lifted her gaze to him. "I would love to join you for dinner tomorrow and meet your family. And I don't have anything planned on Saturday, if you think I'm really needed."

He smiled. "Yes, you'll be needed."

Whether she knew it or not, that kiss was just the beginning.

She nodded. "Good night, Cash."

Cash wasn't ready for the night to end. He was tempted to pull her into his arms again. Give her another kiss. Instead he knew he had to let her go. Besides, he needed to figure out why Brianna Banks had gotten under his skin in a way no other woman had before.

"Good night, Brianna. You were the perfect date."

You were the perfect date...

Cash's words floated through Brianna's mind as she stood by her living room window and watched the lights from his car fade into black. She honestly hadn't thought of it as a date until he'd said it. But now she concurred. After all, he had asked her out, picked her up, taken her to dinner and made sure she enjoyed herself.

And then he gave me one unforgettable good-night kiss.

She touched her lips, still tingling from his kiss. She had never been kissed like that before. Not for a good-night kiss or any other kind. He had taken her mouth like he owned every inch of it, searing her insides with passion.

She moved away from the window and sighed deeply. Her heart beat furiously in her chest. She needed to get a grip. Just because he had invited her to share his weekend didn't necessarily mean a thing. If nothing else, Alan had taught her to only believe in herself and no one else.

But still, there were so many things about Cash that she liked. And for someone who had been prepared not to like him, that said a lot. What really impressed her tonight was his handling of Hal. Although Hal wasn't all that liked around town, people knew not to cross him. Her parents, Mr. Van and Ms. Ellen had been some of the few who had stood up to him. Now she could add Cash to that list. Tonight, he had proven that he was not a man to take lightly. She had a feeling Hal realized that.

As she moved around the bedroom to undress, her spirits were soaring too high to think about going to sleep. She checked her watch. Miesha was a late-nighter and Brianna picked up her phone to call her friend.

"Hello."

"Guess what I did tonight, Miesha."

"Had sex with some hunk with enough orgasms for the both of us?"

Brianna couldn't help but scream in laughter. Her friend could say some of the most outlandish things at times. "No, I didn't have sex, but I did have a date."

"Do tell. You're glowing all the way through the phone."

Brianna figured that could be true because she felt giddy inside. When had a date ever left her feeling that way? "Cash Outlaw returned to town today and asked me out."

"I thought you said he wouldn't be coming back."

"I honestly thought he wouldn't, but he called and said he would be coming back for the weekend." Brianna then told her friend everything, ending with the whopper of a kiss on her porch.

"Hey, I like this Cash Outlaw. And for him to invite you for dinner to meet his family means something."

Brianna rolled her eyes. "It means he appreciates me agreeing to take his family on a tour Saturday."

"I don't see it that way. I've been around more men than you, so I know how they operate. You gave him a tour of the ranch last week, right?"

"Right."

"Then he should be capable of showing everyone around on his own. It shouldn't be that complicated. You know what I think?"

Brianna smiled. "No, what do you think?"

"I think he is using the tour as an excuse to spend time with you. He obviously likes you and that might be a good thing."

"How so?"

"If you decide not to use an unknown donor's sperm, you might want to place him at the top of the list."

Brianna's jaw almost dropped. "You've got to be kidding."

"Why would I kid about something like that? If you ask him, all he can do is say yes or no, Brianna."

"And he would say no, trust me."

"You can't be certain of that. I think it's a wonderful idea, and if you let him know you'll take full responsibility for raising your son, Cash just might be fine with it."

"Yes, but I'm not sure I would be."

"I don't see why not. You thought the world of Ms. Ellen and she thought the world of you. It makes perfect sense to me that you would be the mother of her grandchild."

Brianna didn't say anything for a moment, refusing to let Miesha fill her head with crazy thoughts. "For all I know, Cash Outlaw might be in a relationship."

"Not if he kissed you the way you said he did tonight. I'm not saying he doesn't date, because he probably does. That's not the same as a relationship. Besides, he will let you know if he's unavailable when you broach the subject of fathering your child."

Brianna shook her head. "No, I can't do that. It won't work."

"Okay, it was just a suggestion."

A short while later, after hanging up the phone with Miesha, Brianna began getting ready for bed. Aftereffects from that kiss were still thrumming through her body and a part of her couldn't wait to see Cash again tomorrow.

However, she could not and would not entertain the thought of Cash Outlaw fathering her child—no matter how appealing the idea might be.

Eight

"This is one hell of a nice place, Cash," Garth said as he stood on the porch and looked out over the land. "I can't wait for the tour tomorrow."

Cash smiled as he handed his oldest brother a bottle of beer. Garth had been the last to arrive. Now all his house-guests were accounted for. Most were in the saloon and the others were at the game center, shooting pool. Like Garth, everyone had been taken with the place.

"Hopefully, you'll know by the end of the weekend what you plan to do with it."

"Yes, I should know by then." Cash paused. "Can I ask you something, Garth?"

"Yes, what?"

"It's about Karen."

For years, the family had known never to mention the woman Garth had loved who'd died in a copter accident, because whenever they did, they saw the pain in their broth-er's eyes. But now Garth had moved on with his life. He was married to Regan and the spark was back in his eyes.

Garth lifted a brow. "What about Karen?"

"I recall you saying that from the first time you met her, you knew she was special."

Garth studied his brother as he took another swig of beer. "I did. That's not saying I hadn't dated women I thought were special before. I just knew there was something different about her. I knew she was the one." He leaned against the porch rail. "Have you met such a woman, Cash?"

Cash met his brother's gaze and nodded. "I think I have."

"Brianna Banks?"

Cash didn't say anything for a minute and then, "Yes."

Garth nodded. "Is that why you're taking two weeks off to hang around here? Not that I don't think you deserve the time off."

"I'm not going to say she's the only reason, but I'd be fooling myself to think she doesn't have a lot to do with it."

"Then you're doing the right thing. Hindsight is twenty-twenty. Regan said she'd been in love with me for years. And when I think of the time I could have spent with her being as happy as I am now, I see them as wasted years, Cash. Life is too short to live it with regrets." He paused again. "I think even Bart has regrets."

"You think so?"

Garth smiled. "Maybe not with any of our mothers, but definitely with Charm's. If he could marry Claudia today, he would."

"You think he's learned his lesson?"

"No. Claudia probably does not think he has either, which is why she won't marry him. I honestly don't think he'll ever change. He might be a different person around her, but on the inside he's still the same Bart."

Cash didn't say anything as he took a swallow of his own beer. Then he said, "I invited her to dinner."

"Who?"

"Brianna."

Garth smiled. "I can't wait to meet her."

Brianna saw all the vehicles parked in front of the ranch house the moment she turned in to the driveway. She tried to calm the butterflies in her stomach, telling herself she didn't have a reason to be nervous. Although she didn't know any of Cash's guests, she did know him.

She parked behind a truck, got out of the car and glanced down at herself. She would be looking like a cowgirl tomorrow when she took them on the tour. Today she had dressed up in her long, flowing maxi skirt with a long-sleeve blouse and boots. Her favorite necklace, a gift from her parents on her twenty-first birthday, was around her neck, and the matching earrings were in her ears.

She had taken one step toward the door when it opened and Cash stepped out. If she didn't know better, she would think he'd been waiting for her, but she did know better. "Hello, Cash."

He smiled at her. "Hello, Brianna. You look very nice."

"Thanks."

"Everyone is in the dining room."

"Alright."

He surprised her by taking her hand, something he hadn't done last night. She walked with him toward the dining room, taking time to wave at Dano. She heard loud voices and the butterflies appeared again. Right before she entered the dining room, Cash said, "Thanks for coming."

She smiled up at him. "Thanks for inviting me."

Tightening his hand on hers, he then led her to where several guys were talking. "We have a guest for dinner," Cash said loudly to get their attention.

It seemed all eyes turned their way, giving her curious stares. She figured more so because Cash hadn't let go of her hand. "Guys, I'd like you to meet a friend, Brianna Banks. She and her parents used to work here at the ranch. Brianna will be our tour guide tomorrow."

He then said to her, "Come on, let me take you around to introduce you to everyone. I don't expect you to remember them by name, though."

First, he introduced her to his brothers, Garth, Jess,

Sloan and Maverick. It didn't take long for her to see that Cash's youngest brother, Maverick, was a natural born flirt who enjoyed rattling Cash. Jess was a United States Senator who made his home in the nation's capital. Garth and Jess were older than Cash, and Sloan and Maverick were younger. She could feel a closeness between the brothers. They told her about their sister, Charm, who was a couple years younger than Brianna.

Then he introduced her to his Westmoreland cousins—Zane, Derringer, Jason, Durango, Clint and Bane. There was a striking resemblance between the Outlaw brothers and their Westmoreland cousins. It was uncanny how much Cash and Bane favored. The only difference was their eye coloring. Bane had hazel eyes. However, unless she was standing right in front of them, she wouldn't notice the difference.

Then there were two friends of the Westmorelands, Bane's navy SEAL teammates—Laramie Cooper, who everyone called Coop, and Thurston McRoy, who was called Mac. The two men also owned horse ranches and while away on missions hired trusted foremen to run their spreads. Last, she was introduced to McKinnon Quinn, cousin-in-law of the Westmorelands, who was married to Clint Westmoreland's sister. McKinnon was gorgeous with thick black hair that fell to his shoulders. He told her he was Blackfoot Indian and African American Creole. He and Durango lived in Montana and were the two who had started the horse training and breeding business.

"I can't believe how much the Outlaws and the Westmorelands favor. Especially you and Bane," Brianna told Cash when he seated her beside him at the long table.

He smiled over at her. "Remind me to tell you how I switched places with Bane once, to help bring down a group of bad guys who were threatening his wife."

Brianna lifted a brow. "You're serious?"

He smiled. "Yes, I'm serious."

She enjoyed dining with everyone and although she was the only female in the group, she in no way felt left out of the conversation. These guys were ranchers and she was familiar with a lot of their topics and even added her two cents, especially when they began discussing horses. She could tell they were surprised and impressed with her knowledge.

"How do you know so much about horse ranching? Cash said you worked as the manager of the dude ranch," Clint Westmoreland said, smiling over at her.

"I did, but I was also the daughter of a lifelong foreman. Specifically of this ranch. I grew up here and remember when it was a cattle ranch and there were plenty of horses. I have a barn at my place and keep three horses there and care for them myself."

Dano had outdone himself with dinner and everyone was singing the chef's praises while enjoying the dessert he'd prepared—peach cobbler with what some of the guys claimed was the best coffee they'd ever had.

Every man here was handsome as sin. And she was surprised to learn that they were all married except for Cash's brothers Jess, Sloan and Maverick. Some of the guys and their wives had multiple births...something Cash said was common in his family. Bane was the father of triplets, and Jason and Mac were the fathers of twins. She'd also discovered Clint was part of triplets. He had a brother named Cole, and his sister Casey was married to McKinnon. Bane's triplets were Ace, Adam and Anna Clarisse. Bane's brother Jason had twin girls, one of whom was named Clarisse Hope. Jason and Bane explained they had both wanted to give their mother's name, Clarisse, to their daughters. Brianna thought it was a touching gesture.

When it was time to leave, she stood and said to the

group, "I'm looking forward to showing all of you around tomorrow."

"And we're looking forward to having you as our tour guide," Maverick said, smiling and winking at her.

Cash insisted that he follow Brianna back home to make sure she got there safely, although she had told him that wasn't necessary. It was to him.

He parked his car beside hers and got out to walk her up to the door. "So, what do you think of the Outlaws, Westmorelands and friends?"

She smiled up at him when they reached her door. "The guys are wonderful and I like how they are family men. They love their wives and children."

He lifted a brow. "Isn't that the way it's supposed to be?"

"Yes, but it's not always. I was blessed to have parents who loved each other and who loved me, and the same thing with the kids I grew up with. When I got to college, I discovered that wasn't always the case. My best friend's mom has been married three times and her father, four."

"My father, Bart, has them beat," Cash said. "He's been married and divorced five times and had a son by each of the women. Me and my brothers have different mothers."

"Yet all of you get along."

He chuckled. "No reason we shouldn't. Our father, Bart, raised the five of us and wasn't keen on us having friends. Except for Walker Rafferty. He's been Garth's best friend since they were babies. And Regan, who's married to Garth now. She grew up around us since her father was the corporate pilot for Outlaw Freight Lines for over forty years."

"What about your sister, Charm? Who is her mother?"

Cash was surprised how comfortable he felt discussing his family with Brianna, something he barely did with anyone. "Bart was never married to Charm's mother, and but we know that is something he regrets and would undo if he could. That's a whole other story."

"Thanks for seeing me safely home. Although you really didn't have to, I appreciate it."

He smiled down at her. "Do you appreciate it enough to invite me in for coffee?"

"What about your guests?"

"What about them? Last time I looked they were grown-ass men who can fend for themselves. Besides, a third of them are going to return to playing pool, a third will find their way over to the saloon, and the other third will hang near the kitchen for a second helping of Dano's pie and coffee. Everything was delicious. Thanks for setting up this weekend."

"You're welcome. Do you honestly want a cup of coffee?"

"Yes." He would tell her later he wanted a kiss as well, but he didn't want to do it out here on her porch like he had last night.

"Then a cup of coffee it is," she said, opening the door.

When they were inside and he closed the door behind him, she said, "Make yourself at home and when I return with our coffee, I want to hear all about the time you switched places with Bane to protect his wife."

He chuckled. "Okay."

Cash watched her disappear into her kitchen and went over to her fireplace to look at the framed photographs sitting on the mantel. He figured the older couple was her parents and smiled at her graduation photo.

He recalled what she had told him at dinner last night. Her boyfriend, who was supposed to return to marry her when she graduated, had married someone else. His betrayal was the reason she could never give her heart to another man. Cash could just imagine not only the hurt she'd had to endure but also the embarrassment when he returned with his wife. In a small town like Black Crow, that must have been humiliating. She hadn't deserved that. The guy hadn't deserved her.

Music began playing and Cash immediately recognized the song and the artist. "I'm back," she said, carrying a tray with two cups of coffee. Setting the tray on the coffee table, she handed him a cup.

"Thanks. I take it you like Dylan Emanuel's music."

"I love it. He's a gifted musician and he has such a way with words. And his voice is superb. He's up for another Grammy this year."

"So I heard. I met him once."

Her eyes widened. "You did?"

"Yes. It was years ago. He was seventeen and had won a summer scholarship to attend the University of Alaska's Fairbanks Summer Music Academy. My sister, Charm, had the chance to get to know Dylan when one of her piano instructors also taught Dylan that summer."

There was no need to tell Brianna how Bart had found out about the budding romance between Charm and Dylan and hadn't wasted any time putting an end to what Bart had called utter teenage nonsense.

Brianna eased down on the sofa, tucking her legs beneath her as she stirred her coffee. "Your sister plays the piano?"

He shook his head, grinning. "No. She bummed out on those lessons." He took a sip of coffee. "There is nothing like good coffee. It's delicious."

She smiled. "Thanks. I can't compete with Dano, but I don't do so bad. Dad taught me. He said, 'Don't mess around when it comes to a cowboy's coffee.'"

"Well, I like it. And you know what else I like, Brianna?"

"No. What?"

"Seeing you smile. You have a beautiful smile."

"Flattery is nice, but don't think it's going to get you out of telling me what I want to know, Cash," she said, grinning. "Now, tell me about the time you and Bane traded places."

He couldn't help but laugh. "Okay, here goes."

He spent the next twenty minutes telling her the story. He felt okay in doing so since it had made news when Homeland Security had arrested all those involved.

"Wow! That's just like reading a spy novel. I'm glad Bane and his wife were okay."

"I am, too, but it was never Bane and Crystal who were really in danger. It was those men who thought they could actually take her away from Bane. My family believes in protecting what's theirs."

Brianna nodded. "The one thing I noticed about your family is that they are close. Must be nice."

"It is, especially since the Outlaws and Westmorelands only discovered they were related a few years ago."

She lifted a brow. "You're kidding. How? Why?"

Cash then told her how the Outlaws and Westmorelands discovered they were related. He also mentioned how Garth's best friend, Walker Rafferty, had visited the Westmorelands in Denver to verify the kinship. Walker had met Bailey Westmoreland, the two had fallen in love and ended up marrying. "So there you have it," he said when he finished the story.

"That's way too much action for me," she said, shaking her head. The gesture made a few curls dance around her shoulders.

He wanted to touch those curls, but instead he glanced at his watch and stood. "It's getting late and you need your sleep."

She stood as well and chuckled. "I need my sleep?"

"Yes, we're heading out at dawn, remember?"

"Yes, I remember, and I'll be fine. Baby and I love going out riding that time of morning."

"Baby?"

"Yes, my horse. I'll ride Baby over to your place."

"Okay," he said, following her as she led him to the door. Upon reaching it, she turned to him. "Thanks again for making sure I got home safely and sharing your family with me, Cash."

He took a step closer to her and gave in to the need to push a strand of hair from her face. "You are welcome."

Then he lowered his mouth to hers for the kiss he so desperately needed. The kiss he'd spent most of the night anticipating. The kiss he had gotten addicted to last night.

Everything about her kiss pleased him. The moment she wrapped her arms around his neck, he deepened the kiss. She moaned, and he loved the sound. He loved the feel of her body plastered to his. He greedily took her mouth like it would be his last chance to do so.

Although he wished otherwise, he knew he couldn't stand here and kiss her all night. Slowly and reluctantly, he ended the kiss. But not before sweeping her lips with his tongue.

"I love kissing you," he said against her moist lips. "The first time I saw your mouth, I got turned on by it. Do you know when that was?"

She smiled up at him. "In Mr. Cavanaugh's office?"

"No. Before that."

Her forehead bunched up. "Before Mr. Cavanaugh's office?"

"Yes."

"But I hadn't met you before then."

"True, but I had seen you. The moment I entered town. I was stopped at a traffic light and saw you coming out of an ice-cream shop. Seeing how you were licking that ice-cream cone made my entire body ache."

She didn't say anything. In fact, she actually blushed,

and he thought it was the cutest thing. Not able to help himself, he leaned down and kissed her again.

Moments later, he slowly pulled back, flicked his gaze over her features and saw the expression of a satisfied woman. He smiled, knowing he'd done that. "Good night, Brianna. I'll see you in the morning."

"Baby and I will be there."

He couldn't wait to see the mare she called Baby. He then opened the door. If he didn't leave now, he would be tempted to kiss her yet again.

Nine

"Will you look at that beauty of a horse Brianna is riding?" Zane Westmoreland remarked, staring off in the distance.

Cash turned and like the others, stared at horse and rider. He knew the others were checking out the horse. He was checking out the rider. She looked absolutely stunning galloping across the plains toward them. The mass of hair beneath her wide-brimmed hat was flying in the wind while she sat astride a huge white stallion that looked fierce. Like he could eat you alive. That was Baby?

Cash chuckled, deciding the joke was on him. Baby was not a docile mare like he'd assumed. Zane was right. It was a beauty of a horse. And Brianna was handling him like a pro. He glanced around and saw admiration and respect in his family's and friends' eyes.

"Good morning, guys. You ready?" she asked when she came to a stop in front of them.

"Good morning. Yes, we're ready," Cash said, smiling over at her. "That's a beautiful horse."

"Thanks. Baby has been mine since he was a colt."

"Baby?" Durango Westmoreland said, chuckling. "He doesn't look like a baby. He looks mean."

"He can be to others but not to me. He's very protective of me."

"You handle him well," Clint Westmoreland said.

"Thanks." She smiled at everyone. "By the way, Dano will have lunch ready for us in the lower valley of your property at noon."

Cash lifted a brow. "He will?"

"Yes, that will save us time since we won't need to return to the ranch house."

Cash was glad she had thought of that and taken care of the arrangements. "Where are we headed to first?"

"The range. I want everyone to see how vast it is."

"Then lead the way."

Nearly five hours later, Cash would admit everyone was enjoying themselves. His Denver Westmoreland cousins indicated their land lacked the valleys and plains here, and that the only time they could ride this freely was when they visited Clint's spread in Austin. Everyone was surprised when at noon they returned to the spot where lunch would be served. Dano had a barbecue pit going and had set up tables to accommodate everyone. The meal had been served with baked beans, potato salad and the best-tasting punch. The weather was perfect.

Right before dusk, everyone returned to the ranch, tired and excited about how the day had gone. The guys thanked Brianna for being a great tour guide and told her goodbye since they wouldn't see her again before leaving tomorrow. They then headed inside to shower after what they all considered a wonderful day spent out on the range.

Cash held back to again talk to Brianna before she rode off for home. She was sitting astride Baby and he stood beside her, glancing up. "Everyone enjoyed themselves, Brianna. I could tell they were impressed with the place."

Her smile widened. "I'm glad. It was good seeing you again this weekend, Cash. I hope all of you have a safe trip back home." Then, as if on impulse, she leaned down and swiped a quick kiss across his lips.

Before he could react, she straightened in the saddle and

took off. She and Baby went racing across the yard toward her home. He licked his lips, still tasting her there.

He'd never got around to telling her that he would be staying for two weeks. He grinned. She would find out soon enough.

"So, what do you guys think?" Cash asked the crew around the table later that evening.

It was McKinnon who answered. "You are sitting on a gold mine. This place is perfect for a horse ranch. I can also see you turning it back into a dude ranch. You have enough land to do both. There is one thing I suggest you do, though."

"What?" Cash asked.

"I heard you mention to Zane that you don't have full access to Keystone River from your property."

"That's right. I share it with someone," Cash replied.

"I suggest you contact the owner and make them an offer for it. That could not only be beneficial in a number of ways, but perhaps also necessary."

Cash lifted a brow. "Why?"

"The more water you have for the horses, the better, especially during the year when the water holes on the property become dry. I did my research and that has happened in this area a few times."

"Do you know the person you share that property with? Do you think they would be interested in selling the land?" Bane asked.

Cash didn't say anything. "Yes, I know the owner. In fact, the land was part of the original deed to the ranch before Ellen died."

"Then what happened?"

Cash rubbed his hand down his face before saying, "Ellen divided it up in her will. That part of the property was given to Brianna."

Derringer smiled. "Oh, well, then you don't have anything to worry about. She might just sell it back to you or at the very least, let you lease the land."

"I'd prefer if he made an offer to buy it," Durango said. "McKinnon and I tried leasing land to expand and ran into problems. When it came time to renew the lease, the landowner doubled the price because he knew how essential the land was to our business."

"I can't see Brianna ever doing something like that," Sloan said. It was obvious Sloan had been taken with Brianna.

"Probably not Brianna, but she's young and single. What if she marries one day and her husband is an ass with a lot of influence on her?"

"Brianna can't up and marry anybody," Maverick said matter-of-factly, grinning from ear to ear.

"Why not?" Mac was curious to know.

"Because she's Cash's girl. Didn't you see how he was practically breathing down her neck all weekend? Even on Friday night, his hand seemed to be glued to hers."

Zane rubbed his chin. "Yes, I noticed. I think we all did." He then glanced over at Cash. "Is she your girl?"

Cash found it somewhat amusing how they had been discussing him like he hadn't been in their presence. When he didn't answer right away, an impatient Sloan asked, "Well, is she your girl or not, Cash?"

Cash gave his brother a slow smile. "Yes, Brianna is my girl. She's all mine."

It was strange that he'd just done something he'd never thought he would. Claim a woman as his. But he felt damn good about it, even though he didn't know how Brianna might feel about him stating ownership the way he just had. She had no idea that he wanted to engage in a relationship with her—not just to see where it went, but to make sure it went where he wanted it to go.

Cash then remembered what she'd told him about never wanting to fall in love again for fear of having her heart broken. She'd seemed pretty damn adamant about it. That meant he had to come up with a plan to win Brianna over.

And he would.

Ten

Brianna was surprised when she arrived at the Blazing Frontier bright and early Monday morning to find Cash's rental car still parked in the driveway. Did he not leave with the others yesterday? She didn't recall him saying he would stay longer.

She tried to stop her heart from beating so rapidly as she got out of the car, not sure why she was so anxious when she'd been around Cash all weekend. But then, there had been others around as well. Now they would be alone and the last couple times they'd been alone, he had kissed her. Would he do so again? Did she want him to?

She walked up the steps and before she could knock, the door opened.

"Good morning, Brianna," Cash said, smiling at her.

She tried to ignore the effect that smile had on her. "I thought you would be leaving with the others," she said, walking into the ranch house when he moved aside.

"I decided to stay awhile."

"Oh."

"I looked forward to seeing you this morning," he said.

"How did you know I was coming over today?"

"Dano mentioned you would be returning to go through Ellen's belongings. I was just about to grab a cup of coffee and some of those strawberry muffins Dano made. Will you join me?"

Brianna figured there was no reason she shouldn't. Besides, maybe he would tell her if he had made a decision about the ranch. "I'd love to join you," she said, following him into the kitchen. He looked good in his jeans and shirt. "Why did you decide to remain here instead of leaving with the others yesterday?" she asked before she could stop herself from doing so.

When he turned and looked at her over his shoulder, she quickly added, "Sorry, it's really not any of my business."

He pulled two cups out of the cabinet and poured coffee into them. "In a way, it is your business. I decided to help you go through Ellen's things after all."

The pulse beat in her neck. "You have?"

"Yes."

She met his gaze when he handed her the coffee. What had made him change his mind? Had he gotten around to seeing that packet she had left in his bedroom? Whatever the reason, she didn't want to think about them being in such close proximity.

"How long will you be staying?"

He met her gaze. "That depends on you."

"On me?" she asked, surprised.

"Yes. I plan to be here for as long as you need me here."

She nodded. They were still talking about working together to go through Ellen's things, right? Brianna took a sip of her coffee and tried not to think of him possibly meaning anything else.

Deciding to change the subject, she asked, "Did everyone enjoy themselves this weekend?"

"Yes, they did. They were impressed with the place," he said, setting a plate of muffins in front of her. He had warmed them up and they smelled heavenly.

"Blazing Frontier is a beautiful spread," she said before taking a bite. She glanced up and saw him staring at her.

She licked a crumb off her bottom lip and then asked, "Is anything wrong?"

He shook his head and smiled. "No, there's nothing wrong. You like that muffin?"

She chuckled. "Yes. I love strawberries so these are my favorite muffins." As they ate, Brianna couldn't stand not knowing any longer. "Have you decided whether you're going to keep the ranch or sell it?"

He didn't say anything for a moment. "I've decided to keep the ranch."

A huge smile spread across her face and she couldn't contain her happiness. "You have?"

"Yes. However, there's something I need to talk to you about."

"Oh? What?" she asked, wondering what that could be.

"I want to get the most use out of the ranch and think I can by turning it back into a dude ranch, as well as making it into a thriving horse ranch. There's certainly enough land for both. However, there is a slight problem," he said.

"What's the problem, Cash?"

"Although there are plenty of water holes on the property, they tend to dry up. Before making a final decision, I have to be sure a permanent stream of water will be available for the horses. The best roaming and grazing areas for them are on land near Keystone River. However, only a small portion of the lake is on the section of Blazing Frontier that I own. The largest part of the lake is on the land Ellen gave to you."

He paused and then said, "I need to buy that section of land from you, Brianna."

Cash watched her take another sip of her coffee. She hadn't said anything, although he was certain she had heard him. If she needed time to digest what he'd said, he would give it to her.

A few seconds ticked by before she finally spoke. "I have no problem leasing fifty acres to you, Cash."

"But I'd have a problem with it."

"Why?" she asked.

"Because such an agreement isn't permanent. The amount of money that my investors and business partners will put into this ranch to bring it up to par can't hinge on such an agreement. What happens when the lease expires?"

"Then we enter into a new one," she said.

"We would negotiate for a new one with the hopes that both you and I are happy with the terms. What if we aren't? That would place my investors and business partners at risk."

She studied the contents of her coffee cup before glancing back at him. "Your offer is unexpected. I need time to think about it."

Cash released a sigh. "I wish I could say take all the time you need, but I can't. I will need to know by Friday, Brianna. I'd like to start work on this place before the end of the month."

"That soon?"

He smiled. "Yes, that soon," he said, starting to feel excited about it. "A number of repairs are needed, including a new roof on this house, the barn and several of the cottages. We also need to upgrade the game center and renovate the pool area."

Brianna nodded. "I will have my answer to you by Friday, Cash."

"Thank you. If there was any way I could do what's needed without the fifty acres, I would, but I can't. Otherwise, I will have to sell the ranch to someone who won't need as much water as I will."

"I understand."

Cash wondered if she honestly did. If he put the ranch up for sale, he would have to consider all offers. He was a businessman, after all. But then, what she'd shared with him about Sutherland bothered him deeply, and he knew it bothered her. Therefore, he would not be entertaining an offer from Sutherland, no matter what.

They finished their coffee and muffins in silence. Then he asked, "Where do we start with going through Ellen's belongings."

Brianna pushed her empty plate and coffee cup aside. "Last week I finished in her bedroom after you called to say you were coming. I donated her clothes and shoes to charity." She chuckled softly. "Ms. Ellen had over a zillion pairs."

"She liked shoes, huh?" Cash said.

"Yes."

"So do I. My brothers claim I own more shoes than I will ever wear."

"Then that's something you and Ms. Ellen had in common."

Cash said nothing to that comment as he got up from the table. "So, what's the plan for today?"

She glanced up at him. "We can do the attic."

A few minutes later, Cash followed Brianna and tried not to notice the sexy shape of her backside when she walked ahead of him up the stairs, but he couldn't help doing so. And she smelled good, too. Trying to take his mind off the sexy woman in front of him, he made a mental note to install sturdier railings for the stairs.

When she opened the attic door, he had expected to find a cluttered area but saw the place was tidy, filled with several filing cabinets. Instead of boxes, there were stacks of bins lined in neat rows against the walls.

Cash followed her into the room and saw how spacious the attic was. It didn't have a window, or central air and heat. The room could be converted into a nice-size office. It was on the far end of the hall and in a private corner.

Brianna glanced over at him. "While in high school, I used to earn my money each summer by keeping the attic neat."

He nodded. "What's in the bins?"

"Most contain ranch records dating back to heaven knows when."

"Any reason this stuff can't be shredded?" he asked her.

"No, but the only shredder we have is located behind the check-in desk downstairs," she told him.

"I'll haul it up here, no problem." He rolled up his sleeves. "Okay, let's get started."

They worked in companionable silence for the next couple hours. He had turned on the one ceiling fan in the room, but the air still wasn't circulating sufficiently. He noticed Brianna had rolled up the sleeves of her blouse.

After wiping sweat off his brow a few times, he said, "It's hot as the dickens in here. Mind if I take off my shirt?"

She looked over at him. "No, I don't mind."

"Thanks."

He began taking off his shirt, knowing her gaze was on him. He tried not to make it obvious that he knew she was watching him even though she was pretending she wasn't.

He inwardly smiled.

Brianna would not have minded if Cash had removed his pants as well.

From the first, she had thought he had a nice physique. He looked good in whatever he wore, whether it was a business suit or Western wear. She was just as convinced that he would look good wearing nothing at all.

She didn't want to stare and tried not to make it so obvious she was looking, but she knew he was unbuttoning his shirt and was aware of the exact moment he removed it to show a T-shirt. When he pulled the T-shirt over his head, her pulse began racing.

His muscular bare chest and strong biceps were the kind any woman would want to glide her hands across. Or better yet, she would love to bury her face in the curly hair covering his chest while inhaling his masculine scent. The visual that flowed through her mind nearly made her weak in the knees. Sweaty and sexy was one hell of a powerful combination for any woman to handle. Especially a woman whose hormones were acting out of whack.

"Brianna?"

Her gaze jerked up to his face, and when she saw the smile that curved his lips, she knew she'd been caught staring. "Yes?" she answered in a voice too husky to be her own.

"I just want you to know if it gets too hot in here for you, you can take your shirt off, too."

Cash's gaze lowered to her chest and her nipples hardened. "No, thanks," she said and quickly turned back to finish going through all the papers in one of the bins.

They continued to work in silence and when she glanced over at him again, she saw the rippling muscles of his back when he leaned down to pick up a bin to move it to another area. She forced down a moan and quickly looked away.

He evidently heard it. "Are you okay, Brianna?"

He had a sensual way of saying her name. It seemed to flow from his lips like warm honey. "Yes, I'm fine."

It was getting too hot in here for her and she knew if she didn't get out of this room with Cash, she wouldn't be liable for her actions. Glancing at her watch, she saw they had worked until a little past noon.

"How about if I make lunch?"

He turned and wiped sweat from his brow. "That sounds good. Dano left the fridge stocked, but I'm not sure with what."

"No problem. I'll check to see what I can whip up."

Brianna moved to rush by him, but the heel of her shoe caught on something and she went tumbling.

Right into Cash's arms.

Eleven

Cash caught Brianna, but he was not ready to release her yet. When she'd tripped, her face had landed on his chest, and she still had it there. He figured she needed a moment to get her bearings. That was fine with him.

"Are you alright?" he finally asked her.

Brianna lifted her head, but didn't try to pull away. "Sorry, Cash. I'm not usually clumsy."

There was something sexy about the movement of her throat while she talked. That, combined with such a luscious mouth, sent an adrenaline rush all through him. "No problem. I'm more than happy to catch you anytime."

"Thank you. I'm fine and you can release me now."

Could he? Did he want to? Brianna was the only woman alive who had the ability to shoot his libido up just from the sound of her too-sexy voice. "What if I said I prefer not to?"

She lifted an arched brow as she tipped her head back to look up at him. "Why not?"

"Because of this." Tightening his hold on her elbows, he eased her closer while leaning down to capture her mouth. He paused, waiting for her response, and was rewarded with her leaning in, too.

There was just something gratifying about kissing Brianna. Mating his mouth with hers was intense and so damn pleasurable. There was nothing like sliding his tongue into her mouth and then sucking on her tongue. He liked devouring her mouth in a way that made the muscles in his stomach quiver and the lower part of his body throb.

The deeper he took the kiss, the greedier he became. From the way she was moaning, he knew that she felt it, too. How would it be if they ever made love? They would burn up the sheets and be as sexually compatible as any couple could get.

She suddenly pulled her mouth away and rested her forehead against his chest as they tried to get their breathing under control. She finally lifted her head and looked at him in a way that tightened his gut. He saw her wet lips and glassy eyes, which made his libido soar even more.

"Why do you always kiss me?"

Did she honestly have to ask him that? "I believe your mouth is made for kissing. I can't think of any other woman I'd rather kiss, Brianna."

"I'm not very good at it."

He didn't think she was fishing for a compliment, which meant she honestly thought that. He had no problem putting that assumption to rest. "You *are* good at it, Brianna. You're a natural. That's what makes kissing you so refreshing as well as enjoyable."

She took a step back and dropped her arms from him. "I need to go make lunch now."

"Okay."

She headed for the door, paused a moment and then looked back at him. "I think kissing you is refreshing and enjoyable, too, Cash."

Brianna's heart was pounding hard in her chest. Being around Cash did that to her. Then, whenever he would kiss her, she not only had to deal with her increased heart rate but also lost all sense. Telling Cash that she enjoyed his kisses, too, probably hadn't been a smart thing to do.

Walking over to the refrigerator, she opened it and pulled

out everything she needed to make sandwiches, grateful Dano had purchased enough. She had finished making the turkey, ham and cheese sandwiches, to be served with a pitcher of iced tea, when she heard Cash behind her. Turning around, she saw he had at least put his T-shirt back on.

With great effort she tried maintaining her composure. "Just in time for lunch. I have it ready."

"Okay."

Whether he said one word or several, his deeply male voice had a way of stroking her senses. "I'll go wash up," he said. "I'll be back."

She watched him leave. He had such a masculine walk. His long legs and tight thighs clad in jeans were pure male perfection.

By the time he returned, she had placed their plates on the table. "Thanks for fixing lunch, Brianna. It looks good."

"You are welcome. I think we accomplished a lot so far."

Cash glanced over at her and smiled. "Yes, we have. But we still have a lot more to do. I had no idea there was so much stuff." He paused a moment. "Now I feel bad about expecting you to do it on your own. That was selfish of me."

"No, it wasn't," she said, although she had thought that very thing at the time. "You had no idea all that stuff was up there."

He nodded. "I thought it would just be Ellen's personal things that you'd be more equipped to handle than I would."

For several seconds they said nothing while they ate. Then, out of the clear blue sky, he broke the silence. "You know what?"

She glanced over at him. "No, what?"

"Kissing you brings out the lust in me."

"Oh." She honestly didn't know what to say to that.

"Is there a part of me that brings out the lust in you, Brianna?"

Just because he'd asked didn't mean she had to answer. "I'd rather not say."

In truth, every part of him brought out the lust in her. The way his clothes fit. His smile. That dimple in his right cheek. The touch of his hands. His scent. The magnetism of his eyes could draw her in whenever she gazed directly into them. She could go on and on.

"What if I want you to say?" he asked her.

Those eyes were drawing her in now. She broke contact to look down at her plate. When she glanced back across the table at him, she said, "We can't always have what we want, Cash."

Brianna's words were still weighing heavily on Cash's mind when they returned to the attic. Just like that morning, they worked in companionable silence. The only time they exchanged words was when she asked him about a particular document he'd come across.

He had hauled the shredder up two flights of stairs, and the humming sound helped as she fed documents into it. It didn't help whenever he looked over at her and caught her staring at him, or those times she had caught him staring at her.

He glanced at his watch when he felt a stirring of sexual desire again. "I think we should call it a day."

She looked over at him. "You won't get any complaints out of me. I think we got a lot accomplished."

Cash thought so, too. He watched her pull down the sleeves of her blouse, and then, to make it not so obvious that he was staring, he grabbed his shirt and put it back on. "What are your plans for this evening?" he asked her.

She looked up at him. "I don't have any. Why?"

"I'd like you to spend it with me."

She pushed her hair from her face. "Spend it with you how?"

He could tell her a lot of naughty ways, but instead he said, "I'd like to see what the town has to offer in the way of fun."

She didn't say anything for a moment. "It just so happens the state fair came to town this weekend, if you're looking for something fun to do."

He smiled over at her. "Then let's do it."

They did do it.

Brianna had to admit she had fun. It wasn't just that Cash had taken her to grab something to eat at the town's favorite pizzeria, or that he'd won a huge stuffed bear for her, or that he'd shared his foot-long hot dog with her. It had been how he had walked around holding her hand and hadn't seemed bothered that doing so caught the attention of a number of people.

The one thing that had surprised her was that when they had reached her house, he'd declined her invitation for coffee. But he'd made up for it in the kiss that still had her swooning an hour or so later.

She had just showered and gotten into bed when her phone rang. She recognized the number and her heart began pounding. "Yes?"

"Go to sleep and think about me tonight."

She was tempted to tell Cash that she would do more than just think about him. Deciding to be coy, she smiled and said, "Now, why should I do that?"

"Because you like me."

Yes, she most certainly did. "Maybe."

"Where is Magnum?"

Cash had named the huge stuffed bear Magnum. "He's right here in bed with me."

"I envy that bear."

She didn't say anything but swore she could feel the

crackle of sexual energy through the phone. "What are you doing? In bed yet?"

"Nope. I'm sitting outside on the porch enjoying a beer. What time can I expect you tomorrow?"

"Around nine. I forgot to mention I have an appointment on Thursday so I won't be coming that day." No way would she tell him what the appointment was about.

"Okay, I will see you tomorrow. Give Magnum a pat on his head for me."

She chuckled. "I will. Good night."

"Good night, Brianna."

She had just finished giving Magnum his pat on the head when Brianna's cell phone rang again. She smiled, recognizing the ringtone, and quickly answered it. "Miesha?"

"Yes. I had to put Darrett to bed and then prepare for a meeting with my employees in the morning. But I wanted to know how things went this weekend. Was Cashen Outlaw as hot as ever?"

Brianna chuckled. "Yes." She then told her friend about the weekend.

"When will he make a decision as to whether or not he'll keep the ranch or sell it?"

"Cash already has. He plans to keep it."

After Miesha released a huge yell, Brianna added, "However, there might be a glitch."

"What kind of glitch?"

Brianna nibbled on her bottom lip. "His decision is dependent on me," she said.

"How so?"

Brianna then told Miesha what Cash had told her about the fifty acres.

"He wants your land?" And before Brianna could answer, Miesha exclaimed, "Wow! Now you have bargaining power."

Bargaining power? Brianna lifted a brow. "What on earth are you talking about?"

"Think about it, Brie. You have something he wants, and he has something you want."

Brianna shook her head. "And just what is it he has that I want?"

"Sperm. And I bet he has plenty of them."

Brianna blinked. "What!"

"Why bother going to that fertility clinic on Thursday? Cashen Outlaw would be the logical person to father your child."

"How on earth do you figure that?"

"Because more than once you mentioned he was handsome, but you also said he was intelligent and kind. Those would be great traits to pass on to your child. If you recall, it was just last week when I suggested you place him at the top of the list."

"Yes, I recall the conversation, but at the time you were joking," Brianna said.

"At the time, you didn't have bargaining power. Now you do. I bet the two of you could work out a doozy of a deal if he wants your fifty acres bad enough."

"I don't know, Miesha," Brianna said, not convinced doing something like that was a good idea.

"Think about it, Brianna. You'd know the identity of your baby's father. And more importantly, your baby would know the identity of his father. If Cash Outlaw doesn't like the idea, he can tell you no."

"He *will* tell me no."

"You'll never know if you don't ask."

A short while later, Brianna settled in her favorite position in bed while thinking about Miesha's suggestion. There was no way Cash would go along with such a thing. *Would he?*

But what if he would for the fifty acres?

If he went along with it, and agreed with her terms, at least her child would have a vested interest in both her land and Cash's. But would he see it that way?

Deciding she didn't want to think about it anymore tonight, she did just what Cash had asked her to do earlier. She went to sleep and thought about him.

Twelve

Cash glanced at his watch, expecting Brianna to arrive any minute. It was hard to believe it was the end of the week. She had arrived at the ranch at nine and they would work together until around four in the afternoon. Usually they would break for lunch at noon.

Since she had prepared lunch for them on Monday, he had treated her on Tuesday to Monroe's. On Wednesday, she had brought lunch from home. Cash enjoyed sharing meals with her and liked getting to know her better.

It had become a habit for him to greet her each morning with a brush across the lips. He also gave her the same kind of kiss when he walked her to the door each evening. Cash was trying to practice restraint where Brianna was concerned, not wanting to overwhelm her or sway her decision about the fifty acres in any way. He saw that as business and what was between them as personal.

Yesterday Brianna had taken the day off for an appointment she had in Jackson, Wyoming. He had missed her. Although they would go hours while working through the stuff in the attic without holding a conversation, he would still feel her presence. More than once yesterday he'd glanced over to where she would normally be working and felt lonely knowing she wasn't there.

How would he handle things at the end of next week when he left to return to Fairbanks? He didn't want to think about that. It took a lot for a woman to capture his interest—and what felt like his very existence.

Maybe that's why he was standing on the porch waiting for Brianna to arrive this morning. He knew the moment her car pulled into the driveway. He stood, leaning against one of the posts, and watched her get out of the car. She looked pretty today, wearing a long, flowing printed skirt and pink blouse.

In truth, he thought she looked pretty every day. The moment she set foot on the porch, he walked over to her, pulled her into his arms and kissed her. In broad daylight. Not caring if the foreman or any of the ranch hands saw them. And it wasn't a mere brush across the lips.

He needed to taste her, mingle his tongue with hers, hold her close in his arms and inhale her scent. When he finally released her, he could tell by the look on her face that she had been surprised by his bold action. His public display of affection.

"Welcome back, Brianna," he said, but not before giving her lips another swipe with his tongue. "You look beautiful this morning. I love seeing you in the color pink."

She smiled up at him with moist lips. "Do you?"

"Yes, most definitely. It brings out the beauty of your eyes even more."

"Um, flattery will get you everywhere. Should I assume you missed me yesterday, Cash?"

He chuckled. "Yes, you can assume that. I went into town earlier and grabbed take-out breakfast from Brewster's Café. All we have to do is warm it up."

"Thanks. Did you get a lot done yesterday while I was gone?" she asked, following him into the house.

"No," he said, deciding to be honest. "I was bored."

"Poor baby."

He chuckled. "Yes, poor baby."

Cash warmed up the food in the microwave, and whenever he glanced over at her, she was staring out the kitchen window as if deep in thought. It was Friday. Did she remember that today she was to give him an answer on the fifty acres?

What if she didn't want to sell the land to him? He honestly didn't want to think about that possibility, although the businessman in him thought he should. He would admit being here on the ranch for the past nine days had spoiled him. Or could it be that he hadn't realized how much he had needed a break from Outlaw Freight Lines, and that any place would have worked?

He refused to believe that. He had a feeling it had everything to do with waking up at daybreak and breathing in the brisk Wyoming air.

And maybe spending time with Brianna.

He set the plates in front of her and then poured the coffee into cups before joining her at the table. The pensive look on her face bothered him. "Brianna, is anything wrong?"

Brianna shook her head. "No, why do you ask?"

"Usually you're more talkative than you are this morning."

Yes, usually she was. There was no way she would tell him that her meeting in Jackson at the fertility clinic hadn't gone quite the way she'd hoped. Everyone at the facility had been nice and positive, yet when she reviewed the bios of the men they'd selected for her to consider, she had found them all lacking.

Now she wished Miesha hadn't planted that seed in her head about Cash becoming the father of her child.

"I just have a lot on my mind."

"Anything I can help you with?"

If only you knew, she thought. Instead she said, "It's something I need to deal with on my own."

"Alright. If you change your mind, let me know."

She nodded. She would be letting him know soon enough. They didn't say much as they climbed the stairs to the attic, and once there moved to their respective areas of the room.

As she was about to go through the bins, she found an envelope with her name on it. She glanced over at Cash, but he had his back to her. She opened the envelope to find a note.

I really did miss you yesterday.
Cash

Brianna couldn't help but smile as a warm feeling flowed through her. It touched her deeply that he'd missed her and hadn't had a problem letting her know it.

She thought he deserved the same. "Cash?"

He turned around. "Yes?"

She gave him a bright smile. "I missed you yesterday, too."

He returned her smile. "Good."

Was it good? Would he still think it was good after she told him the decision she had made about the fifty acres? A decision that had taken her a few sleepless nights and thought-provoking days to ponder.

It hadn't been easy, but Miesha was right. Brianna couldn't think of any other man she would want to father her child. There were a number of reasons she felt that way, but she knew the main one—the one she could not deny—was that she had fallen in love with Cash.

Brianna honestly believed a part of her had given him her heart that day, close to nine years ago, when she had come across his picture. Whether he knew it or not, he had replaced the pain in her heart with hope. Seemed that was still true.

"I guess we better get to work," she then said, rolling up her sleeves.

Pretty soon a few hours had passed and Cash said it was time to stop for lunch. Glancing over at him, she said, "I'm not hungry. I think I'll work through lunch."

He stared at her for a minute and then nodded. "I'm not hungry either. I suggest we work for couple more hours and then call it a day."

It seemed as if the two hours had rushed by when he said, "That's it for today. How about if we share a glass of lemonade?"

"Sounds good," she said, moving across the room.

She was walking past him when he reached out and took her hand, studying her features. "Are you sure you're okay, Brianna?"

She was about to nod and tell him yes, and then thought better of it. It was time for her to give him her answer about the land and then face the consequences.

"I need to tell you my decision about the land, Cash."

He leaned against a wall, still holding her hand. "And what is your decision?"

She nervously nibbled on her bottom lip as she looked at him. "I will sign over all fifty acres to you, Cash, free and clear, if you give me something in return."

He bunched his forehead. The look on his face clearly showed his bemusement. "And what is that?"

Brianna didn't say anything as she nervously gnawed on her bottom lip and glanced away. She needed to focus on anything but him. She could feel the heat of his stare on every part of her body.

After forcing a deep whoosh of air through her lungs, she said, "I will *give* you the fifty acres, Cash, in exchange for your sperm."

Thirteen

Cash stared at Brianna. There was no way she'd said what he thought she'd said. He must have misunderstood. "Excuse me, but could you repeat that?"

She held his gaze and repeated it.

So she *had* said that. "My sperm?"

"Yes."

"Why do you need my sperm?"

"Because I want a baby."

Duh, Cash thought. That had been a stupid question for him to ask. What other reason would there be for a woman to need a man's sperm? "Why do you want a baby? You aren't married."

"If I was married, I wouldn't be needing your sperm. You don't have to be married to have a baby, Cash."

He knew that. Maybe he wasn't asking the right questions. Maybe it was the heat in the attic frying his brain cells, or the fact that normally, women didn't go around asking men for their sperm. "Let's get out of here." He needed something to drink, and for him it had to be something stronger than lemonade. "We're going to sit down at my kitchen table and you're going to tell me what the hell is going on, Brianna."

"That's fine."

"After you," he said, standing back for her to move ahead of him. He hung back a minute to get himself together.

When they reached the kitchen, she went straight to the refrigerator for the lemonade and he went to the liquor cabinet. He pulled down a bottle of vodka and a shot glass.

When he walked back to the table, she was already seated, staring into her glass. She looked nervous. Hopefully, that meant she didn't make it a habit of going around asking a man for his sperm. He honestly didn't think she did, but he would know for certain in a minute.

He slid into the chair across from her, placed both the bottle of vodka and the shot glass on the table and poured. "So, why a baby and why *my* sperm, Brianna?"

Brianna took a sip of lemonade before she said, "I've always wanted a family, Cash. I was an only child, so I dreamed of one day getting married, becoming a mom with lots of kids. At least four. Alan had wanted a large family, too. That was one of the things we agreed on."

She paused. "I had everything planned. We would marry like he promised, the year I graduated from high school, and I would travel with him and support his military career and have his babies. It was my dream to have all four before my thirtieth birthday."

She couldn't help but smile at the lifting of his brow. "I know that sounds crazy because it means my being pregnant most of the time, but I was okay with that. Alan was, too. The kids would each be two years apart. Like I said, I had it all planned out."

The smile on Brianna's face faded when she continued. "But none of those plans happened. My dreams were destroyed."

He nodded. "Yes, you told me."

She took another sip of her lemonade. "Nobody knew how much I wanted a family more than my parents. Especially Dad. I think at one time that's all I ever talked about. Marrying Alan, being a good wife to him and a good mother to our babies. Dad knew the pain Alan's betrayal caused me and I told him I would never marry. He believed me."

Brianna paused again. "Dad knew he was dying and wanted to prepare me for a life without him. He didn't want me to be alone. He knew it was likely I would never fall in love and marry, which meant I would never have a child and be the mother I'd always wanted to be."

She fought back tears. "The night before he died, Dad sat me down on the sofa beside him and made me promise him that I wouldn't be alone on my thirtieth birthday. And that I would have the one thing I'd always wanted."

"A baby?"

"Yes."

He looked at her. "A child and not a husband?"

"Yes. Dad figured I would get pregnant without a man's involvement like Miesha did."

He lifted a brow. "Who's Miesha?"

"Miesha James is my best friend from college. She still lives in Atlanta and owns a communications firm there. For reasons I'd rather not go into, Miesha wanted a baby, so she went to a sperm bank. She had the procedure done, got pregnant, and now Darrett is six and in first grade." Brianna paused. "Dad figured right. I had planned to do the same thing when it came time to have my baby."

She took another sip of her lemonade. "However, I recently discovered the sperm bank might not be the best approach to motherhood after all."

"Why not?"

She poured more lemonade before answering. "It was a hard decision to make, but there were no donors there who felt right to me."

"Why me, Brianna? Why would you want me to father your child?"

Brianna gave him the reasons that had convinced her

she would be doing the right thing. "You are kind, thoughtful and caring, Cash. Besides, you don't live here. You said you would be living in Alaska and would hire someone to run the ranch for you. That means I could raise the child on my own. You and I wouldn't have to see each other. But more than anything, I believe you would do right by our child and take responsibility for him or her if something happened to me."

When he didn't say anything, she pressed on. "I wouldn't want anything from you, Cash. This won't be a love match and I'll sign any papers waiving my rights to your possessions. I can afford to raise my child on my own. This will strictly be a business arrangement. You get the fifty acres. All I want is your sperm."

"How?"

Now she was the one lifting a brow. "How what?"

"How am I supposed to give you this sperm, Brianna?"

By asking that question, did that mean he was at least considering it? "By artificial insemination. That way you won't have to be concerned about any physical contact between us."

Brianna stood, took her glass over to the sink and washed it out, noting he hadn't said anything. She came back to stand by the table. "I realize you're going to need time to think about it, Cash. However, if you can let me know something by next week, I would appreciate it."

Without saying anything else, she grabbed her purse off the counter and walked out the door.

Cash sat at the kitchen table until he heard Brianna's car drive off. Then he threw back the shot of vodka.

He wanted fifty acres of Brianna's land and she wanted to use his sperm to have a baby. By artificial insemination.

A slow heat stirred in his groin when he thought of another way that he could share his sperm with her. He quickly brushed the thought from his mind because he wasn't sharing his sperm with anybody. What made her think that if he got a woman pregnant, he wouldn't want to be a part of the child's life?

Damn that guy who had destroyed all her dreams of becoming a mother and wife. Now she was willing to become a mother without a husband. She deserved her whole dream. She said she thought Cash was kind and caring. Well, he thought the same thing about her. He had seen firsthand how she'd gotten along with his cousins and friends last weekend. And those times when he had accompanied her in town, it was obvious to him how well liked she was.

The one thing she was wrong about was her assumption that she knew Cash. If she did, then she would know there was no way he would get a woman pregnant and not want to be a part of his child's life. Especially after his mother had chosen not to be a part of his. He would not make that same mistake with his own child.

Then there was the way she said she would get pregnant. Artificial insemination? Not hardly. And what did she say about eliminating any concern about physical contact between them? Did she honestly think that was a concern of his? Especially when there had been an overabundance of sexual chemistry between them from the start?

Brianna never did say what would happen if he didn't go along with this idea of hers. Did that mean she would approach someone else? He rubbed his hands down his face in frustration. The bottom line was that there was something he wanted more than those fifty acres of land.

He wanted her.

She wanted them to handle this like a business deal. In that case, she would see just how he operated. Other than Garth, Cash was the Outlaw who didn't pull any punches when it came to negotiation. When he had a challenge, he overcame it each and every time. He could be steadfast and unmovable, and could play hard better than anyone. In other words, when confronted with opposition, he could be a force to reckon with.

Cash grabbed his Stetson off the hat rack as he headed for the door. He intended to ride around the range and was confident that when he returned, he would have come up with a plan.

Brianna had eaten and cleaned up the kitchen by the time the sun went down. She had then showered and changed into a comfortable sundress. Now she was enjoying a glass of wine in the swing on the porch.

She couldn't help wondering if Cash was giving her proposition any thought. Asking a man to father her child was a very bold thing to do. But then, desperation would give a person the courage to do just about anything. She had given him until next week for an answer, but what if he didn't agree to it? Would she withhold the land from him? Probably not, but at least she would have tried playing her hand.

Hearing the sound of a car approaching, she tilted her head to see the driveway. It was Cash. Her heart began beating fast in her chest, like it did whenever Cash was around.

Why was he coming here? Did that mean he had made a decision already? If he had, that also meant he really hadn't given her proposal much thought. Was he here to tell her he had no intention of being the father of her baby?

Placing her wineglass aside, she stood when he came up the steps. She saw he had that just-showered look and had changed into another pair of jeans and a Western shirt. He smelled good. Too good.

Whatever he'd come here to say, the best thing would be for him to say it and leave.

"Hello, Brianna."

The deep, throaty sound of his voice put sensuous goose

bumps on her arms. "Cash? I am surprised to see you. Is anything wrong?"

"No. I came to deliver my answer to your proposition."

It was just as she'd assumed. He hadn't given it much thought if he was turning her down already. "I was enjoying a glass of wine. Would you like one?"

"I prefer a beer if you have one."

"I do. Come on in," she said, entering the house.

He followed her into the kitchen and leaned against one of the counters. "You've eaten already?"

She grabbed the beer out of the refrigerator. "Yes. If you want something, I—"

"No, thanks," he interrupted to say. "I have a taste for a hamburger and fries and was on my way to Monroe's."

She nodded, handing him the beer. "You're getting addicted to the place like the rest of us."

"Looks that way." He took a slug of his beer and then licked his lips.

Watching him do that made her pulse rate increase. She didn't want to wring her hands together but was doing so anyway. "What is your answer?"

"I'm here to make you a counteroffer, Brianna."

That's not what she'd expected to hear. "A counteroffer?"

"Yes."

"What kind of counteroffer?"

Covering the distance separating them, he came to stand in front of her. She tilted her head back to look up at him. "I will give you the baby you want, but there will be something I want from you," he said.

Brianna lifted an arched brow. "In addition to the fifty acres?"

"Yes, in addition to the fifty acres."

She nervously licked her lips, not knowing what that could be. "What is it you want from me?"

"Marriage."

Fourteen

Cash saw Brianna's eyes widen. "Marriage?"

"Yes, marriage. The only way you can have my sperm is to marry me. Also, when I get you pregnant, it won't be by any insemination procedure. It will be the traditional way with us sharing a bed as husband and wife."

He saw the color drain from Brianna's face.

"But why would you want us to get married? That doesn't make sense," she said, honestly looking confused.

"I happen to think it makes perfect sense. You want my baby and I want marriage."

She shook her head as if still not understanding. "But why would you want marriage?"

"There are a number of reasons. The foremost is that I'll be thirty-five at the end of the year and it's time for me to settle down," he said, knowing it was a bald-faced lie even as the words flowed from his lips. He could have gone through life and never married, and he certainly hadn't given any thought to settling down before now. But she didn't have to know that.

"What do you mean, 'it's time'?"

He shrugged. "What I mean is that it is expected. My older brother Garth married last year. My brother Jess would be next in line to tie the knot, but he'll need a wife who wants to be married to a politician, so we're giving him more time."

He took another swig of his beer. "Being married comes in handy when you're negotiating business deals with men with single daughters who think it should be a package deal."

Brianna frowned. "But I have no intention of ever moving to Alaska."

"And I have no intention of ever living here. For us, it wouldn't matter since our marriage will only be a business deal." That was another lie. "I will come and visit from time to time to see my child."

She didn't say anything for a minute and then asked, "In other words, you want the status and not a real marriage?"

A smile touched his lips. "No, I wouldn't say that. I want all the things that come with being married, including sharing my wife's bed."

Before she could respond, he said, "I think there is something you should know about me, Brianna. Because of the kind of relationship I had with Ellen, there is no way I would want to have that same kind of relationship with a child I created. There is no way on this earth I could get you pregnant and then pretend you and the child didn't exist."

"What about other women?" she asked.

He lifted a brow. "Other women?"

"Yes. Although it wouldn't be a traditional marriage, would you still stick to your marriage vows or would you feel you have the right to sleep with other women?"

He held her gaze, needing to make sure she understood him. "You will be the only woman I make love to, Brianna. And I expect the same on your end."

When she didn't say anything, he pressed on, hoping what he was about to offer would be the icing on the cake.

"Also, as my wife, you will share the Blazing Frontier with me. All of it, and not just what Ellen left to you. If anything were to happen to me while we are married, it will belong to you and our child."

She stared at him. "Since you are demanding marriage, how long will this marriage have to last?"

Demand? Was he demanding marriage? Yes, in a way he was. "Forever."

"Forever!"

He crossed his arms over his chest. "Yes, forever."

"Impossible. I told you I never intend to marry."

"And I refuse to get a woman pregnant without marriage. Then, after that, it is important that I remain married to the woman for my child's sake. I refuse to divorce my child's mother the way my father did his wives."

She didn't say anything for a moment, then asked, "Just what will this marriage entail?"

He dropped his hands to his sides. "I've told you one aspect of it, regarding our sleeping arrangements. I also mentioned you didn't have to move to Alaska unless at some point you wanted to. Most of my time will be in Alaska, but I will visit here from time to time to see my child."

"And the ranch?"

"As part owner, you can run the dude ranch like before. The horse training and breeding part of it will require help and you will get it."

"You're entrusting me with all the Blazing Frontier's business?" she asked in amazement.

"As my wife and business partner, I see no reason I shouldn't. However, there is the matter of the times you might need off during your pregnancies."

"Pregnancies?"

He smiled. "Yes, pregnancies. Like you, I also want a lot of children and agree that four sounds good." That wasn't true since he honestly hadn't ever thought of having children until she'd made her request. But if she wanted four babies, he could certainly give them to her.

"Who knows? Multiple births run in my family, so we

might hit the jackpot and have triplets or twins, which will decrease the number of times you'd be pregnant." He only added that part because he'd overheard her tell his cousin Bane that she would love to have twins or triplets.

"What do you think of my counteroffer, Brianna?"

She was nibbling on her lips and wringing her hands together. "I need time to think about it."

"Okay. I want your answer on Monday morning."

She drew in a deep breath. "If I decide to go along with your counteroffer, Cash, how soon would you want this marriage to take place?"

"Within forty-eight hours of when you say yes."

Her eyes widened. "Why the rush?"

He raised a brow. "Maybe I misunderstood you earlier today, but didn't you say something about wanting a child before your thirtieth birthday? I figured you would want to get started on one right away. I plan to leave for Alaska next weekend. After that, you will have to let me know your body's best time for fertilization, and then I'll make arrangements to return."

Cash knew he was giving her the impression that the only reason he would make love to her was for a baby. His goal was that making love would be so enjoyable that she would want to continue for more than just making a baby.

"Why not artificial insemination?"

He placed the empty beer bottle on the table, deciding not to answer. He glanced at his watch. "I need to leave to get something to eat. Will I have your decision Monday morning, Brianna?"

She released a deep breath and then said, "Yes, you'll have it."

He leaned down and brushed a kiss across her lips. "This way, we both get what we want, Brianna."

And then he turned and left.

*** *

"What are you going to do, Brie?"

Sitting on her back patio, Brianna looked over the land she was proud to call hers while sipping her coffee. It was her second cup that morning after getting up early, before sunrise, after a sleepless night thinking about Cash's counteroffer.

"I don't know, Miesha. None of what he is offering is what I asked for."

"Yes, but you're getting a whole lot more. Just think. He is offering marriage."

Brianna rolled her eyes. "He is *demanding* marriage, Miesha. Why can't he just do things my way?"

"I think he's told you why. Cash Outlaw wants a wife, not a woman to impregnate. He wants more than one child, just like you do, and he prefers the same woman birthing his children. I can appreciate that. What I appreciate even more is that he is willing to share what's his with you."

Hoping she had Brianna thinking, Miesha pressed on. "Just think. He is giving you control of the ranch. Not as an employee but as co-owner. That sounds pretty darn generous to me. Some men would stick you with a prenup so fast your head would spin. Don't let your hang-up about never getting married keep you from what I see as a pretty darn good deal."

Brianna took another sip of coffee. "It seems like he's trying to get the upper hand."

"Why? Because he's found a way to get you into his bed?"

"In a way, yes."

Miesha giggled. "Excuse me. But haven't you said his kisses left you so hot you were tempted to jump his bones?"

"I was all talk and you know it."

"Well, now you can put your 'all talk' into action. What are you afraid of?"

Brianna knew the answer to that question easily. Her heart.

"I got a crush on him from just looking at his picture, Miesha. What if I fall for him again? Harder this time. Do you know what that could do to me?"

"You were vulnerable back then because of Alan, and Cash Outlaw was your escape from reality. There was nothing wrong with that. If you recall, all the time I was pregnant, I fantasized Shemar Moore was my baby's daddy."

"I know, but—"

"But this is now, Brianna," Miesha interrupted to say. "If he's good to you and treats you right, would it be wrong to fall in love with him? He's not setting a time limit on your marriage. It sounds to me that he expects it to last. A lot of things can happen. A lot of emotions can develop on both sides."

"What about being the town's scandal again?" Brianna said.

"Honestly, girl? You were planning on having a baby without the benefit of a husband. How is marrying a man and having his baby more of a scandal than that? Think about it."

An hour later, Brianna had saddled Baby to go riding, and to think. Out on the open range, she couldn't help but laugh out loud as they raced across the plains and valleys. Because Baby was used to the land, Brianna allowed him the freedom to roam wherever he pleased. She was so caught up in her thoughts about Cash's counteroffer that it took a while for Brianna to notice she was now on Blazing Frontier land.

She tightened her hold on Baby's reins to turn him back when she saw a lone rider galloping toward her.

Cash.

She quickly assessed her options. She could pretend she hadn't seen him and race Baby back home, or she could stay and acknowledge his presence. She chose the latter, but the closer he got, the more she wished she'd chosen the former.

It seemed every time she saw Cash, he was even more handsome than the last. He was sex-in-jeans, sex-drinking-a-beer and now sex-riding-a-horse. She'd thought the same thing the first time she saw him slide into a saddle, and watched how his thick, masculine thighs flanked the animal in a way that made Brianna want to fan herself.

He definitely knew how to handle a horse and sat erect in the saddle the way a rider was supposed to. He finally brought his horse to a stop a few feet from hers.

"Good morning, Cash."

"Good morning, Brianna." He tilted his Stetson in greeting. "Looks like we had the same idea. Nice morning for a ride," he said.

"Yes, it is."

"You're heading back?" he asked, looking at her intently.

"That was my plan," she said, holding tight to Baby's reins.

"Would you ride with me for a while?"

Brianna didn't think that was a good idea and should have declined his invitation. However, when those penetrating dark eyes stared at her, the next thing she knew, she was nodding her head.

They took off galloping across the plains, going deeper and deeper onto Blazing Frontier land. When they slowed the horses, she glanced over at him. He rode his horse well. Why on earth was she suddenly imagining him straddling her and then riding her the same way? The thought made a shiver rush through her, and when he watched her with such smoldering intensity, she suddenly felt extremely hot.

"I thought about you last night, Brianna."

She had news for him. She had thought about him, too. "Did you?"

"Yes. You might not know this, but lately you've taken my dreams hostage."

Probably no more than he had taken hers, but she was surprised he would admit such a thing. "Why?"

He chuckled, and the sound made even more intense heat pass through her. "That's easy enough to answer. I see you and I want you. I don't see you and I still want you. Point blank. I want you, Brianna."

Fifteen

"You shouldn't say such things, Cash."

He leaned back on his horse. "Why not? It's the truth. But you already know that, right? I'm sure my desire for you comes through loud and clear every time we kiss, and we've kissed quite a bit."

"Not this week."

She quickly looked away, as if she'd been embarrassed to make such an observation. Too late, she had made it. Did that mean she had missed their kisses as much as he had? That could easily be remedied, but first he felt the need to tell her why he had toned them down.

He brought his horse to a stop and so did she. "The reason I haven't kissed you much this week, Brianna, is that whenever I kiss you, I don't want to stop. I want to take it to the next level." He was certain she clearly understood what that next level was.

She looked back at him with a glare in her eyes, and he knew she'd taken offense. "Like I wouldn't have had anything to say about it?"

He smiled. "I'm sure you would have, but mostly what I would have heard from you would have been moans of pleasure."

While she angrily spluttered her denials, he dismounted. He then moved to her horse and reached up for her.

"What do you think you're doing?" she asked in a voice filled with annoyance as she batted his hands away.

"I am helping you down. The horses need to rest a spell. I won't bite you." But he sure as hell wouldn't mind kissing her.

She hesitated, but then, as if deciding he was right and the horses needed to rest, she took his hand. Then it happened. The moment their hands touched, total, complete and unharnessed awareness shot through his entire body. Cash glanced up at Brianna and knew without a doubt that she had felt it, too. There was no way she had not.

"Maybe I should go," she said in a soft voice.

"The horses need to rest, Brianna. You're safe here with me."

She gave him a doubtful look, but she didn't pull her hand away. When her feet touched the ground, she said, "Thanks, Cash." When he continued to hold her around her waist, she added, "You can let go of me now."

"Brianna…"

He was about to say something, but for the life of him, he wasn't sure what it was. So he tried again. "Brianna…"

She held his gaze and nervously licked her lips. "Yes?"

Instead of answering, he moved his hands to her waist and nudged her closer. Then, as if his mouth had a mind of its own, it lowered to hers.

The moment their mouths touched, Brianna felt her insides tingle as if she'd come in contact with a live wire. A series of responses, none she felt capable of controlling, ripped through her body. Cash's kisses were her weakness because she enjoyed them so much.

She knew she should push back, stop him from deepening the kiss more than he already had. But all her common sense left her, vibrated off into the wind. All she had the ability to do at that moment was get wrapped up in his incredible taste.

And it was incredible.

Brianna was convinced there was nothing else quite like it. Not that she had kissed a lot of guys, but Cash Outlaw's taste created a yearning within her that made her entire body ache.

He suddenly released her mouth, and she pulled in air and the scent of man through her nostrils. Then he was kissing her again, his mouth more demanding and greedier than before. She heard herself moan under the onslaught of the deep glides of his tongue.

Then she felt his hand leave her waist to fondle the buttons on her blouse. Brianna knew she should stop him, but that thought vanished when he deepened the kiss even further. She heard herself purr again as toe-curling sensations rippled through her.

She knew he had unbuttoned her shirt when she felt a breeze across her chest. He broke away from her mouth to trail tongue-licking kisses against her jaw and neck and along the edge of her collarbone.

"Cash…"

She closed her eyes, absorbing all the sensations he was making her feel. She hadn't realized he had used his fingers to undo the front clasp of her bra until his mouth was right there, sucking her nipple into his mouth.

Brianna threw her head back, and the movement seemed to thrust her nipple farther into him. He took advantage by exerting more pressure and sucking her nipple in earnest, like he'd been greedy for it forever.

Those actions made a series of moans flow from her lips at the same time she grasped the back of his head to hold his mouth right there. Never had she felt such intense desire.

She and Alan had made love only twice. The time right before he was supposed to leave for the military, and when he'd come home right before getting deployed to Germany. He had taken care of his own needs without hers, but at the time she hadn't minded.

Now she saw how selfish that was. He had never taken her breasts into his mouth and lapped on them the way Cash was doing. Suddenly, her entire body felt as if it was on fire.

Her body jerked. It seemed as if a bolt of lightning had lanced through her and she convulsed in unthinkable pleasure. Brianna gasped aloud at the unexpected, unadulterated carnality that tore through her, then screamed Cash's name.

Then he was back at her mouth, kissing her while a barrage of sensations bombarded her, followed by spasms that ran through her body. He released her mouth and pulled her into his arms while gently stroking her back as the spasms continued.

"You're okay, sweetheart. I got you."

Brianna knew what had just happened. She had experienced her very first orgasm and it had been unbelievable. It had happened not in a bed but out on the plains. On Blazing Frontier land. If she had to do it again, she wouldn't change a thing. It had been natural and perfect.

"Brianna?"

She leaned forward and buried her face in Cash's chest, not ready for him to look at her yet. When he said her name again and asked if she was okay, she finally lifted her face and met his intense gaze. "Yes, I'm okay. And thank you."

He snapped her bra back in place and began rebuttoning her blouse. "What did you just thank me for?"

Brianna figured he had to know. A man with his experience could tell. He probably just wanted her to admit it. "I was thanking you for giving me pleasure. No man has ever done that before."

His hand on her buttons went still, and he glanced down at her. "Are you saying Alan never…"

"No. He never. We only made love twice and both times he was in a hurry."

Brianna saw the tight frown that settled over Cash's face. "A real man is never in too much of a hurry to satisfy his woman."

She didn't know what to say to that. The only thing she knew was she needed to get away from him and fast before she was begging for an encore. When she took a step back, she nearly lost her balance from feeling weak in the knees. Totally drained.

"Hold still. I'm taking you home."

She lifted a brow. "How are you taking me home?"

"We're riding double on my horse. I'll tie Baby to the back."

"That's not necessary. Just put me on Baby. He knows the way home. I'm fine."

He just looked at her and said, "I'm taking you home, Brianna."

And as if that settled it, he lifted her up and placed her on his horse like she weighed nothing, before straddling his horse and holding her in front of him.

"You can lean back against me if you want," he invited.

She did. His chest felt strong, warm, comforting. Brianna closed her eyes, lulled by the slow rocking motion of the horse and the feel of resting her back against Cash's chest. She must have fallen asleep because she recalled him gently rubbing the side of her face to let her know they had arrived at her house.

He dismounted and then reached up for her. But he never let her feet touch the ground—he swept her from the horse into his arms.

"Cash, you can put me down."

He smiled down at her. "I will, but not now."

When they reached her door, he asked for her key. She shifted in his arms to tug it out of her pocket and handed it to him. He opened the door and carried her inside and straight to her bedroom, where he placed her gently on the bed. Right next to Magnum. Then he backed up.

"I suggest you take a nap."

"A nap?"

"Yes."

She shook her head. "I'll take a nap later. I need to take care of Baby."

"I'll take care of Baby. You rest."

She frowned, tempted to tell him she'd had her first orgasm, not open heart surgery. "I'm fine, Cash. But I am curious about something."

"What?"

She began nibbling on her bottom lip, and she could tell he knew she was nervous about whatever it was she wanted to ask him. "You can ask me anything, Brianna."

"Are all of them like this? This powerful?"

His expression said he knew exactly what she was asking. "Most are way more powerful than that. On a scale of one to five with five as the max, you experienced a level-one."

Her eyes widened. "That's enough about levels of passion. Take a nap and rest. I'll stop by later to check on you."

She pulled to sit up and he gave her a look that had her easing back down. "You don't have to do that."

"I take care of what's mine, Brianna."

She glared at him. "I'm not yours."

"Not yet."

He moved toward the door, paused and glanced back at her. A smile curved his lips when he said, "If you want to experience a higher level of passion than you did today, Brianna, you'll have to marry me."

Brianna continued to lie in bed long after Cash left. Why was he so insistent that she marry him? And she wasn't sure she liked him assuming she was his. At that moment she couldn't help but remember their kiss and how it had moved to another level when he had put his mouth on her breasts.

Even now, her pulse kicked up thinking about it, and she could recall every single sensation that had swamped her body. She had been filled with pleasure she hadn't known anyone was capable of feeling.

What was happening to her? There was no doubt in her mind that Cash presented a temptation causing an edginess within her that couldn't be normal. At least not for her. And what had he said before leaving? She would not experience a higher level of passion with him until they got married.

She was convinced a higher level just might take her out. The thought of it made lust hum through her veins, had her pulse kicking, her nerves dancing and her brain becoming dysfunctional.

Brianna yawned, still feeling a bit lethargic. Shifting in bed to her side, she decided to do just like Cash had told her to do and take a nap. He liked giving orders. He liked making demands. She smiled, thinking that she liked him.

As she closed her eyes, her mind was filled with Cash.

Sixteen

It was Monday morning.

Cash glanced at his watch as he stood on the porch in the exact location where he'd stood on Friday. Like then, he was expecting Brianna to arrive any minute. However, today her arrival meant something else as well. He was anticipating her answer to his marriage proposal.

Granted, she might not think of it as a real proposal since he hadn't gotten down on one knee, nor had he slid an engagement ring on her finger. He knew Brianna hadn't expected either. In fact, it was quite obvious she hadn't expected his counteroffer of marriage. But he had made it and he had no intention of withdrawing it.

He had no choice.

Little did she know that it had nothing to do with the fifty acres like she assumed. His counterproposal came from his need to claim her as his wife, the mother of the children he hadn't even known he wanted.

It was obvious to him that not only had Alan Dawkins betrayed her, he had failed to do right by her in the bedroom as well. Both were bad, but the latter was inexcusable. Cash's goal, for as long as it took, was to get her to see, and accept, that she was worthy of a man's respect.

When he had returned to her place on Saturday with food that he'd gotten from a restaurant in town, she was still sleeping. Chances were she hadn't slept well the night before, and he figured he was partly to blame for that. There was no doubt in his mind that his counteroffer had thrown her for a loop, and he'd not given her much time to answer him.

That part had been intentional.

As a businessman he knew not to give an opponent too much time to make a decision. Overthinking anything could cause problems and unnecessary delays. Delays he didn't want.

Brianna didn't have a clue as to the extent of his desire for her. There was more going on between them than a sexual attraction, even if he couldn't name what it was. That was the real reason he'd made the counteroffer for marriage. Point blank, he couldn't imagine any other man making her his.

On Saturday he hadn't bothered waking her. He had left the food on her table with a note that he would see her Monday morning. He wanted to give her time by herself to make her decision without any influence from him. He just hoped she made the right one.

Brianna saw Cash the moment she pulled into the long driveway of the Blazing Frontier. Butterflies were going off in her stomach. She knew what her answer would be.

She'd never wanted to get married after the pain and humiliation Alan had caused. Therefore, her decision should have been a no-brainer. But all it had taken was to wake up Saturday after her nap to find the food Cash had brought to her along with the note he'd left. Then to think about the relationship they'd shared over the past two weeks. The sexual chemistry had been there from day one, but he certainly wasn't the obnoxious type. Cash Outlaw in the flesh was everything she had fancied him to be when he'd been her fantasy boyfriend.

Now she had decided to make him her in-the-flesh husband. She would be entering this marriage with blinders off. She would get what she wanted—a baby—and Cash would get what he wanted—her fifty acres. They would both be happy. Besides, he'd given her another incentive. Marrying him would make her co-owner of the Blazing Frontier. In a way she felt good knowing that her child's... *their* child's...future would be secure.

Now if she could only accept his way of wanting to make a baby. After what happened on Saturday, she wasn't certain sharing a bed with Cash would be wise. There was no doubt it would be pleasurable, but the last thing she wanted to do was let off-the-charts sex take over her common sense.

If a kiss could make her feel the way she had on Saturday, she didn't want to imagine what making love with him would do. Unfortunately, she *was* imagining, even those times when she did not want to do so. Like now. Seeing him standing on the porch in such a sexy pose while drinking a cup of coffee was stirring her blood.

When she brought the car to a stop and got out, she saw the smile that curved his lips. A smile that made her insides feel like mush. "Good morning, Cash."

"Good morning, Brianna."

He always said her name in a deep, husky tone. Today, his voice sounded even huskier. "I hope you have a cup of coffee for me," she said as she stepped up on the porch to stand in front of him.

"I've got something better than that. I went back to that café and grabbed breakfast. I hope you're hungry."

She was, and when she saw his mouth move—the mouth that had given her so much pleasure Saturday—she had to force air into her lungs. "Yes, I'm hungry."

"Good." He opened the door, and she followed him into

the kitchen. "Go ahead and have a seat at the table and I'll warm everything up for you."

"Thanks."

First he poured her coffee, and she was glad of that because she needed it. Then she settled in the chair and watched him move around the kitchen, appreciating—as she always did—how he looked in his jeans. Today he was wearing a T-shirt that showed the muscles of his upper arms and tight abs.

The aroma of what he was warming up flowed over to her. "Strawberry muffins."

He chuckled. "Yes."

Moments later he placed the warm plate of muffins in front of her and took his seat. They began eating in silence. "How was the rest of your weekend?"

She shrugged. "Quiet." No need to tell him that she hadn't ridden Baby yesterday for fear of running into him again if she ventured off her property. "What about your weekend?" she asked, knowing they were stalling to avoid what was really on both their minds.

"Yesterday I decided to go through more of that stuff in the attic. I missed having you there working alongside me."

Brianna didn't say anything because they never really worked alongside each other even when she was there. That would have been too close for comfort, but she knew what he meant. He had missed her yesterday. That was good to know.

They continued to eat with little conversation, but she knew he was watching her. She dared not glance up and catch him staring.

"Brianna?"

She looked over at him, certain what he wanted to know. They had stalled long enough. "Yes?"

"What is your decision?"

Brianna drew in a deep breath as she placed her coffee cup down and met his gaze. Just staring into his eyes made her pulse rate increase.

"Yes, I will marry you, Cash."

Seventeen

Cash released the breath he'd been holding. He was getting the marriage he wanted. He stared at Brianna, wishing desperately he could read her thoughts to determine her true feelings about the decision she had made.

He wanted to ask her if she was sure, but he wasn't certain he wanted to hear what she might say. In time he would prove to her that marrying him was the right thing to do and he intended to make her happy or die trying.

Now, with her decision made, he wouldn't waste time. Before he could broach the subject, she said, "However, I prefer we wait a couple of weeks, even a month, before we marry."

"Why?"

"I need time to adjust to the idea."

Cash thought any adjustment time she needed could be done while married to him. "I told you I wanted to get married within forty-eight hours and I meant it, Brianna. I won't change my mind on that. I checked and there's no waiting period in Wyoming."

"What's the rush?"

"I need to secure my investors and get things moving around here." Honestly, that was the least of his concerns, but he wouldn't tell her that. "We're getting married Wednesday."

"Wednesday?"

"Yes. That will give you time to do whatever you need to do before then. In fact, I suggest we take the rest of the day off here. That will give you even more time. If you prefer, I'll make all the arrangements."

Brianna gave him an irritated look. "Fine, make all the arrangements."

She began nibbling on her bottom lip and he knew something was bothering her. "Is there anything else, Brianna?"

"I suggest that we marry someplace other than Black Crow."

He figured she had her reasons for making that suggestion. It really didn't matter where they got married, as long as they did so, legal and binding. "What about Jackson? I can fly us there in my plane."

He saw relief in her eyes. "Jackson will be fine."

"And be prepared to stay until Sunday."

Her expression showed that she was surprised by his request. "Until Sunday? Why?"

"A honeymoon. I want one, although it will be rather short. We'll take a longer one later."

"We don't have to take one now or later. It's not as if it's a real marriage."

Was now the time to discuss just how real he wanted their marriage to be? She would find out soon enough. "It's the only one I ever intend to have, Brianna, so let's make plans to stay in Jackson until Sunday."

"Whatever." She stood to take her plate to the sink and rinsed it out to place in the dishwasher. He saw her tense when he carried his own plate to the sink and stood beside her. "I don't bite, Brianna. Why are you acting so skittish today?"

"I'm not acting skittish."

"Yes, you are."

She turned to him. "If I am, then it's because I've agreed to do something that I swore I would never do."

He reached out and touched her cheek, feeling her emotions in every word. "I'm not a bad guy, and you do want the best for our child, right?"

"Yes."

"Then I'm asking you to believe I will do right by you both." He paused a moment, then asked, "Do you trust Henry Cavanaugh's office to keep things confidential?"

She lifted a brow. "Mr. Cavanaugh will, but Lois Inglese won't. She's been known to talk. I figured that's how word got out that Ms. Ellen had a son days before you showed up for the signing of the will."

Cash frowned. "Why does he keep her on?"

"She's worked there for years. He has counseled her about loose lips but I'm not sure how well that has worked. Why?"

"I want you to know I will do right by you, and I'm having my cousin draw up a legal document to that effect."

"Your cousin?"

"Yes, Jared Westmoreland. He practices family law. I suggest you consult your own attorney to review everything with you before Wednesday."

"I can take the document to Mr. Cavanaugh as a consultation without him keeping a copy on file. That way there will be no need for Lois to see it."

Cash nodded. "Okay, then. I will get the document to you."

Brianna grabbed the mail out of her mailbox before entering her home. She had called Mr. Cavanaugh's office to make an appointment for tomorrow morning. Cash had assured her his cousin would be faxing the documents over to her by three this afternoon.

Drawing in a deep breath, she tossed the mail on the coffee table before dropping down on the sofa. She wanted to believe that being married to Cash would be okay. He would be spending the majority of his time in Alaska. If anyone asked her about her husband's long and periodic absences, she would merely tell them he had a business to run in Alaska and she was in charge of their operations at the ranch. At least during his visits his child would get to know him. She was comforted to know he'd have a part-time dad rather than not having one at all.

Brianna stood. She had a lot to do by Wednesday. Taking out her phone, she began making calls and setting appointments. Her hair needed to be done, and she would get a manicure and pedicure.

She had finished making her calls and was about to pick up her mail and go through it when her cell phone rang. It was Cash. "Yes?"

"I just talked to Jared. His office will be faxing the documents to you in a few minutes."

"Okay."

"And I've made all the arrangements with the airport. I will pick you up Wednesday morning around seven."

"I'll be ready."

When she ended the call, she glanced at her watch. It wasn't yet noon, but she needed to get away. Since she had so many appointments lined up tomorrow, now would be a good time to drive to Laramie to shop for several outfits and items.

If she went shopping in town for the clothing she needed, someone would speculate as to why. The last thing she wanted was for anyone to get into her business. They would find out soon enough.

"You're marrying Brianna?"

Cash heard the disbelief in Garth's voice. "Yes, I'm marrying her."

"Please don't tell me you're doing so because of those fifty acres."

Cash rubbed his hand down his face, knowing he could BS answers with Sloan and Maverick, but when it came to Garth and Jess, Cash never had such luxury. They could read him like a book each and every time.

"I had something she wanted, and she had something I wanted, so we agreed to compromise."

"By getting married?"

"Yes, by getting married."

Cash knew his brother was trying to take it all in. It didn't take Garth long to ask, "When will the wedding take place?"

"We're eloping."

"To Vegas?"

"No, to Jackson, Wyoming. Like Nevada, there's no delay in getting married in Wyoming. We're applying for the license on Wednesday morning and will get married that evening."

"No honeymoon?"

"There *will* be a honeymoon. We won't return to the ranch until Sunday. I know I said that I would be in the office on Monday and I still plan to be."

"You're bringing Brianna back with you?"

"No."

"You're moving to Black Crow?"

"Not at first."

"The two of you plan to have a long-distance marriage?" Garth then wanted to know.

Cash eased off the sofa, went to the window and looked out. The sun would be going down in a few hours and he wanted to ride the range before it did. "Such an arrangement will work for us."

"You think so?" Garth asked.

"You don't?" Cash countered.

"No. I watched you with her, Cash. I also know the reason you went early to Wyoming and why you stayed behind had everything to do with Brianna Banks. She has come to mean a lot to you. I would suggest you accept that." He paused. "Maybe you already have."

Knowing it was time to end the call, Cash said, "I'd appreciate it if you don't mention my plans to anyone, especially Bart. I'll tell everyone when I return home next week. That's when I'll let them know it's a deal with the Blazing Frontier becoming a horse ranch as well as being a dude ranch again."

A couple hours later, Cash returned to the ranch house after going riding. There was something about this place that renewed his energy. Made him feel as if he was in his element. He was honestly getting used to the place, but he knew he would get even more used to it when he was here with Brianna as his wife.

Eighteen

"Are you sure you packed everything you're going to need, Brie?"

Brianna smiled as she moved around her bedroom. It was Wednesday morning and Cash would be arriving in less than an hour. "Yes, Miesha. I packed last night. I'm just putting together my toiletries and makeup."

"Your dress is beautiful."

A few minutes ago she had taken a picture of the dress and sent it to Miesha over the phone. "Thanks. You don't think it's too fancy, do you?"

"No. I think it will look beautiful on you. I wish I could be there with you today."

"I wish you could, too, but like I said, it's not that kind of ceremony. You know after Alan I never intended to get married anyway, so I don't plan to make a big deal of it."

"Regardless of what you might not have planned, you should be happy if for no other reason than knowing you'll get the baby you wanted."

Brianna knew that to be true. "Hopefully you and Darrett can come visit this summer once we get the dude ranch up and running again."

"Trust me, we will. He's fascinated with horses so maybe he can learn to ride while we're there. That has to make you feel good, knowing Cash is putting you in charge of everything."

Brianna paused what she was doing and drew in a deep breath. Cash had given her everything he'd promised in the documents that he had faxed to her. She would be co-owner of the Blazing Frontier while they were married.

There were a number of other things he had included that she hadn't expected, and Mr. Cavanaugh had concluded that her husband-to-be had been very generous and there was no reason she should not sign the documents. She had signed them and had faxed them back already.

"I know you packed a lot of sexy stuff, right?"

Brianna laughed. "I packed enough."

"Are you ready for Cash Outlaw to rock your world?"

She hadn't told Miesha what happened on Saturday and how he had not only rocked her world, he had literally made her weak in the knees. "As prepared as I'll ever be, I guess." She then glanced at the clock. "I need to get off the phone and finish doing everything. I've been so busy I haven't even read the mail. I figure most of it is junk anyway since I pay the majority of my bills online."

"Enjoy your day, Brianna. You might be lucky and get pregnant tonight."

"I wish."

"Then that will be my wish for you, too."

After ending the call, Brianna watered her plants. Ted would be taking care of Baby while she was gone and she appreciated it. She glanced at her watch. Cash would be arriving any minute. Moving to her fireplace, she looked up at the picture hanging there of her parents. Seeing them together and knowing how much they'd loved each other gave her the will to make it through today and believe everything would work out alright.

When she heard a car pull up outside, she knew Cash had arrived.

* * *

"This is nice, Cash," Brianna said as they boarded the small plane.

"Thanks." He tried not to stare at her, but from the moment he had picked her up he couldn't keep his eyes off her. Her hair was different, styled in a way that complemented her features. He had told her more than once how much he liked it.

The flight from Laramie to Jackson went smoothly. Brianna sat beside him in the cockpit, although she slept most of the way there. He figured she hadn't gotten a lot of sleep the night before, and if he had his way, she wouldn't get much sleep tonight either.

It would be their wedding night.

She woke up when he landed the plane, and she quickly sat up and glanced around. "We're here?"

He smiled over at her. "Yes, we are here."

Cash had made all the arrangements for the day. Once they left the airport in a rental car that he had reserved for them, they stopped for breakfast before driving to the courthouse to get a marriage license. Surprisingly, the process took less than thirty minutes. Then he drove them to the hotel after informing Brianna the wedding ceremony would take place at five o'clock in a chapel not far away.

The hotel was beautiful, a five-star, and they had connecting rooms. Glancing around her suite, Brianna was truly impressed. It was huge, larger than most studio apartments, and beautifully decorated. What she truly liked was the separate living areas. She could dress for the ceremony in her own space.

She saw no reason to unpack since Cash had said they wouldn't be spending the night here. After the ceremony they would leave for Jackson Hole, a section of Jackson that was a valley between the Teton Mountain Range and the Gros Ventre Range.

Jackson Hole was known as a place where celebrities and those persons with plenty of money to spend migrated for fun and enjoyment. She and Cash would be there for a three-day honeymoon of sorts. At least, he was referring to it as that. She only thought of it as baby-making time.

She checked her watch and saw it wasn't quite noon but close to it. Since Cash hadn't mentioned anything about lunch, she figured he intended for this to be a do-your-own-thing time, which was fine with her. She needed all the time possible before the ceremony to think about how her life would be changing.

Then again, maybe it was better if she didn't think about it at all.

The more she thought about it the more apprehensive she got, and it was too late to get cold feet now. For a woman who'd always dreamed of a fairy-tale wedding day, this certainly wasn't how she'd thought it would be. But then, Alan had destroyed a lot of things for her, when she thought of the time spent planning their wedding, sending invitations. Luckily, she hadn't had any wedding gifts to return.

Sighing deeply, she decided not to look back but to look ahead. The thought of one day holding a child in her arms—her child—would be worth working through any misgivings she had.

She'd walked to her luggage to pull out something that was more comfortable to put on, when her cell phone rang. It was Cash. She had given him a special ringtone.

"Yes, Cash?"

"I'm going downstairs to grab lunch. Would you like to join me?"

"No, thanks." No need to tell him she was too nervous to eat right now. "I'm still full from breakfast. If I get hungry later, I'll order room service."

"Okay. And just so you know, I have plans for dinner after the ceremony."

"Oh? Where?" she asked him.

"It's a surprise."

She would rather it not be, but instead she said, "Alright. I'll wait for the surprise."

"You won't be disappointed. I'll see you at the chapel at five."

Another thing he had told her was that he had made arrangements for them to arrive at the chapel separately. He wanted to get there early to make sure everything was as he'd requested. A private car would be picking her up around four thirty.

Although she knew they would be spending a few days in Jackson Hole, she had no idea where. She had only herself to blame for not knowing any details since she had passed all the marriage arrangements to Cash. It would appear rather petty of her to question anything now.

She figured she would grab an hour of sleep before she showered and got ready. She really wasn't sleepy since she had slept on the plane, but she was getting antsy and needed to calm her nerves. Just the thought that this was her wedding day—and then to think about the wedding night—was enough to make her heart beat too fast.

She had kicked off her shoes and slid half out of her jeans when there was a knock on her door. She quickly pulled her jeans back up and wondered if that was Cash. Did he think she had changed her mind about lunch?

After giving herself a quick look in the mirror and fluffing her hair back from her face, she moved toward the door. Pausing, she glanced through the peephole and nearly screamed. Then she could not open the door fast enough.

"Surprise!"

"Miesha!" Brianna exclaimed, pulling her best friend into the hotel room. "What on earth? What are you doing here? How did you know where I was? You didn't tell me you would be here. You had me send you a picture of my dress and everything, and you didn't say a word."

Miesha laughed. "Cash arranged everything. He contacted me yesterday morning at my office and invited me, but told me not to say anything to you about it. He wanted it to be a surprise."

Brianna couldn't help but grin as she and Miesha sat down on the sofa. "But how did Cash get your number?"

"He said you told him my name and the type of business I owned, and he looked me up on Google. Girl, I was totally surprised. He was so thoughtful to want to have me here with you."

Brianna couldn't believe it. "All this time Cash had me thinking it would be a small and private wedding with just me and him. Now I wonder if his brothers will be attending."

"Just his oldest brother, Garth, and Garth's wife, Regan."

Brianna tilted her head to look at Miesha. "How do you know?"

Miesha smiled. "Because Cash not only invited me to the wedding, but he provided transportation to get here. Garth's wife is their company pilot. She and Garth flew the company jet to Atlanta and picked me up and then we flew here. I thought it was cute how they took turns piloting the plane. They are super nice people. You're getting great in-laws."

Brianna nodded. She had met Cash's brothers and was looking forward to meeting Garth's wife. "It doesn't matter how nice my in-laws are. You know as well as anyone that Cash and I won't have a real marriage."

"Well, evidently his brother and sister-in-law didn't get that memo. They are excited about the wedding. So am I, and I'm here to be with you. Darrett is with my folks."

"Are you staying at this hotel?"

"Yes. My bedroom is across the hall. Garth and Regan's room is also on this floor, but down the hall. They will fly me back home tomorrow, then fly to Florida to visit Regan's father. Garth said his other brothers don't know about the wedding. Cash wants to tell them himself when he returns to Alaska next week."

Brianna thought about everything Miesha had just told her. Cash was putting more into their wedding than she had expected him to. Just the idea that he'd made arrangements for Miesha to be here with her was special.

"What are you thinking about, Brianna?"

She met her best friend's gaze and said, "Cash is making it hard for me not to love him."

"But you do love him."

Brianna lifted her brow. "I never told you that."

Miesha's smiled. "You didn't have to, Brie. I could hear it in your voice, and I know that voice. I heard that same excitement when you returned to college that fall telling me all about your fantasy boyfriend."

"You know why, Miesha."

"Yes. Cash replaced Alan in your mind that summer and it worked. In fact, I think you fell in love with him then, Brie."

Recently Brianna had begun thinking the same thing.

Miesha glanced at her watch. "Come on. Let's grab lunch. Garth introduced me to Cash in the lobby when we first arrived. Definitely eye candy, girlfriend. He was on his way out, said he had to pick a few things up." She chuckled. "I heard he even hired a photographer so you'll have memories of today. Cash Outlaw is really taking this wedding seriously. He is trying to make sure today is special for you."

"It definitely seems that way," Brianna said thoughtfully.

"Cash also told me you hadn't eaten anything since breakfast. The last thing I want is for you to pass out from hunger during the wedding ceremony."

Brianna didn't want it to happen either. Standing, she grabbed her purse off the table. "Okay, let's go."

Nineteen

Cash knew the moment Brianna walked into the chapel. He had been talking to Garth and when he turned, she was there, standing in the doorway with her best friend, Miesha, and Garth's wife, Regan. Garth had mentioned that Regan had gone to Brianna's hotel room and introduced herself, to see if she needed help with anything.

He felt a sudden tightness in his throat when his gaze roamed over her. She looked amazing, beautiful. She was wearing a pink silk dress. It stopped at her knees with a beautiful lace hem border. He remembered once telling her how much he liked the color pink on her. Had she worn the color just for him? Pink made her appear feminine and sexy. The color also enhanced her complexion as well as highlighted the darkness of her eyes.

She wore a pair of silver stilettos, which looked to have a four-inch heel. He'd never seen her in heels that high and they enriched the beauty of a gorgeous pair of legs. When she began nibbling on her bottom lip, he knew she was nervous, probably from him staring so hard. But he couldn't help it. His heart began beating nearly uncontrollably. Brianna Banks was his.

"Are you going to just stand here and stare or are you going to claim your bride to get this wedding underway?"

Cash glanced back at his brother. "I am claiming my bride."

He walked off toward Brianna, holding her gaze with every step he took. Coming to a stop in front of the three women, he noticed Garth had walked over with him and stood by his side. "Regan. Miesha," Cash greeted the two women. He then glanced at Brianna. "You look beautiful."

She seemed to blush. "Thanks."

Offering her his arm, he said, "Let me introduce you to Reverend Epps."

In less than five minutes, Cash and Brianna were facing each other in the chapel. He had hired someone to decorate it and she had said she liked it. She also said she liked the bridal bouquet of hollyhocks he had presented to her. One day while out riding she had mentioned her favorite flower was hollyhocks and he had remembered.

Garth was his best man and Miesha was her maid of honor. She'd obviously asked Regan to be her attendant. When Reverend Epps told them to hold hands, he reached for Brianna's hand and felt her tremble. She tilted her head up to meet his gaze as they followed the minister's instructions and spoke their vows.

The words flowed from his lips freely and her responses were clear as she continued to hold his gaze. He took that as a positive sign.

"By the powers invested in me by the great state of Wyoming, I now pronounce you husband and wife. Mr. Outlaw, you may kiss your bride."

Cash smiled when he saw apprehension in her features. He knew as well as she did that their kisses could take on a life of their own. He winked to let her know he wouldn't do anything to give the minister heart palpitations, and Garth a reason to jab an arm in his ribs.

He wrapped his arms around Brianna's waist, leaned in and captured her lips in a kiss that wasn't chaste, nor was it as hot and greedy as he could have made it. Those kinds of kisses would come later.

Upon releasing her mouth, he smiled at her. Then the minister beamed his approval and said, "Congratulations, Mr. and Mrs. Cash Outlaw. I wish the two of you the very best, and may you have a long and happy life together."

Without breaking eye contact with Brianna when he replied to the minister, Cash said, "Thank you, Reverend Epps. I'm going to make sure of it."

More words of congratulations came from Garth and Regan and of course Miesha, who was shedding happy tears. Brianna still couldn't believe her best friend was here and that Cash had made it happen. Regan had shown up at her hotel door, introducing herself and offering to do whatever she could to make Brianna's day special.

Brianna had liked Regan immediately and she could see how Garth had fallen in love with her. There was no doubt in Brianna's mind it was a love match. She had seen the look in Garth's eyes the moment his wife had arrived at the church.

Brianna had also seen the look in Cash's eyes when he had seen her. She knew it had been lust and not love, but she would take it.

The photographer had taken a ton of pictures and she was glad. She would need them to convince herself she was truly married. Especially those times when he left her for days, for months, and she waited in Wyoming for his return.

She felt Cash's arms slide around her waist seconds before he leaned down and whispered, "It's time for us to go. We have reservations for dinner at six."

Nodding, she gave everyone hugs and waved goodbye. Cash then took her hand in his as they walked out of the chapel. She remembered her luggage was in the private car that had transported her, Miesha and Regan to the chapel. She glanced around for the car.

"What are you looking for?" Cash asked her.

"That private car with my luggage. I don't see it."

"The driver has taken our things on to Jackson Hole. Your luggage, as well as mine, should be in our room when we arrive after dinner."

Our room.

His reminder that they would be sharing a bed tonight sent shivers through her. Mistaking the shivers as a sign she was cold, he wrapped his arms around her shoulders and led her to the car.

He opened the car door for her and as soon as she slid onto the seat and snapped her seat belt in place, questions formed in her mind about just what the night held in store. Would it be anything close to the fantasies she'd had of him?

That kiss on Saturday had pretty much proven he would use his mouth in ways that should be forbidden. Even now when they were both seated in the car and he was about to start the engine, she could feel his sensual heat. Was such a thing normal? She wasn't sure because it hadn't happened to her with any other man, but then, Cash had been the first for her in many ways.

"The ceremony was nice, Cash. Thanks for arranging everything. I am especially grateful that you thought to have Miesha here. That was special."

"You are special."

Brianna wished she could believe he really thought that, and he wasn't just getting caught up in anticipation of a lustful night. Either way, she owed him a response. "Thank you. I think you are special, too."

The car had come to a traffic light, and he looked at her and smiled. He then reached out and took her hand in his and carried it to his lips. "Then I guess we are two special people who were meant for each other."

She was about to set him straight and tell him that it wasn't necessary to lay the compliments on so thick, then decided to just go with the flow. Besides, whenever he looked at her like that, she wasn't capable of setting him straight on anything.

"We're here."

Already? She glanced out the window at the extravagant restaurant. Although she hadn't ever eaten here, she had heard about it. The Jagged Edge was a popular place in Jackson that catered to an elite and extravagant crowd. She was neither, so she'd never put this place on her radar to visit.

A valet parked their car, and a smiling maître d' met them at the door. "Mr. and Mrs. Outlaw, congratulations. Your table is ready."

Brianna was surprised by the man's words. "You know him?" she asked Cash, trying to ignore the warmth of his hand at her back as they followed the man. The restaurant was huge and impressive, especially the triple stairs that led to other dining areas. The top was a cathedral ceiling with the largest chandeliers Brianna had ever seen. The back wall was completely glass to take advantage of the view of the lake.

"No, I don't know him personally. However, we met yesterday when I flew in to make all the arrangements."

He'd flown here yesterday? What kind of arrangements required him to come here in person? She got her answer the moment the maître d' opened the door to a private room.

Like the church, it was decorated with balloons and a banner that said Best Wishes Cash and Brianna. In the middle of the candlelit room was a table set for two with a beautiful view of the lake as a backdrop. A bottle of champagne was in a bucket, and soft music was playing.

"This is our own private wedding reception," he said, leading her to the table. "We will have an official one later where we can invite family and friends."

We will? That was news to Brianna, but she was too caught up with how beautiful the room looked to dwell on it now. She hadn't expected this. But then, she hadn't expected Miesha to be there for her either. Cash Outlaw was definitely full of surprises. Overcome with emotion, she had to struggle to collect herself before saying, "I hadn't expected any of this, Cash."

"I wanted to make things as special as you are, Brianna."

If he was working for brownie points, then he was doing a good job of getting them. "Thanks."

When they sat down, he grabbed the champagne bottle out of the bucket, opened it and poured some into their glasses. He lifted the glass in a toast. "To my beautiful wife."

She drew in a deep breath before she took her sip. Knowing she needed to add to the moment, she lifted her glass and said, "To my very thoughtful, kind and handsome husband."

After clinking their glasses, he threw his head back and laughed before taking a sip of his champagne. "You are laying it on rather thick, Brianna."

She smiled sweetly at him. "No more than you, Cash."

It seemed as if he would argue that point. Then, as if he thought better of it, he said, "I took the liberty of preordering our meal. I hope you don't mind."

"No, I don't mind." She was too nervous to study a menu anyway.

"I know how much you like salmon, and they have a superb dish that's baked with steamed carrots and pears over a white wine sauce."

"Sounds delicious."

"I had a sample tasting yesterday."

The waiter came with their meal. It looked pretty on their plates and she bet it was just as delicious. He had ordered the same thing for himself. Before leaving, the waiter poured more champagne into their glasses.

Over dinner she told him she had never learned to ski.

He had informed her that since Jackson Hole was known for some of the best ski slopes, he intended to teach her. He didn't tell her much else about where they would be staying in Jackson Hole, and she figured she would have to wait to see it. He had said it was not a hotel, though.

When the music in the room seemed to get a little louder, Cash glanced at his watch. "Right on time. I instructed them that after we completed our meal, I wanted at least one dance with my wife before we left."

His wife...

Why did she feel a tingling sensation all through her body whenever he referred to her that way? She tilted her head up when he stood beside her chair and offered her his hand. "May I have this dance, Mrs. Outlaw?"

Mrs. Outlaw... Hearing him call her that made goose bumps form on her arms. Made her breath nearly catch. She stood and took his hand, and the moment they touched, a jolt of sexual energy passed between them. He tightened his hold on her as he led her to a shadowy section of the room.

Cash drew her into his arms, and as if it was the most natural thing, she went there without any hesitation. Resting her head on his chest, she got caught up in the sound of the soft romantic music that was playing while their bodies swayed.

It felt good being held in his arms as they slowly moved in rhythm. Blood rushed through her veins and her pulse rate increased.

Suddenly Cash stopped, although the music continued to play. She lifted her head from his chest to look up at him. Even in the semi-darkened room, she could see into his eyes from the moonlight shining off the lake.

She knew what was coming next and welcomed it. When he lowered his head, she tilted her chin up to meet his mouth. The connection fired her blood, made her heart rate kick up even higher, made her purr.

Only Cash could elicit such a response from her. He could do what others had failed to do. Although she had tried to deny it, she would admit now that this was the man she wanted, not just to father her child, but to be a part of her life.

At nineteen he had been her fantasy boyfriend, the man she had always wanted. Now he was her real husband.

He deepened the kiss and she let him. Cash had a way of breaking through her guard walls, lowering her defenses. Miesha had been right. Brianna needed to take charge, not let him be a drop-in husband. What she needed to do was use the days they spent together to give him a reason to visit her in Wyoming every chance he got. Could she pull off such a thing with her limited experience? She would certainly try.

He broke off the kiss and whispered against her moist lips, "It's time for us to leave."

Yes, he was right. It was time to leave. "Alright."

She was ready to act on the intense heat blazing between them.

Twenty

"This villa is beautiful, Cash."

Cash leaned against the closed door and watched as Brianna stood in the middle of the living room. As a romantic gesture he had carried her over the threshold and doubted he would ever forget the look of surprise on her face when he'd done so.

There was still a little daylight outside, so they had seen the beauty of the area when he'd driven across the scenic valley before crossing several snow-covered roads. The villa was at the top of one of the mountains in Jackson Hole.

It was part of a prestigious ski resort, and he had leased it for five days. This was one of their most secluded villas, and the two-story structure consisted of four bedrooms, three baths, a living room and a spacious eat-in kitchen. It was nestled among low-hanging trees, right by a huge lake with a view of much larger snowcapped mountains. There had been a drop in the temperature the higher he had driven up into the mountains.

"I'm glad you like it," he said, removing his tuxedo jacket and stepping away from the door to move toward her. "Did I tell you how beautiful you look?"

She nodded. "Yes, you told me."

"Everything about you today was perfect."

He meant it. She looked beautiful in pink. Her dress was exquisite, her makeup flawless and her hair—which was curled and pulled up with a bevy of ringlets around her face—made her look both serene and sexy.

More than once he had lost his train of thought while staring at her from across the dinner table. And at the wedding, while reciting his vows, he'd had to fight to retain his concentration. All he could think about was that by the end of the day, she would belong only to him. Not as a possession but as a treasure.

She didn't back up when he stopped in front of her. To him that was a good sign. Instead, she tilted her head back to meet his eyes while nervously licking her lips.

"Do you know what it does to me whenever I see you lick your lips like that, Brianna?"

She immediately stopped doing it. "No. What does it do to you?"

"It makes me want to be the one to lick them for you."

He saw the flash of heat in her eyes. Then, as if his words brought out a boldness in her, she deliberately licked them again, and whispered, "I welcome you to go for it, Cash."

That was all the invitation he needed. The moment their tongues touched, he had to fight for control. Brianna kissed him back with a need he felt all the way to his groin. Her response forced him to deepen the kiss. He wanted her to feel his hunger from the top of her head to the bottoms of her feet.

Her mouth tasted like the champagne they had consumed earlier. He wrapped his arms around her so tightly, he could feel the hardness of her nipples against his chest— nipples he had tasted once and looked forward to tasting again.

Knowing where this kiss would eventually lead and wanting them both naked when it did, he broke away and slowly lifted his head to stare down into her eyes. The intensity in the dark gaze staring back at him made his heart pound.

Drawing in a much-needed breath, he asked, "Do you want to get naked out here or in the bedroom?"

"In the bedroom," she said in a soft voice that fired up his libido even more.

Images of the two of them in bed, naked and making love, had him struggling for breath again. Without wasting any time, he swept her into his arms.

After Cash placed her on the bed and stepped back, Brianna could feel the intensity of his gaze as if it were a physical caress. She might not be experienced in some things, but at that moment, she was aware of the magnetism between them.

When he reached out his hand to her, she took it and stood beside the bed with him. He released the clips holding her hair, making it flow around her shoulders. Then he reached behind her dress to slowly inch down the zipper.

Brianna forced breath through her lungs at the thought of Cash's hands touching her. These were the hands of her husband, the man she loved.

Yes, she loved him. Her love for him was absolute, even if he never felt the same. As long as he kept all the promises he'd made to her child, she could handle anything.

While holding her gaze, he stepped back and let the dress flow down her hips and land at her feet. His gaze went to her bra and this time he was the one who licked his lips. Seeing him do so reminded her of what happened the last time he'd enjoyed her breasts. The reminder made heat settle in the area between her legs.

Brianna had always liked matching bra and pantie sets, and while shopping in Laramie, she had purchased a few of them. The one she wore today was the exact shade of pink that matched her wedding dress.

"Thanks for making things easy for me," he said when his fingers went to the front clasp of her bra and removed it with the proficiency of a man who'd done so many times. That thought didn't bother her. She believed him when he'd said she would be the only woman he slept with now.

She watched when he knelt before her to inch the thong down her legs and suddenly, she felt bashful. No man had ever undressed her before, and Cash was taking his time doing so.

When she lifted her legs to step out of her thong, she wondered why he hadn't removed her shoes first. She got her answer when he glanced up at her and said, "Seeing you naked in a pair of stilettos is a vision that will be branded into my mind forever. You look so hot and sexy. So damn desirable it makes me ache."

He was still down on his knees in front of her and she held his gaze. His words made every pulse point within her body come alive. Every inner muscle tightened. Her nipples hardened.

She knew he saw her reaction.

Then he grabbed her thighs and buried his head between her legs. When she felt his tongue invading her womanly core, she clutched his shoulders. Otherwise her knees would have given out on her, right then and there.

Using his tongue as a sensuous weapon, he dived deep inside of her, and she moaned at the intimate invasion. He drove his tongue even deeper and sucked harder, greedily, as if he loved her taste and couldn't get enough.

Alan had never done this to her, but she'd heard talk at college about guys doing this and what a mindblower it was. Her friends were right. She wanted to scream for him to stop in one breath, and then beg for him to continue in the other. How could she feel so brazen to let a man do this to her?

But then, Cash wasn't just any man. He was her husband. Whatever she allowed him to do was fine. Then she felt his hands tighten on her thighs as he wiggled his tongue inside of her. She gave up fighting the sensations that took over her mind and body.

Grabbing the back of his head, she tried pressing him more intimately to her, wanting more of what he was doing. When she felt a sharp pleasure hit her just where his mouth was connected to her body, she screamed and fell backward on the bed as her legs gave out.

Cash didn't stop. He couldn't. His mouth remained clamped tight to her feminine mound, while his tongue drove even deeper inside of her. He loved her taste. He loved the sounds she was making and he loved her scent.

Brianna Outlaw.

Her name was now his.

He hoped they created their baby tonight. Not because she wanted a child, but because he wanted one, too. Suddenly, more than anything, he wanted a baby with Brianna.

When the last of the tremors finally left her body, he pulled his mouth from her, removed her shoes and readjusted her position on the bed before tackling the chore of removing his own clothes. Through a pair of exhausted eyes, she watched him.

He smiled at her. "Don't get sluggish on me now, sweetheart."

She looked totally sexy lying on her back, naked, with her legs slightly spread. Her eyes closed as she tried to regain control of her breathing. With each intake of air into her lungs, her breasts moved, and the sight of the darkened nipples was arousing.

She opened her eyes to look at him. "I honestly don't know if I have the energy for anything more, Cash," she said in a tone that he would have found convincing had he not known better. Whether she knew it or not, his wife was a passionate woman. That was obvious in the way she returned his kisses.

"Trust me. You will find the energy."

Brianna looked skeptical, but he had a feeling her body would be ready whenever his was. Even now, there were signs of her vitality returning as she watched him undress. He could see it in the eyes watching his every move, the rise and fall of her chest that denoted the heaviness of her breathing.

When he slid his tuxedo pants down his legs along with his briefs and stood before her completely nude, he even heard her purr.

"Your body is beautiful, Cash."

He smiled at the compliment. "Your body is beautiful, too. Are you ready for me, baby?"

Without taking her gaze off his midsection, she nodded. "Yes, I'm ready."

Cash smiled, looking forward to teaching her all the ways they would pleasure each other. "Good, because I'm ready, too." He got back on the bed and slowly eased up her body.

When he was in the right position, he stared down at her and saw the intensity in the eyes staring back at him. That look tempted him to lean in and kiss her. She was his. He had gotten more than the marriage he demanded. He had gotten the wife he desired.

He captured her mouth with his.

Brianna was convinced no man could kiss better than Cash. He not only used his mouth and tongue to bring her to an aroused state, but he also used them to push her close to the edge then snatch her back.

She moaned in protest when he finally released her mouth, and gazed up at him while trying to get her breathing back in sync. That's when she felt him nudge her legs apart with his knee. As he held her gaze, he slowly slid inside of her, stretching her body to accommodate him.

Sensations overtook her the deeper he went, and she couldn't stop the moans that slipped past her lips. "Cash…"

"I'm here, sweetheart." And then, as if to prove that he was, he held their joined hands above her head. That made her breasts lift with the nipples pointing at his mouth. She saw the fiery look in his eyes when he noticed as well.

Two things happened simultaneously. He leaned in and latched onto a nipple, easing it into his mouth, and her inner muscles—as if with a mind of their own—clamped down. It was as if they were trying to pull everything out of him.

That's when she heard his moan, but he didn't let go of the nipple in his mouth. While her body was milking him below, he was using the same technique on her breast. That realization sent shivers down her spine.

He released the nipple to gaze down at her as he moved, thrusting in and out, slowly at first. Making sure she felt every incredible inch of him. She wrapped her legs around him as his body began pounding her hard into the mattress, pushing her over the edge and making her scream his name.

And he screamed hers.

Not only did he scream her name, but she felt him let loose inside her. The very essence of him coated her insides. She screamed his name again when the sensations kept coming, kept tearing into her with a force she had never felt before. The violent tremors took her breath away.

Then the shudders slowed. The intensity of her pleasure made her whisper his name in admiration and awe. She hadn't known making love to someone could be like this. Overpowering. Satisfying. Full of contentment.

She felt drained, totally sapped. The last thing she recalled before drifting off was Cash kissing the side of her face, whispering for her to rest because there was more to come.

* * *

Daylight streaming in through the window brought Cash awake. He glanced around the room, knowing where he was and who he was with. There was no doubt in his mind whose legs were entwined with his and whose warm body he held in the spoon position.

My wife.

He smiled, liking the sound of that.

She was still asleep and he understood why. It had been one wild night. Brianna hadn't thought she had energy left for round two or three. She'd surprised herself.

Now Cash was glad he hadn't planned any activities for them today, other than eating and making love. He glanced at the clock. It was eight in the morning. He had ordered their breakfast to be delivered to their villa at nine. To ward off the cold, he started a blaze in the bedroom's fireplace. In no time, it was throwing off good heat in the room.

This was a beautiful villa. It was larger than what they needed, but he'd loved the layout when he'd seen it online. He had chosen this particular villa because of the location. He wanted complete privacy with Brianna. It wouldn't hurt his feelings any if they didn't see another human being for as long as they were here together.

Making love to her through the night had been one of the most pleasurable things he'd ever done. That had him wondering how he would handle those nights in Alaska when she would be in Wyoming. Hopefully he wouldn't have to. When he returned to Alaska next week, he had an idea he would run by Garth.

Brianna shifted in his arms and then slowly rolled over to face him. When their gazes connected, he felt a spark of renewed arousal and knew she felt it, too. There was no way she couldn't when his erection pressed hard against her.

"Good morning, Cash," she said in a soft voice.

"Good morning, Brianna. However, I believe the morning-after greeting should go something like this."

Then he kissed her. Finally releasing her mouth, he snuggled her closer.

"What's planned for today?" she asked him.

"Breakfast will be delivered at nine. Lunch at one. Dinner at six. Very good reviews on the food and service here."

"And in between lunch and dinner?"

He smiled. "For me it will be Brianna at ten, eleven and twelve. Then again at two, three, four and five. Then the rest of the day after dinner."

She giggled. "Is that your way of letting me know you plan to pretty much keep me on my back?"

"Yes, I guess you could say that. Of course, you can request to put me on my back whenever you want."

She laughed. "Thanks for being so accommodating."

"You're welcome. I guess we need to get up and throw something on for breakfast. Or better yet, we can always eat in bed." That was an idea he rather liked.

"Either way is fine with me."

He was glad to hear that. "We have activities planned for tomorrow. We're taking a cable car tour of Mount Laver."

"Sounds like fun."

"Um," he said, leaning in and kissing her on the side of her neck, "not as much fun as staying inside the villa with you."

Then he straddled her body, knowing he needed to make love to her before he could possibly get his day started. And from the sound of her breathing, she was all in.

Good.

Twenty-One

"How did I do today?" Brianna asked Cash after taking a shower and putting on a comfortable maxi dress. She loved how the linen material felt on her skin. However, what she liked most was the front zipper that ran the length of the neckline to the hem. Easy on and easy off.

For the past two days, he had taught her how to ski. They had rented everything they needed, from clothing to equipment. Today was their last at the Jackson Hole ski resort and she was missing being here already.

Thursday had been a stay-in-bed day, but Friday and today they had gotten out so Cash could teach her how to ski. More than once, she had stared down at her hand to see the beautiful wedding ring he had placed there as proof they were truly married. She had never thought having a husband would be so much fun, both in and out of the bedroom.

"You did well, but you're not ready for the slopes yet," Cash said, grinning.

They were high up in the Wyoming mountains. It was cold and the snow was heavy and thick. Whenever they returned to the villa, the fireplaces had the inside all warm and toasty. She loved being here with Cash. Whenever she thought about all the things they had done together, all the ways they had pleasured each other in the bedroom, she got both bashful and giddy inside.

They would be returning to the ranch tomorrow, and

then he would leave for Alaska before daybreak Monday morning. She couldn't help wondering when he would return. Would he miss her when they were apart?

On the drive from Black Crow to the Laramie airport, she had told him she would be going to the doctor next week to get a temperature kit. That way she would know the best times to get pregnant. She figured those would be the only times he would return. Until then…

Because she would be wearing her ring, it wouldn't be long before word of her marriage got around. This morning at breakfast he had surprised her when he said he wanted her to move into the ranch house and turn it into a home. She figured he wanted the place to feel like a home whenever he dropped in.

Since the wedding, not once had they talked about the reason for their marriage. Others probably assumed they were a newly wedded couple who were madly in love.

"Do you like this place, Brianna?"

She glanced over at him. He was sitting on the rug in front of the fireplace. It had become one of their favorite spots at night to unwind and sip glasses of wine. Huge pillows were placed all around—a comfortable place to sleep or even make love.

"Yes, I really like it. Thanks for bringing me here." She paused. "Ready for our glass of wine?"

He glanced up at her. "Yes, I'll get it."

"No, stay put. I will get it."

Cash smiled up at her. "Okay."

She returned a short while later with a tray carrying their glasses and a bottle of wine. Each day a different bottle had been delivered to the villa, compliments of the resort.

She placed the tray by him and then eased down in front of the fireplace beside him. "You did a good job arranging everything, Cash."

She meant it. In less than two days he had made all the

wedding arrangements as well as the ones for their five-day honeymoon. Not only was the resort itself wonderful, but the service was excellent, especially the food.

"It was all for you, sweetheart," he said.

He was gently caressing her cheek while gazing into her eyes. It was during tender moments like these when she truly felt like her fantasy husband. He had a way of making her think he was sincere in everything he said and did. Even when he used terms of endearment, which he'd been doing a lot, they flowed naturally from his lips.

She watched him pour wine into their glasses and then he handed her one. He held up his. "Let's toast our last night here together. The days were great." His smile transformed into a sexy grin. "I especially enjoyed the nights."

She held up her glass and agreed. "Yes, especially the nights."

They stared at each other over the rims of their wineglasses as they leisurely sipped. He had told her she was a very passionate woman and she was beginning to believe him. Although certain parts of their lovemaking could still leave her weak, it was a satisfying feeling.

In just three nights Cash had shown her that no two sessions of lovemaking were the same. *You get out of it what you put into it, granted your partner isn't a selfish or inconsiderate bastard.* Those were his words, not hers. Her excuse was that she and Alan had both been young and inexperienced.

As they continued to stare into each other's eyes, she could feel the sexual energy flowing between them. There was a buildup of need and desire slowly overtaking them. He was aroused, which was something a man couldn't hide. And their chemistry was more powerful than ever.

She knew Cash would soon act on all that hot, carnal awareness. However, tonight she intended to act first. Placing her wineglass aside, she stood. Knowing he watched her every move, she slowly lowered the zipper of her dress. If he had suspected she hadn't been wearing anything underneath, he knew it for certain now.

When she stood naked in front of him, she said, "Now for your clothes. Stand so I can take them off you." She was doing what she hadn't done yet—undressing him.

Brianna watched how he eased to his feet; even that was sexy. Without wasting any time, she moved to him and began unbuttoning his shirt, feeling the rapid beat of his heart against her fingers.

Next came his jeans, which proved to be difficult because of his aroused state. He took pity on her and helped her out. When he finally stood naked before her, she just stood there a moment looking at him. The firelight flickered across his body, making him look like a deep bronze Adonis.

She moved back toward him when he extended his arms to her. She went into them. "This is my night for you, Cash. One I want you to remember during your nights in Alaska without me."

She hadn't meant to say that, but now that she had, she didn't regret it. She wanted him to miss her. She wanted him to come back to her often. She wanted to have a purpose in his life that was more than the woman he had agreed to impregnate. The woman who had the land he wanted.

On tiptoe, she wrapped her arms around his neck, tempted at that moment to tell him that she loved him. However, she didn't feel brave enough for the words. She had said enough already.

So she kissed him.

She kissed him in all the ways he had taught her over the past few days. And when he kissed her back, she almost lost control of her senses. That was the last thing she wanted. Without knowing he'd done so, each and every time they had made love, Cash had branded her his. Now she wanted to brand him hers.

Without breaking their kiss, she began easing down to the floor with him, and then, when she did break off the kiss, she gently pushed him onto his back to straddle him.

She liked looking down at him, seeing the surprise in his eyes as well as the heat. There was something else there, too, a look she couldn't define. At that moment, he was as aware of her as she was of him.

When she deliberately lowered her midsection to rub her body against his, he moaned out her name.

"Brianna..."

"Yes?"

"Put me out of my misery."

He hadn't experienced her brand of misery yet. Instead of granting his request, she lowered her mouth to kiss him. Using the technique he had taught her, her tongue dueled with his.

When she broke off the kiss, she began kissing his chest, then moving lower to his stomach, and then she slid lower still. Before he could stop her, she had taken him into her mouth.

Cash was convinced Brianna was trying to kill him. He should have known he was a goner when she unzipped her dress to reveal her perfect body—beautiful shoulders, a pair of firm breasts with luscious nipples, a small waist, flat stomach, curvy hips and shapely legs.

The icing on the cake had been the dark triangle at her center. It didn't matter that he had tasted her there and had gone inside of her every day since they'd married. Every time he saw her womanly mound, he wanted as much of it as he could get.

Cash let out a moan at the way Brianna was working her mouth on him. He grabbed her head, having a mind to make her stop. Instead of stopping her, he held her head right there as her mouth continued to greedily consume him.

He closed his eyes at the feel of her tongue wrapping around the head of his shaft. Nothing had prepared him for this. When she widened her mouth to take in the full length of his manhood, the bottom half of him nearly shot off the floor.

A growling sound escaped his lips, and when he felt his body getting ready to explode, he knew he wanted to be inside of her when it happened.

With all the strength he could muster, he grabbed hold of her shoulders and pulled her up over him. "I need to be inside of you. Now!"

He thrust upward and slid into her at the same time she came down on him. The connection was so intense, it shook them both. She then began moving up and down him, riding him hard.

He did upward thrusts and she did downward plunges. Together, the strokes intensified, electrified and nearly pushed them over the edge. It seemed neither was ready for this to end, so he deliberately snatched them back just to repeat the process over and over again.

Then Cash couldn't hold off any longer. When he exploded, it was so severe, it felt like it would shake his entire insides loose. From the trembling of her body, he knew she had felt the same thing. That's when he grabbed the back of her neck and brought her mouth down to his, and kissed her with a hunger that only intensified their orgasms.

It was only when the last shudders had left their bodies that he released her mouth and gathered her into his arms. They faced the fireplace to watch the flames and get their breathing under control.

Cash knew that leaving Brianna to return to Alaska would be the hardest thing he'd ever done, but now his trip home had a purpose. When he returned to Wyoming, he didn't intend to ever leave without her again.

Twenty-Two

"There you have it, Garth. Do you think it's a workable idea?"

Although the plan had been for Cash to return to the office for today's midday meeting, he'd honestly considered calling in to request more time off. After all, he had gotten married less than a week ago. But he'd needed to explain his idea to Garth in person.

Garth leaned back in his chair, nodding. "Yes, it's workable and a damn good idea. It would require the shifting of job duties between you, Sloan and Maverick, but I think they are ready for a change anyway. Sloan has hinted that he's getting tired of traveling so much. Now he can take over your duties here in the office."

Garth paused and then added, "And Maverick has been champing at the bit to work internationally for years. If we ever need you to attend an in-office meeting, your flight time between Wyoming and Alaska is less than five hours."

A huge smile spread across Cash's face. "Thanks." Setting up a satellite office of Outlaw Freight Lines in Black Crow, Wyoming, at the Blazing Frontier Ranch was a good idea. Cash would handle the company's expansion into various other states.

"So, when are you going to tell everyone that you're married?" Garth asked.

"After today's meeting. I plan to fly back to Wyoming

tomorrow morning and then return with Brianna to introduce her to Dad over the weekend." Their father and Charm's mother, Claudia, had flown to see a Broadway show in New York and wouldn't be back until the end of the week.

"Just prepare yourself, and you might want to prepare Brianna. Bart still likes to think he's in control and calling the shots. He isn't going to like that you got married without consulting him first," Garth said.

Cash rolled his eyes. "I stopped consulting Bart about anything years ago. I usually take his advice with a grain of salt."

Garth chuckled. "Don't we all?"

Back in his office, Cash was glad things had turned out so well. Of course, Sloan and Maverick, although surprised to hear he'd gotten married, were happy for him since they liked Brianna. He hadn't told Charm because she hadn't attended the meeting. She would have to wait and hear it from him at the same time he told Bart.

He leaned back in his chair as he remembered how he had awakened at the ranch house before dawn that morning to make love to Brianna before he left. She hadn't asked when he would be returning, so when she saw him tomorrow, she would certainly be surprised. And there was no doubt in his mind she would be surprised to know he was staying.

He had called to let her know he had arrived safely in Alaska. She was still in bed and said she would make this a lazy Monday for her. She would arrive at her house later today to check on things and go through her mail. It was her plan to return to the ranch house to spend the night and then begin moving her stuff this week.

Cash liked the thought of knowing that when he arrived at the ranch early tomorrow morning, she would be there in his bed. Then he would be there to help her move her stuff to the ranch. It was her home now and he intended for them to live together as husband and wife. Any misgivings about how she would feel about it had come to an end when she had unintentionally whispered that she loved him before drifting off to sleep after they'd made love this morning. Chances were she wouldn't remember saying it, but he had definitely heard her.

Hearing the words had made him finally understand what he'd been feeling all this time, why he knew he had to make this move to Wyoming.

He loved his wife.

More than anything, he looked forward to having her back in his arms again.

Brianna had thrown the last of her clothes in the dryer and decided to take time to eat lunch. She would definitely be busy this week. Cash had asked that she move into the ranch house and she'd promised she would. That meant she would start moving her things a little at a time.

When they'd talked that morning, she had been tempted to ask him when he would return, but kept herself from doing so. She had known what their marriage arrangements would be when she'd agreed to marry him. Just because they'd had a wonderful time on their honeymoon, that didn't mean anything had changed—although she had tried her best to make sure he would miss her while he was in Alaska.

Leaving the laundry room, she saw all the mail stacked up on her kitchen table. It was mail she'd been too busy to look through before leaving for the wedding. Most was junk mail anyway.

Thirty minutes later she had tossed most of it away when she came across a letter addressed to her from the law firm of Denese, Fryson and Cohen in Los Angeles. She frowned. Why would a law firm be writing to her? And where had she seen the name of that firm before? For some reason, it sounded familiar.

She tore open the letter, and as she read what it said, intense anger consumed her. Cash was going to contest the will? When had he planned this? The letter was dated more than a week ago. Before she had agreed to marry him. It had been delivered Tuesday.

Was this plan B in case she had turned down his counteroffer of marriage on Monday? From what the letter said, it seemed he had already put a plan into motion to take her to court and contest Ms. Ellen's will, not just for the fifty acres but for everything his mother had left her. That included her house, and the thought had her fighting back tears.

How could she have been so wrong about him? How could she have let another man play her for a fool? Tears she couldn't hold back streamed down her face. Never again. Never again.

Cash glanced down at his cell phone when it rang and smiled when he saw it was Brianna. He clicked it on. "I was just thinking about you, sweetheart."

"Were you? Why? Did your attorney let you know he had jumped the gun in sending that letter since I *did* consent to marry you?"

Cash frowned. "What are you talking about?"

"I am talking about the letter I got from your attorneys, Denese, Fryson and Cohen, stating your plans to contest the will. I guess that was your plan B in case I decided not to marry you."

"I have no idea what you're talking about."

"Tell that to someone else, Cash. Just so you know, I plan to get my own attorney and file for a divorce. I refuse to stay married to a man I cannot trust." And then she hung up on him.

Cash sat there holding the phone, not believing the conversation that had just transpired. He had no idea what Brianna was talking about. He'd never dealt with any law firm by the name of Denese, Fryson and Cohen.

He tried calling her back, but she wouldn't answer. Damn! Getting up from his desk, he crossed the hall to Garth's office and barged in without knocking. Garth snatched his head up from the papers he'd been reading. When he saw the anger on Cash's face, he stood and asked, "Cash, what's wrong?"

Cash then told Garth what Brianna had told him. "Damn it, Garth, I've never even heard of that law firm."

Garth's jaw tightened. "I have. They used to be Dad's attorneys out of LA."

"Dad?"

"Yes, but I had no idea he still had them on retainer."

Cash's frown deepened as he rubbed the back of his neck. "I swear, Garth, if Dad is responsible for this, there will be hell to pay. How dare this firm send any document on my behalf when they don't represent me. I can't believe they would notify Brianna that I would be contesting Ellen's will."

"How soon are you leaving for Wyoming?" Garth asked his brother.

An angry Cash met his brother's gaze. "I'm leaving as soon as I can get my plane ready."

Around midnight, Brianna was awakened by pounding on her door. Turning on the lamp by her bed, she got up and slid into her robe. She had a sinking feeling who it was. A quick look out the peephole confirmed her suspicions.

"What do you want, Cash?"

"Open the door, Brianna. We need to talk."

"No. We have nothing to say to each other. Just go away."

She was about to return to her bedroom when he began

pounding on her door again. "I am not leaving, Brianna. Open the door."

Brianna drew in a deep breath. Before going to bed, she had talked to Miesha, and her best friend had found it hard to believe Cash would do such a thing. Brianna hadn't wanted to believe it either, but she had those attorneys' letter to prove it.

"Brianna!"

She could hear the anger in his voice. What did he have to be mad about? She was the one who'd been played for a fool. "We have nothing to say, Cash."

"Yes, we do. Now open the door."

Fine, they would get it all out, but there was nothing he could say that would make her forgive him. She opened the door and looked at him. He stood under the porch light, his features tight and brooding. He was wearing a business shirt and slacks. Had he come straight from his office?

"Please say what you have to say and leave, Cash," she told him, closing the door behind him when he entered her home.

"You are wrong about me, Brianna."

She crossed her arms over her chest and glared up at him. "I got the letter from your attorneys, Cash. Now I know the truth. You were going to take everything Ms. Ellen left me. You pretended to be fine with my inheritance, but deep down you resented it and didn't want me to have anything. You were going to toss me out of my home like Hal Sutherland planned to do. You are no better than him."

Her words seemed to have struck him. His eyes lit with even more anger. "I did not have those attorneys send that letter, Brianna. Why would I send a letter contesting the will when I planned to marry you?"

"It was a plan you put in place just in case I turned you down."

He shoved his hands into the pockets of his jeans. "I

planned to marry you whether you turned me down on Monday or not. You would have been my wife regardless."

His words infuriated her. "Are you saying I would not have had a say in the matter?"

"No, what I am saying is that you would have eventually said yes because we're good together. Because I couldn't live without you. Because I would have convinced you how much I want you. How much I love you."

She backed up as if his words were a weapon. "You don't love me."

"I do love you. I love you as much as you love me, Brianna."

She lifted her chin. "What makes you think I love you?"

"You told me this morning before I left. You said it right after we climaxed together that last time and before you drifted off to sleep."

Had she? "What I said after sex means nothing now. I am filing for a divorce." She watched him rub his hand down his face as if he was agitated. Brianna cared less how he was feeling when her heart had been broken.

Cash looked straight at her and said, "That firm does not represent me and I did not have them send you that letter. However, I think I know who did."

"Who?"

"My father."

Her frown deepened. "Why would your father do such a thing?"

"Because Bart Outlaw thinks he has the right to control every situation. Even those that involve his grown-ass sons."

"You want me to believe your father would do something like that knowing you would eventually find out about it?"

"Yes, because in his mind, he honestly believes he's looking out for our best interests."

Brianna didn't say anything because what he'd told her was pretty much what Ms. Ellen had said about her ex-husband. Suddenly, Brianna remembered why the name of that law firm sounded familiar. "That same firm also sent Ms. Ellen letters when she tried reaching out to you."

Cash lifted a brow. "Ellen tried reaching out to me?"

"Yes, for years. That same firm would return her cards and letters, threatening to sue her if she continued to contact you. It's all in that packet I told you about in your bedroom. She even hired a private investigator to send her periodic reports on how you were doing, when you refused to have anything to do with her."

Cash frowned. "I didn't know she tried reaching out to me. I figured she was no different than my brothers' mothers. That she never wanted to have a connection to me."

"Well, you were wrong."

I have been wrong...

Cash didn't say anything as his mind absorbed what Brianna had said. She had told him about that packet weeks ago, but he had refused to look at it. Now he wished he had, and tonight he would, but first he needed to make sure Brianna believed him.

"It seems Bart's deceit is deeper than I thought."

"I don't understand why your father would want to keep you away from your mother."

"Like I said, he thinks he has the right to control every situation when it comes to his sons. He gives orders and expects us to obey, but we never do."

Cash remembered that time Bart didn't want to accept the Westmorelands as the Outlaws' kin even though they all favored. His sons hadn't gone along with that directive either.

He moved to stand in front of Brianna. "I meant it when I said I love you. I've probably loved you from the first. I did not have any attorneys send that letter. I knew nothing about it. You have to believe me, Brianna."

"You father didn't want us to be together?"

Cash shook his head. "It's not about you, since he had no idea how I felt about you. For Bart, it's about him believing I am getting cheated out of something he feels is rightfully mine." He paused. "I recall him saying something to that effect when I returned to Alaska after the reading of the will and mentioning Ellen had left parts of her land to you. He said then that he thought I should get all of it. My mistake was dismissing what he thought. I hadn't figured he would do what he did."

"Do you think you're being cheated out of something that is rightfully yours, Cash?"

He shook his head. "No. The land was Ellen's to do with as she pleased. I was honestly surprised she left me anything. At the time, I thought she hadn't wanted any dealings with me. That's why I didn't want to keep the land. I hadn't wanted anything from her."

"And now?"

"You are the reason I changed my mind about the ranch, about my mother. Falling in love with you was the clincher."

"You do love me? Honestly?"

He reached up and caressed her chin. "I do love you. Honestly. I want to see what's in that packet to find out the truth. But first, I need to know that you believe me, Brianna. That you still love me. That is what is most important to me now."

She met his gaze and nodded. "Yes, I believe you."

Cash released the breath he'd been holding. He hadn't wanted to imagine her not believing him. He pulled Brianna into his arms and captured her mouth with his. He needed this. He needed her. Moments later, when he broke off the kiss, he whispered against her moist lips, "I love you."

Teary eyes stared up at him when she said, "And I love you."

He swept her off her feet and headed to her bedroom.

Twenty-Three

"Yes, I'm okay, Garth, but I'll be a whole hell of a lot better after I confront Bart," Cash said. "It's bad enough he had that law firm send that letter to Brianna, but to discover Bart also used them to keep Ellen from being a part of my life is unacceptable."

"I agree. Are you still returning this weekend?"

"Yes, and I'm bringing my wife with me. What Bart did was unforgivable."

Cash, with Brianna by his side, had gone through the packet. He saw all the birthday cards Ellen had sent that the attorneys had returned, along with their letters threatening what they would do if she continued to reach out to him. He'd also seen the private investigator's periodic reports on him. It changed everything he thought he knew about his mother. It hurt to think of all the time they'd missed.

"I told the brothers what Bart did, and we support you," Garth said. "Bart was wrong."

"Yes, he was."

When Brianna came into the living room with a cup of coffee for him, Cash said to Garth, "I'll talk with you later. Brianna and I will be coming in on Friday. I don't want anyone to mention anything to Bart."

After hanging up, Cash took the coffee cup Brianna offered him. After taking a sip, he put it aside to pull her into his lap. Seeing those cards and reading the private investigator reports had been emotional for him, and Brianna had been there to help him through it.

"When?"

He glanced down at the woman he held in his arms. "When what, sweetheart?"

"When did you know you loved me?"

He smiled. "I honestly think it was when I arrived in town and saw you with that ice-cream cone. I thought about you the rest of the day and night, and then to see you again at the reading of Ellen's will was mind-blowing. All I knew was that I wanted to see you again, which was why I rushed back to Wyoming on Thursday. I finally accepted I loved you when you whispered the words to me, but I should have known based on how I felt when you asked for my sperm."

She covered her face. "I can't believe I asked you that."

"As you can see from our sexual encounters, I am all in." He uncovered her face with his hands and said, "Now tell me when you fell in love with me."

She smiled up at him. "It was the summer after my first year at college."

"But we hadn't even met," he said.

"I know. It was the first summer I returned home from college after my breakup with Alan. I hung around the ranch, too embarrassed to go into town. Ms. Ellen got me to organize the attic to keep me busy. That's when I came across that PI report with your college graduation picture."

She shifted in his lap and wrapped her arms around his neck. "I saw it, thought you were quite a handsome young man and decided to make you my fantasy boyfriend."

He chuckled. "Your fantasy boyfriend?"

"Yes. The more I thought about you, the less I thought about Alan and the pain he had caused me. Needless to say, that summer I got all into you, Cashen Outlaw. Then when I saw you that day at the reading of the will, I knew you could be my fantasy everything. I realized I loved you when I was trying to make up my mind about your counterproposal. I decided that if you never fell in love with me, I would love you anyway, and I would love the baby you would give me."

"Um, the baby I *have* given you," he said, touching her stomach. "I have a feeling you got pregnant during our honeymoon."

A huge smile spread across her face. "I have that same feeling. I hope so."

"I hope so, too. And what we have has nothing to do with the land, Brianna. It's about me loving you, you loving me and us wanting a baby together. It's all about love."

And then he lowered his mouth to hers.

Bart Outlaw walked into his study at the Outlaw Estates in Fairbanks after being told by his housekeeper that his son Cash wanted to see him. He saw Cash with some woman and wondered what this was about.

"What's going on, Cash?"

Cash turned to his father. "First, I'd like you to meet my wife."

"Wife?"

"Yes, I got married last Wednesday. This is Brianna Banks Outlaw. Brianna, this is my father, Bart. Now, with that out of the way, I want to know why you had your attorneys send Brianna a letter saying I was contesting my mother's will?"

"Because you should have contested it! And why did you feel the need to marry her?" an angry Bart asked. "I had things under control. You would have gotten everything."

"As usual, you stuck your nose where it didn't belong, Dad. I told you from the beginning I thought Ellen did the right thing in her will. And to set the record straight, the reason I married Brianna had nothing to do with the land. It had to do with me falling in love with her. And what about all those times you refused to let Ellen reach out to me while I was growing up? Who gave you the right?"

"It was a decision I made as your father. Had she really wanted you she would have gotten you."

"She tried. I know she took you to court to get custody of me."

"And she lost. I had to teach her a lesson about what can happen when anyone tries to go against Bart Outlaw."

Cash didn't say anything. At that moment he knew his father didn't regret anything he'd done because he felt he was justified.

"I'm moving to Wyoming," Cash said.

"You're what!"

"You heard me. I am moving to Wyoming."

He saw the color actually drain from Bart's features. "You're leaving the company?" Bart asked in a shocked voice.

A part of Cash wished he could say yes, he was leaving the company, knowing how much such a thing would hurt the old man. Instead he said, "No, I will still be working for the company, but not here. Now more than ever I need to get away from here. Get away from you. Hopefully, one day you will realize what a huge mistake you made in trying to control my life. Goodbye, Dad."

And without saying anything else, Cash took Brianna's hand and walked out of the house.

Epilogue

A month later

It was a beautiful day for a wedding celebration in honor of Cash and Brianna Outlaw. The affair was hosted on the grounds of the Blazing Frontier Ranch. Family, friends and plenty of townsfolk were in attendance to celebrate the affair.

The couple walked around greeting their guests. Brianna got the chance to introduce Cash to a lot of the locals he hadn't yet met. Everyone was happy to welcome him to town, especially after hearing the announcement that he would be reopening the dude ranch. They knew that would be a big boost for the economy.

Brianna met the members of Cash's family that she hadn't yet met, including his sister, Charm. She and Charm became friends immediately. She also met those other Westmorelands, including motorcycle legend Thorn Westmoreland, and bestselling author Rock Mason (aka Stone Westmoreland).

The announcement that the ranch would also be a horse ranch was met with loud cheers. There was another announcement, too. However, it was one Brianna and Cash wanted to keep between themselves for a while. They were expecting their first child. She had indeed gotten pregnant during their honeymoon.

The happy couple were talking to Garth and Regan when Garth glanced over Cash's shoulder and said, "Look who's here."

Cash turned and saw his father had arrived with Claudia. Although Bart had called weeks ago and apologized to Cash and Brianna for what he had done, Cash hadn't known whether or not he would come to the wedding celebration.

Since Claudia was with Bart, Cash had a feeling she was responsible for both the apology and Bart's appearance today. They had heard from Charm that Claudia had raked Bart over the coals after hearing about what he had done to Cash, in the past and the present.

Cash and Brianna had accepted Bart's apology. They just wanted to look to the future and not dwell on the past. Cash was looking forward to a long and peaceful life with his wife and family at their ranch home in Wyoming.

Cash and his brothers knew they needed to have a heart-to-heart talk with their father about a lot of things. It was time he leveled with them about why he still felt the need to run their lives and why he still could not accept the Westmorelands as their kin, when it was obvious that they were.

That talk would not take place today. Today was Cash and Brianna's time to celebrate their marriage. As Cash gazed down at his wife, he was glad the marriage he'd demanded had landed Brianna right where he wanted her to be, a permanent part of his life.

* * * * *

BLUE COLLAR BILLIONAIRE

KAREN BOOTH

One

"Lexi, sweetheart, you don't have to do this."

Lexi Alderidge adored her father, Winston, but how she hated his instinct to shelter her. It had been one thing when she was a little girl, but she was a thirty-eight-year-old divorcée now. It was time for him to get a new hobby. "I *do* have to do this," she replied. "If I'm going to stay in Royal, I need to work. I can't sit around all day, waiting for life to come to me."

This had been a recent realization for Lexi. Recent, as in it had only dawned on her since she'd moved home to Royal, Texas, several months ago in the wake of her divorce. She'd been all too quick to fall back into old habits and under the spell of her high school sweetheart, which ended up with her getting dumped the night before they were to be married. Lexi and romance had gone off the rails. Hence, her determination to forget about men and focus on her new job as VP of marketing for Alderidge Bank, owned by her father.

Sitting behind his humongous mahogany desk, her father crossed his arms over his chest, rocking back in his well-worn leather chair. The morning April sun streamed in through the windows behind him, glinting off his salt-and-pepper hair and adding a softer edge to his sometimes-dark demeanor. "I still don't like the idea of you visiting a construction site by yourself."

"It's my job. The bank is one of the biggest sponsors of Soiree on the Bay, and I need to oversee our involvement in it. Don't you want a status update on how they're progressing on the site construction?" The food, art and wine festival was precisely the sort of social event the bank needed to be involved with. It had the potential to bring in a much younger and hipper clientele. Alderidge Bank was stuck in the past, much like her dad. And Lexi intended to shove it—and him— into the present.

"You're too pretty to spend time with construction workers." Her father was not about to let this go, nor was he capable of seeing his own impossibly narrow-minded views.

"Now you're being ridiculous." She opened her laptop bag, which was sitting on one of the chairs opposite her father's desk, and stuffed a stack of papers into it. "I'm going."

"Look at what you're wearing. A dress and heels? What if you get catcalled? I don't even want to think about what some of the workers might say."

"I've worn a dress nearly every day of my adult life. This is my look. And I promise you, I can hold my own on a construction site. Don't worry about me." *Honestly, a catcall might make me feel better about myself.*

He pounded a fist on his desk, shocking Lexi in the process. "Alexis Simone Alderidge, I will worry about you until the day I die. You're just going to have to get used to that." Her father only called her by her full name when he wanted to underscore his point. "You're in a fragile state right now."

Lexi could admit to herself that she was a bit unsteady these days, but she was trying her hardest to put that all behind her. "If I've learned anything since my marriage ended, it's that I'm not going to break."

"At least take the helicopter down to Appaloosa Island. It's a six-hour drive round trip. There's no reason for you to be behind the wheel for that long."

Lexi had looked forward to some time alone in her new car, a pearl white Jaguar F-Pace SUV. It had been a gift to herself after her divorce. It was supposed to be a symbol of a fresh start and a new beginning, but she'd stumbled since she got back, and all of it could be blamed on her weakness for the opposite sex. She'd no longer be giving in to any of that. Love, and romance, were off the menu for the foreseeable future. "Will it make you feel better if I do that?"

"Yes, actually, it will. I know you'll be able to make a quick escape."

She nearly laughed at the mental image of herself running across a construction site in heels, trying to reach the helicopter while several construction workers were in hot pursuit. If only the men of the world were that interested. "I'll take the copter to save time. I want a few hours in the office this afternoon so I can work on my list of prospective new clients. Lila

Jones from the Royal Chamber of Commerce has a few ideas for me."

"I really don't want you going out into the community trying to drum up business. I have never, ever courted a customer. People come to us, not the other way around."

"We'll talk about it, okay?" Lexi stepped behind the desk and kissed her dad on top of his head. She loved him deeply, even when he could be a thorn in her side. "There might be some things that need to change around here."

She turned and headed for the door of her dad's office, but his voice stopped her dead in her tracks. "Just remember, Lexi. There's no fault in deciding this job isn't for you. Between your alimony and your trust fund, you certainly don't need the money."

Lexi sucked in a deep breath. Yes, her finances were in good order. But she did need something other than a man to cling to. "I'll be fine. Don't worry about me." Lexi ducked out of her dad's office before he could argue with her again. She didn't go far though, stopping at the desk of her father's assistant.

"Can I help you?" Vi asked, her drawl as thick as molasses on a cold, winter day. Her spiky hair was a shock of pure silver that beautifully complemented her tan skin tone. Lexi hoped she looked that good when she was in her late fifties.

"Yes. I need to go to Appaloosa Island and my father is insisting I take the company helicopter. Can you arrange that for me?"

"Absolutely. I'll call right now. You can meet the pilot out at the pad. Is fifteen minutes okay?"

A pilot was always on càll for her father. The bank's

clientele was old money, and in her experience, quite impatient. "Sure thing. Thank you."

Lexi stopped at the ladies' room to neaten her hair and check her makeup. She smoothed her red tresses, fighting the frizziness that started in the spring in Texas and continued right through the fall. It was only April. She'd be attempting to tame her hair for months.

Afterward, she headed for the rooftop access of Alderidge Bank, where the small helipad was situated. Sure enough, the black-and-gold helicopter was waiting for her. She put on her sunglasses and rushed ahead, helped inside by the copilot. She sat next to the window in the small but comfortable cabin, and buckled herself in. Moments later, they were airborne, floating in midair above her hometown of Royal. Then, they headed south.

Lexi immediately became entranced by the view below. She loved her state and the varied terrain— stretches of bright green intermixed with urban outposts and dusty rural patches. When they reached the outskirts of Houston, the city that had been her home for the entirety of her marriage to Roger, her stomach soured. It only got worse when she spotted the northern edge of sprawling Memorial Park. Just south of that, over the Buffalo Bayou River, was the ultraexclusive River Oaks neighborhood where she'd lived with her ex.

Their fairy tale had lasted for fifteen years along the golf course, where they made dozens of fabulous friends and hosted countless parties. Roger spent his days at his investment firm, and the weekends hitting the links. Lexi busied herself with charity work and Pilates. But he had never wanted her to work. That should have been her first hint that Roger was more interested in her as an ornament—a *belonging*—rather than as a woman. The life she'd had with her ex might seem clichéd to some, but Lexi still loved it. Roger was the perfect guy—handsome, well-educated, and most important, her parents adored him. He was exactly what they had always wanted for her—an upstanding man from a well-known, old-money Texas family.

But that life was no more. She was all on her own now and she needed to prove, to herself at the very least, that she could make a life for herself. A tear gathered in the corner of her eye at the thought. She had so far to go. Sighing, she looked up from the view of the city and waited several minutes until she dared to look again at the ground below. They were approaching Mustang Point, an elite waterside community with a large marina for yachts. When the Soiree on the Bay festival happened, visitors would catch a ferry from there, over to Appaloosa Island.

They were only over the clear blue of the Gulf of Mexico for a few minutes before they were closing in on the isle. This dot of land had been owned by the Edmond family for years. The western side had a small resort and a handful of mansions running along the coast, but the eastern side, where she was headed, was still largely undeveloped. Hence the importance of construction.

The helicopter dropped down onto a large patch of dirt, close to the bustling building site. Nearly every worker turned to watch the landing, shielding their eyes from the midday Texas sun. Lexi hadn't really bargained on how much of a commotion she was going to make by arriving like this. She knew for a fact that her dad hadn't thought about that, either.

Lexi grabbed her purse and sunglasses and climbed out of the helicopter in as ladylike a fashion as she could. As the rotors stopped spinning and kicking up dust, she heard the sound of swinging hammers and men shouting at each other. This was an impressive operation already, with heavy machinery pushing dirt and cranes moving steel girders. In all honesty, Lexi was a bit out of her element here. She knew absolutely nothing about construction, and it suddenly occurred to her that she hadn't asked her father whom she should speak with now that she was on-site.

She considered calling her dad, but her phone had zero bars. Guess she was going to have to wing it. She straightened her skirt and decided to forge ahead, which meant approaching the man straight ahead, probably fifty or so yards away. As she got closer, her shoes teetered on the uneven and rocky surface, but no matter how unsteady she felt, she couldn't help but appreciate the view. This guy was big like a lumberjack, leaning over what looked to be a set of plans. His white T-shirt pulled tight across the defined muscles of his biceps and shoulders. Upon further examination, she noted that his taut forearms were bronzed from the sun, and his slim-fitting jeans hinted at the contours of his long legs.

Could she be so lucky that he was in charge? The person she needed to speak with? Even though she was done with men, that would still feel like a pleasant turn of events. There was no harm in looking, right?

"Excuse me," Lexi said when she was a few feet away. "Are you the site supervisor?" Was that the right term? She honestly had no idea. "Or I guess the foreman?" She hated being so far out of her depth, but she reminded herself that this was part of jumping into a new job and learning the ropes.

The man turned and straightened, nearly blocking out the sun. The full view of him knocked the breath right out of her. He was magnificent and deliciously imposing. The man stood at least a foot taller than her five-foot-two-inch frame. His face had strong lines, and he had close-cropped brown hair that made him almost look like a drill sergeant.

She was intimidated. And intrigued.

"Who wants to know?" he asked, his expression stern.

For a moment, Lexi wondered if she'd made a horrible gaffe. "Lexi Alderidge. From Alderidge Bank. We're one of the presenting sponsors of the Soiree on the Bay festival."

"Checking up on us, huh?" He stared right at her, but he was wearing aviator sunglasses, so all she saw was her own reflection.

She hadn't expected such a gruff reception. After all, she had a legitimate reason to be here. "Yes, that's right. I'm making sure we're getting the most out of our investment. It's my father's bank and he expects a report."

The man's stern expression cracked into a brilliant white smile that first caught Lexi by surprise, then made her knees go weak. "I'm sorry. I'm just giving you a hard time. It's been a tough day on-site, and we can always use a bit of levity." He swiped off his sunglasses and laughed. His whole face lit up, the most enchanting features of which were his warm brown eyes and mesmerizing dimples.

Lexi nervously tried to match his laughter, but it came out as a pathetic titter. She'd never spent much time around men like him, so deliciously rough around the edges. "Oh. Okay." She took a deep breath, doing her best to keep her cool. "So, your boss? Is he available? Or she? I suppose a woman can work construction, too, can't she?"

"Absolutely." He surveyed her up and down, his gaze lingering for a few nervous heartbeats. "Are you looking for a job?"

"No." She felt ridiculous the minute she'd answered. He wasn't taking her seriously and she didn't appreciate it. "I'm not. I'm looking for your boss."

"Lexi!" Another man's voice sounded behind her.

She turned, just as Ross Edmond, son of Royal billionaire businessman Rusty Edmond, approached. He was quite literally one of the last people she wanted to see right now, but she wasn't surprised he was there. As a member of the festival advisory board, it was understandable that he'd be on site at least some of the time. Lexi had met hundreds of guys like Ross in her life—effortlessly handsome, born with a silver spoon in his mouth and accustomed to getting exactly what he wanted. His family owned this island, and their fathers were old acquaintances.

Despite their families' familiarity, chatting with Ross was not going to be fun. Ross's mom, Sarabeth, had recently returned to Royal, fallen head over heels in love and gotten engaged. The man who put a big fat diamond on Sarabeth's finger and professed his undying devotion? Brett Harston, Lexi's first love, and the man who six short weeks ago, had left her at the altar.

Jack Bowden didn't quite know what to make of Lexi Alderidge. Sure, he knew what he'd thought on first sight, that this redhead with the bright green eyes and killer curves was one of the sexiest women to stroll into view in quite some time. She might be petite in stature, but everything about her attitude said she was a spitfire. He had a real weakness for a spirited woman.

Oh, how he loved a challenge…

Still, he was feeling a bit guilty for toying with her and not owning up to the fact that he was not only the boss on this construction site, he was the owner of Bowden Construction. He'd have to get around to sharing that once Lexi was done talking to Ross Edmond.

"How are you holding up? I'm so sorry about everything." Ross's voice dripped with pity as he spoke to Lexi. That made Jack's ears perk up, even when he was trying to focus his attention on the festival site plans. What could a woman like Lexi Alderidge possibly have in her life that would make anyone feel sorry for her?

"I'm fine. Totally fine." Her spine stiffened and she proudly stuck out her chin, but Jack saw right through it. Lexi was definitely *not* okay. She was deflecting.

"I'm sure it's hard." Ross reached out and gently patted her shoulder. "I just wish everyone back in Royal would finally let it go for your sake. But you know how it goes. Royal loves a juicy story, and you don't get much juicier than a bride and a runaway groom."

Runaway groom. Oh, crap. Jack realized then that he'd heard about Lexi; he simply hadn't made the connection between her and the bank with her family's name on it. She was the woman from Royal who'd been left at the altar. *Ouch.* He had been dumped before, and the timing had been very similar, but it had happened long ago and not in such a publicly humiliating way.

"Well, you know what it's like when everyone talks about you, right? All I've been hearing about is your fight with your dad. Please tell me that he hasn't actually disowned you." Lexi's tone was sweet, but there was no mistaking the bite behind it. It was all "bless your heart" without actually meaning the words she was saying.

Jack loved hearing her stick up for herself, but he couldn't ignore his protective urges, the way he wanted badly to intervene and put a stop to this. He had three younger sisters, after all, and he didn't know another way to react to a woman in trouble.

"My dad doesn't matter. I wouldn't trade my life with Charlotte for anything. I'm with my soul mate," Ross said, trying to play it off. "I hope the same for you, Lexi. That you can find happiness like I have. Plenty of fish in the sea, and you have a lot to offer. I'm sure you'll meet someone."

She'd been left at the altar, and Ross was reminding her that she was apparently unattached at the moment? That last part was a slice of good news for Jack, served with a side of bad for Lexi. Jack couldn't witness any more of this. He cleared his throat and hoped to hell Lexi wasn't going to react to what he was about to say by elbowing him in the groin. "Now hold on a minute."

She turned toward him, her eyes wide with bewilderment.

Jack had to keep going. He'd started this and now he was going to finish it. Resolute, he reached for her hand. Her skin was just as velvety smooth as it looked, and his fingers practically swallowed hers up. "Lexi, you'd better set the record straight with Ross, don't you think? It's early days, but we've got a pretty good thing going." As he peered down at her, wordlessly trying to explain his plan, he was tempted to dive right into her crystalline green eyes. Especially when she arched one eyebrow at him, silently telling him that he was nuts.

But then she surprised him by knocking back her head and unleashing a musical giggle. She returned her sights to Ross. "I was a little afraid to say anything since the rumor mill refuses to stop talking about me."

Ross's stare narrowed. "You and Jack? You're dating?"

Jack realized what a close call that had been. He hadn't even told Lexi his name. "Yep," Jack said. "How lucky am I?"

A skeptical smile crossed the other man's face. "That's great. I'm very happy for you."

Jack squeezed her hand a little tighter.

"Thanks," Lexi said. "That's why I came to the festival site today. Had to check up on him."

"Checking up on the boss. I like it." Ross's cell phone rang and he fished it out of his pocket. "Oh, shoot. I really need to answer this. It's one of the other festival board members. I'll talk to you two soon." He wandered off, leaving Jack and Lexi alone.

It took a fraction of a second before she yanked back her hand. "The boss? *You're* the boss?"

Jack swallowed hard, sensing exactly how angry she was. It was radiating off her in waves. He would've been lying if he said it wasn't a turn-on. "That's me.

Jack Bowden. Bowden Construction." He extended his hand, admittedly afraid she might bite it off.

She shook her head in utter disgust, surely not realizing what it did to him, sending wafts of her sweet perfume in his direction. "And was there a reason you lied to me when I asked to see the site supervisor?"

Jack didn't have a good answer for that. He'd only looked at Lexi, with her designer clothes, sky-high heels and flawless face, and assumed she was going to give him trouble. That had been the totality of his life experience with women who came from money, and he knew the Alderidge family was as wealthy as they came. "I was just kidding around."

"Is it your gut instinct to give a woman a hard time? Just because I don't look like I belong on a construction site?"

Jack felt bad now. His propensity for joking around often got him in trouble, but he'd learned long ago not to take everything so seriously. "I'm sorry. Truly, I am."

"I just don't think it's appropriate in a professional setting. I'm here to discuss business, and you're trying to play a prank on me? And then you jump in with that ludicrous story about us dating? It's *preposterous*!"

Jack took issue with that last part. "Why exactly is it, as you put it, preposterous?"

"I think that's fairly obvious."

He tried not to be too insulted, reminding himself that he was wearing jeans, a T-shirt and work boots. Lexi was obviously more accustomed to men like Ross, who didn't think twice about wearing a Rolex and eight hundred-dollar shoes to a site that was all dirt and grime. "I was trying to help you out of a jam."

"I don't recall asking for your help."

Something told him that it wasn't going to go over well if he explained that he had a real weakness for a damsel in distress. He'd save that excuse for another time. "I couldn't listen to him talk to you like that. I don't know what happened with your wedding, but I'm sure that whoever left you at the altar is a certifiable idiot. No woman deserves to be on the receiving end of that, but especially not one who's so beautiful."

Lexi's posture softened and Jack was struck by an image of her in his arms, breathless from his kiss. Logic said he should swipe it away, but he didn't want to. "I'm the dumb one. But thank you. I appreciate that."

"Can we start over?" He offered his hand, trying to shake free his illicit thoughts of Lexi and the way he couldn't stop wondering if the rest of her delectable body was as soft as her hand. "Jack Bowden. Bowden Construction."

The faintest smile crossed Lexi's luscious lips, which wasn't helping Jack focus. "Lexi Alderidge. Alderidge Bank."

"What can I help you with today, Ms. Alderidge?"

"I came to check the progress on the festival construction. I was hoping you could tell me more about it. Show me around a little bit."

Jack didn't want to ogle Lexi in a professional setting, but his vision dropped to the impractical heels she was wearing. They made her lithe legs look impossibly good. The contrast of the sleek black leather and her creamy skin was too much to take. "I'm sorry, but I can't let you walk around the site in those shoes. It's not safe. You'll hurt yourself, and if that happens, it'll be my fault. I could never forgive myself."

"Are you saying I came all this way for nothing?"

"If you'd let me know ahead of time that you were coming, I could have planned accordingly."

"You can't show me anything? I need to be able to tell my dad something when I get back to the office." There was an edge of desperation in her voice that hadn't been there a few moments ago, not even when she'd had Ross reminding her of her personal problems.

"I take it your dad is Winston Alderidge?"

"He is. You aren't one of our customers, are you?"

Jack cleared his throat and tried to not let the memory of his one run-in with the banking mogul ruin his day. "No. Definitely not."

"I didn't think so."

Jack ignored the subtle inference that a guy like him wouldn't have an account with Alderidge Bank, what with their sizable account minimums. He wasn't about to inform her that a man who owned a construction company, but who also wasn't afraid to get his hands dirty on-site for a highly important project, might have more money than he knew what to do with. "I could show you the plans. At least tell you where we are in the process."

"I guess that could be okay."

"Come on." Jack waved her over to the worktable where he kept the site plans. He got another whiff of her sweet floral scent when she stood next to him. It was heavenly, like a meadow of wildflowers at the peak of a Texas summer. "There's a lot to do before the festival. Here's where the stages are going, but we're also constructing outbuildings for the various VIP areas, facilities for food preparation, and bringing water and electricity to this side of the island. You name it."

"Wow." Lexi leaned closer to him as she surveyed the plans. She clearly had no idea of the effect she was having on him, but Jack was painfully aware as a wave of tingling warmth came over him. It hadn't been long since he'd been this close to a woman, but it had been a lifetime since he'd had one pique his interest like this. "Do you think you'll have enough time to get this all done?" She turned around and looked out over the work site. It was still largely a vast pile of dirt. "I don't know much about construction, but it seems like a very big job."

Jack had known from the beginning that they were biting off a bit more than they could chew with this festival, but with Rusty Edmond bankrolling the project, he believed they could pull it off. Money had a way of making everything easier. Having come from very little, Jack had learned that lesson many times. "We'll get it done. We're about to start rotating crews and working longer shifts."

Lexi smiled at him sweetly, delivering another pang of guilt over having given her a hard time when she'd arrived. "If I wear different shoes, can I come back to see the progress?"

Jack was hit with a glimmer of optimism at the thought of that. "Of course." He reached into his pocket and pulled out a business card. "Here's my number. Just call or text me ahead of time and I'll be sure to clear my schedule."

Lexi looked at the card. "There you are. Owner, Bowden Construction. Very impressive."

Something told him she wasn't all that impressed,

but he'd take it. "You know, I'd like to apologize again for the way I acted when you first arrived. I shouldn't have done that."

"Apology accepted, Jack. It's old news at this point."

"I'd like to make it up to you if I can. Dinner? In Royal?"

"Do you live there?"

"I do. Out in the sticks." Jack skipped the part about twenty acres of land and a magnificent custom home with a massive pool. He wasn't the bragging type. And would rather *show* a woman what he was worth, not tell her about it.

"Well, sure. That would be fine."

"I mean, we *are* dating," he said with a wink. "We should probably be seen in public. At least once."

Two

Jack wasn't proud of it, but he'd looked up Lexi Alderidge online as soon as he returned home from the job site Thursday evening. It was a move made solely for self-preservation. He already knew he didn't like Lexi's dad, Winston, so he had to know what his offspring were like. He'd made a few mistakes when it came to women over the years, and he wanted to know exactly what he was getting into by taking Lexi Alderidge out on the town.

Much of what Jack found online was reporting on Lexi's recent divorce. Her now-former husband was Roger Harrington from Houston, a man of considerable means. Lexi and Roger had been married for nearly fifteen years before the split, but they hadn't had children, which was probably a good thing considering how things ended. Jack's parents were happily married, but he had plenty of friends who'd struggled with it when their parents split up.

Irreconcilable differences were cited as the reason for the divorce, but Jack had suspicions that might not be the whole story. Roger was photographed weeks later at a charity event with a much younger woman on his arm. Jack knew guys like Roger, who were born with a big bank account, attended the finest of schools and never wanted for a single thing in life. Although Jack didn't want to invest much energy into thinking about how his own life had wildly differed from that path, he did hate that the arrogant jerk had insulted Lexi by picking up so quickly with another woman. Perhaps Jack could take away some sting from that rebuke. It sure made him want to treat her like a queen.

A few minutes before seven on Friday night, he pulled up to the guarded entrance of Pine Valley, the ritzy gated golf community where Lexi had told him she lived. "Jack Bowden. Lexi Alderidge should have left my name," he said to the man working security.

"Yes, sir. Do you know where you're headed?" The guard stepped out of the small outbuilding and pointed off to the east. "The Alderidge family compound is along that end of the golf course."

"Family compound?"

"Yes, sir. Winston and Annemarie have lived here since their girls were little. Ms. Lexi is staying in their guest cottage. Once you get past their gate, keep to the right of the main house and continue until you run out of road."

For an instant, Jack considered turning around. Lexi had left out the part about living on her parents' property. He didn't relish a run-in with her father. The one he'd had several years ago had not ended well, and Jack didn't want to embarrass Lexi. Then again, it might be good for the Alderidge family to have someone like him shake up their utopia. "I'll find my way. Thank you."

As Jack drove down the winding tree-lined streets of Lexi's neighborhood, with its stately mansions and pristine lawns, he knew very well that he couldn't be any farther removed from the life he'd had before he came to Royal eleven years ago. This much money and prestige had never been part of his upbringing in San Antonio, and frankly, he preferred it that way. He took immense pride in how hard he'd worked to be driving a Bentley Bentayga SUV with a panoramic sunroof, custom leather upholstery, and some serious horsepower under the hood. The first time he'd driven into Royal, heartbroken but determined to succeed, he'd had nothing but big dreams and a rusty old Ford pickup. How times had changed.

He finally reached the Alderidge home, which in all reality looked more like a fortress. A tall ivy-covered stone wall surrounded the property, with a large wrought-iron gate. Lexi had given Jack the security code, but it didn't make him feel any better about pulling into Winston Alderidge's driveway.

The house was still several hundred yards ahead, with a wraparound front porch and plenty of Southern charm. There were lights on inside the house, and he did wonder for a moment if Lexi's dad was the type to peer out the window to see who was driving around back to pick up his daughter. Jack didn't put too much thought into it though. He'd have his moment with

Winston someday, and then he'd tell him exactly what he thought of him.

As directed, Jack pulled around the side of the main house, driving past a five-bay garage, then a lush pool area and even a putting green. Ahead, he could see the guesthouse, an elegant white cottage, complete with flower-filled window boxes, tall lead-paned windows, and an arched portico to shield the entrance from the elements. It was the upgraded version of a fairy tale, and in Jack's mind, the sort of place a princess would live. He pulled up in front and strolled to the front door, wondering for about the one hundredth time what in the world he was getting himself into. Maybe he should have just let Lexi twist in the wind when Ross had been talking to her yesterday.

But then he rang the bell, and as soon as she answered, he realized he'd done the exact right thing. She was breathtaking in a simple sleeveless red dress with a plunging neckline. It was hard to know where to look. She had so many spellbinding curves and was truly a feast for the eyes.

"Hi," Lexi said softly. "Did you find the place okay?"

"I did." He folded his hands in front of him and peeked inside, waiting for an invitation.

Lexi shook her head as if she was distracted. "I'm sorry. Why don't you come in for a minute while I grab my bag?"

Jack stepped inside and closed the door behind him. All he could think as he took in a view of the house was that the Alderidge's guests were very lucky to be able to stay in such a finely appointed place. It was decorated with elegant, but comfortable furnishings like overstuffed sofas and chairs, but everything was upholstered in bright white. Definitely not the place for dogs or children or anything messy. "Beautiful place you've got here."

"Thanks. I'm not staying. This is…temporary. It was an easy choice when I came back to Royal, but I can't live under my parents' noses forever."

"How long have you been back?"

"It's been almost five months. I was in Houston before this."

"Gotcha." Jack didn't want to let on that he knew about her divorce. But the one thing he didn't know the details of was the part about being left at the altar. There may have been buzz around Royal, but he hadn't seen anything online. Perhaps he'd ask about it over dinner. After several glasses of wine. "Are you ready to go? I made a reservation at Sheen for seven thirty."

Lexi turned and checked her makeup in a mirror hanging on the wall. "You shouldn't feel like you have to impress me, Jack. I'm happy going anywhere. We could go to the Royal Diner if you want. Great pie. Sheen is so pricy. Or we could go dutch."

Sheen was a newer restaurant in Royal, housed in a remarkable building made entirely of glass. The cuisine was top-notch, but it did indeed have the price tag to match. "That's where I want to go. I love the food. That dish the chef makes with the braised beef over Thai noodles? It's amazing."

She dropped a lipstick into her bag and cast him a look of surprise. "You've been?"

Jack would've corrected her if he wasn't so amused by the things she loved to assume. Plus, he felt that this was a bit of a test of her true colors. "Many times." He offered his arm. "Now giddyap or we'll be late."

Lexi hooked her arm in his and out the door they went, but they didn't get far before she came to a stop. "Is that your car?"

"It'd better be. It's what I drove here."

She cast him a sideways glance. "You love to joke around, don't you?"

"Guilty as charged. Were you expecting me to be driving something else?"

"No. I mean, yes. Frankly, it does surprise me. I had no idea the construction business was so lucrative."

Jack rounded to the passenger side and opened the car door for her, laughing under his breath. Any other guy would be more than insulted by Lexi's comment, but he wasn't about to let it bother him. If anything, he saw it as a challenge to show her exactly what and who he was. "Lexi, I'm the *owner* of Bowden Construction. We have millions of dollars in projects going at any one time. You'd be surprised." She climbed in and he shut the door behind her. "Apparently," he muttered under his breath as he ambled to his side of the car and climbed in.

She fastened her seat belt and planted her hands in her lap, seeming a bit uncomfortable. "I'm sorry. I wasn't trying to be rude. I didn't know."

Jack slid her a grin and started the ignition. Fake date or not, he didn't want her to have a bad time. "It's okay. I don't judge people. That's one of the first things you need to learn about me."

Lexi had to wonder how many more surprises Jack was going to spring on her tonight. First there was the suit—in fine charcoal gray wool, probably Italian, and certainly custom tailored to accommodate his wide, muscled frame. It was a complete turnaround from the T-shirt and jeans he'd been wearing yesterday, and inexplicably, Lexi couldn't decide which look she liked better. They each held their own sexy appeal. Second was his sleek, refined choice of car. Third, she never imagined he'd opt to take her to a place as chic and sophisticated as Sheen.

Jack had upped the stakes with their fake date. All sorts of people from Royal would see them together at Sheen, including the likes of the Royal Reporters, her ex's nickname for the locals who circled around juicy pieces of gossip the way bees swarmed to honey. They'd all relished the epic way in which Lexi had been dumped. Her fall from grace had been too delicious for them to pass up. If she was lucky, being on the arm of handsome, impossible-to-miss Jack Bowden might get them to stop chattering about her or at least get them gossiping about her in a different way.

As Jack drove to the restaurant, Lexi couldn't help but notice the way his big hands handled the steering wheel. She could imagine that if they ever got into a scrape, he would protect her. No man had shielded her from much of anything, aside from perhaps her dad. Maybe that had been her problem when it came to romance—she'd never chosen the right guy.

Stop it, Lexi, she reprimanded herself. This was not a real date. She had zero business getting involved with any man, including Jack, no matter how sexy and intriguing he was. Tonight was for having a bit of fun and for shutting up the Royal rumor mill. If she never heard "left at the altar" again, it would be too soon.

"I don't want to pry, but I feel like I should ask you about something before we get to the restaurant," Jack murmured.

Lexi feared what was going to come next, but they were only five minutes or so from arriving at Sheen, so hopefully it wouldn't be too much of an ordeal. "No guarantees that I'll answer but feel free."

"I was hoping you'd tell me what exactly Ross was talking about yesterday. I didn't want to say anything where someone might overhear. Like at the restaurant. And if it's too painful to discuss, feel free to punch me in the arm or tell me to mind my own business."

Lexi couldn't help but smile, even when this was her least favorite subject of all time. Jack was more than a surprise; he was a true Texas gentleman. She'd been embarrassed more often than she could count in the last six or seven months, and here he was trying to prevent that from happening again. She greatly appreciated the gesture. It almost made her want to tell him every last painful detail. *Almost.*

"Brett Harston and I were to be married, but he dumped me right before the wedding. He was my high school sweetheart, and we got back together when I returned to Royal after I went through a divorce." Lexi looked out the window, watching the Royal scenery, wondering if she'd ever stop feeling so damn weepy when telling this story. "Brett and I were drawn together. I think it felt familiar. I convinced myself we were in love again, but we weren't. It was comfortable." She turned to look at him, admiring his strong profile. "Does that sound crazy?"

He gave her a reassuring glance. "Not at all."

It wasn't much consolation, but she'd take it. "I pressured him into the wedding. It was my fault. My father's opinion of him didn't help."

"He didn't like Brett?"

"My mother helped me plan the wedding because that was what I wanted, but my father still saw him the way he was when we first met. Not the sort of guy he wanted for his daughter." Lexi stopped there, knowing that if she explained further, she'd likely insult Jack. Her father had objected because Brett had a very modest background. "That's probably more than you ever wanted to know."

Jack shook his head. "No. I just don't like hearing you blame yourself. I realize I don't know you well, but it doesn't strike me as right." He turned into the parking lot at Sheen. The glass structure was all lit up against the dark Royal sky. Then, after pulling up to the valet stand and killing the ignition, he turned over his keys to the attendant and met Lexi on the sidewalk. Just like he had at her place, he offered his arm, but he stopped before they went inside. "I have a proposal for you, Lexi." His voice was deep and calm as he peered down at her.

She found it difficult to swallow. His eyes were so warm and comforting, and after the things he'd said in the car, she didn't quite know what to make of him. Even with her determination to stay away from men, she could imagine how nice it would be to have Jack Bowden's eyes be the last thing she saw before she went to sleep. Or the first thing she saw when she woke up. "What's that, Jack?"

"Let's not talk about any man who couldn't find a way to be good to you. Let's let tonight be all about looking ahead."

Lexi was flabbergasted. Where in the heck had this man been all her life? Maybe she needed to go on fake dates more often. This one was going perfectly. "You're full of surprises tonight, aren't you?"

He grinned and reached for the door. "The night's not over yet."

Lexi was swept inside, immediately inundated by the sights and sounds of the bustling restaurant. The place was packed, with customers dining at every table, enjoying cocktails in the bar, and a sizable line was waiting to speak with the host. Jack and Lexi took their place in the queue, and she tried to ignore the conflicting thoughts that were whirling through her. Part of her wished no one would see her, and she could enjoy her evening with Jack, getting to know more about him. Another part of her hoped *everyone* would see her and become convinced that she had rebounded from her heartache in spectacular fashion.

A willowy woman with bronze skin and thick brunette hair swept up in an elegant twist came from the back of the dining room and spoke to the host. She surveyed the line of waiting diners, then her eyes lit up when she seemed to see Lexi and Jack. She waved, and to Lexi's surprise, Jack waved back.

"I don't think we'll be waiting much longer," he muttered into her ear as the woman approached.

"Jack! I knew I saw your name on the reservation list." The woman and Jack embraced warmly, making Lexi wonder if she was an ex. "I can't believe you didn't call me directly. You know I'll always get you a table."

"Faith, I'd like you to meet Lexi Alderidge," Jack said, turning to Lexi. "Faith is the manager."

Lexi then remembered that the entire Sheen staff were women, a detail put in place by their head chef, Charlotte, Ross Edmond's fiancée.

Faith shook Lexi's hand. "It's nice to meet you. Jack and I go way back."

"Oh, really?" Lexi was sure she was right. This was an ex. Why did that bother her?

Jack laughed, and she yet again noticed his dimples. They made him a little more perfect. "We knew each other in high school. In San Antonio."

"How nice," Lexi said, mentally tucking away every bit of info about Jack she gathered.

"Let me get you two to your table," Faith said. "We're insanely busy tonight." She waved them through the throng of waiting customers and whisked them to the back of the restaurant, where she seated them at a beautiful table. "I'll have Charlotte send out something special for you. Can I get a bottle of wine or champagne started?"

Jack slid Lexi an inquisitive look, like he was sizing her up yet again, but he didn't ask a question. "I'm thinking champagne tonight, Faith. Your best bottle. Thank you."

"Absolutely." She patted him on the shoulder and turned on her heel in the opposite direction.

"You didn't have to do that," Lexi murmured as she got settled in her seat.

"We're celebrating."

She quirked a brow. "What are we celebrating?"

"Your freedom."

Lexi hadn't thought about her situation like that. She'd spent her entire life under someone's thumb, having gone from her parents to Brett in high school, then

Roger in college and beyond, only to end up back with Brett. She was free now. Or she would be once she was off the family compound.

Just then, she spotted Rusty Edmond coming up behind Jack, along with Billy Holmes, the mastermind behind the Soiree on the Bay festival. Rusty's daughter Gina and stepson Asher were with them, as well. Lexi felt her spine stiffen. If she was about to get the same treatment from Rusty as she'd gotten from Ross, this nice evening was about to evaporate.

"Are you okay?" Jack asked.

"Yes. We're about to get a visit from more of the Edmond family. I'll introduce you."

Jack turned and rose out of his seat, completely blocking Lexi's view of the restaurant with his size, although she appreciated the new vista of his backside in that impeccable suit. He stepped aside and she saw him shaking hands with Rusty, the two men laughing heartily. Lexi had once again made a bad assumption. Of course, they knew each other. Rich tycoons like Rusty loved to build things. Jack must have done some work for him. Plus, they shared ties to the festival, since the older gentleman was bankrolling much of that enterprise.

Rusty caught sight of Lexi and seemed surprised, looking back and forth between her and Jack. "Ms. Alderidge. I didn't see you there. Probably because you were hidden by this big guy." Rusty slugged Jack in the arm.

Jack stood back. "Yes. Lexi and I met on Appaloosa yesterday. As you know, her family's bank is one of the sponsors."

Rusty nodded and Billy took notice of the turn in

the conversation. "We're happy to have the support," Billy said to Lexi.

"Is everything coming along?" Rusty asked Jack.

"By the skin of our teeth, but yes. We'll get it done," he answered.

"Excellent," Rusty said. "I'll let you two get back to your meal."

The four of them breezed past with Rusty leading the way. Jack rejoined Lexi at the table.

"I'm sorry. I didn't realize you knew Rusty," Lexi said, still feeling bad that she'd jumped to yet another wrong conclusion about her dinner date.

"Oh, yeah. We've done dozens of projects together."

Lexi was still assembling the pieces of the puzzle that was Jack Bowden. Perhaps she'd never heard of him because she'd spent so many years in Houston, removed from the social circles of Royal. "Are you happy to be working with him again?"

"With Rusty? Sure. It's the supposed mastermind of the project I'm more worried about."

"Billy Holmes?" Lexi didn't know much about Billy, other than the fact that he and Ross were old college buddies and that he'd worked his way into Rusty Edmond's good graces with lightning speed. Rusty could be a ruthless man, and very few people made it into his inner circle. "Is it because the project is so huge and the timeline so tight?"

Jack tapped his fingers on the table. "That's definitely a concern, but I've had plenty of unreasonable schedules over the years. It's part of the game, especially when there's so much money involved."

"Then what is it?"

He shrugged. "Not sure, exactly. But I can't help but think that something's not quite right. It seems strange that he's getting closer to Rusty while Rusty and his own son are at odds."

"Families can be difficult sometimes. And maybe Billy's trying to get them to mend fences."

"You might be right," he acknowledged. "I hadn't thought about it like that."

The sommelier appeared with their champagne. She presented the bottle to Jack, who consulted the label carefully.

"Faith made a fantastic choice," he said. "I've had this many times."

"Are you a big wine drinker?" Lexi asked.

"I dabble." He cocked an eyebrow, and his devastating dimples made another appearance. With Jack around, Lexi didn't need champagne. She was already light-headed.

The sommelier poured a taste for Jack, which he knocked back. "It's perfect. Thank you."

She grinned and filled the first glass, which he took and handed to Lexi while his was being poured.

"Thank you," he said again to the woman, then raised his glass to Lexi once they were alone again. "To the future."

"To the future." She took a small sip and the bubbles tickled her nose. Lexi realized this was the first time in a very long time that she'd had any fun. "I'm glad I met you, Jack." Perhaps it was the initial buzz from the wine that made her feel bold.

"I'm glad I had the good sense to pretend you were my girlfriend."

Her face flushed and she turned her attention to

the menu. She could enjoy herself this evening, but she couldn't afford to get carried away.

The meal was incredible—Jack ordered the noodle dish he said he'd been craving, and Lexi had salmon with a bourbon glaze and beautiful local veggies. As they ate, he told her about how he got into construction, about growing up in San Antonio, and about having three younger sisters. Lexi had a far better time than she ever would've imagined, laughing more than she'd ever thought possible, and feeling at ease for the first time in ages.

After their entrées, the waitress delivered Sheen's signature dessert, a peach mirage torte with chocolate crumbles and a dollop of Chantilly cream, with two spoons. Between the champagne and watching Jack lick the sweet treat from the corner of his mouth, Lexi was definitely rethinking the concept of a fake date. She didn't need a boyfriend, but she could absolutely be up for a good-night kiss.

"Should we get out of here?" she asked.

Jack regarded her for a moment, and Lexi held her breath. It felt like he understood what she was asking and was totally on board. "Yes." He signaled for their waitress. "I'll pay the check."

The drive home was a test in patience, but she occupied herself by peppering Jack with questions. "Where do your sisters live?"

"Two are still in San Antonio. The youngest, Angie, lives in Royal now. She's going through a divorce right now, and I thought I'd give her a new start and a job."

Lexi reached over and touched his forearm. "That's

so sweet." Honestly, he was one of the most thoughtful men she'd ever met.

When they arrived back at her place and Jack put his car in Park, she wasn't quite sure what to say. "Thank you for a lovely night."

He smiled and snapped his keys up in his hand. "It was a ton of fun. I'll walk you to the door."

Of course, she'd never say no. "That would be great."

With his hand at her back, he escorted her up the walk. Every step closer made Lexi's heart beat a little faster. "May I kiss you, Lexi?" he asked when they arrived.

She turned and gazed up at him in the soft light of the wrought-iron carriage lamp next to her front door. And while she positively ached to feel his lips on hers, she was also incredibly nervous about what might happen if they actually kissed. She didn't trust herself to not get involved, especially with a man as appealing as Jack. "We're still pretending this is a date, right?"

He turned away for a moment, looking out over the family compound. She'd once thought of this as home, but it was her parents' place now. The lights in her father's study were on, and Lexi knew from experience that her dad had an excellent view of her front door from there. She hoped to hell there weren't any prying eyes on them.

Jack turned back and reached for her hand. "The night started that way, but I felt like things changed over the course of the meal. Toasting with champagne. Talking about family..."

Lexi's heart seized up in her chest. He was right. She'd felt it, too. Something *had* shifted. In her case, she felt a little less vulnerable. A little braver. Her eyes drifted over his chest, her brain full of questions about what it might feel like to be in his arms. Before she knew what she was doing, her hands were on Jack's rock-hard biceps, so large that her fingers hardly went halfway around them. She scanned his handsome face, expecting shock, but a satisfied grin crossed his lips.

"I can't date anyone, Jack. I just can't do it. I'm not ready." It was her only condition. "But something tells me I'd be an idiot to turn down a kiss."

His smile broadened, and once again he flashed his dimples. Then, ever so slowly, he made his approach. He leaned down while Lexi craned her neck and raised herself up on her tiptoes, holding on to his strong arms. Time seemed to move at a snail's pace as his lips came closer and the sweet anticipation of what was to come made her heart flutter uncontrollably. His mouth met hers, soft at first, and she became putty in his hands. He seemed to sense her weakening, wrapping his arms around her and pulling her against him. Lexi wanted to take things slow but that kiss was too damn good, and she tilted her head to one side and parted her lips, teasing his tongue with hers. His mouth was warm and perfect.

Meanwhile, her inner dialogue was a race of competing thoughts. *He's amazing. He has a million muscles. I wonder what he looks like under that jacket. Stop it, Lexi. Stop it.* She had no business getting involved. She *had* to stick to her plan. At least for a little while longer…

Lexi pulled back, breathless. Her eyes wildly scanned his face.

"For not a real date, that was one hell of a kiss." His eyes had changed. They were dark and full of desire, stoking the fire inside her. He wanted her. She could have him if she wanted.

"I'm sorry. I guess I got carried away. I do that." So much for the promises she'd made to herself.

Jack reached up and tenderly brushed her cheek with the back of his hand. "I like the idea of you letting loose, Lexi. Something tells me you need to do that. Maybe get a few things out of your system."

Was he right about that, too? If so, something told her that Jack might be the perfect guy to help her straighten things out. She decided then and there to keep Jack in her orbit but take things slow. She wouldn't entertain a single thought of anything serious. "You're probably right about that. Maybe we can see each other again?"

He nodded and kissed her cheek, sending another wave of warmth through her. "Absolutely. You know how to reach me. Good night."

Lexi watched as Jack strolled down the sidewalk to his car and climbed inside. The ball was officially in her court. She might be terrified to lob it back, but something told her she'd be a fool to not find some excuse to see Jack Bowden again.

Three

Lexi woke to the sound of her doorbell ringing. She rolled over and pried one eye open to catch sight of the time. "Who in the world is at my door before seven on a Saturday?" For a split second, she wondered if it might be Jack. Her heart did a little flip just thinking about that kiss last night. The memory of it was still reverberating in her body. The man was not only an excellent kisser, he was a *different* kisser. The painful truth of Lexi's life was that she'd only kissed two men—Brett and Roger. Neither had ever taken control like that, leaving her with little doubt that she was actually worth kissing.

The bell chimed again, and she remembered that Jack only had the temporary passcode to her family's security gate, and she never knew when it would change. Her dad insisted that only family should be given the permanent one. As Lexi's parents got older, she appreciated the security the gate provided, but she didn't like the way it made her feel like a princess locked up in a tower, or in her case, in a corner of an exclusive Texas neighborhood. But because of the passcode, it might not be Jack.

Lexi tossed back the covers and beelined for the door. She opened it and saw her sister, Bianca, staring at her phone, designer handbag looped on one arm, sucking on a bottle of green juice through a straw. Bianca was dressed for a workout, wearing dark purple leggings and a black tank that showed off her toned shoulders. Her sister was two years younger than Lexi, happily married to Kevin, a day trader, and they had two beautiful children together. In so many ways, Bianca had everything Lexi had ever wanted. Lexi did her best to not be jealous, but it still creeped in every now and then.

"Took you long enough to answer," Bianca said, breezing past Lexi into the house.

"Please. Come in," Lexi said with all the sarcasm the invitation warranted. Her sister treated the guesthouse like it was hers, even when Lexi was the occupant.

"You slept in," Bianca said with an accusatory tone.

"It's before seven on a Saturday. Don't try to make me sound lazy."

"I can only stay for a minute. I have yoga at eight, but I stopped by to see Mom and Dad, and figured I'd walk over and pester you."

Their parents were very early risers, even on the weekends. "So nice of you," Lexi retorted, plopping down in one of the armchairs in her living room.

"Dad and I just had a *very* interesting conversation."

Bianca perched on the arm of the chair opposite Lexi, crossing her legs and bobbing a foot, seeming wholly satisfied with herself.

"Interesting how?"

"You went on a date and didn't even tell me? I'm more than a little insulted."

"How do you know about that?" Lexi asked.

"Dad saw you kissing some guy at your doorstep. A big guy he didn't recognize."

It came as little surprise that her parents would be nosy about this, especially her dad. Something told Lexi that they would love it if she became romantically involved with another man, only so they could have something to tell their friends, rather than making excuses about how she was still pulling her disastrous life together. The only problem was there was no way Jack was that guy. Her parents appreciated old money and the families swimming in it. She wished she could drag them into the present day, where a person's money, how long they'd had it, or where it came from was zero indicator of their character. "I really need to get my own place. I'll never be able to move on with my life with my own parents spying on me."

"Call that real estate agent I told you about."

"I will."

"And stop avoiding the subject," Bianca chastised. "Tell me about this mystery man."

Lexi's instinct was to keep Jack all to herself. She wanted him to be her delicious secret. Unfortunately, since they'd been seen together at Sheen, that was no longer an option. Also, she couldn't hide Jack from her sister, especially when the corners of her mouth quirked up into a smile when she thought about him. "It wasn't a date. At least not a real one."

"Unless you've taken to hiring male escorts, I have no idea what that means."

"Oh, stop. His name is Jack Bowden. I had to go to the Soiree on the Bay construction site Thursday afternoon, and we met." Lexi wasn't quite sure how to explain what had happened next. In many ways, it was still so inexplicable. One minute she was enduring Ross Edmond's pity-laden small talk and the next, a handsome man she'd known for mere minutes was pretending he was her boyfriend.

"I thought you had sworn off guys, completely."

"I have. Totally." Even Lexi wasn't so convinced anymore. "But Jack swooped in when Ross Edmond was asking a few too many prying questions about everything that happened with Brett. I think the minute Jack overheard the part about being left at the altar, he felt sorry for me. So, he told Ross that we were dating." Since that moment, Lexi'd had some time to think about it, and had wondered whether he'd been motivated to do it simply because he felt sorry for her. She appreciated the gesture, but she didn't want that from anyone.

"Wow. Bold move on his part. And you just went along with it?"

"What else was I supposed to do? I wanted Ross to go away, and I'll do anything to get people to stop talking about me. Especially the Royal Reporters."

"So. Tell me. What's this Jack like?" Bianca took another long sip of her juice.

Lexi had to think on that one. Jack was unlike any man she'd ever spent time with. He was formidable, but kind, seemingly an open book, but one with lots of revelations she hadn't expected. "Handsome. Funny. Full of surprises."

"Is he one of the financiers of the festival?"

Lexi shook her head. "No. He owns the construction company that was contracted for the festival. It's a little embarrassing, but when I met him, I thought he was one of the workers. He was dressed in jeans and work boots."

"Ooh. A working class guy. That's a big change for you. Is he in really good shape?" Bianca had a mischievous glint in her eye.

Lexi bit down on her lip just thinking about Jack's muscle-bound frame and what it had felt like to be swept up in his very capable arms. "Unbelievably good shape."

"Okay. I need to meet this guy. Like right away." Bianca rose from her seat and shot a pointed glance at Lexi. "Bring him to the library fundraiser Friday night."

Oh no. She had completely forgotten about the literacy event Bianca had been planning for months. It was being held at the Texas Cattleman's Club and would be a veritable who's who of Royal. "I can't go if Brett is going to be there. I've only seen him once since the wedding and that was plenty. I really can't be around him if he's going to be with Sarabeth."

"Do you honestly think I would make you come if Brett was going to be there? I purposely sent his invitation late. By the time he received it, the tickets were already sold out. He did write us a sizable check though. I call that a win-win."

Lexi felt a small measure of relief, but something

else was bothering her. Would she seem desperate if she asked Jack out so soon? Then again, Lexi didn't want to go alone. Her sister would be no company at all, too busy chatting with the library's many supporters and dealing with things like the silent auction. "I don't know if that's a great idea. I'm trying to stay away from men, remember?"

Bianca cast her a dismissive look. "Lexi, sweetheart. You were making out with a construction worker on your front porch last night. I'd say you're failing at staying away from men."

"Don't you have a yoga class to get to?"

She grinned, then leaned down to kiss the top of Lexi's head. "Nice job deflecting. Let me know if you decide to bring Jack Friday night. But just for the record, I will be deeply disappointed and never forgive you if you don't."

Lexi blew out a long sigh as she watched her sister let herself out. Bianca had a real talent for backing her into a corner. She not only had to ask Jack, she had to hope he'd say yes. Because if Lexi showed up on Friday night without him, Bianca would give her a hard time about it forever.

Unfortunately, it was too early to call Jack to extend the invitation. But maybe that was a good thing—it gave her a bit of time to formulate her plan and figure out what to say. In the meantime, she threw in a load of laundry, changed into leggings and a tank top, then went for a run through Pine Valley. As her legs began to warm up and she hit her stride, she wound her way down the wide tree-lined streets, past the mansions and picture-perfect custom homes with their well-tended landscaping and manicured lawns. This idyllic neighborhood had brought her so much comfort as a kid. It was a safe place to grow up where nothing ever went wrong. She knew now how poorly it had prepared her for real life. It certainly hadn't equipped her to deal with the fallout of her divorce, everything that had happened with Brett, or her still-healing broken heart. Things did go wrong in real life. She wished she hadn't been so sheltered from it. *Time*, she told herself. All she needed was time…to figure out who she was, who she wanted to be and where she was going.

As to how a man fit into that equation, Lexi was still firmly in the camp of thinking that romance was not a good choice for her right now. But even so, Jack still had her second-guessing that. Perhaps some male companionship could be good for her, as long as there were no strings attached. She could focus on having fun and building a friendship with him, things she'd never managed to accomplish before. Now might be a good time to start.

She arrived back at the cottage an hour later and decided to try Jack a little after nine. His phone rang and rang, and Lexi paced, wondering if he was the sort of guy who might opt to not take her call. She was just about to hang up, when he finally answered.

"Lexi? This is a surprise." His voice was breathless, but warm. It did something to her, overwhelming her with a feeling that was equal parts excitement and anticipation.

"Are you okay? You sound out of breath," she said.

"I was in the pool. Doing some laps. I needed some time to think." He cleared his throat. "About last night."

Her immediate reaction was to grin like a fool. The vision of Jack in a swimsuit had her imagination running wild. And his words had her heart doing somersaults. "What exactly about last night?"

He unleashed his hearty laugh, which sent a thrill down her spine. "Are you really going to make me say it out loud?"

Lexi loved the playful tone of his voice. She loved that they could flirt, and it could be nothing more than a bit of sexy fun. "Too embarrassing?"

"I'm not shy, Lexi. You must have figured that out by now."

"What is it then?" Deep down, she knew exactly where he was going with this, but there was still an uncertain part of her that wanted him to say it first.

"Fine. Elephant in the room. That was a pretty amazing kiss last night."

Heat rose in her like steam off the asphalt after a hot summer rain. "It was, wasn't it?"

"To be honest, I can't stop thinking about it."

Lexi gnawed on her thumbnail. She felt like she was playing with fire, but Jack was too damn tempting to pass up. "I thought about it all night too."

Jack groaned quietly over the line. "I don't want to let our chemistry go to waste by not seeing each other."

"Me neither."

"What do you say to lunch?"

"Yes," she blurted, then took a deep breath to slow herself down. She'd been worried about asking to see him in six days. And he wanted to see her *today*? She'd be stupid to say no. "I mean, a girl's gotta eat, right?"

Jack worried he was barreling for a heap of trouble by seeing Lexi again so soon. She was coming off two epic cases of a broken heart. While he was trying to keep his life uncomplicated, not make it messier. However, their kiss last night had changed the game. He'd told himself it would merely be fun, but it had been a lot more than that. Lexi had sent him a clear-cut message—she had something fiery pent up inside her—and he'd have to be a dead man to not be intrigued by that. In fact, he'd have to suppress every primal urge in his body to deny himself the chance to see what might transpire between the two of them.

Still, Lexi was not simply a woman to be seduced. There were roadblocks and hazards ahead. It wasn't that Jack wasn't equipped to deal with a woman who had problems. His youngest sister had them in spades, and he took pride in trying to make her struggle easier. But she was family. Those ties were the strongest. And in Lexi's case, they led straight to her father, who thought very little of Jack. He knew that because Winston Alderidge had told him as much. Their run-in might have happened several years ago, but he was certain that a man like Winston didn't go around changing his mind about people. Jack could deal with any insults that might be lobbed at him, but he didn't want to cause a rift in Lexi's world. She had more than enough to worry about.

Jack also hadn't counted on a call the day after their date. He'd thought it would be at least next week until he heard from her. But just as he'd surprised her last night, she'd turned the tables on him. And she was right. A girl *did* have to eat, as did he. In fact, he was starving. Just the thought of a hearty meal from the Royal Diner, capped off with a slice of pie, had his stomach rumbling loudly.

They'd opted to meet at the restaurant. He took a

different car this time, his black BMW M3. Although it was sleek and sporty on the outside, it had so much headroom that it was one of the preferred sports cars of professional basketball players. Jack was a big guy and he needed the space, but he also loved the lion of an engine under the hood, and the way it took tight corners with ease. He zipped up in front of the diner just as Lexi was walking up to the door. Unable to help himself, he stole an eyeful of her as he killed the engine then climbed out.

Holy smokes.

"Jack!" Lexi spotted him, smiled and approached, carefully removing her oversize black sunglasses. Everything about her was perfect—her lush red hair tumbled over her shoulders as the Texas sun caught the highlights. Her deep blue dress skimmed the sumptuous curve of her hips, with a low scoop neck showing off her mind-boggling décolletage, and her perfume trailed its way to his nose with that beguiling mix of flowers and summer rain.

"Hello there." He gripped her elbow and kissed her on the cheek, her skin soft and supple. "You look so pretty today."

"Do I? I just threw this on."

Jack cast her a disapproving look. "Lexi. Take the compliment."

Crinkles formed between her eyes. She didn't seem convinced. "You're right. I'm a little self-critical."

"I got that impression."

She looked beyond him to where his car was parked. "A different set of wheels today? Are you trying to impress me?"

He wasn't surprised that she would zero in on the

vehicle, but part of him was still disappointed. He wasn't trying to impress her, and if he ever were, he wouldn't try to make an impact with something he owned. "What can I say? I have a weakness for things that go fast."

"Construction really does pay, doesn't it?"

"Considering that I met you through my job, I'd say that it absolutely does."

Her cheeks blushed with a bright and vibrant pink. "You're such a flirt."

Jack knew better than to lay it on so thick, but the reality was that he was drawn to her like a moth to a flame. "Just stating the obvious." He offered his arm, fighting a grin. "Shall we?"

They strolled into the cheery diner, brightly lit from the big picture windows facing the street. The hostess quickly saw them off to a comfortable booth near the back and handed them menus. "Your server will be over in a minute."

Jack was fixated on lunch, but Lexi seemed keenly attuned to everyone around them. His hot take was that she wanted to see who was there, and more importantly, what their reaction would be to seeing them together. She cared far too much about what the people in Royal thought. He wanted her to stop doing that. "What are you thinking about for lunch?" he asked.

"I usually do the Cobb salad," she answered. "You?"

"Burger, fries and a slice of pie."

"Sounds like a lot of calories."

"Sounds perfect to me."

Jack closed his menu and sat back on his side of the booth, spreading his arms across the back of the banquette. There was a part of him that wished he and Lexi

could sit on the same side, but if she was worried about
what people might say, their current seating arrangement was best. The bell on the diner door jingled and
Jack looked up to see Lila Jones from the Royal Chamber of Commerce, along with Valencia Donovan, direc-
tor of the Donovan Horse Rescue. Both were members
of the Soiree on the Bay festival advisory board, but
Jack had very little in the way of direct dealings with
them. Rusty was paying the bills, and he ran interference most of the time.

The two women spotted Lexi and him, and waved,
then beelined over to their table. Lexi turned as Valencia and Lila walked up.

"Jack Bowden," Lila said, pointing at him. "We were
just talking about you." Lila was an earnest person,
hardworking and rather serious, so her greeting came
across more like an accusation than a warm hello.

"We were talking about the construction," Valencia quickly added, gathering her long wavy blond hair
and pulling it back, then planting her hand on Lexi's
shoulder. "Hello, Lexi. How are you?"

"I'm good, thanks. Lila, it's nice to see you."

"Nice to see you, too," Lila replied. "Are you two
meeting about the festival?" Her big blue eyes darted
back and forth between Lexi and him.

"Yes. That's exactly what we're doing," Lexi blurted.

Jack was getting whiplash from spending time with
her. She calls him, readily accepts his offer of a lunch
date, then covers her tracks by saying they were having a business meeting?

"If you're already on the subject, I hope you won't
mind if I ask how construction is coming along,"
Lila said.

"It's getting there, but the schedule is incredibly tight. I predict a photo finish, but I'll do everything in my power to get it done on time and on budget. By the end of the month." Jack didn't want to paint an unnecessarily rosy picture, but he also didn't want them to question whether he could get the job done. He absolutely could.

"Oh, good. I'm glad," Lila said.

Valencia nodded, also seeming satisfied with Jack's answer. "That's good to hear. I think our biggest obstacle right now is getting the word out. I don't have a good sense of what public opinion is on the festival. That's part of why we came downtown today. We were hoping to walk around and find out more about what the average Royalite is saying about it."

"Jack can probably help you with that," Lexi offered.

Jack quirked an eyebrow at her, silently asking what in the hell that was supposed to mean. Was she saying that he was an "average" guy?

"He's so hands-on at work. He talks with all of his workers, and I'm sure the festival's been a topic of conversation." Lexi's face flushed with uncertainty.

"Well, Jack? Do you care to fill us in? Has anyone been talking about it?" Lila asked.

"The truth?" he answered.

"Of course," Lila said.

He cleared his throat and prepared his unvarnished words. "Outside the TCC, I'm not sure the festival is on anyone's radar. My guys know about it, but only because that's what's paying the bills right now."

"Do you think we should be doing more advertising?" Valencia asked.

"That could work, but if I'm being honest, I think

the real problem is the advisory board. You all travel in the same circles. You need to get people outside of that insular world involved."

"We've been speaking to a documentary filmmaker named Abby Carmichael about filming the festival. That might help to build some buzz if we can talk about that," Lila said.

"That's a start, but I think it might be wise to get some free PR, too. Maybe find some social media influencers to talk up the festival. That's how you'll gain traction outside of Texas. If you've got people flying in from other parts of the country, then you change the game completely."

Lila and Valencia looked at each other, nodding eagerly. "That's great advice. I will work on that," Lila said, turning her attention back to Jack and Lexi. "Thank you so much for giving us your take on it, Jack."

"No problem. Anytime."

"And feel free to reach out to me," Lexi added. "As you know, I'm handling the bank's involvement in the festival. Give me a call if you ever think of any opportunities for us to get more involved."

"Sure thing," Lila said. "We'll leave you two alone and let you get back to your meeting." With that, Lila and Valencia wandered back to the hostess, who saw them to a table on the other side of the diner.

"Meeting, huh?" Jack asked. "I thought we were on a lunch date."

"I'm sorry. I just sort of panicked."

"Lexi, I need you to know something. I don't have some hidden agenda here. I like you. I enjoyed our date last night, and I'd like to see you some more. But

I'm also not going to pretend to be something that I'm not. When you're surprised I own more than one car, and tell Lila Jones that I can be the voice of everyday people, it's pretty clear that you don't see me as being up to snuff. I don't need to spend time with a woman who looks at me that way."

Lexi frantically shook her head from side to side. "No. No. It's not that." She closed her eyes for a moment, drew in a deep breath and brought her shoulders nearly up to her ears. When her eyes popped back open, they were so full of vulnerability that it was an arrow straight to his heart. "I like you a lot. You're just very different from any guy I've ever been out with. That's all. And I'm afraid that certain reflexes die hard. I come from a family that's ridiculously fixated on things like money and influence and power. But I'm not like that. Really. I'm not. Still, it's hard to not notice those things when you've been spent your whole life around people who do."

"Fair enough. I just need you to make a conscious effort to tone that down a bit. Maybe find a way to relax and have fun."

She smiled sweetly. "Yes. Fun. I desperately want to do that. I'm sorry, but I will do better."

"Okay, good. Because I don't want to think that you're embarrassed to be seen with me."

"I'm not. At all."

"Okay." Jack wasn't entirely convinced. "Maybe you'll have a chance to prove that to me at some point."

"Actually…" Lexi's eyes sparkled from behind a thick fringe of dark lashes. "Do you have a tux?"

"I do. Why?"

"My sister organized a fundraiser for the children's

literacy program at the TCC, and I want you to be my date for it."

Jack wanted to laugh. Being with Lexi was a roller coaster. Just a minute ago, she'd been covering her tracks and saying they were having a meeting. But now she wanted him to be her date at a fancy charity event. "When is it?"

"Next Friday. It'll give you a chance to meet my sister and my parents."

"I've already met your dad."

"You have?"

Jack didn't want to get into it now. Maybe Winston Alderidge had changed. And if not, he would deal with the fallout then. "It was a while ago."

"Oh, okay. Well, I hope you'd be willing to go with me. I think it will be fun." She extended her hand across the table.

Jack took the invitation, wrapping his fingers around hers. He wasn't sure where this was going, but he was damn curious to find out. "With you, I have no doubt it'll be a night to remember."

Four

Lexi worried her dress was too much. "I'm not going to be able to breathe at all tonight," she muttered to herself as she turned before the full-length mirror in her bedroom. It felt like the five-hundredth time she'd scrutinized what she was wearing. The gown was a strapless emerald green satin with a gravity-defying deep V neckline and a mermaid skirt that left nothing to the imagination. Her butt, hips and breasts were not merely flaunted in this dress, they were impossible to miss. "Hopefully it'll be worth it."

She could admit to herself that she looked good. But she still wasn't sure a dress this daring was the right call. She only knew that she wanted to be sexy for Jack. And she also wanted to show everyone in Royal that she had not been defeated by the things that had happened to her over the last year. But even more important, she wanted to show Jack that she was not embarrassed to be seen with him. Lexi knew she would draw attention in this dress, just as Jack did wherever they went. She was proud to have him as her date tonight.

The doorbell rang and Lexi darted for the door, but her progress was painfully slow as she learned the art of walking in her dress. Full strides required an exaggerated wag of her hips. Still, it got her where she was going. When she pulled open the door, she realized how poorly prepared she was for the sight of Jack in a tux. Wrapped up in classic black and crisp white, he was the embodiment of a dashing, elegant man. The cut of his jacket accentuated the strong lines of his shoulders and the way his trim waist narrowed. But the real showstopper was his smoldering dark eyes as they raked over her from head to toe—it was like watching a spark turn to a four-alarm fire.

"Well?" she asked. It felt as though he'd been eyeing her for a full five minutes. She had to know in words what he thought of her in the dress.

"Sorry. I'm still taking it all in. Or more specifically, *you*, all in."

Goose bumps raced over Lexi's bare shoulders and heat spiked between her legs. Her brain flashed with a visual of Jack unzipping her dress, then exploring her naked body with his big manly hands. She wanted to return the favor, to tear off that perfect tux and drag her fingers all over every inch of him. Just thinking about it made it even harder to breathe. "I hope that's a good thing." She bit down on her lower lip, a little harder with each passing second while she waited for an answer.

"You're one of the sexiest women I have *ever* had the pleasure to see, Lexi. You need to know that."

She wasn't sure about the other women who had come before her. Ex-girlfriends? Casual dalliances? Jack hadn't spoken at all about his history. Her romantic frame of reference was painfully narrow, and she suspected that his might be the exact opposite. Looking at him now, it was impossible to come to a different conclusion. "You look so handsome in your tux. I know I'll have the hottest date in the whole place tonight."

One of Jack's devilish grins cropped up, which brought out his dimples. He took a step closer until they were nearly standing toe-to-toe, making Lexi hyper-aware of the way her breaths made her breasts heave. "We should probably get out of here before I figure out how to get you out of that dress. I'm guessing that would disappoint your sister."

Lexi felt as though her heart was in her throat. She wanted Jack. There was no point in pretending otherwise. She just needed to find a way to keep things light and fun between them while still leaving room for hot sex. That was a balance she'd never achieved before, but she desperately wanted to try. "Bianca would not be happy if I missed her event."

He nodded in agreement and lightly traced the line of her jaw with the back of his hand. "We have to save some things for later, right?"

Lexi swallowed back her uncertainty about being both casual and seductive. "At the very least, you can help me with my zipper later."

"Then I'm your guy. I have very talented hands." Jack auditioned for the job by pulling Lexi closer by her hips, his fingers insistently pressing into the soft flesh of her butt.

She rose up on her toes for a kiss, soft and wet, tongues tangling. Jack was the *best* kisser. It would've been so easy to get carried away with him. But if she didn't make it to the TCC, Bianca would kill her, and she'd never live it down. "We should go, huh?"

"Yeah. I think that's for the best."

Lexi grabbed her handbag from the foyer table, as well as a cashmere wrap. The April nights in Royal could get chilly, although if Jack kept this up, she wouldn't need it at all.

It was a short drive to the Texas Cattleman's Club and they arrived just shy of seven o'clock, when the cocktail portion of the party was set to start. Jack took a spot in the parking lot and insisted on opening her door for her. He truly was the consummate gentleman. So much so that Lexi had to wonder how he was still single. His assets were considerable—wit, looks, charm. A highly successful business. And those dimples. She *couldn't* forget those. In total, she failed to see the downside of Jack. Lexi only hoped that the timing wouldn't ultimately prove to be their downfall. She wasn't ready for a relationship. But she *was* ready to explore what was under that tux.

Ahead of them sat the TCC, the rambling single-story structure of dark stone and wood that had been in Royal for more than one hundred years. The crowd funneling in through the main entrance was sizable. It seemed like all of Royal was here, which made Lexi all the happier that she'd thought to ask Bianca ahead of time about whether Brett might be in attendance.

Bianca and her husband, Kevin, were right inside

the doors, greeting guests after they checked in and picked up their name tags. Bianca was absolutely gorgeous, decked out in a midnight blue gown with skinny straps and a full skirt. Kevin looked handsome in his tux, although he couldn't hold a candle to Jack as far as Lexi was concerned.

"Bianca. Kevin. I'd like you to meet Jack Bowden." Lexi watched as her sister's eyes lit up and she enthusiastically shook his hand.

"Jack. I've heard so much about you," Bianca gushed, clearly sizing him up and appreciating what she saw. Lexi loved her sister, but she could be so transparent. "I understand you're the brains behind Bowden Construction. Or should I say brains *and* brawn?" Bianca smiled and patted his upper arm, then shot Lexi a look of pure envy.

Jack laughed. It was always his tendency to dismiss comments that marveled at his finer attributes. "I don't know about either, but it's nice to meet you both." He shook Kevin's hand and the two men exchanged pleasantries.

Lexi took the opportunity to pull Bianca aside. "Are Mom and Dad here yet?"

Her sister shook her head. "Not unless they managed to sneak by me. You know Dad. He loves to make an entrance. I'm sure they'll be some of the last to arrive." Bianca glanced past Lexi in the direction of Jack and Kevin. "Are you worried about seeing if Jack passes muster with Mom and Dad? Because he seems like a great guy, Lex. Well done."

"Don't say it like we're a thing. This is just casual. And yes, of course, I'm worried about Mom and Dad, exactly for the reason you just stated. Jack is a good guy. He doesn't deserve to meet the Alderidge family's grand inquisition."

Bianca patted Lexi on the shoulder. "You worry too much."

"Easy for you to say. You're my younger sister and you have it all figured out. Great marriage. Two beautiful kids. You're the golden child and I'm…" Lexi had to stop herself before she spiraled down into overly negative thoughts. "I'm a work in progress."

"Trust me. We all are. Now go get a drink with your guy." Bianca glanced back at the crowd gathering in the great room. "Hey, Jack. I'd love it if you and Lexi could get the dancing going. It always takes forever for someone to have the nerve to get out there."

"Uh. Sure." Jack seemed uncertain about the assignment her sister had given him.

"We'll do our best," Lexi said, kissing her sister on the cheek. "Great job with planning this, by the way."

"Thanks, Lex. I hope you have fun tonight." Bianca, ever the kidder, elbowed her in the ribs.

Lexi hooked her arm in Jack's and they made their way over to the line at the bar. She did her best to focus on Jack, but she couldn't stop glancing at the entrance, looking for the arrival of her parents. Meanwhile, there were definitely people in this room who were looking at them. Possibly talking about them. Lexi feared that none of it was good, that she'd yet again become the subject of unpleasant gossip. Whatever confidence and determination she'd felt back at home was quickly fading.

"You okay?" Jack asked quietly. "You seem on edge."

Lexi managed a small smile as she looked up at him.

Good God, he was handsome. It was her best distraction right now. "It's the dress. I can't breathe, so I'm basically just hyperventilating."

He unsubtly eyed her cleavage, one corner of his mouth twitching with a smile. "I'd say I'm sorry, but I'm not. The view is spectacular." He gently placed his hand on her elbow, dragging his fingers down the length of her forearm until he reached her palm and grasped her hand. Then he raised her fingers to his lips and kissed them tenderly. That one innocent gesture did nothing to soothe her nerves. It only amped up her desire to have him kiss the rest of her. "I'm also not sure you're being entirely truthful with me, but it's okay if you don't want to talk about it."

Lexi didn't want to ruminate over the things that were worrying her. She wanted to grab Jack's hand, race out of the building and kiss him ravenously. For a moment, she even wondered if his SUV had a generous back seat, although, if she thought people were gossiping about her now, having sex with Jack in the parking lot of the TCC would really get them talking. The bottom line was he was the only person in this crowd of hundreds who was making her feel good about herself. For the woman who was trying to move forward with her life, coming here tonight felt too much like she was moving backward.

They reached the bar and Jack ordered Lexi a glass of champagne and a bourbon, neat, for himself. He spotted an available bar-top table, but it was very close to the center of the action, meaning it felt as though they were on display. From what she could tell, Jack seemed to be enjoying himself, waving at some people and saying hello to others. Meanwhile, Lexi took deep breaths and tried not to think about what those other guests might be thinking. Was Jack crazy to be out with a woman who'd been left at the altar mere months after a divorce? Had Lexi allowed herself to be distracted by another handsome face?

Lexi, stop. How she hated this cycle of negative thoughts that sometimes crept into her head. She had to stop caring about what other people thought of her. And that needed to start right now. Lexi downed the last of her champagne and plunked her glass on the table. "I think we should dance."

"Really?" Jack took survey of the room. "I know your sister said she wanted us to, but there's not a soul out there yet. I'm not usually the first guy on the dance floor."

"Why not? You like to have fun, don't you?"

"Well, yeah, but that's not really my idea of a good time. Especially with the DJ's music choices."

The song faded from an upbeat country song to a slower, romantic ballad, which Lexi took as further encouragement. She wanted to be in Jack's arms right now. He was the only thing making tonight enjoyable. And if she was going to stop thinking about what others thought, her best course was to focus on him. Completely. "Just one song." She tugged on his hand until he relented and followed her out to the dance floor.

"Okay. But I'm in charge." As soon as they stepped onto the parquet wood, Jack pulled her into his arms and they spun in a circle. "Is that good with you?"

Lexi felt dizzy in the most delicious way. As she looked up into his face and soaked up his self-assured expression, she couldn't have contained her smile if she'd wanted to. "I expect nothing less."

* * *

Jack wasn't much of a dancer. He could hold his own, but as a big guy, he'd always felt like all eyes were on him. Swaying back and forth in the middle of the dance floor in the great room at the Texas Cattleman's Club, this was one hell of a place to put yourself at center stage. A good chunk of people in this room had been his clients at one point, and the rest were folks he'd love to get some business from. It was in his best interest not to make a spectacle, but he and Lexi had already succeeded in that. Everyone seemed to be watching.

"Either these people all need to get a life or we've made a horrible mistake by coming out here," Jack said into Lexi's ear. He loved every instant when her soft skin touched his.

"So, it's not just me? You noticed it, too?"

"It would be hard not to," he quipped.

"Remind me to yell at my sister. This was all her idea. Why isn't anyone else dancing?"

"Maybe it's your dress. They're all mesmerized by you."

Lexi peered up at him. "Somehow, I doubt that. Maybe it's the incredibly handsome ten-foot-tall guy I'm dancing with."

Jack laughed and pulled her a little closer. The silky fabric of her dress was smooth against his skin, but it was nothing compared to the tender warmth of her hand. She felt so right pressed up against him. He had no idea what they were doing or where this was going, but he only knew that at that moment, he didn't want to be anywhere else but with her. "I'm only six-two."

"Hey. Don't say only. You're a full foot taller than me."

"Are you seriously only five foot two?" Their height difference was the perfect illustration of how opposites sometimes really did attract. Jack loved that they were mismatched in so many ways but were still so drawn to each other.

"Yes. I have to wear four-inch heels just to be average."

"Trust me, Lexi. You're not even close to being average." He meant it. She was extraordinary, and he hated that she didn't seem to know that. The song began to fade and segued into a faster tune. Jack was eager to exit the dance floor. Because as much he loved having her in his arms, he wanted to be somewhere out of the public eye. "Another drink? It looks like we managed to convince a few other couples to come out here."

"Sounds great."

He and Lexi walked off the dance floor, hand in hand. Just as they were about to reach the carpeted perimeter of the room, Winston Alderidge stepped into view, along with a woman Jack could only assume was Lexi's mother. She was of a similar height as her daughter, with the same red hair. Lexi reacted first, her hand dropping from Jack's. She stepped right between him and her parents, almost like she was trying to block him from view, which was not only an absurd idea, it made things awkward from the start.

"Dad. Mom. You're finally here," Lexi said.

Winston embraced his daughter, but he'd narrowed his sights on Jack. "Yes. We are. Are you going to introduce us to your companion?"

Jack tensed up the minute Winston opened his mouth. Memories of their run-in years ago barged into his mind. He had a hard time imagining he would ever like this man, however fond he was of his daughter.

Lexi's mother smiled weakly. She seemed as uncomfortable as Jack felt. "Perhaps we should go talk over in the corner. Your dad and I have a private table."

Lexi cast an anxious glance in Jack's direction then scurried off behind her parents. He hadn't actually been invited to join them, but he presumed that was the plan, so he followed. When he arrived at their table, Winston turned and thrust his hand at Jack.

"I'm Winston Alderidge, Alexis's father. This is my wife, Annemarie."

Jack could admit there was an amusing edge to this awkward scenario. Mr. Alderidge needed no introduction, and he had hoped he hadn't needed one either. "Jack Bowden. We've met, sir. Three years ago." He made sure to return an especially strong handshake.

"Jack is the owner of Bowden Construction," Lexi interjected. "We met last week when I went to Appaloosa Island."

"Bowden Construction. Hmm. I've never heard of it." Winston shrugged. "So many start-ups in these parts. It's hard for me to keep up."

Jack wanted to be nothing less than polite and cordial during this interaction, but the truth was that Lexi's father was so condescending it made it incredibly difficult. "Not a start-up, sir. We've been in business for eleven years. We're the sole contractor for the Soiree on the Bay festival."

"Ah. I guess it's good to know Rusty Edmond is supporting the little guys."

Jack was intent on keeping his cool, but Winston

was grating every last nerve. "You don't remember meeting me, do you?"

Lexi's dad frowned. "I don't. But I meet a lot of people. It's impossible to remember them all."

Jack was *this* close to telling Winston that he was a pompous ass. But he decided it would be better to illustrate it and let everyone else reach their own conclusion, rather than say it right out loud. "You don't remember everyone you personally turn down for a significant business loan? Even when you met with them in your office?"

Winston reared his head back. "Is that how we met?"

"It is. I came in for a multimillion-dollar loan to expand my business. Even though I had the personal assets to guarantee it, you said I was too big a risk. Told me you would rather lend to someone who was better established in the community."

A hesitant smile crossed Winston's face as his memory seemed to kick into gear. "Ahh. Now I remember you. Things got a bit heated between us, didn't they?"

Jack nodded in affirmation. He might have said a few choice words that day, but he'd been justifiably angry. "They did. I'm an extremely hard worker, Mr. Alderidge. I have considerable assets and have built them with my own two hands. I wasn't asking for charity or a favor that day. On paper, there was no reason to deny the loan. But I have a feeling I know why you did." Jack took a step closer, doing everything he could to tamp down his temper. The problem was that every minute facing Winston made the memory of that day all the more acute.

He had left Alderidge Bank feeling humiliated and insulted.

"You took one look at me and decided there wasn't anything in it for you, aside from some interest. I didn't come from your social circles. I wasn't acquainted with your cigar-smoking buddies. I was the man who wasn't afraid to get his hands dirty. You didn't see the point, did you?"

"Well, I…" Winston's voice trailed off. "I can't grant a loan to someone I hardly know. That's not how I do business."

"You don't need to tell me how business is done. Your competitor across town greeted me with open arms. I now run my entire business through them. Millions of dollars every month, flowing like water." Jack looked at Lexi. All color had drained from her face and her eyes were like saucers. He reached for her hand, but he wasn't sure she would take it. Part of him feared she would stay with her parents and tell him to shove off. If that was the case, he'd have to live with the disappointment, but it was going to sting. "Lexi, I'd like to go. You're welcome to join me or stay. It's your choice."

She looked back and forth between Jack and her mom and dad. The wait for her answer felt like it stretched on for an eternity. "No. I'm coming with you." She slid her hand into Jack's and gave it a gentle squeeze, then turned to her parents. "Please let Bianca know I left."

Jack wasn't about to wait for more. He marched to the great room doors, Lexi in his wake. She caught up to him and took his hand again. It brought him more comfort than he cared to admit. "Jack. Stop," she said when they'd reached the hall just outside the room. Luckily, they were mostly alone—only a few stray guests were out there. "I'm so sorry. I had no idea that was the reason you knew my dad. Why didn't you tell me?"

He scanned her face, which was full of sincerity. That made him feel bad, even when his blood was right on the edge of a rolling boil. He prided himself on being the guy who stayed calm and even, but that was no longer possible. "You shouldn't have to answer for the things your father has said or done."

"You're right… I shouldn't. But I also deserve the chance to make things right, don't I? I understand everything you *didn't* say back there. I know how my dad is, how he looks down on people and makes assumptions. I hate it. He did it to Brett all the time."

Someone stepped out of the great room and Jack caught a glimpse of the crowd of people inside, wearing tuxedos and gowns. Would he ever truly fit in here? Did he actually want to? Jack was proud of his roots *and* the success he'd worked so hard for. And he didn't need invitations to garden parties and country club golf tournaments as validation. "I don't want to be a prop, Lexi. I don't want to be the blue-collar guy you parade around as a novelty. That's not me."

She grasped both of his arms, adorably craning her neck to look him in the eye. "You're not a prop, Jack. I like you. A lot."

He froze for a moment as her words sank in. He'd told himself he wouldn't get in deep with Lexi, and here she was, confessing her feelings. The trouble was that he had the exact same feelings. Even when he'd said he wouldn't go there…that he wouldn't get involved. "I like you, too, Lexi."

"Can we go talk in the car? Where we can have some privacy?"

"Yes. Good idea." Jack was sick of being here. He just wanted to be alone with her.

Lexi didn't waste any time when they got back to his car. "Do you remember that moment out in front of Sheen, when you said that you didn't want to talk about any man who didn't have the sense to treat me well? I don't think you know how much that meant to me. To have my feelings validated like that."

"It wasn't some big act of heroism, Lexi. I was being a decent guy. You should expect everyone to treat you that way."

"But they don't. My parents blame me for my divorce. I know they do." She looked down at her lap, seeming ashamed. How he hated seeing that look on her face. "They don't actually say it. They tell me that it's all for the best, but I know they don't really believe that. Deep down, they think I didn't try hard enough to be a good wife. That I should have done more to make Roger want to hold on to me. And maybe those things are true, but I also feel like if you love someone, you should want to be with them. And if you don't, then it's time to let them go."

Everything Lexi was saying was a big part of what he liked about her so much. She had a huge heart, but it seemed as though she'd been taught not to trust it. Jack liked seeing her work these things out for herself. He liked seeing her come into her own.

His phone rang. He didn't want to answer it, but there was too much going on with the Soiree on the Bay construction for him to ignore it. "Dammit. It's Rich, my business partner. I need to see what he needs."

"Yes. Of course."

Jack accepted the call. "What's up?"

"We're short a foreman out on Appaloosa for the night shift. Larry's wife went into labor," Rich said. "I know you're at a function, but is there any way you can come out here? There are a whole lot of guys standing around right now, and I can't do it all on my own."

Jack looked at Lexi. He didn't want to end their night, but duty was calling, and perhaps this was for the best. "Send the helicopter for me, okay?"

"Your house?"

Jack's property on the outskirts of Royal was over twenty acres, most of it nothing but open ranch land. "Yes. I'll be there in forty-five minutes."

"Got it."

He ended the call and placed his phone in the cupholder. "Lexi, I'm sorry, but I have to go back to Appaloosa. There are problems. And maybe tonight didn't quite turn into what either of us were hoping for."

Lexi nodded slowly. "Of course. Whatever you need to do."

Jack wasn't sure of much, but he was sure of one thing as he peered down into her flawless face—he couldn't deny how much he wanted her. But he felt like Royal, her family and his crazy schedule were smothering them. There were too many prying eyes, too many outside forces getting in the way.

"Come away with me."

"What? When?" Her voice was full of surprise, but the look on her face was one of utter delight.

He reached for her hand, then leaned down to place a soft kiss on her cheek. It took every bit of self-control he had to not take it further, to pick up where they'd left things at her house. "I like you, Lexi, but I feel like everything and everyone in Royal is sabotaging us.

Let's go away for a night next weekend. I have a function I have to attend in Houston. I'm being recognized by the children's hospital foundation for an expansion I did for them last year. The Soiree on the Bay project is going to be hell for the next few weeks, but I've had this event on the books for months." He smiled down at her. "I promise I'll make it fun. I think you need to be able to let your hair down. And I know I could use a chance to breathe."

"Houston is where I lived for years. I'm bound to run into someone I know. I'm not sure it'll be much of an escape for me."

He hadn't thought that part through, but he was determined to make this work. "I already have a suite booked at the new hotel downtown. We'll go to my event, but we won't stay long. We can get to know each other on a whole new level." He drifted closer to her and kissed her cheek again, then he brushed his lips across her ear and finally, her graceful neck. Jack closed his eyes, praying for strength as her sweet smell filled his lungs. He wanted to make love to her right here and now. But she was upset, so was he, and work was calling. The time wasn't right.

"I would love to go away with you. I want you, Jack."

He grinned. The unhappiness of the earlier exchange with her dad was quickly fading. He and Lexi didn't need the rest of the world to get in the way of what was growing between them. They only needed time. Alone. "Good. Because I want you, too." He cleared his throat, distracted by her sweet smell and the display of her luscious cleavage before him. He didn't like to wait, but he would for her. "So you'll accompany me next weekend?"

"Yes." She nodded eagerly. "A million times yes."

"Perfect." He pressed the ignition button and the engine roared to life.

"What do I wear for this event?"

"You could wear that dress again if you want. You look unbelievable in it. Every guy in the place will be insanely jealous."

"Jack, you're hilarious. I'm not wearing the same dress."

"Why not?"

"My wardrobe is one of the few things I've done right with my life. I have just the thing, waiting for exactly an event like this. It still has the tags on it."

He pulled out of the parking lot, leaving the TCC behind. "What does it look like?"

Lexi drew a finger up the length of his forearm. "It's red. Silk crepe to make it cling in all the right places. And it's so low cut, I can't really wear a bra."

Jack felt a noticeable tightening in his pants. Waiting an entire week to be with her was going to be sheer torture. But he had a feeling the reward was going to be so worth it. "I can't wait to see you in it." He glanced over at her. "And then I look forward to seeing you out of it."

Five

Jack was set to pick up Lexi for the trip to Houston in two hours, and he was nervous. So much so that he wasn't doing a great job staying focused on work, which was a real problem because he, Rich and Jack's sister Angie were having their first in-person meeting in weeks. The Soiree on the Bay schedule was so crazy, they rarely had the time to sit down and hash things out.

If anyone would sense his distracted state, it was these two. Rich had been Jack's best friend since fifth grade. He'd taken a real chance on Jack by agreeing to move to Royal with him to start Bowden Construction eleven years ago. Jack had needed a fresh start in a new city after his fiancée, Marcella, had dumped him, and he'd been smart enough to know that he couldn't get a new business off the ground on his own. Thankfully, that chance had more than paid off for both Rich and Jack.

"Let's take a look at the numbers for the Soiree project." Rich hit a few keys on his laptop, and the master spreadsheet was projected on the screen at one end of the small conference room.

"We're showing a slight overage right now of about two percent," Angie said. She'd only been working for Jack for a few months, ever since he brought her to Royal after she separated from her husband, who had a volatile temper. Jack had wanted to give his sister that same fresh start he'd given himself, but he also needed to keep her safe. Angie hadn't wanted to come to Royal. *Too many rich people*, she'd said. *They make me uncomfortable. I feel like they're all looking down on me.*

Jack had swiftly reminded her that he was quite wealthy now, with a sprawling home and a fast-growing business, and that people with money were just like anyone else—some were wonderful and others were not. Luckily, Angie had acquiesced to the move to Royal, and since then, she'd not only learned the ropes of managing construction, she was a whiz with the figures.

"Do you think we'll be able to hit our numbers?" Rich asked.

"If we do, it's going to be super close," Angie said. "The cost of moving supplies over to the island has been much higher than the budget allowed. That's the big reason for the difference. Jack, it might be a good idea for you to have a conversation with Rusty Edmond and let him know."

Jack heard his name. He just hadn't heard the other

words that had come before or after it. Or they'd gone in one ear and out the other. "I'm sorry. Can you repeat that?"

"Angie said you need to talk to Rusty about the overage," Rich said.

"Oh, right." Jack scribbled a note to himself. "I'll call him on the way to Houston."

"No, you won't," Angie said. "You're going to be with Lexi Alderidge, and you won't be able to focus on anything. Just like in this meeting."

"What's that supposed to mean?"

"It means you've lost your mind for this woman, Jack. And I don't like it." She sat back in her chair and crossed her arms over her chest, shooting him a piercing glare. Angie had never been one for beating around the bush. She had zero filter. "We all know where this is going. It's not only going too fast, it's going to a very scary place."

Rich closed his laptop, which made the spreadsheet disappear from the wall. "Wow, Ang. You're going to bring this up now? I thought we agreed that we wouldn't say anything until after he got back from Houston."

"Hold on a minute," Jack said. "You two have talked about this?"

"Well, yeah," Angie answered with a shrug, as if it was completely obvious that they would discuss Jack's personal life behind his back. "When a guy who once got dumped by his fiancée two weeks before his wedding gets involved with a woman who apparently doesn't know how to do anything *but* get married, it makes me worry."

Jack drew a deep breath through his nose. "My situation with Marcella was a long time ago. It's water under the bridge. I'm fine."

"You haven't had a single serious girlfriend since then," Rich said. "That doesn't seem to me like you've gotten over it."

"I've been busy." He couldn't help but notice the defensiveness in his own voice. "Getting Bowden Construction to where it is has been a monumental task. I haven't had time to get serious."

"And now you *do* have time?" Angie asked. "Your number one complaint since I moved here is that the Soiree on the Bay project is the biggest one you've ever taken on, and that the timeline is impossible. So that argument doesn't really add up. You're barely sleeping, Jack. So I don't see how you have time to date right now."

Angie and Rich had made a few halfway decent points, but that didn't stop Jack from wanting to fight back. "Lexi and I are having fun. Am I not entitled to that? This isn't serious. It's a casual thing."

Angie rolled her eyes, which Jack did not appreciate. "I've heard the things people say about Lexi around town," she said.

"You can stop right there. I don't care about gossip."

"This isn't that. Her sister Bianca goes to the same yoga studio I go to. From everything she said, her sister hasn't been single since she was seventeen, and every guy she's been with she either married or tried to marry. That doesn't seem like the track record of someone who is capable of keeping things casual."

Jack didn't want to listen to any more of this nonsense. "You're being ridiculous. Both of you. Lexi and I are not getting married. We hardly know each other."

He got up from the table. "Plus, her dad doesn't like me, and I'm guessing her mom doesn't either after what happened at the TCC last week, so it doesn't even matter. It's a nonstarter. I'm not about to get serious with a woman whose family doesn't approve of me. You both know that's way too important to me."

Rich nodded. "I get it. Lexi's dad is a real piece of work, Jack. But I also don't think it's smart to get even with him by whisking his daughter away. He's a powerful man and people in this town talk like crazy. I really think you should rethink this whole idea."

Jack couldn't believe what he was hearing. He wasn't trying to get even with Winston Alderidge. Or *was* he? Was that part of what made things so hot with Lexi? The fact that her dad so clearly looked down on him? Was this so forbidden that it made him want her that much more? "All of these points would have been more helpful to me after my first date with her, you two."

Rich and Angie exchanged plaintive looks. "We know. We just weren't sure how to bring it up with you," Angie said. "You've been busy and stressed. We aren't trying to make your life more difficult, Jack. But we're worried about you. And frankly, we're a little worried about Lexi, too. I mean, I don't know her at all, but it can't be good for her to get involved with another guy right now, especially one who her father doesn't like"

Jack felt like he had no choice but to engage in the self-reflection he'd been avoiding, but he couldn't call Lexi and cancel their getaway. She'd be disappointed, and quite frankly, so would he. He'd been looking forward to getting lost in a beautiful woman for at least one night.

"Look," he said to Rich and his sister. "I love you both. But you need to back off and let me do my thing. Lexi and I are both consenting adults. We want to get away for a night and have some fun. That's all."

Angie and Rich looked at each other, seeming to have a silent conversation, all of which suggested that they thought he was being foolish. "Suit yourself," Angie said. "I'll be here to help you pick up the pieces when it all falls apart."

"Trust me. I'm not going to get hurt," Jack retorted on his way out the door. "I don't want serious and neither does she."

He stalked down the hall to his office to check his email while trying to shake off the sour mood he was in after his conversation with Rich and Angie. Was this really that bad of an idea? It was one night.

What could possibly happen?

Lexi wasn't so worried about her dress this time. Now that she had a better sense of what Jack liked, she was certain the red one she'd told him about hit the mark. Unlike the green gown she'd worn to the event at the TCC, she could breathe in this one, and that was a very good thing. Oxygen made it easier to manage the anticipation for what was ahead…a romantic evening at a five-star hotel, dinner and perhaps dancing, followed by their escape to his luxury suite. They could finally be truly alone, and she couldn't wait. She wanted Jack so badly it burned inside her, just as hot and crimson as the gown she wore.

Jack had asked Lexi to meet him at the airstrip outside of town, as they would be taking a helicopter to Houston. With his crazy work schedule, it was the best way to get away for a night and not spend too much time traveling. Her suitcase was in the back of her car, packed full of cute outfits, heels, a bathing suit, probably too many toiletries, and a few choice pieces of very expensive lingerie. Lexi liked having options, even if she knew she wouldn't come close to using everything she'd brought along.

Outside, the charming Royal countryside rolled by, a reminder of her lifelong ties to this place. She loved being back here, despite the recent trouble with her dad. The state of their relationship was a bit of a gray cloud hanging over her getaway with Jack—Lexi and her father were barely speaking after the dustup at the TCC. She knew a big talk was coming, but she'd wanted them both to cool off first.

Lexi's phone rang. It was Bianca. "What's up?" Lexi answered. "I'm almost at the airstrip, so I only have a few minutes."

"You can't go to Houston, Lex."

"What? Why? You said you thought it was a good idea for Jack and me to go away. You told me to go have fun. Why are you telling me this now?" Lexi didn't want to be so annoyed, but her sister's timing was wretched.

"I came across a news story about this charity event you're going to. Do you know who's hosting it? Savannah Lee."

Her stomach knotted so tight she thought she might get sick. Savannah was the woman who Lexi's ex-husband Roger had started dating soon after she left Houston. "Do you think he will be there?"

"Even if he's not, and I'm guessing he will, you won't be able to get away from the bigger story here. Savannah and Roger just got engaged."

Ahead, Lexi saw the gated entrance for the airstrip. Jack was likely waiting for her on the other side of that fence. What was she supposed to do? Cancel on Jack? Or don't tell him and deal with seeing her ex and his new fiancée?

"Lexi? Are you still there?" Bianca asked.

"I am."

"Are you okay?"

Lexi sucked in a deep breath. "I guess." She pulled up to the electronic keypad, rolled down her window and punched in the code Jack had given her. "I don't know what to do." Straight ahead, Jack was standing next to his car, typing something on his phone. He was sporting sunglasses, wearing another of his perfect-fitting suits, looking as devastatingly handsome as ever. She'd so looked forward to this and now it felt like the universe was trying to send her a signal that this was a bad idea. "Bianca, I need to go. I'm here."

"I'm so sorry. I didn't want to ruin your weekend. But I also couldn't let you walk into that event with no idea of what's going on."

"Thank you. I appreciate it."

"Love you, Lex."

"Love you, too." She hung up the phone just as she was pulling into the space next to Jack's.

A few seconds later, he was opening the driver's side door. "Hello, beautiful." Jack smiled down at her, offering his hand to help her out of the car. "I can't wait to see you in that dress."

She climbed out, her leg naturally slipping out of

her gown's high slit. That should have been a very sexy moment, a precursor to their night ahead, but Lexi was feeling like far less than a seductress right now. "Hi." That was all she could manage before she was drifting into the safety of Jack's arms, resting her head against his chest.

"What's wrong?"

"Am I that transparent?" she asked.

"You're shaking like a leaf."

"I am?" Lexi hadn't noticed, but now that he mentioned it, she realized her shoulders were quivering.

"Yes. Talk to me. Is it something with your dad?"

If only Lexi could be so lucky. She had a tiny shred of control when it came to him. "Bianca just called me. Turns out my ex-husband got engaged and his new fiancée is hosting your event tonight."

Jack blew out a big breath and pushed his sunglasses up on top of his head. He scanned her face like he was looking for answers, but she felt like she had absolutely none. "Okay, then. Plan B. We'll go somewhere else."

Lexi was confused. "No. Jack. We can go. I'll be fine. I might need a stiff drink before I walk through the door though."

Jack reached down for her hand. "Lexi. I am working like crazy right now and the promise of tonight is the only thing that got me through this week. I'm not going to drag you to some event that might only upset you."

"But you're supposed to get an important award tonight."

Jack waved it off. "It's a plaque. I couldn't care less about that. I'd rather be with you."

Lexi's heart was being so fast that her brain couldn't

keep up. She knew she was getting swept away by Jack, which she'd told herself dozens of times was a very bad idea. "I don't want you to have to rescue me again. You did that the day we met."

"Don't think of it that way. I did what anyone would have done. I know you would've done the same for me."

She wanted to think she had the nerve to save Jack, but she wasn't sure. She hadn't been tested like that before. "Where can we go if we don't go to Houston? We talked about getting out of Royal."

"I think we should go to Appaloosa Island."

"The construction site?"

Jack unleashed his hearty laugh. "No. I promise you that where we're going is a lot nicer than that."

Lexi looked down at her gown. "Whatever it is, I'm totally overdressed."

"No. You're perfect. I love seeing you in that. Not that I don't want you to be undressed later."

Heat rose in her cheeks. She swatted Jack on the arm. "You're bad."

"Or maybe very, very good." Jack's eyes glimmered. "Come on. We'll grab your bag and I'll speak to the pilot."

Lexi gathered her purse and phone charger from the front seat of her car as Jack brought her suitcase to the helicopter and briefly conferred with the pilot. Then he waved Lexi over and helped her on board. The cabin was even nicer than the one the bank owned, with white leather upholstery and enough room for six. Lexi took a center seat, with Jack next to her.

"Are we going to the hotel on Appaloosa?"

Jack shook his head as he buckled himself in. "I rented a house on the island a few weeks ago. It was too much to go back and forth all the time, and the owner is out of the country for at least six months. I figure that'll give me a prime spot for Soiree on the Bay." He swept her hair to one side and kissed her neck.

Lexi's eyes fluttered shut as she soaked up his warmth and the enticing brush of his skin against hers. It was the perfect reminder of why she was here—so she could finally have what she'd wanted since the moment she met this amazingly sexy man. "Jack, if you're going to kiss me like that, I don't care where we go. I only know that I'm ready to get there."

"I promise you it'll be spectacular." Jack reached for her hand as if it had become the most natural thing in the world. No, they weren't truly a couple, or boyfriend and girlfriend. She and Jack were just having fun. But as the helicopter took flight and Royal became a dot on the Texas landscape, it sure was starting to feel like something more than casual.

Six

Once again, Jack had proven himself to be full of surprises, pivoting from their Houston plan to one Lexi had never expected—an escape to Appaloosa Island. She had relished the thought of the five-star hotel, but there was something equally appealing about coming here. With little access from the mainland, they were essentially cut off from the world, if only for one night.

It was shortly after sunset when they arrived on the island, which Lexi realized left them the entire evening ahead. The mere thought sent goose bumps racing down her spine. She wanted Jack so bad, and there had been too much waiting. It felt as though she'd spent an eternity tasting his kisses on her lips, but never getting more. Perhaps that had been Jack's game all along, exercising his endless patience while she did nothing but squirm in her own skin. And right now, her desire for him was reaching a fever pitch, because all she could think about was getting him out of his suit, and him getting her out of this dress.

"Are we almost there?" she asked as they rode along in a small SUV that Jack had arranged for when the helicopter dropped them off. Although the island was far more developed on the western side, there was still very little in the way of streetlamps or normal city infrastructure. All around them was nothing but the slowly deepening blue of night, the softly moon-lit sway of tall palms in the wind and somewhere off in the distance, the Gulf. It was beautiful and serene. It reminded Lexi to take a breath and enjoy her time with Jack, even when she didn't want to wait anymore.

"Just a few more minutes." Jack slowed down and turned left on to a narrow gravel drive. The car pitched and rocked for several hundred feet, then they hit asphalt and the ride smoothed out.

Ahead, Lexi saw the outline of a massive white house. She knew that Rusty Edmond only let his closest friends, people of extreme means, build on the island. Still, Lexi hadn't expected such a grand structure. "Wow. This is it? What I can see is absolutely beautiful."

Jack pulled up and parked the car. "You will love this house. I have it rented for six months so I can be on the island for Soiree on the Bay, but honestly, I'm thinking about trying to buy it. The owner is an old friend of Rusty's, but he does so much business in Asia, that he's almost never here."

Lexi was interested in the backstory, but then again, she wasn't. She leaned over the center console and reached up, placing her finger against his warm lips.

"Jack. If you don't take me inside and take off my clothes, I will never forgive you."

He smiled widely. Even in the dark, there was an unmistakable glimmer in his eyes. "I don't need to be asked twice. We'll leave the bags. I'll come out and get them later."

Or never, Lexi thought to herself. She did have some truly exquisite, very expensive lingerie in her bag, but she also felt like being naked would suffice, too. She didn't wait for Jack to open her door, hopping out of the car and hiking her dress up with one hand so she could hurry over to him. He took her hand and they ascended the full flight of stairs up to the house. After stealing a quick kiss, Jack entered a code on an electronic keypad.

When the lock clicked open, it was like a starting pistol. Lexi felt as though her heart was going to rocket out of her body. They stumbled through the front door, Jack closed it and her hands were all over him. Thank goodness she'd left her heels on or she'd be at a serious disadvantage here.

She kissed him without inhibition while she threaded her hands inside his jacket and pushed it from his shoulders to the floor. Her fingers scrambled to untuck his shirt, then went straight for the buttons. She flew through them like a woman on a mission. When she finally pulled the garment down his arms and was able to see his smooth bare chest and run her hands over it, it was like she'd unwrapped the best gift she could ever receive. As she'd hoped, he was pure muscled perfection, but feeling the warmth radiating from his skin and seeing the look on his face when he watched her touch him made it all the more real.

"You're amazing," she whispered, leaning in and kissing one of his defined pecs.

A deep groan escaped his throat. "You're the amazing one. And I want you closer to a bed." He swept her feet out from under her with what seemed like zero effort, carrying her up another flight of stairs. Then as he strode down a hall, she wrapped her arms around his neck, clinging to him and breathing in his smell, a heady mix of bourbon and cedar. He turned and angled her through a doorway and set her on the floor.

Lexi was in awe of the room, which had a generous king-size bed arranged with a perfect view of an entire wall of windows. Outside, the moon lit Trinity Bay, highlighting what was surely a beautiful vista by day. "It's so incredible, Jack," Lexi said, placing her hand on the wood molding between the windows. "This place is magical. I can't wait to see the view tomorrow."

Jack came up behind her and placed his hands on her shoulders. "I can't wait to see the view of you right now."

Lexi watched her reflection in the window as Jack slipped the straps of her dress from her shoulders and pulled them down her arms. Her nipples drew tight with the rush of cooler air against her skin. Watching him admire her body made the moment that much more intoxicating—she felt wanted. Desired. He kissed her shoulder one more time, then turned her around and dropped to his knees. Lexi kicked off her heels, leaving Jack's mouth at the perfect height to suck on one nipple and then the next. He looped his tongue around the hard bundle of nerves, sending zaps of electricity straight to her core. His generous hands cupped her breasts, lifting them higher and together in the center, while his eyes darkened as they raked over her.

Meanwhile, heat gathered between her legs and Lexi dug her fingernails into his shoulders, kissing the top of his head, holding his face to her bosom. Every kiss or lick he bestowed on her body felt like a message. *I want you.* If only he knew how badly she'd needed to feel like that.

She was intent on returning the sentiment, raising his face to hers and kissing him with as much raw passion as she'd ever shown. Even she marveled at her own boldness, the way she owned her movements and took what she wanted. Perhaps Jack had been right. Maybe she needed to get a few things out of her system. If so, being with him felt like it was opening the door on a whole new world, and Lexi was eager to explore it all.

Jack's hands were at her waist, but then he dropped them to her hips and pulled the dress down until it pooled around her feet. She was wearing only a pair of lacy red panties, a whisper of fabric between her and what she really wanted. Jack groaned when he sat back and looked at her, then stood and once again picked her up, taking only a few long strides before placing her on the bed.

Lexi stretched out on the cool linens, arching her back, and watching him study her body as he unzipped his pants. She raised one hand to her mouth, running a finger along her lower lip as he finished undressing and finally showed her everything she'd been waiting for. The moment was so worth marking—Jack was absolutely magnificent. Every inch of him was sculpted, and it was impossible to ignore the way he was so primed for her.

He stretched out next to her and Lexi rolled to her side to kiss him. Her desire for him was too great— nothing seemed like it was happening fast enough, even when she wanted every moment to last. She hitched her leg up over his hip and got as close as she could to him, her apex hungry for his touch. He trailed his hand up and down the channel of her spine, then rolled to his back, pulling Lexi along with him until she was straddling his waist. She sat up and Jack molded his hands around her breasts, rubbing her nipples in tiny rotations with his thumbs. Lexi gasped at the pleasure and reminded herself to enjoy herself, to not be so impatient. Let Jack have control.

He gripped her rib cage and pulled her so close that her knees were nearly bracketing his chest. Then he bent down and drew one tight bud into his mouth, drawing circles with his tongue and sending Lexi into near oblivion as she felt bold enough to watch him. His lips against her skin, his dark eyes looking up at her— each inviting detail only stoked her desire for him. She wanted him with every molecule in her body.

Lexi rolled back onto the mattress and kneeled next to him, near his waist. She drew a line down the center of his chest, starting at the base of his throat, between his pecs, to his belly button and finally lower. Jack sucked in a sharp breath when she wrapped her fingers around his stiff erection. She was desperate to figure out what he liked, so at first, she took slow, gentle strokes. Jack mumbled his approval, something that sounded like *yes* over and over again. He seemed content, enjoying every instant of her touch, but when she tightened her grip, that made a very sexy rumble leave his throat. The satisfaction of having Jack at her command was far more than she'd bargained for. She felt strong. Powerful. And had never felt so alive.

"Do you have a condom?" Her voice was breathless and a little desperate. "I brought a box, but they're packed away with my toiletries. I guess that was stupid of me."

"Of course. I came prepared." He hopped up from the bed, giving Lexi the chance to watch his muscled frame in motion. Every inch of him was perfect, but his butt was particularly breathtaking.

Once again, she stretched out on the bed, swishing her hands against the silky linens as the seconds ticked by and anticipation boiled up inside her. Jack turned back to her, and his smile as he approached made her so dizzy that she nearly passed out. The only thing that kept her wits about her was the fight inside her—she would not be denied. She was finally going to have Jack.

That first glimpse of Lexi on the bed, wearing nothing more than sexy red panties and a knowing smile, ripped Jack's breath from his lungs. He'd imagined this a few times, but her beauty was so much more potent in person, far hotter than anything he ever could have dreamed up in his own head. Just kissing her in the foyer downstairs, with the knowledge that nothing was going to stop them, had been a lot to wrap his mind around. And now the moment was here.

He needed her with every inch of his body, but there was one part of him that was begging for her, so he tore open the foil packet and rolled on the condom. Jack was certain he'd never been so hard, was positive he'd never wanted a woman as much as he wanted Lexi right now, perhaps because he'd waited so long. But he also wanted to help her feel as good as she could possibly feel.

He stepped to the very end of the bed, nearest Lexi's feet. "I want you to do something for me."

"Anything."

How he loved the way she trusted him. "Clasp your hands and raise them up above your head."

Her sights narrowed on him, seeming skeptical, but she followed his directive, leaving her hands together up near the pillows. "I want to be able to touch you, Jack."

"Believe me, beautiful, I want that, too. But for now, I want you to think only about your own pleasure." He reached down and tugged her panties down her hips, past her knees and then her ankles, before dropping them to the floor.

Lexi wiggled in place, arching her back. "Jack. This doesn't seem fair."

He loved seeing her so impatient. "Oh, it will." With both hands, he urged her to spread her legs, then placed a knee on the bed. He drew his fingers along her inner thigh, then placed one of his knees on the bed so he had a better chance to slip his hand between her delicate folds and find her apex. She was so wet, so ready for him, it made yet another rush of blood race to his groin, amping up his need for her. He'd wait a little longer though.

Jack rubbed in gentle circles, studying her face as her eyes drifted shut then watched as she rolled her head to one side, her lips going slack. She was the most beautiful creature he'd ever seen, and that was not overstating the fact. He took immense pleasure in watching her reactions as she relaxed a little more and surrendered to his touch. With every circle he drew with his fingers, Lexi's breaths grew shorter. He knew she was close. That was all he wanted right now—just to push her to the edge, then tease her back from it. He knew from experience that it would make her climax that much more powerful.

Stretching out next to her, he pressed his lips to hers, his arms pulling her close. He listened for the changes in her breath as they were drawn back into another heavenly kiss, but she wasn't disappointed. She wasn't even frustrated with him. In fact, she was on board with everything he did.

With a move Jack had not anticipated, Lexi pressed her hands against his chest, pushing him to his back. She climbed on top of him and Jack watched in utter fascination as she reached for his length and guided him between her legs. As she sank down onto him, a storm of heat threatened to swallow him whole. She fit perfectly around him, warm and soft. Being inside Lexi made his thoughts disjointed, so he focused on the physical sensations. The wait for this had been so worth it. They moved together, Lexi lowering her chest to his, not actually resting her body weight on him but instead rubbing her nipples lightly against his bare chest. No one had ever done that to him before. It nearly sent him over the edge.

Lexi's breaths were short once again. His own were rough and jagged. Pressure was building and he was in that intense place where you want to reach your destination, but you don't, because every second of the journey is so rife with pleasure. Lexi rolled her head to the side, eyes shut and pouty mouth slack, and he sensed she was close to surrendering to her peak.

Then she turned back to him and her eyes opened again, a wild and untamed green in the dark. She pressed her chest against his, and he was able to kiss her deeply and wrap his hands around her hips, dig his fingers into the lushness of her bottom. He thrust more forcefully, but it took very little to lift Lexi from the bed. The pent-up need coiled tight in his groin. It wouldn't be long before it would all break free. He pulled hard on her hips and rocked his pelvis so he could be even deeper inside her. That one change seemed to speed everything up as Lexi started to call out, then gasped for breaths, her mouth wide open as the orgasm hit her and she pulsed tight around him.

His own pleasure rocketed from the depths of his belly, a relentless cycle of tension winding up and letting go. Lexi gasped again and fell flat against his chest, kissing his neck over and over again. Jack rolled to his side and they were in each other's arms, breathless with contentment.

Lexi nuzzled his chest with her face, dotting his skin with delicate kisses. "That was amazing."

"It was." Jack's thoughts hadn't quite gathered yet, although he did know that he needed so much more of this incredible woman. "I want to remind you that we would be sitting in a stuffy hotel ballroom right now. And I'm positive this is so much better."

She kissed him softly. "I feel bad about that, Jack. You missed out on your award. Because of me and my pathetic history."

He shook his head. "Lexi. Stop saying things like

that. You've been through a hard time. It's not a reflection on you."

She blew out an exasperated sigh. "You're right. Bad habit."

"Are you doing okay, though? How long had you known that your ex got engaged?"

"About ten minutes before I saw you," she admitted. "Bianca called me while I was in the car."

"I'm glad she saw that and was able to warn you. Although, we would've just dealt with it if we'd had to run into him. I would've pulled you in my arms and laid a hot kiss on you to make him jealous."

Lexi laughed, but there was an edge of melancholy to it, too. "I don't think there's any making him feel like that. He's the one who wanted to split. He'd probably be relieved if I met a guy, got serious and got married so he didn't have to pay me alimony anymore. Well, that's not happening any time soon."

Jack's feelings could've been hurt by Lexi's words if he didn't understand why she felt that way. She'd been badly burned and would do anything to not experience that again. He still couldn't fathom how any man could walk away from Lexi, and he sensed that there was part of her that wondered the same thing. Jack wanted her to know that she wasn't alone in feeling rejected. She wasn't the only person who'd suffered such a heartache. "I have a confession."

"Then I want to hear it."

"Before I moved to Royal, I was engaged. My fiancée dumped me a few weeks before the ceremony. It's not quite the same as what you went through, and I have a feeling it must be far worse for the bride than the groom, but that was part of what made me jump in and say something to Ross the day we met. I know at least some of what it feels like, and I wanted to take that away."

Lexi looked deeply into his eyes. "Is that why you were okay with not going to Houston?"

"That was a bit more selfish, if I'm being honest. I have been looking forward to this all week, and I didn't want anything to get in the way of us being together, at least for a night."

Lexi smoothed her hand over Jack's chest, making desire bubble up inside him again. "What was your fiancée like? Had you been together a long time?"

Jack didn't think about Marcella very often now. It was a lifetime ago. He'd moved on. "She was nice enough to tell me that she wasn't really in love with me. At the time, it hurt like hell, but now I'm thankful. It never would've worked, and we both would've been miserable."

"I guess Brett was nice enough to call it off, too. I hadn't thought about it like that. I mostly thought about the mistakes I made."

"Like I said, Lexi, you need to stop focusing on your missteps and focus on the good choices you've made."

"Like coming with you to Appaloosa Island for a night?"

Jack grinned wide. He hadn't been this relaxed or happy in a very long time. "You know, I've been thinking. There's no reason why you can't stay until Sunday night or even Monday morning. Even if they need me on the job site, I can pop over there easily, and being able to come back to you will be pretty amazing." He was struck by the thought of Lexi waiting for him, and of them spending more nights together. The idea suggested what might eventually be a serious relationship, and they weren't there yet, but he could imagine wanting to go there.

If only he could be sure that Lexi would want that, too.

and of them spending more nights together. The idea
suggested what might eventually be a serious relationship, and they weren't there yet, but he could imagine
wanting to go there.

Seven

Saturday morning, Jack tried to convince Lexi they
should go swimming. In the bay.

"Jack. It's April. I don't care if we're in Texas. The
water will *not* be warm." Lexi was wrapped up in nothing but a light blanket, comfortably perched in a white
rocking chair as the sun warmed her face and ocean
breezes blew back her hair. As far as she was concerned, she was going to finish her cup of coffee, then
take Jack back upstairs and let him set her world on
fire as many times as humanly possible. Last night
had been epic, but that didn't mean they couldn't try
for more.

He leaned against the railing, facing her and wearing only a pair of board shorts and a smile. It wasn't
fair. He was not only blocking out the sun, he was so
spectacular, she could hardly think straight. "We'll

run in for a few minutes. I promise it'll be exhilarating. Then we can get in the hot tub."

"There's a hot tub?"

Jack pushed off from the railing and pointed down to the floor below. "Right there."

Lexi got up from her seat to check it out for herself. Sure enough, down on the ground level was another deck, with an outdoor kitchen and spa. "How did I not see that?"

"I haven't given you the full tour." Jack placed his hand on her hip, tugging her closer. "We've been too busy."

Lexi rose up on to her tiptoes and kissed him. Even the most innocent of kisses felt hot right now. She knew what he was capable of now, and it made her hunger for him all the more. It was as if she'd been asleep her whole life, waiting for Jack's touch to awaken her. "I was hoping we could go back upstairs to the bedroom."

"A quick swim first? I promise I'll make it worth your time in the hot tub." He bounced his eyebrows up and down.

"Condoms and water don't mix."

"There are other things we can do."

That certainly sounded promising, and there was no denying that every minute with Jack was an adventure. "You're lucky I brought a bathing suit."

"I would've been fine with you skinny-dipping."

"Hmm. I hadn't thought about that." It wasn't the worst idea in the world. A tiny number of people were on the island at any time, and there were no permanent residents. But Lexi could also imagine some massive yacht toddling by, possibly owned by someone her parents knew, and her flame red hair would stick out like a neon sign. Probably best not to take that chance. "I think I'll stick to my bikini, though. It's too cute to leave in the suitcase."

"Sounds like I win either way." Jack smiled, showing her those dimples she was somehow even more entranced by.

"Two minutes and I'll get changed."

"Sounds perfect. I'll grab some beach towels."

Lexi flitted upstairs and carefully sifted through the contents of her suitcase, pulling out her black bikini. She cast aside the blanket and put it on, stopping in the bathroom to brush her teeth. Glancing in the mirror, she couldn't help but notice the rosy glow in her cheeks and the way even her eyes looked brighter. Even better, she felt like she looked—like the day was full of possibilities, all because of Jack.

She met him down on the main floor, where the living room, kitchen and several other bedrooms were located. They walked out to the deck where she'd just been occupying the rocking chair and descended a staircase at the far end, taking them to the lower patio area, at the same level as the grass-topped dunes lining the beach. Hand in hand, they padded down the boardwalk and onto the pale gray sand. The wind whipped around them, and seagulls swooped out over the water while wisps of white clouds floated against a gauzy blue sky. Ahead, the deep azure of the Gulf was indeed inviting, but Lexi knew better than to jump right in. Her worries about it being cold were well-warranted. Depending on the currents, the water temperature could be in the sixties, a bit chillier than the air temp, which was in the low seventies at best.

They approached the waterline, where the sand was darker and the tide had revealed countless tiny shells. Looking down the beach in either direction, there wasn't another soul as far as the eye could see. The closest house, another stunning mansion, had to be at least a fifteen-minute walk away. Jack had been right. She could have skinny-dipped and no one would've known. They were all alone in what she saw as paradise.

Lexi squeezed his hand, feeling like she needed to mark the moment. She hadn't felt so free in a very long time. Possibly ever. Every worry she held so tightly in her head seemed insignificant right now. And it was all because of Jack. "Thank you for bringing me here. I'm sure our stay at the hotel in Houston would've been lovely, but this feels really special."

He turned to her and took her other hand, smiling and squinting at her as the sun hit his handsome face. "I'm so glad you said that. I was thinking the same thing."

"You're really serious about going in the water, aren't you?" Another gust of wind hit them, making goose bumps dot Lexi's arms and shoulders.

"I'm not going to force you."

However much she did not enjoy being cold, she wasn't about to be timid. There was this sense of adventure that followed Jack wherever he went, and she'd be stupid to pass up this chance to have an experience she might always remember. "I'm not a wimp."

"Of course not." He inched closer to the lapping waves, with Lexi in tow. "I usually run in up to my knees, dive under to get my head wet, swim out a few strokes and get out of the water."

Lexi could do that. No problem. And she wanted to show Jack that she could be bold, so she let go of his hand and did exactly what he suggested. The first few strides into the shallow water felt fine, so she went for it and dove in. She felt the cold first in her face, then her stomach, but it wasn't a shock—it was more of a pleasant jolt into the here and now. Her feet found the sandy bottom and she pushed off to surface, shaking her hair when she came up for air.

Jack was out of sight, and Lexi's heart was fiercely beating. "Jack?" She frantically looked all around her then screamed when she felt hands around her waist.

Jack rose out of the water like a god, pulling her into his arms and spinning her in the waves. "Well? What do you think?"

Honestly, the only thought that came to mind as he pressed his warm bare stomach against hers and water drops glistened on his face, was that he was perfect and she wasn't sure what she'd done to deserve this time with such a singular man. "It's amazing. *You're* amazing." She smashed her lips against his, her arms resting on his shoulders and her fingers digging into his hair. The kiss was just like the water in the bay—unpredictable and untamed, but nothing was forced. Everything felt right.

"Do you want to stay in?" Jack asked when he broke the kiss.

Lexi was out of breath. "Absolutely not. I'm freezing."

He laughed and scooped her up in his arms, showing off his strength by carrying her to shore. She could get so used to this. Then he gently set her feet on the sand and she grabbed the towels, tossing one to him and wrapping herself up in the other.

"Hot tub?" he asked.

"Yes."

They ran up the beach to the boardwalk, and after rinsing the sand from their feet, Jack opened up the hot tub cover and turned on the jets.

"Ooh. It feels a little hot after our swim," Lexi said, easing into the water.

Jack was less tentative, climbing right in and reclining in one of the seats. "You'll get used to it."

Lexi was already relaxed, but now that she was becoming accustomed to the warm water, she felt her muscles unwinding even more. "You're a smart man. You know that, right? I feel incredible right now."

Half a smile cracked at a corner of his mouth and she saw the familiar glimmer in his eyes. "I don't know about smart, but I'm sure I'm not dumb. All I want is whatever will make you happy."

Jack's words were everything she'd ever hoped to hear from a man. "That's so sweet of you. This whole trip has been wonderful. Thank you." The one thought persisting in her head was that the rules she'd given herself about not getting serious might not apply to Jack. He wasn't Brett. He wasn't Roger. He wasn't a man who'd broken her heart.

Jack held out his hand in invitation, his eyes heavy with desire. "Come here, beautiful."

She'd never taken a suggestion so readily. She slipped her hand into his and he tugged her closer through the water. His other hand cupped the side of her face, making her feel once again like she might melt. His touch was both firm and tender—how did he do that? How did he treat her with such regard while making it so clear that he wanted her?

Lexi leaned into him and shut her eyes, soaking up the instant when their mouths met and she could slip into the warmth of his kiss. Once again, that perfect mix of strong and soft. She tilted her head to the side and parted her lips, their tongues teasing and toying with each other. As each heavenly second ticked by, her body heat spiked hotter. She felt like she was on fire and not merely because she was up to her shoulders in hot water. Needing him, she placed a knee on the bench and straddled his lap.

He groaned into her mouth as her legs gripped his hips and she planted her elbows on his shoulders. Lexi dug her fingers into his hair, never allowing their kiss to break. She only wanted more. More heat. More intensity. She gently nipped his lower lip and she felt him get harder against her center. The faintest waves of his heady, masculine scent filled her nose, while his damp hair rubbed against the tender underside of her arms. He dragged his hands up and down her sides, squeezing and pressing into her skin like he couldn't get enough. It soon became evident that he wanted more, when he sneaked one hand to her back and tugged at the string across her back. As the garment came loose, Lexi pulled it over her head and tossed it on to the deck.

"That's so much better," she muttered, pressing her breasts against his bare chest. Her nipples tightened at that small bit of friction. The need inside her rolled to the boil and she rocked her hips, grinding against him, needing the gratification of his touch. "I need you, Jack."

He moved his mouth to her ear. "I need to hear you say that." It sounded like he was on board, but he still held on to her so tight that it seemed like he didn't share her immense sense of urgency.

"Then let's get out."

"In a minute." Jack flattened his hand against Lexi's belly and slid it down into the front of her bikini bottoms.

She gasped when his talented fingers found her apex. Her eyes slammed shut, and she pitched forward, nestling her face in Jack's neck. He continued in determined circles, not stopping, only changing the pressure. The tension in her body doubled, then doubled again.

"Kiss me, Lexi."

The deep tenor of his voice was only more of a turn-on. She dragged her cheek across his stubble and kissed him with as much unbridled enthusiasm as she could muster. He met her effort, and it was like they were trying to outdo each other. The only difference was that Lexi was right at the brink, her attention spiraling between the sensations—the kiss and the spellbinding action of his hand.

The peak rolled right over her, causing her to cry out and knock back her head as she dug her fingers into his shoulders. He stilled his hand, then dragged it along the center of her torso, between her breasts, then back down, as her body shuddered with the exquisite pleasure. As those final waves receded, she sought the comfort of his arms. Lexi could be as vulnerable as she wanted with Jack, no strength to speak or stand, and it didn't matter. She'd never felt safer.

There was something about watching Lexi unravel, with the beauty of Appaloosa Island all around them, that made Jack impossibly happy. Yes, he was overwhelmed by her beauty, but he was equally blown away by the difference in her since they'd arrived. Lexi was unwinding here, not worried about what anyone thought about her. She wasn't fixated on the forces in their world that thought the two of them as a couple was a bad idea. And the joy that brought him scared him a bit—he hadn't realized that he'd been waiting for her to show him a sign that there was a chance for them to have more.

Of course, Jack wasn't thinking about those things either when he had Lexi at his mercy. He was only relishing what she was at her core—a sensitive, sexy and smart woman. A person who had been read wrong by a lot of people. Jack had been underestimated many times in his, life and he knew exactly how much it hurt. Lexi wasn't the poor little rich girl people gossiped about, and if she *was* that, he sure didn't see her that way. Part of him wanted to rage against everyone who had ever whispered about her behind her back. Another part of him thought those people weren't worth the trouble.

Lexi spread her hand across Jack's chest and kissed his wet skin. "I need to take care of you now."

As appealing as that was, he needed to clear his head. He'd told himself that he had zero problem with things staying casual, just as Lexi wanted. Now he wasn't so sure, not when his only thought was to keep her on Appaloosa forever. That didn't sound like a noncommittal frame of mind. "You know, I'm starving. Maybe we can grab some lunch first. Then I'll have my strength back."

Lexi narrowed her eyes, seeming suspicious, but

ultimately nodded in agreement. "I guess I'm pretty hungry, too." She climbed out of the hot tub, wrapped herself up in a towel and grabbed her bikini top from the deck.

Jack closed up the hot tub and they headed upstairs to the kitchen. He didn't bother getting dressed, content to walk around in his swim trunks, but Lexi ran up to the bedroom, quickly returning barefoot and wearing a black-and-white-checkered sundress with skinny straps. She had no makeup on, and her hair was pulled back in a high ponytail that really showed off the natural color in her cheeks. This was not the everyday Lexi, with her flawless appearance and designer wardrobe, and Jack knew for a fact that most people never saw her this way. He felt damn lucky to be with both versions of her.

It was really nice to make lunch together, just some sandwiches with fixings he had stocked the fridge with a few days ago. Lexi made an amazing side salad with a vinaigrette she whipped up on the fly, and they sat out on the deck while they ate, just watching the waves, breathing in the salt air, laughing and talking. Jack couldn't think of a time when he'd been this at ease with a woman, and so soon. He had to remind himself that he and Lexi had hardly known each other for two weeks. But that didn't even seem possible. Because he felt like he'd known her forever.

"How's the search for a place to live going?" Jack asked.

"It isn't. I've been so crazy busy at work I haven't had a chance to call the real estate agent. I guess I'd better get on that."

He was surprised she hadn't even started the process. For someone so eager to get out from under her parents' control, he thought she would've set the wheels in motion by now. "Well, whenever you're able to go look at some places, I'll be happy to go with you if you want. I can spot poor construction from a mile away."

"That would be great! Bianca has offered to go with me, too, but she's more worried about how far away I'll be living from her. She'd like me to be close."

Although that hinted at more familial interference, he appreciated her bond with Bianca. He had a similar relationship with his sister Angie. "What do your parents think about all of that?"

"They're happy with me being in the guesthouse, to be honest. But I think they're just being protective. They're convinced I'm going to fall apart at some point, and I think my dad in particular likes the idea of being the one to pick up the pieces."

It wasn't hard to imagine Winston wanting to fill that role. "How are things with your dad? I still feel bad about that night at the TCC. I'm really sorry I reacted that way." Now that Jack had long since cooled off, he knew that he'd been stewing over the way Winston had treated him for years. He'd let that boil over that night, and it wasn't fair to Lexi.

"To be honest, they're strained. I'm mad at him for the way he treated you, Jack, and he knows that. But he's so stubborn that he won't admit that he was wrong. He might never admit it."

"I bear at least some of the responsibility for what happened that night. I could've kept my cool."

Lexi shook her head and looked at him with determination blazing in her eyes. "No. He started it. As far as I'm concerned, the blame all lies with him."

That didn't sit well with Jack—if he could take some of the heat for the situation, it would lessen the tension. Hopefully he could find a way to have a chat with Winston and smooth things out. "All I'm saying is that there are two sides to every story, and I'm not afraid to own up to my part in this one."

"I appreciate that. Seriously." Lexi reached over and traced her finger up and down his forearm. "You know, Jack, I have to say thank you for bringing me here. I think this was exactly what I needed. It's been fun and relaxing, and we get along so well."

"You're most welcome. I couldn't agree more about all of that. Especially the last part."

Her face lit up with a smile. "It's funny, isn't it?"

"How so?"

She shrugged and looked out over the water. "We're very different people. We come from such different backgrounds. And yet we naturally get along."

"People don't have to be the same to be compatible."

"I know. I'm just glad that something for once is easy. That I don't have to try to be something I'm not around you."

Jack was doing his best to take her words in the spirit in which he believed they were intended. "You never have to pretend around me, Lexi. In fact, I'd rather see the unvarnished version of you."

She turned back to him and smiled sweetly. "And that's what's so awesome about you, Jack. As a woman who just spent fifteen years with a man who expected perfection, it's a refreshing change of pace."

Jack decided he would leave it at that. He wasn't going to get caught up in semantics or dig for more. Lexi was happy right now. She liked that the two of them together, at least on Appaloosa Island, was a simple proposition. He could be content with that. For the time being.

Lexi got up out of her chair and reached for his empty plate. "I'll clean up the kitchen and then we can go upstairs?"

"Sounds perfect."

Once the dishes were loaded into the dishwasher, they headed upstairs. Jack decided to hop in the shower to wash off any residual saltwater from their swim. When he was done, he dried himself off and walked into the bedroom with the towel wrapped around his waist, but he didn't get far. There on the bed was Lexi, leaning against the headboard, wearing a sexy black lace negligee that accentuated every enticing part of her. It was cut low in the front, drawing attention to her luscious breasts, and impossibly short, showing off her beautiful legs. Her hair tumbled across her shoulders, and the clever grin on her face told Jack everything he needed to know.

His body responded immediately, every muscle drawing tight with the need for her. But as he cast aside the towel and set a knee on the bed to get closer to her, he knew this was about to be way more than sex. He was falling for Lexi. And there wasn't a damn thing he could do about it.

Eight

Jack and Lexi couldn't bear to leave Appaloosa on Sunday, so they said their goodbyes before dawn on Monday morning, in the parking lot of the airstrip. "This weekend was amazing." Lexi wanted to say more, to let him know exactly how much it had meant to her, but she also didn't want to lay it on too thick. She knew her own tendencies too well…that she was apt to go overboard. *Slow and steady*, she reminded herself. *You and Jack have plenty of time.*

"It was the most fun I've had in a really long time," Jack said. "I feel bad dropping you off so early. The sun just came up. That doesn't seem quite right."

"I don't mind at all. You know, it'll probably be good for me to get into the office early this morning. Before my dad arrives."

Jack nodded. "Speaking of work, I need to get home,

change, pack and then head back to the island. We have a big week ahead of us."

Lexi was going to be so glad when the festival construction was over and she and Jack would have fewer obstacles to spending time together. "I'll let you go." The bittersweet tone of her voice said it all—she didn't want to do that. Despite her trepidation about getting involved with a man, there was one fact she couldn't deny. This weekend had not been enough.

Jack leaned down and pressed his forehead against hers. "I don't want to go, if that makes you feel any better."

Lexi couldn't help but smile. "It does make me feel better. A lot better." She raised her lips to his. Even now, when they'd kissed millions of times, he still managed to make it incredibly exciting. "I'll see you on Saturday, right? Angie's birthday at your house?"

"Yes. Absolutely. Remember your bathing suit. We'll be in the pool. I like the one you wore on the island."

"At your sister's birthday party? I'm thinking I'll go with something a little more conservative." She kissed him again.

"Party pooper."

"You'll get to see the black bikini again. But it'll be a time when it's only the two of us." Lexi realized that she and Jack were officially making plans—lots of them. Part of that thrilled her, but it also made fertile ground for the seed of doubt in her head, the one that worried things were going too fast.

"That sounds wonderful."

Jack kissed her one last time and then Lexi climbed into her car, stopping to wave goodbye to him when she pulled out of her parking space. As she drove off, she realized that she felt like she was walking on air. She knew this feeling…she'd felt it with Roger once and with Brett twice. Infatuation. Preoccupation. The start of the feelings that sometimes led to love. But she couldn't afford to be starry-eyed about it this time around.

Lexi strolled into the Alderidge Bank office by eight o'clock, arriving before most of the executive staff, including her dad. She loved being at work before everyone else. It gave her a sense of autonomy she rarely enjoyed when her father's presence was impossible to ignore.

It was too early to call most people, but she fired off several emails—one to Lila with the Chamber of Commerce to see if Lexi could get the first jump on any upcoming events the town might be holding. Another message went to the real estate agent Bianca suggested. She even sent along some links to a few houses she was interested in—homes that were closer to her sister, but on the opposite end of town from Pine Valley. Her last message went to Mandee Meriweather from the local gossip TV show *Royal Tonight!* It wasn't like Lexi to encourage tabloid journalism, but she did want to talk about the bank's involvement in Soiree on the Bay. She was serious about positioning the bank as hip and accessible, rather than the ultraexclusive image her father had cultivated.

What Lexi hadn't counted on was getting a phone call from Mandee less than five minutes after she sent the email.

"Lexi Alderidge. I am so excited you contacted me. I'd love to do an interview with you." There was something about Mandee's tone that sent a shiver up Lexi's spine. The reporter was known to be a bit of a shark, and from her tone she smelled blood in the water.

Still, Lexi felt as though she had to play along. "Oh, great. We can talk about the bank's involvement in Soiree on the Bay. Maybe get one of the people from the festival advisory board to join me."

"We can talk about that, but what I *really* want to hear about is your relationship with Jack Bowden. There's quite a buzz around town."

"There is?" If that was the case, Lexi was oblivious to it, but she'd spent very little time running around town, and of course, she and Jack had just disappeared for nearly three whole days.

"Lexi, can I record this? Then I can add our conversation to tonight's show."

"I'd really prefer it if you didn't. I'd rather talk about the festival."

"Soiree on the Bay will be a hot topic of conversation when it happens, but until then, I think people want to hear your story, Lexi. It doesn't have to be a negative thing. People want to hear about you moving on after your divorce, and that whole messy situation with Brett Harston leaving you at the altar." Mandee cleared her throat. "And then there's the latest story about your ex-husband getting engaged."

Lexi's stomach lurched. Had she opened Pandora's box by contacting Mandee? It sure felt like it. She had to protect herself, but more than anything, she felt she needed to shield Jack from this, as well. "Jack and I are friends. That's all I'm going to say about that. Thank you for the offer of an interview, but I'll have to pass for now. Let me know when you want to talk about Soiree on the Bay."

"That's disappointing, Lexi."

"Sorry. I don't want to talk about my personal life right now."

"Call me if you change your mind. And in the meantime, have fun with Jack. He's a hottie. I know fifty women who would *love* to be with him."

Lexi knew she was lucky to have caught Jack's eye. However, she didn't enjoy the reminder. "Bye, Mandee."

"See you around, Lexi."

"I hope not," Lexi muttered to herself after she'd ended the call. She looked out the window of her office, wondering what Jack was doing, if he was out on Appaloosa Island by now. Their weekend together still fresh in her mind, she couldn't help but wish she was back there with him. Having that respite from everyday life had been amazing. And the call with Mandee was a reminder of how nice it was to get away.

A knock came at her office door, followed quickly by her father opening it and strolling inside. "Good morning, Alexis."

Lexi got up from her desk to greet her father. "Good morning. Also, you should wait until someone says, 'come in' before you walk into their office."

"I own the bank, Lexi. I own that door. And that desk. In fact, I own everything you see."

Lexi fought her inclination to roll her eyes. "I realize that, Dad. But it's still the polite thing to do." She returned to her chair and took a seat. "Do you need something from me?"

"I was disappointed to see you were gone all weekend and didn't think to tell us that you wouldn't be home. Your mother and I were worried sick. We called Bianca. She told us where you went."

Lexi wished her sister was a little less open with their parents. She could've covered for Lexi and said that she'd gone to a spa for the weekend or something less controversial than spending several days with a man her father didn't seem to like. "I'm sorry, but I'm thirty-eight years old. I didn't think I needed to report to you."

"While you're staying on the family compound, I'd appreciate the courtesy of an update. It's only natural that we would want to know where you are and that you're safe."

He wasn't wrong, but this was certainly cause for ramping up the timeline on moving out. "I'm sorry, Dad. It won't happen again. Plus, you won't have to deal with it for too much longer. I've reached out to a real estate agent. I'm hoping she can show me a few houses this week."

"There's no reason to rush. You're welcome to stay in the guesthouse as long as you want."

"I appreciate that. I do. But I need my independence. Do you realize I've never lived in my own place? I went from living at home, to a dormitory, to Roger, and then back home. I need a house of my own."

Her father nodded and stuffed his hands into his pants pockets. Lexi always worried when her dad got quiet. It usually meant he was mad, or at the very least unhappy. "Are you going to admit to me that you spent the weekend with Jack Bowden?"

Here we go. Apparently, they were about to have this discussion. "I don't have to admit anything. I'm not embarrassed. Yes, Jack and I went away. He's working incredibly hard on the Soiree on the Bay project and only has time on the weekends."

"Is it serious?"

Lexi shook her head adamantly, even when she wasn't certain her response warranted that much of a definitive slant. "It's not."

"Why do I feel like you're just telling me what I want to hear?"

Because I am? Because I don't know what else to say. Even I don't know what's going on between me and Jack. "It's the truth. I thought you'd be happy to hear those two things match up."

"I don't want you getting in too deep, Lexi. A guy like Jack is okay for dating. But you know, when the time comes, you'll want to set your sights a little higher."

Lexi knew very well that her father had some pig-headed ideas lodged deep inside him. But she was still surprised when she heard those things come out. She'd listened to this speech as it pertained to Brett many times. And she wasn't going to make the mistake of nodding her head like a good daughter and letting him get away with this close-mindedness again. "Dad. You don't know Jack. I can assure you that he's of the highest character. He treats me better than any man has ever treated me, and that includes my husband." It was the truth. Jack regarded her like she was a queen. And when they were together, she never doubted that she was his sole focus. "And honestly, you should be thanking Jack because he saved me from some epic embarrassment on Friday night. We were going to a charity event in Houston and Roger was going to be there. With his new fiancée. Jack changed our plans, even though he was supposed to get an award."

Her dad cast a dubious look her way. "My guess is that he had other objectives."

"Dad. Listen to yourself. Jack's instinct was to protect me. If anyone should appreciate that, it's you."

"I'll decide what's worth appreciating."

Lexi decided this was going nowhere. She got up from her desk, walked past her dad and waited at the door, hoping he'd take the hint that he was cordially invited to leave. "If you don't mind, I should get to work. I'm expecting a call from Lila with the Chamber of Commerce. There's an arts fair this fall I think we should sponsor."

"Arts fair? I'm not sure that attracts the sort of people who might want to bank with us."

As much as Lexi was tired of this conversation, this was the perfect illustration of his troublesome attitudes. "And that's the problem. When a man like Jack Bowden, who is hardworking, honest and owns a solid business, walks away from our bank feeling as though he isn't welcome, that spells trouble for our business. We need to be welcoming, not sitting in an ivory tower."

Her dad opened his mouth to respond, but just as fast, he closed it.

"Dad. Whatever it is you have to say to me, come out with it. I'm tired of tiptoeing around these things. I know you feel like I'm trying to change everything, but I only want you to open your eyes. I love you, and I don't want to see your life's work go down the drain. But I think it will if you don't take the time to consider that the old way of working was never a very good way."

He sighed and wandered over to the window. "Do you ever feel old, Lexi?" He turned back to her. "Because I do. And every time we have this conversation, I feel a little bit more so. I've been in charge of things for so long that it's hard to let go. And I can't help it. I feel better when I'm in charge of things."

"You're still in charge, Dad. I'm just steering you in a slightly different direction. One that I think will seal your legacy and the future of the bank. That's all I want."

He smiled thinly. "Do you know what I want?"

"I don't."

"For you and me to be able to work together, happily."

"Okay. That's going to require some flexibility on your part."

"I'm beginning to see that." He strolled back to the door. "And I will try. I will."

Lexi wasn't sure she should broach the other subject looming overhead, but now seemed as good a time as any. "I would feel better if you and Jack could make another run at getting to know each other."

"I thought you said it wasn't serious."

"It isn't," she admitted. "But I like him a lot, and I'd like to date him. I'd like my dad to know and appreciate a man I'm involved with."

"Since when does my opinion matter on the subject of your love life?"

Lexi laughed. She couldn't help it. That was the only obvious reaction to his absurd question. "Since forever.

I don't feel like you ever approve of my choices. And I'm tired of feeling like that."

"The divorce wasn't your choice."

"But you blame me for it, don't you?"

He frowned and marched right up to her, gently caressing her shoulder. "Never, Lexi. Roger hurt you. I would never blame you for that."

"Seriously?"

"Seriously. I only want you to be happy. Roger made you unhappy, and that makes him the wrong person for you. That is the extent of my opinion on the matter." He let go of his grip on her and strode back to the door. "As for Jack, let's play it by ear."

It was late on Monday night when Jack arrived back at the Appaloosa house to grab a few hours of sleep. Just like when he and Lexi had done when they'd first arrived Friday, Jack practically stumbled inside. He sat on the stairs in the foyer and untied his work boots, casting them aside. He was exhausted. Dead on his feet. It was past ten o'clock, and if he didn't get to bed soon, that exhaustion was only going to get worse tomorrow.

He trudged up the stairs and down the hall to his bedroom, immediately confronted by the memory of his weekend with Lexi. They'd made love in nearly every corner of this room. It used to be that he would go to the window and look out at the water, but now he was struck by the mental image of the first time he saw Lexi naked, her luscious body reflected in the glass and lit by the soft glow of the moon. And then there was the bed, where time and place had meant virtually nothing because they were so wrapped up in each other. Even this room smelled like her, and that made the rest of the workweek staring him down that much more depressing. He wasn't sure he could make it without seeing her. And that was a worry in its own right. He wasn't supposed to get in so deep with Lexi.

Damn. What kind of spell was this woman casting over him?

To wash away his day, he walked into the bath and turned on the shower, then shucked his dirty work clothes and stepped inside. As the warm spray hit his back and shoulders, the temperature in the room began to rise. Jack closed his eyes and made a conscious decision to relax, but that made the visions of Lexi that much more real, especially in the shower, where everything was hot. And wet. As he lathered himself up, he couldn't stop thinking about her, about kissing her, touching her and being inside her. His entire body went tight at the thought, then with a rush, the blood in his body seemed to head straight for his groin.

He opened his eyes and looked down, confronted with his own arousal. Logic said he could easily satisfy this urge on his own, but the truth was that the mere thought of Lexi made his chest ache. Rinsing, he wondered if she would be up for a late-night phone call. *All I can do is try*, he thought as he turned off the shower.

He grabbed a towel and dried off his chest and shoulders, then stretched out on the bed and called Lexi.

"Hello?" she answered, her voice light and bubbly.

"Hello, beautiful." He nearly growled out his response. One word from her and his whole body felt like it was going to explode.

"I'm surprised you called. I figured you would be too busy. Or sleeping. I didn't want to bother you."

Jack stared up at the ceiling, but in his mind, all he saw was Lexi—her gorgeous red hair and bright green eyes. "You couldn't bother me if you tried. What are you doing?"

"Just getting ready for bed. I was going to read for a bit then catch up on sleep. Somebody kept me up all weekend."

Jack laughed and closed his eyes, luxuriating in Lexi's sweet, sultry voice. Indeed, they hadn't slept much over the course of the weekend, but rest was the last thing he cared about right now. "Have you already dressed for bed?"

"That's sort of a weird question."

"You wouldn't say that if you knew what state I'm in right now."

"And what would that be?"

Jack was having a hard time putting this into words. How he wished she was here, in some mind-blowing lingerie, and he could take off every enticing stitch of it and make love to her. "On the bed. No clothes. And hard."

"Oh. I see…"

Lexi wasn't giving him much to work with here, and he couldn't help but feel like he was standing on a precipice, staring down his own future. If he leaped, would she follow? Or would she say it was too much? *Life is too short to second-guess yourself, Jack.* "I swear, Lexi. One step into this bedroom and all I could do was think about you and how badly I want you. How amazing our weekend was. And how much I can't wait to do it again."

"That's so sweet, Jack. Truly."

It still felt like she was missing the point. He wanted to be talking to the Lexi who was bold and not shy. He wanted her to show him just how uninhibited he knew she could be. "I'm not trying to be sweet, Lexi. I'm trying to seduce you. I want you to undress and tell me what you're doing. Tell me what you're feeling."

Several moments of quiet played out on the other end of the line. The wait was excruciating. "Of course I will. Anything you want."

"Just tell me everything, okay?" Jack put his phone on speaker and laid it next to him on the bed.

"Got it. Yes. Hold on." In the background, there was the sound of drawers or doors opening and closing. "Okay. I took off my dress. I'm going to climb up on my bed now."

"Does that mean you're naked?"

"No. Of course not. I still have my bra and panties on. I know you like lingerie."

Jack swallowed back a groan, and slid his hand down his stomach, but he didn't touch himself yet. He wanted to savor this. "Tell me more. The color. What they feel like."

"They're dark purple. Like a plum in the middle of summer. They're silky soft, but they have lace, too. At the edges."

Jack saw the whole scene in his mind's eye. "I can imagine," he said gruffly. "I'm sure you look absolutely ravishing. I can't wait until I can touch you again. Until I can taste your skin again."

Lexi hummed her approval over the phone. "I can't wait either, Jack. You're making me want you so bad right now."

"How bad?"

She nearly made him rocket into space when she told him how just hearing his voice made her nipples hard. How she wished he could touch every inch of her. He wrapped his hand around himself, but it was Lexi's velvety fingers he felt against his skin. So warm. So perfect. Exactly what he wanted.

The pressure built as she narrated taking off her panties, when she told him that she was touching herself but imagining it was him. Even with her heavenly scent all over the pillows, the experience wasn't the real thing, but for right now, it was as close as he was going to get. The tension in his hips was so tight he felt like he might snap in half. He told her how he imagined her kisses, and she moaned into the phone, making it clear that she was near her own climax. Jack silently begged for release and his body answered, the pleasure roaring through his body like a rockslide down a mountain face. Thankfully, Lexi followed almost right after him. He sank into the mattress, breathless.

"Lexi? Are you there?"

She giggled. "I am. I'm sure you're sick of me saying this, but you are full of surprises, Jack. When you called tonight, I was not expecting *that*."

Jack's chest, neck and face flushed with heat. Even after their wickedly hot phone call, he wanted more. "It's all you, Lexi. Just thinking about you and hearing your voice gets me all worked up."

Nine

Saturday afternoon, on her way to Jack's house for his sister's birthday party, Lexi was unbelievably nervous. Her outfit wasn't making things any better. She shifted in the driver's seat, tugging at the dress that she'd agonized over. Was it too dressy? Too casual? Would his sister hate her? She wasn't sure how her brain made that particular leap, but it kept doing it.

With only ten minutes until she'd arrive at Jack's house, Lexi decided to make a desperate call to Bianca. She needed a cheerleader right now.

"Hey, you," her sister answered.

"Help me calm down."

"I'm currently quizzing Maisie for her history test, so it'll have to be fast."

As if Lexi needed more pressure. "I'm on my way to Jack's. He's hosting a birthday party for his younger sister. His best friend Rich will be there, too."

"And you're worried they aren't going to like you?"

Thank goodness Bianca understood her so well. "Oh, my God, yes."

"This is not good."

"What? You're supposed to be reassuring me right now that everything is going to be okay. And hurry up. According to the GPS, I'm going to be there in five minutes."

"I meant it's not good that you're worried. If this wasn't serious, we wouldn't be having this conversation. And since you decided to call me, I have no other choice than to assume that you're getting in deep with Jack."

Lexi's navigation system chimed in. *In five hundred feet, turn left. Destination will be on your right.*

"I don't know how many times I have to tell you this. It's not serious. We're having fun."

"Does the way you feel right now seem like fun? Because it sure doesn't sound like it."

Lexi made the turn onto the private drive leading up to Jack's house. Up ahead, at the top of the hill, sat a beautiful sprawling home, charcoal gray with exposed dark wood beams and creamy white trim, surrounded by green rolling vistas as far as the eye could see. Of course, Jack would have a showstopper of a home— she wasn't sure why she'd expected anything less. "I don't know what I'm doing, to be honest. And I have zero time to figure it out because I'm basically here."

"Fine. Then let me give you some quick advice. Have a glass of wine. Don't bring up anything too serious. And more than anything, be yourself. Either they'll like you or they won't. That's not up to you to decide."

If only it was so simple. Lexi pulled up and parked in an open space off to the side of the garage. There were two other cars parked outside—a big black pickup truck and a silver mini SUV. Luckily, she was apparently one of the first to arrive. It would be easier if she could ease into this rather than walk into a house full of strangers. "Okay."

"You don't sound convinced."

"I'm not. But I'll do my best."

"If this isn't serious, don't take it seriously," Bianca said. "I think that's the best way to go."

Lexi thanked her then hung up, her stomach wobbling with unease. She grabbed her bag and the gift she'd bought for Angie and climbed out of the car just as Jack stepped out the front door onto his wraparound front porch. That one glimpse of him and his broad smile made all the worry evaporate. She hadn't seen him since early Monday morning at the airstrip, and although they'd talked on the phone every night all week, it didn't come close to matching the sight of him in person. She nearly ran to him, even in heels, flinging her arms around him, or as close as she could get considering their size difference. For Jack's part, he threaded his arms under Lexi's and her feet left the ground when he lifted her for a kiss.

"It's so good to see you," he said.

"Nice to see you, too," Lexi murmured.

From somewhere behind him, someone cleared their throat.

Jack whipped around. "Oh, Angie. I'd like you to meet Lexi. Lexi, this is Angie."

Jack's sister stepped forward, tall like he was, but willowy. Her hair was a shade darker brown than

Jack's, and she had a natural beauty accentuated by her strong features, wide sable eyes and full lips. She was dressed in a flowing red sundress and flat sandals. "Finally, I meet the famous Lexi. Thank you for coming." She sized her up, then offered a hug.

Lexi was relieved, figuring no one hugs a person they think they might ultimately hate, and she eagerly accepted the embrace. "I'm glad we finally get to meet. Happy birthday." She handed over the gift, again feeling uncertain.

"Thank you. I'll open this later. With the rest of the presents."

A very tall man Lexi didn't know emerged through the front door. "I've been looking for you guys."

"Rich, come meet Lexi," Jack said, waving him over.

So, this was Rich, Jack's best friend. He towered over Lexi, just like Jack, nearly as muscle-bound and broad-shouldered. He offered his hand. "I've heard a lot about you."

She hoped that was a good thing. "It's great to finally put a face with the name."

Several more cars pulled up into the driveway. "I should go greet my guests."

Angie grabbed Lexi's hand. "Go. Lexi and I will get to know each other."

"It's your birthday," Jack said. "Don't you think you should come with me?"

"They're your friends, Jack. Remember, I'm the new girl in town. I can meet them later. This might be the only chance Lexi and I get to talk about you."

Jack slid his sister a skeptical look and put on his sunglasses. "Be nice."

"I always am."

Lexi followed Angie inside, into a soaring open foyer. Off to one side was a formal dining room, and on the other side there seemed to be a study. Straight ahead was a wide corridor, leading them to the back of the house. At the end of the hall, the space opened up into a great room with a gourmet kitchen to the right, with pale gray cabinetry, white marble countertops and a beautiful glass mosaic backsplash in a muted color scheme. On the left was a living room with the largest sectional sofa and entertainment center Lexi had ever seen. Everything about this house was like Jack—the furniture was big, the ceilings were tall, but the casual elegance of the decor put a person at ease right away.

"Come on and get a load of the pool." Angie led the way to the windows, which overlooked an expansive patio area and large pool with waterfalls, natural clusters of stone, and even a waterslide. It was a true oasis, but it was also a place to play and have fun.

Lexi didn't pin any of Jack's worth on his financial status, but there was still a part of her that wanted her dad to see all of this. It might change his mind. "It's beautiful," she said to Angie.

The other woman nodded. "My brother put his heart and soul into this house. But he does that with everything."

"You two are close, aren't you? You'd have to be to move to a new town and start over, just so you could be in the same place."

Angie leaned against the wood frame between windows. "It was a little more than that. Not sure if Jack told you, but I just went through a divorce. I feel a little pathetic since I'm only twenty-nine. I figured I'd at least get to thirty before my life started falling apart."

Lexi's heart went out to Jack's sister. She understood everything Angie was saying. "I was married for fifteen years before my husband dumped me. That's a lot of time, and it's hard not to feel like I wasted it by being with the wrong person."

"Did you have kids?" Angie asked.

Lexi shook her head. "No."

"Me neither."

"I wanted them, but my husband didn't, and I never forced the issue. I know people say that it's better to have not had children when you go through a divorce, but it's still a big regret of mine. I wish I had spoken up for what I wanted."

Angie looked back in the direction of the front door. Jack was walking in with a group of five or six people. She returned her attention to Lexi. "The flip side of that is you tell him exactly what you want and it turns into a big fight. That was the case for me."

Lexi hadn't considered that possibility. She'd had several months to reflect back on her marriage to Roger, and she'd worried many times that she'd allowed herself to be a doormat. "I guess we've both been through the wringer."

Angie drew a deep breath through her nose. "Definitely. The question is where do we go from here? I don't know about you, but I'm not ready to tie myself to another guy."

Lexi truly felt put on the spot, but she had to be honest. "I'm not ready either, but I do like your brother a lot. We have so much fun together."

"I don't know that it's possible to not have fun with my brother."

From across the room, a woman Lexi didn't know was laughing and grabbing Jack's biceps. She did her best to tamp down her jealousy, but it was next to impossible.

"Case in point," Angie said, with a nod toward the woman. "The ladies find him endlessly entertaining."

Lexi couldn't help think about the comment Mandee Meriweather had made about how she knew fifty women who would love to date him. Jack hadn't talked at all about his romantic past, other than to share the story of his own failed engagement. "You've probably seen him with lots of different women."

Angie twisted her lips into a bundle, as if she was considering how much to say. "I don't want to lie to you."

"It's okay. I suspected as much."

"Let's just say he hasn't taken anyone seriously since his fiancée dumped him," Angie confided.

"He told me about that. One of those odd things we have in common."

"If it makes you feel any better at all, I haven't seen him be so over the moon with a girlfriend in a long time."

"I don't know that I've earned the girlfriend designation," Lexi said. "Jack definitely left that out when he introduced me to you and Rich."

Angie frowned. "Really? I hadn't noticed."

Lexi had, right away. But she didn't want to make a big deal about it, especially since the other woman would likely bring it up with Jack. "It's nothing. And believe me, I'm not pushing for the label. I'd rather just be Lexi, and he can be Jack. That's enough."

But was that true? *Was* it enough? Lexi glanced over at Jack and caught his eye, his lips turning up in a smile before he returned his attention to the conversation he was having. She couldn't ignore the way she was happier when she was around him, the way he made everything better and brighter. It was like there was a big flashing sign in her face, telling her to not mess this up. She only wished the timing was different, that she'd made more headway with being her own person and standing on her own two feet before Jack came along.

"Come on," Angie said. "We should probably go join the rest of the party."

"Lead the way."

Although playing the role of host had been a big job, tackling everything from ordering Angie a cake to organizing the guest list, Jack still found it a welcome respite to have a weekend away from the Soiree on the Bay construction. He'd need to be back on site first thing Monday morning for the final push on the project. It exhausted him to think about it, so he didn't, instead having a few margaritas and enjoying several hours out by the pool with Lexi, Angie, and his other guests. Now that the festivities were winding down and only a few people remained, it would've been easy to start worrying about work again. Luckily, he had Lexi to distract him.

"You throw quite a party," she said. It was just the two of them sitting under an umbrella in lounge chairs side by side.

Jack was enjoying the spectacular view of her in a

bikini. This one was also black but a bit more modest than the other one. It didn't matter too much to him. He was content looking at her curves and the stretches of her bare skin. "I hope you've enjoyed yourself. I know it's been a lot. You've met a ton of people you didn't know." He would never say a word to Lexi, but he had worried about whether she would fit in at this party. Not only did she have to navigate conversation with his sister, which could be tricky in its own right, she had to make small talk with strangers, many of whom were tied to Bowden Construction. That was not Lexi's world. Just like banking was not his.

"You make everything fun." Lexi leaned over for a quick kiss. "Your sister and I actually chatted about that."

Jack had been wondering how he was going to find out what those two had talked about. He was glad Lexi had brought up the subject herself. "You care to share any other parts of your conversation?"

"It might sound horrible, but we sort of bonded over our divorces. It was nice to confide in someone else who has gone through it."

Jack was glad they'd found common ground. He knew that Angie could put up roadblocks and she would always be protective of Jack, just like he was protective of her. "That makes sense. You've both been through a hard time. I'm glad you were able to talk to her about it. You might have some helpful perspective for her. I think Angie still feels like her life has ended. I'm trying to remind her that she has lots of time to build a life."

Jack felt like that was solid advice, but he didn't necessarily think it pertained to him. He didn't have as much runway ahead of him as his sister. At thirty-nine, with his career well established, Jack was starting to think he should get serious. Funnily enough, Lexi was the person who'd made him doubt the very notion of keeping things casual when he'd been perfectly content with it for a long time. He understood why she wanted it that way—her personal history demanded it. But he also knew the other reason he'd gone along with it from the start. He'd worried they wouldn't get along. However, as it turned out, quite the opposite was true.

Angie wandered over. "I don't want to sound completely lame, but I think I'm going to head home. I'm beat."

"Are you okay to drive?" Jack asked.

"Rich is going to drive me. He hasn't had anything to drink. I'll come back tomorrow to get my car."

Jack got up from his seat to give his sister a hug. "I hope you had fun."

"I did, Jack. It was awesome." She patted him on the shoulder, then turned to Lexi. "It was great to meet you. Thank you for the bracelet. I love it." Angie held up her arm, showing off the very thoughtful gift Lexi had bought.

"Oh, good. I'm really glad you like it. It was nice to meet you, too," she said.

Angie pulled Jack aside. "Actually, can I steal a minute? Inside?"

"Yeah. Of course." He turned to Lexi. "I'm going to help Angie grab her stuff."

The pair made their way inside to the living room, where she'd opened her presents. They both sat on the couch, Angie loading up a gift bag with her birthday haul, while Jack gathered spent wrapping paper bound for the recycling.

"I want you to know that I like her. A lot. I thought she was going to be a bubbleheaded rich girl, but she's not that at all. She's very thoughtful and down to earth."

Jack was fairly certain that was the case, but he was still relieved to hear it from his sister. "I'm really happy to hear that. Thank you."

"But there's one thing you need to realize."

Here we go. "Yeah. Of course. Tell me."

"Knowing the way I feel right now, she's still really hurting from her divorce. There will be some days when she's over the moon with you and others when she's not sure. I'm learning that it's part of the process. Your whole life gets shaken up, and it makes you question everything."

Jack nodded, solemnly, taking in the things his sister had said. "Keep taking it slow."

"Exactly."

"Okay. I appreciate you telling me that."

Angie got up from the couch and picked up her gift bag. "One more thing. She noticed that you didn't introduce you as her girlfriend. I think that's probably a conversation you should have."

"Was she upset? And how is that supposed to be part of taking it slow?" Jack felt more than a little overwhelmed by all of this.

Angie placed her hand on his forearm and shook her head. "She wasn't upset. In fact, she said she'd prefer that you be Jack and she'll be Lexi. So, I think you're good. But I also think you should probably talk about it."

"Got it." One thing Jack knew for sure was that Lexi

had made serious inroads in his world today. If their romance was going to progress, he was going to have to find a way to fold himself into hers. That meant at some point he'd have to find common ground with Lexi's dad.

Angie kissed Jack on the cheek. "Thanks again for everything today. Now go spend some time with Lexi and I'll talk to you on Monday."

Jack watched as Angie found Rich in the kitchen and they turned down the central hall to leave. When Jack got back out to the pool, the final guests were heading out. "Thanks for coming."

"Thank you for a great day," they replied.

Jack joined Lexi under the umbrella again, sitting rather than reclining, and reached for her hand. A few minutes later, they were alone. That moment of recognition hit him every time this was the case—that he wanted her. Needed her. "Will you stay the night?" He stroked her fingers softly, but even that innocent touch had his body on high alert.

"I don't know if I can sleep over. Bianca dragged me to yoga this morning, so I made her promise me that she'd come over and help me go through the boxes in my garage. The only time she can get away from the kids is at 8:00 a.m."

"Ouch."

"I know. Right? Anyway, I want this move to a new house, once I find a place, to be a clean slate. There are a lot of memories of Houston and my marriage in those boxes. I think I'll feel better if I just get rid of all of it."

Jack was happy to hear that. Lexi was taking strides forward, and he saw that as an essential part of their future. "I'm happy to haul stuff away if you need it. I sure as heck have a big enough truck."

"That would be great. Can you come by tomorrow? Late afternoon or tomorrow night?"

"Sure thing." Jack decided then and there that if Winston was on the family compound tomorrow, he would talk to him. It wouldn't be a showdown, but rather he would try to patch things up.

"What else do you have going on tomorrow?"

"It's my only day off, so I'm definitely sleeping in. It'll be my last chance to catch up on some z's before I head back to Appaloosa."

Lexi smiled at him wistfully. "I can't wait until I can go back there."

"I'd suggest next weekend, but since we're supposed to finish up this week, I think I'm going to want a break from the island for a while."

"Perfectly understandable."

Jack lifted her hand to his lips. "But I promise we'll go back for another sexy escape."

Lexi climbed off her chair and stepped over to him. The sun was setting behind her, casting her beautiful body in a soft glow. "I think we can have our own sexy escape right here. It's early. I can stay for at least a few hours."

"That is music to my ears."

Ten

Jack was on his way to Lexi's late Sunday afternoon when his phone rang. It was Angie. He pressed the button on his in-dash display to answer the call.

"Hey. What's up?" he asked.

"I'm catching up on bookkeeping. The last check we got from the Soiree on the Bay festival bounced."

Jack was confounded. That had never happened before. "Seriously?"

"Yes. And it was presented at the bank twice."

"What was the amount?"

"Two-fifty."

Jack knew that his sister meant hundreds of thousands. A quarter of a million bucks. Still, he wasn't worried. Rusty Edmond would make it right. "Okay. I'll give Rusty a call."

"You on your way to Lexi's?"

Jack pulled up to the Pine Valley security gate and slowed down, but the guard waved him right through. Apparently, he'd been here quite a lot. "I am. Why are you asking with that tone?"

"No reason. Just thinking about how taking things slow means not seeing someone all the time."

A grumble left his throat. "It's our last chance to see each other before I have to finish up on Appaloosa. And I'm helping her get rid of some boxes. It's not exactly a romantic visit."

"Something tells me you'll make it romantic."

"I'm not having this discussion with you." Jack really hated how much his sister was capable of making sense and driving him crazy at the same time. "I need to call Rusty, okay?"

"Sure thing. I love you, Jack. That's the only reason I'm saying any of this. I like Lexi and I'd like to keep it that way. If she breaks your heart, or vice versa, it'll be bad for everyone."

"I'll keep all of that in mind. Goodbye, Angie." Jack ended the call and dialed Rusty's number. He was almost to Lexi's house and wasn't sure how long this call would take, so he pulled up to the curb in front of the Alderidge estate.

"Jack. This is a surprise," Rusty said when he answered.

"I know. I'm sorry if this is out of the blue and I'm sorry if it's an odd time to call."

"What can I do for you?" he asked, cutting right to the chase.

"I'm calling because the last check we got from the festival board didn't clear the bank."

"That must be a mistake."

"We sent it through twice. Maybe an accounting mix-up?"

"I sure as hell hope not. I never want to hear about people not getting paid, especially someone who's working as hard as you are."

"What you would like me to do? It's a quarter of a million dollars."

"I'll cut you a check myself. I'll talk to Billy and get it straightened out on our end. I'll have a courier bring it to your office first thing tomorrow morning."

"Sounds great. Thank you, Rusty, for taking care of this for me."

"I trust you're going to be at the cocktail party to celebrate the completion of the construction?"

As if he needed more pressure on him, Rusty had scheduled a postconstruction event for Wednesday night. That meant Jack *had* to hit the deadline. "As long as we finish on time, I'll be there. I might show up in work boots, but hopefully you'll still let me in the door."

Rusty managed a quiet laugh. "Bring a date. Lexi Alderidge if that's still going on."

"I'll see what I can do."

"I look forward to construction wrapping up so I can put a drink in your hand on Wednesday night."

That was only a few days away, but it seemed like a lifetime. Jack had so much work to do before then. So many things to accomplish. "Thanks, Rusty. I'll talk to you soon."

Jack ended the call and pulled up to the Alderidge's personal gate and entered the code. The light flashed red at him, so he punched it in again. "Dammit," he muttered to himself, calling Lexi's cell. Before she had a chance to answer, the gate rolled open. Jack ended the call, looking for Lexi on the other side of the entrance. But when he drove into their driveway, he saw Winston Alderidge standing there.

Okay then. I guess we're doing this right now. He put the car in Park and climbed out. Lexi was running down the driveway from her house. Jack really wished she wouldn't interfere. He wanted to have this conversation with Winston one-on-one.

"Mr. Alderidge." He extended his hand. "I'm sorry you had to open the gate for me. I couldn't get the code to work."

"The visitor codes automatically change every two weeks." To his credit, Winston *did* shake Jack's hand. Still, it wasn't a warm greeting.

Lexi arrived, breathless, barefoot and wearing one of her many dresses. "I wasn't thinking. The codes changed over."

Jack smiled at her. "It's no problem. If it's okay, I'd like to speak to your dad for a few minutes."

Lexi looked back and forth between him and her dad. Surely she sensed the tension between them. All the more reason to excuse herself. "Okay. I'll be home whenever you want to come over. I'm just going through some boxes." She took a few more steps over to him, popped up on to her tiptoes and went to kiss his cheek, but Jack had to lean down to let her do it. He appreciated the sentiment, and he had to admit it made him happy that she was willing to do that in front of her father.

With that, Lexi walked back down the driveway.

"Would you like to come in?" Winston asked.

"Really?" Jack didn't want to sound so surprised, but he was. "I mean, yes. Thank you."

"For a minute. My daughter doesn't like to wait for anyone or anything, but I'd also rather not have this conversation in the driveway."

"Perfectly understandable." He trailed behind Winston, filled with trepidation, but also a tiny glimmer of hope. Surely the man wouldn't invite him in just to yell at him.

When they walked inside, it occurred to Jack that this was a glimpse into Lexi's life that he hadn't been privy to before. This was the original ivory tower his favorite princess had grown up in. It was pure luxury, of course, with an added edge of stuffiness that came as no surprise. There were formal settees in the marble-floored foyer and crystal chandeliers overhead. Winston led Jack down a long hallway lined with dark wallpaper and dozens of family portraits. He caught a glimpse of one of Lexi as a teenager and had to pause to look. She had a mouth full of metal.

Winston stopped and laughed when he saw the picture Jack was looking at. "She hated those braces. Couldn't wait for them to come off."

Jack was a bit shell-shocked. He hadn't known Winston was capable of expressing humor. "She's still cute." Jack dared to make direct eye contact with the older man, and it felt as though they had an entire conversation, acknowledging that Winston loved his daughter deeply and would protect her at any cost, and that Jack was her unwavering admirer who would not back down, even when faced with her dad's wrath.

"Indeed." Winston continued down the hall, and through a door at the very end.

Jack stepped into Winston's study. It practically looked like a museum dedicated to Alderidge family history in Royal. The walls were covered with framed awards and photos of the man with local dignitaries, the shelves lined with golf trophies. As he took survey of it all, he realized that perhaps the reason Winston was so stuck in Royal was because he'd been immersed in it for so long. That wasn't necessarily a bad thing. Jack had once felt that way about San Antonio and his circle of friends there. Hell, he'd dragged Rich and his sister here just so he could feel connected to someone and something. Although he didn't agree with snobbery, especially when it came to money, he might be understanding Winston a bit better.

"You play golf, Jack?" Winston asked.

"I've done it a few times, sir, but it's not really my forte. I enjoy other sports, though. I play a lot of one-on-one basketball with my best friend. Laps in the pool. Things like that."

"I see. Well, if you ever decide to try your hand at it, let me know. I'll gladly take you out."

Jack appreciated the offer, but he was skeptical of what was going on here. "Can I ask why the change of heart, sir? That moment we met at the TCC, you looked like you were ready to skin me alive, and all I'd done was dance with your daughter. I know for a fact that I wasn't the first man to do that, so I couldn't help but think that I was the *wrong* one."

Winston leaned back against the edge of his sizable mahogany desk and folded his arms over his chest. Jack couldn't help but notice that through the windows directly behind Lexi's, there was a perfect view of her cottage, especially the front door, where Jack had kissed her after their first date. That couldn't have helped his case that night at the TCC. "I like you, Jack."

"You'd better be sure about that, because if it's the truth, I'm going to hold you to it."

Winston quirked an eyebrow and nodded. "See? Right there. That's what I like. You're direct. You don't beat around the bush."

"I don't see the point."

"Neither do I." He cleared his throat then went on to say, "I wanted you to know that I went back and looked at the loan application you submitted all those years ago. The source of the rift between us."

"And?"

"In my defense, you hadn't been in business in Royal for very long."

"Seven plus years had been more than enough time to get myself established," Jack informed him. "I was turning down work at that time, which is why I needed the capital to expand."

"I understand. But there's something about Royal. It's a wonderful place to live, but it takes time to get in deep and gain people's trust. And this is where I get to the part where I admit to my mistake, which was that I didn't know you or your company at that point, and so I assumed you were a fly-by-night operation. I hadn't given the numbers a close enough look. Your projections were solid and I should have granted the loan. I apologize."

"If I can be frank, it was more than the rejection, sir. It was your tone. It sent a pretty clear message that I was not only not part of the inner circles of Royal, but that I might never be." Jack realized his retort had been bottled up for a long time.

Winston nodded. "I know. And I'm sorry for that, as well. Lexi and I have had many conversations about exactly that since she's come to work at the bank. You know, when you're the boss, and you've been doing your job for a long time, you don't always stop to think about the ways you present yourself." He hesitated for a moment, then confided, "Business is going great and you assume that everyone loves you and wants to work with you. But I've been learning from Lexi that I might catch a few more flies with honey than with vinegar."

Funny, but Angie had accused Jack of being grumpy in the office just the other day. "I understand. I'm glad Lexi has shown you a different way to do business."

"I was reluctant to step into the future because the history of our bank is one of our biggest selling points. People want a financial institution that's been around for a long time. But they also want one that's pleasant to work with. I need to remember that."

Jack felt the need to bring up the elephant in the room—Lexi. "I care about your daughter deeply." His voice cracked at the end of his sentence, emotion welling up inside him.

"I understand that. And I believe she cares about you, too."

"Does that mean things are square between us?" Jack asked.

"More or less. I mean, I am still her father, and I will fight you to the death if you dare to hurt her."

"Good to know."

The older man looked him square in the eye. "Tread lightly, Jack. The girl has been through the wringer."

So he'd been told. "I will, sir. I promise." Jack reached over to shake Winston's hand one more time.

"I'd better go. I'm sure Lexi is wondering what we're talking about."

"Oh, I guarantee she's dying to know."

Lexi was supposed to be going through the boxes she'd brought in from the garage, but she kept pulling back her living room curtains, trying to deduce what was going on in her dad's study. He and Jack were definitely in there. What were they talking about? Were they having another argument? Lexi really hoped not because she didn't want to have to do damage control. She'd said her piece to her dad. He needed to get with the program.

Maybe it's for the best, she thought to herself, although just as fast, she banished it from her brain. She didn't want to walk away from Jack. The problem was that she felt like circumstances were pushing them in that direction of serious—the weekend away, the pool party, the phone sex... Jack had opened up her whole world, and she wasn't ready for that to end. But every shared experience they had brought them closer to what Lexi was rightfully scared of—commitment.

Lexi took another peek outside, and Jack was headed up the sidewalk in front of her house. She let go of the curtain and allowed it to fall back into place, then rushed to the door. "What happened?"

Jack came to a dead stop and his killer smile crossed his lips. Every time he did that, her fears evaporated, even if it was only for a few seconds. She adored him. She wanted him. And against all odds, wanted things to work between them. "Were you worried?"

"Of course I was. Have you *met* me?" She stood back to let him in, then closed the door behind him.

"How could I not worry? I know my dad and I know you, and never the twain shall meet."

"Actually, we had a good conversation. He apologized."

Lexi felt like she might need to have her ears cleaned out. Was this a trick? "You're not serious. I've never heard him say he was sorry. About anything."

Jack ventured into her great room and took a seat at the end of one of the couches. He patted the empty spot next to him. "Come here, beautiful. I'll tell you everything."

Lexi eagerly took the invitation, settling in on the cushion and immediately leaning into Jack's firm, solid frame as he put his arm around her. "So it was good?"

"It wasn't perfect, but I think we understand each other. He said he was sorry about the loan, and he explained that he has a blind spot for the established Royal businesses and families. He actually admitted you've been a big part of convincing him that he needs to open his eyes to everything around him."

She still found it hard to believe what Jack was saying. "I feel like I'm drilling that into his head all day long. There is so much business available in Royal, and we could do such a better job being a part of the community. He's just so stuck in his ways."

"Or, as he sees it, he's loyal to the town where he's raised a family and lived his whole life," Jack said. "There's nothing wrong with remembering where you come from and the people who helped you get where you are today. That's important to me, too."

"Like Angie and Rich."

"Yes. Exactly."

It occurred to her that they'd each basically gotten

the stamp of approval from their respective loved ones. That left only Lexi's muddled brain as she tried to figure out of what she was truly ready for with Jack. "So, what else did he have to say?"

"He said I need to tread lightly when it comes to you. And that he'd hunt me down and kill me if I ever hurt you."

"You have nothing to worry about. I can't imagine you ever hurting me." Lexi feared it was the other way around. She didn't question Jack's feelings about her, even though neither of them had put it into words beyond saying that they liked each other and had a lot of fun together. But she was in zero rush to get to big important labels. She knew the way he made her feel—like she was cherished. That she mattered. That her thoughts and feelings were real and she was entitled to process them in her own time.

But she also wasn't stupid. She'd seen the way other women looked at him—at Sheen, at the TCC, and even at his own pool party. She also knew that once a woman got to know Jack the way Lexi knew him, she likely wouldn't ever let him go. Angie had said that he'd spent years not taking relationships seriously, all because he'd had his heart broken more than a decade ago. Didn't it reason that at some point, Jack would decide he wanted to settle down? He was almost forty. Would he wait around for her to get over her hang-ups, or would he grow impatient and want to move on?

"I'm glad you have confidence in me." Jack took her hand and they twined their fingers together. It was a bit comical the way his were so much bigger than hers, the way they almost threatened to swallow hers up, but however funny, it was also the perfect illustration of them as a pair. They were very different people, who somehow worked together.

"I knew from the moment I met you that you were a man of your word."

"That's not true. I was giving you a hard time and not being entirely truthful about who I was or what I was doing."

"Okay. That's fair." She playfully swatted his leg with her one free hand. "But that's also the day you came to my rescue. And I'm very grateful that you did. If you hadn't, we never would've gotten to know each other." Lexi was suddenly hit with a vision of what would've happened if Jack hadn't acted that day, or even worse, if she hadn't accepted his invitation. She would've missed out on so much—which added up to a lot more than hot nights and unbridled passion. There had been laughter, contentment and tenderness, too.

"One of the smartest things I ever did." He leaned over and kissed her temple. "I will give you all the time you need, Lexi. Your dad asked that of me, and I intend to do that. I'm happy with the way things are right now. But I also need you to know that you do mean something to me. This isn't just a fling for me."

Lexi's heart started to hammer. She'd just been thinking about how she didn't need words. "Yes. I'm happy with the way things are right now, too. I have a lot of changes ahead. Finding a house. Moving. I'm still figuring out my job. I like that we've kept things casual and fun."

Jack cleared his throat. "It's definitely been fun. That's for sure."

She wondered if she'd said the wrong thing, but decided her truth was always right. That was what Jack would want from her. "I hate to say this, but I should probably finish going through these last two boxes. You can relax and we can talk while I work."

"I thought I was here to be the muscle."

Lexi laughed, appreciating that the mood had been lightened a bit. She patted his thigh before getting to her feet, then reached down for his hand in an effort to pull him off the couch. "Fine, Muscle Man. I'll show you which boxes can go in the truck."

Jack feigned a scowl but rose out of his seat. Lexi walked across the room to the stack of boxes filled with things she wanted to get rid of. He came up behind her and placed his hands on her hips, leaning down and snuggling her neck with soft kisses.

"Jack. This doesn't feel like lifting boxes. This feels like something else."

He pressed against her backside. "How does *this* feel?"

She giggled, but it came out more like a moan. He didn't have to work very hard to make her want him. "It feels like you're wanting to go in the other room."

"Or here. I'm up for whatever you want." He brushed her hair to one side and kissed her neck while he gathered the hem of her dress in his hand then palmed the upper part of her bare thigh, his fingers dangerously close to her center.

A gasp left Lexi's lips as she rolled her head to one side to let him take full purchase of her skin. "I just want you, Jack. That's as much brain power as I can put into it right now."

Jack needed no further invitation. He took charge like he always did, scooping her up in his arms and carrying her off to her bedroom. "I've been in your dad's office. I know what a good view he has of your house. At least things are private back here."

"Smart man."

Jack set her feet on the floor then lifted her dress over her head and unhooked her bra. He sat on the edge of her bed and she stood between his legs. Their eyes met and held. Then he bent down, taking her nipple between his lips, sucking and rolling his tongue over the firm bud. All of Lexi's blood left her head, aiming straight at her center, which was now ablaze with desire for him. She removed his shirt, then he wriggled her panties past her hips.

Lexi climbed up on the bed, straddling his lap. He reclined back on the mattress while slipping his hand between her legs and caressing her most delicate spot. The rough denim of his jeans rubbed against the tender skin of her inner thighs, but she loved the contrast between the sensations. Like every other time he'd touched her, it felt impossibly good, but it was like he automatically knew now exactly what she liked. He paid attention. He...cared.

"We need to get you out of these jeans." Lexi shifted from his lap and rummaged through her bedside table drawer for a condom.

Jack stood and shucked his pants, then took the foil packet from her and rolled on the condom. Lexi was about to stretch out on the bed, but he surprised her and picked her up again. Pressing her back against the wall, he wrapped one of her legs around his hip and she followed suit with the other. She had never done it in this position, but then again, she'd never been with a guy as strong as Jack. He drove inside and she pulled him closer, with her ankles crossed and her heels pressing on his backside. His kisses came hot and wet, and the pressure built impossibly fast, even more so than the other times they'd made love.

Jack was taking hard, fast thrusts, forcing her hips into the wall, and ragged breaths from her lips. She was already at the edge of her peak. Hovering. Reaching. So close. But not yet. Lexi let her mind go and focused on his kiss, the touch of his skin against hers, and how she could be totally uninhibited with him without worry. She trusted him. Implicitly.

When her body gave way, she burrowed her face in his neck, biting down on his skin while the stubble along his jaw dug into her cheek. She called out against his skin and Jack did, too, only he wasn't quite so quiet. His body convulsed and neither said anything, arms wrapped tightly around each other, both of them struggling for breaths.

Jack gently set her down and stepped into her bathroom to dispose of the condom. When he walked back into her room, Lexi was sprawled on the bed. He happily stretched out next to her.

"That was unbelievable," she said, rolling to her side and placing her hand on his chest.

"Really? It seemed totally believable to me. We work well together."

Jack had an excellent point. Their chemistry was so electric that this part of their relationship was undeniably perfect. The rest of it was great, too, for that matter. "Are you thirsty? Hungry? Can I get you anything?"

"I'd love a glass of water for now." Jack scooted back on the bed, then pulled back half of the duvet and climbed underneath it.

"I'll be right back." Lexi grabbed her silk robe from the closet and wrapped herself in it before padding off to the kitchen. She stood at the fridge, filling two glasses from the water dispenser. Through the kitchen window, she could see the lights on in her parents' house. She still couldn't really believe Jack had made peace with her dad. It was remarkable.

Glasses filled, Lexi also grabbed a package of chocolate sandwich cookies from the pantry to deliver it all to the bedroom. But the instant she walked through the door, she saw the loveliest sight. "Aww. He fell asleep." Jack had turned onto his side, tucked one arm under the pillow and was deep in a peaceful slumber. His eyes were closed, his mouth slack. She set down the glasses of water, perched lightly on the edge of her bed and took out a cookie, nibbling on it as she watched him sleep. Jack had never slept over at her place before, and Lexi knew for a fact that her dad was aware that he was there. Heck, his truck was still in the driveway. But Jack had been working so hard, she couldn't bear to wake him.

She went into her bathroom to brush her teeth and wash her face, then turned off the lights and climbed into bed next to him. It wasn't easy to snuggle with Jack—he was so big. But she could mold her body next to his, and that was what she did. Her only thought as she drifted off to sleep was that she was in big trouble. Not so much with her dad, but with her own heart.

Eleven

Waking up in Lexi's bed shortly before five in the morning was the worst possible start to Jack's week. He stumbled around in the dark, searching for his clothes in the somewhat unfamiliar landscape of Lexi's bedroom, trying not to wake her. When he stubbed his toe on her dresser, he failed.

"Ouch!" He did his best to swallow back his outburst as he hopped around the room on one foot.

"Jack?" Lexi's sleepy voice sounded as disoriented as he felt.

"I'm so sorry I woke you. I'm trying to get my clothes so I can get out of here. I'm going to be late. I'm supposed to meet Rich at the landing strip at six."

Lexi switched on the small lamp on her bedside table, blinking as she got used to the sudden burst of light. "I'm sorry."

Jack grabbed his remaining clothes to finish getting dressed. "You should have woken me last night. My car is out in the driveway…which means your dad knows I slept over. I told him I'd take things slow, and then I do this?"

Lexi laughed quietly. "I'm pretty sure he knows we're having sex, Jack."

"It's not funny. He probably does, but it's the principle of the thing. I want him to know I'm an upstanding guy. This is not what an upstanding guy does."

"It's no big deal. So, you fell asleep. You're exhausted, which is no surprise. You're working like crazy."

Jack drew in a deep breath, trying to clear his head and calm down. He didn't want to blow things with Lexi, and that included messing things up with her dad. "I'm sorry. I guess I'm stressed. The next three days are going to be a nightmare."

Lexi climbed out of bed and grabbed her robe, which was draped over the back of a chair. "I know. And I'm sorry. But try to focus on the big party at Rusty's Wednesday night. You'll be done then." She gently placed her hand on his arm, peering up at him.

As soon as she touched him, he felt a bit better. "You're right. I just need to get through this final push."

"You'll do great."

"Thanks. I should get going." Jack made sure he had his keys and wallet, then walked out into Lexi's living room with her trailing behind him. "Oh, damn. I can't take these boxes for you right now. Can I do it this weekend?"

"Yes. Of course. Don't worry about it."

Jack felt like he was letting everyone down. "I'm sorry. That was the whole reason I came over in the first place."

"Last night was great, Jack. You talked things out with my dad. We got to have some superhot sex. Try to look on the bright side. The boxes can wait."

She was right. Of course. "Thank you for being so amazing."

"Anytime. Now get going." She shooed him toward the door. "Call me if you have a spare minute over the next few days?"

"I'll make time." He pulled her into his arms and kissed her, knowing this blip of time with Lexi would have to fuel him for the next few days. "Talk to you soon."

Jack walked double-time to his car, being very careful to close his door quietly. Moments later, he zipped out the security gate and through Pine Valley, racing home to grab his bags, then turning around to get to the airstrip. Rich and the pilot were waiting for him, but he was only about fifteen minutes late. It could've been worse.

"You okay?" Rich asked as they both buckled in.

"Yeah. Fine. Just preoccupied with the job." In truth, it was more than that. There was this emptiness inside him that refused to go away. He felt unsettled. Off his game. The two things he wanted most felt just out of reach—finishing this job and getting Lexi to take the idea of them as a couple more seriously. All he could do was forge ahead. Do his best. Let things play out as they would.

"You and me both," Rich said. "You and me both."

* * *

As per usual, construction wrapped up with zero time to spare, and it wasn't 100 percent done. There were still a few tiny details to finish, but Rusty had been insistent that they proclaim the project complete. He'd invited a heap of people to the Edmond estate for the celebratory cocktail party, and he said it would've been an embarrassment to postpone. And, despite his trepidation, Jack saw where the old man was coming from. Delaying the shindig would most assuredly cast a pall over the excitement surrounding the Soiree on the Bay project. But the worst part about being late was that he'd had to ask Lexi to meet him at the party. Once again, he felt like he was falling short.

Jack called her as he approached the security gate on the perimeter of the Edmond estate. Ahead, a long line of cars trailed up the driveway, brake lights glowing red against a darkening night sky. Surrounded by miles of pristine ranch land, the property featured a pool, stables and several guesthouses. It was notorious in Royal, one of the largest private tracts within the county limits. Currently a bachelor, Rusty lived here with his daughter, Gina, and stepson Asher. Soiree on the Bay mastermind Billy Holmes also resided on the grounds, currently occupying one of the guest cottages.

"Are you stuck in this traffic jam outside the house?" Jack asked.

"I just parked," Lexi answered. "I'll wait for you outside."

"Perfect. Thanks." Jack drummed his thumbs on the steering wheel, feeling impatient. All he wanted was to see Lexi, have a drink and find somewhere to sit down. Attending a cocktail party was quite literally the last thing he wanted to do right now, but he'd make the best of it.

"It just occurred to me—I don't think I've been to Rusty's since I was a teenager," Lexi said.

"It's been a few months for me. Rusty sometimes invites me to his poker parties."

"I'm surprised you never ran into my dad here," she remarked. "He's not much of a card player, but he loves to smoke cigars with Rusty so he'll sometimes come for one for those games."

"I don't always accept the invitation. Mostly because I don't enjoy losing thousands of dollars in one night the way Rusty does. I'd rather hold on to my money. I guess you could say that old habits die hard." As soon as the words came out of his mouth, he realized that he had one old habit he was eager to cast aside—his penchant for keeping things casual with a woman forever. He'd spent a lot of time thinking over the last three days, imagining what came next for Lexi and him— months of casual dating, long, passionate nights, and a lot of back and forth between their two houses, no matter where she ended up living. He loved what they had together, but there was a voice in his head saying it wasn't enough.

"These cars are not moving fast," Lexi lamented.

"Rusty told me the guest list is huge."

"Are you nervous?" she asked as he got closer to the massive house, which was all lit up in dramatic fashion.

It wasn't nerves he was feeling. "No. I need a nap though. I'm definitely sleeping in this weekend."

"I know you're exhausted. It was so adorable the way you fell asleep the other night at my place."

"Don't remind me," he grumbled. "I'm still unhappy about that."

"Pretty soon, we won't have to worry about it at all. I'll be at my new place."

It made Jack feel a bit better to hear her say "we" along with mention of future plans, but as he got closer to the house and he saw the news van parked out front, his stomach sank. "Oh, crap. The *Royal Tonight!* van is here. That means Mandee Meriweather is going to be there. She's so nosy."

"Seriously. I spoke with her a week or so ago, to tell her about the bank's involvement with Soiree on the Bay, but all she wanted to focus on was you and me."

"You didn't tell me that."

"I guess I forgot."

Finally, the cars were moving ahead. Jack was directed into a parking space in the expansive stone driveway in front of the house. "I'm going to do my best to avoid her. She's given me a hard time in the past, and has this deluded idea that I'm a playboy. Which is utterly ridiculous."

"From everything I've heard it's the truth."

Jack knew that Angie had run her mouth about how many women he had dated. But he didn't want Lexi thinking about that. Ever. "Whatever my sister told you, I'm positive she embellished. She does that."

"Last time I checked, you were happy that your sister and I get along."

He drew in a deep breath. "I am happy about that." He climbed out of his car and clicked his fob to lock the doors. "Where are you?"

Lexi laughed, but the sound wasn't coming only from his phone. "Right behind you."

Jack turned around, confronted by the beautiful sight before him. She was absolutely gorgeous, in a sparkly black dress that made her red hair flame. He couldn't help but gather her up in his arms, spin her around. His whole body felt lighter, just from seeing her. Her kiss was sweet and familiar. Perfect.

"You seem really tense, Jack," she said when he put her back down on the ground.

If only she knew that seeing her made any tension go away. "I'm just tired."

"Let's get you inside and get you a drink. Hopefully that will reenergize you."

"First, I need to tell you that you look absolutely stunning tonight." The words felt so inadequate. She was more than beautiful and sexy. She was everything he'd never known he wanted.

"And *you* look incredibly handsome. But, then again, you always do." She spread her hand across the lapel of his charcoal gray suit.

Jack smiled at the praise. Having her look at him like that was like being under the gaze of an angel. "Thank you." He leaned down and kissed her cheek. "I love having you with me tonight."

Lexi beamed up at him. "I love that you asked me."

A sigh left his lips as he took her hand and they walked up to the wide steps leading up to the Edmond home. Although he appreciated every sweet thing she said, he wanted more. He could admit that to himself. The question was when he could feel good about admitting it to her.

As soon as Lexi and Jack stepped over the threshold of the Edmond home and were greeted by Rusty, she started to feel on edge. She loved Royal, but the pressure in these old money circles, where people came to a party to see and be seen, weighed on her. There was so much judgment and appraisal in the air, everyone trying to outdo each other, and stake their claim in the social pecking order. She may have grown up in this sort of environment, and she may have even thrived in it at times, but in the aftermath of being left at the altar, Lexi had truly learned just how empty and ruthless the trappings of wealth and power could be.

"Jack!" Rusty exclaimed, clapping him on the shoulder. "You're the man of the hour. I'm so glad you're here. There are so many people wanting to talk to you tonight. Including some other investors you should have a chat with. I'd also like you to talk to Mandee Meriweather from *Royal Tonight!* She's doing a big story on the festival. We've got to light a fire under the PR machine."

Jack pulled Lexi closer to his side. "If it's all the same to you, Rusty, I'd like to first focus on getting Lexi and myself a drink. We both could use it."

The tycoon smiled. "Oh, yes. Of course. Please help yourselves. I'll hunt you down in a little bit."

Lexi couldn't help but notice that Rusty had hardly acknowledged her. There had been a time when that really would've irked her, but she could let it go now. That was really progress for her. "What do you want to drink?" she asked Jack as they approached the bar.

"Rusty always has the best of the best, so I'll definitely go for a bourbon. What do you want, sweetheart?"

Lexi was about to tell Jack that she wanted champagne, but she first had to address something else. *"Sweetheart?"*

"What?" Confusion clouded his expression. "Does it bother you that I called you that?"

Lexi enjoyed the expression of affection, but he'd made an unfortunate choice. "I think it's sweet that you want to call me that, but that's the endearment Roger used for me. So, it doesn't feel great to hear it."

Jack's face immediately fell. "I'm so sorry. I didn't know."

"You couldn't have. It's okay. It was still such a sweet thing to say." She hated the thought of hurting Jack's feelings.

"I'll think of something better, okay?"

Lexi pulled him closer as they stepped up to the bar. "Perfect."

Jack ordered their drinks, and they walked over to a relatively quiet corner. The room was packed with people milling around, conversation and music steadily gaining volume. "I don't know how much of this I can take," Jack said.

"But you're the man of the hour."

"That's just an excuse for Rusty to hype the festival."

"Or maybe he sincerely wants to celebrate your accomplishment." Lexi was about to share more encouragement when she saw a bright light out of the corner of her eye. Making her way through the crowd was Mandee Meriweather and a cameraman from *Royal Tonight!*

"Jack Bowden!" Mandee exclaimed, wagging a finger at him. "You've been hiding from me."

"I haven't. Just got here."

"Well, I need an interview with you right now. We *have* to discuss Soiree on the Bay."

Jack didn't seem happy about it but agreed. "Sure. Okay."

Mandee glanced at Lexi. "Hey, Lexi. Do you mind moving out of the shot?"

She had to swallow back how insulted she felt by the request. It hadn't been that long ago that Mandee was eager to interview her, but she reminded herself that tonight was Jack's night. Lexi was here for support. "Gladly."

Mandee cozied up to Jack and Lexi slugged back her champagne, hoping it would help to tamp down her jealousy. The reporter exchanged words with the cameraman, just as Rusty arrived to watch. Jack became noticeably more tense. Lexi's heart really went out to him. She knew how much he did not enjoy being the center of attention.

Mandee looked directly into the camera. "Mandee Meriweather here, broadcasting live from the lavish Edmond estate. Tonight is the scene of a grand cocktail party, where the Royal elite are gathered to honor Jack Bowden, whose company just completed construction on the Soiree on the Bay festival site on Appaloosa Island."

Mandee smiled widely, then turned her attention to Jack, asking about the upcoming festival and the hoops he and his crews had jumped through to get the construction completed on time. Jack provided succinct answers, thinly veiling his annoyance that he had to endure this at all.

"Now, Jack—" Mandee planted her hand on his shoulder "—the last time we talked, you were single.

Since then, lots of folks in Royal have spotted you and Lexi Alderidge together, but when I recently asked her about you, she said that you were just friends. She was adamant that you were nothing more."

Lexi felt as though her stomach had just dropped to her knees. She had given that answer to protect Jack and her. And certainly hadn't meant it the way Mandee made it sound. Lexi stepped closer to the cameraman, trying to catch Jack's attention. When their gazes connected, the disappointment on his face was so profound, it was a dagger plunged straight through her heart. All she could do was mouth, *I'm sorry.*

Jack cleared his throat, then directed his attention to Mandee. "Yes. That's true. Lexi and I are friends. That's it."

Mandee unleashed a sly grin that made Lexi nauseous. She turned to the camera. "You heard it here first, ladies of Royal. Jack Bowden, the man behind the Soiree on the Bay construction, is single."

Jack waited for only a few more seconds before he asked, "Is that it?"

"I got everything I wanted," Mandee answered.

Jack stepped out from the bright camera light and took Lexi's hand. "We need to talk." As ominous as that sounded, she was eager to explain herself. Jack turned to Rusty. "Is there anyone in your study right now?"

Their host shook his head. "No. The door is closed."

"Perfect. Is it okay if I steal it for a few minutes?"

Rusty seemed utterly confused. "Is everything okay, Jack?"

Jack's grip on Lexi's hand loosened ever so slightly, but it felt like he was sending her a message about exactly how unhappy he was. "Everything's perfect. Lexi and I just need to have a chat."

"Don't be long. I have a lot of people I want you to speak with tonight."

"Got it." With Lexi in tow, Jack stalked through the door on the far side of the room and down a quiet hall. He seemed to know exactly where he was going, opening Rusty's office and slipping inside.

"I'm sorry, Jack," Lexi blurted as soon as the door was closed.

"Did you mean it? That we're just friends and that's it?"

"Well, yes. I mean, what else would you have wanted me to say to her? You hate gossip just as much as I do. Did you actually want me to tell her that we were involved?"

He stared down at her, a muscle ticking in his jaw. "I would've hoped that you would tell her the truth. I don't have a lot of patience for skirting that."

Lexi could hardly believe what he was saying. "Her whole job is twisting people's words to try and make them sound more exciting and salacious. I wasn't going to feed into that."

"I see your point. It still doesn't mean it isn't disappointing." Jack shook his head and paced to the other side of the room. "Or frustrating. Or slowly driving me crazy."

Lexi felt as though she was completely out of her depth. "Frustrating you how? I don't understand what you're trying to say."

He came to a stop and looked her square in the eye. "I love you, Lexi. I love you and it hurts like hell to know that you aren't where I am. It hurts to know that

I've finally found the person I want to be with and she's not sure."

Lexi needed a minute to absorb the things he'd just said. The thing was, the idea of love wasn't as outlandish as the reason why she couldn't bear to hear him say it. "I—I don't know what to say."

"You don't feel like I do. I get it. I don't want you to tell me something you don't feel." He turned to the window and hung his head. "And now I feel like a jerk for putting you on the spot."

"It's not that, Jack. Don't feel bad. I don't want that."

"Then what *do* you want, Lexi?"

There was something so simple and yet so devastating about that question. Part of her wanted to go back, to a time when she hadn't been hurt so badly. When she was the old Lexi who took things in stride and had very few troubles. And yet, she knew that she couldn't go back. She knew it as well as her own name. "I want those three words to not hurt so much."

He turned back to her, betrayal blazing in his eyes. "How could it hurt to hear that I love you? You spend so much time questioning the way people feel about you, the way they see you." He stepped closer, his physical presence overwhelming her senses. "And I'm telling you that I look at you and all I know is that I want to see you every day. All I know is that you make me happier than I've ever been."

"Jack. We've known each other for a month."

He froze and his eyes glistened with emotion. "I know. That's what's so scary. I feel like this after a month. Doesn't that mean that what's between us will just grow into more?"

Lexi wished she could feel so optimistic about the

future. Now she really did want to go back—to a mere hour ago, when the genie hadn't yet been let out of the bottle and he'd said those three little words. "Do you want to know why it hurts when you tell me that you love me?"

"Yes. I need to know. Because it doesn't make any sense to me."

"Because the other two men who said those words to me didn't mean it." She heard her voice cracking and wobbling. "I built my life around two people who told me they loved me, but ultimately didn't. And the thought of one more person saying it and later changing their mind? I can't live through that, Jack. Not again."

"I'm not going to change my mind, Lexi."

"You don't know that. They did."

He sucked in a deep breath. He'd never seemed more exasperated. "I don't know what I can do to convince you. And whatever it is, I don't see a way I'm supposed to persuade you in five minutes when we're standing in Rusty Edmond's study."

"What are you saying, Jack? Are you saying you don't want to see me anymore?"

He pressed his lips together firmly. "I don't think I can move forward if we aren't on the same page. I'm a patient man, Lexi, but there's a limit to that. I think we need to take a break. You need to spend some time thinking and I need to do the same."

Lexi choked back her tears, mindlessly nodding, even when she didn't agree with what he was saying. A break was stupid. It meant breaking up, when she'd felt like they were only getting started. "Okay, then. I'm going to go home."

"You don't have to go. Stay. Have fun." Jack reached for her hand, but Lexi stepped back and headed for the door. It was only going to hurt to touch him. It was just going to break her heart.

"You know as well as I do that there's nothing fun about this."

Twelve

Lexi couldn't sleep after the cocktail party at the Edmond estate. Her bed felt cold and lonely, but it also felt like what she deserved. Everything that had happened last night tumbled through her head like a boulder rolling down a hill—building speed and gaining momentum. The faster her thoughts traveled, the worse they seemed to get.

She couldn't escape the sense that she'd made a huge mistake by telling Jack that it hurt to hear "I love you." It was the truth, but it wasn't the *whole* truth. It wasn't Jack. It wasn't the words. It was the echoes of the pain they'd created. They wouldn't stop reverberating through her head. Through her body. She had to stop giving her history so much power over her. But she didn't know how to do that. Meanwhile, a once-in-a-lifetime man might be slipping away.

A little after 4:00 a.m., she'd had enough of tossing and turning, and decided she had to do something. Going through the final box from Houston seemed like the most obvious choice. If she was going to keep her past from ruining her future, she wanted to discard the remaining physical vestiges of it.

Lexi turned on the overhead light in the living room and walked over to the corner where the boxes sat. She picked up the one unopened carton and lugged it over to her coffee table, cutting the packing tape with a pair of scissors. When she pulled the flaps open, she found a smaller box inside. She already knew what was in there. Lots and lots of old photos. Part of her wanted to simply set it aside for another time. Another day when she wasn't feeling quite so broken.

But no. It was time to do this. She tossed aside the lid and grabbed a stack of photos. They were candids of her and Roger with their friends at a bar. It was the night he'd proposed. Her first reaction was that her hair looked ridiculous. She wasn't sure what she'd been thinking. Her second thought was that she was wearing her fake smile in every picture. She knew that expression. It was the one that appeared when her parents dragged her to an event she didn't want to be at. It was the one she painted on her face when she knew everyone expected her to just be happy.

As she flipped through the final photos, she realized what had been the highlight of that night. It hadn't been the thought of a life with Roger Harrington. Or even the big fat family diamond he gave her. It had been the moment when she'd called her parents and they both cried over the line, telling her how excited they were to tell their friends, how wonderful it would be to plan an enormous wedding.

What she felt with Roger wasn't love. And she was fairly sure that the same went for her feelings for Brett. She was spending time mourning the loss of something that had never been there. And then Jack walked into her life and she'd told herself she still needed to heal because that was what everyone around her was saying. But did she *really* need to heal? Or did she just need to take a single step forward into her future, with the only man who'd managed to make her happy?

Her heart was saying yes, but she wanted to make sure she was thinking straight. She needed Bianca.

You up? She texted her sister a little before 7:00.

I already did my workout. Getting the kids ready for school soon.

Do you have a minute to talk?

Sure.

Lexi dialed her sister and flopped down on the sofa in her living room, staring up at the ceiling.

"What's up?" Bianca asked when she answered.

"I think I ruined my life. Again." She explained everything that had happened last night. "What do I do?"

"I can't answer that for you. Only you know what the solution is."

Lexi picked at her fingernail, thinking about how much she disliked her sister's reply. "That's not helpful."

"Fine. Let's look at the reality. I mean, a guy like

Jack won't stick around forever, especially after he said I love you and you didn't respond in kind."

Her heart lurched at the thought of her panic last night. "That was definitely a mistake. I messed up."

"Well, do you? Love him?"

"Yes." As certain as Lexi was of the answer, the word nearly came out as a whisper.

"Are you sure?"

"I am. It just feels foolish. I thought I loved Brett. I thought I loved Roger. Then I thought I loved Brett again. But none of that worked out, and I don't think I can go through that again. It hurts too much to be rejected."

"And yet that's exactly what you did to Jack last night."

Lexi's stomach sank. "I know. I feel terrible."

"At the very least, he deserves an apology, right?" Bianca asked. "And maybe he's willing to talk it through with you."

"I definitely need to tell him I'm sorry. I just don't know what comes after that, and I know he's going to want to know what I think about a future."

"I want you to close your eyes," her sister told her.

"What? Why?"

"Just do it, okay?"

Lexi grumbled but did exactly what Bianca said, shutting her eyes and staring off into black and nothingness. "They're closed."

"Now imagine you've moved into your own house. Think about one of the places you've looked at. Don't think about tomorrow. I want you to think about a year from now. Imagine your furniture placed exactly the way you want it. Think about what it's going to be like on a Saturday morning, when you have the whole weekend ahead of you."

"Okay."

"What does it look like?"

Lexi imagined the house she'd liked most from the online listings. She imagined the photos she'd seen, pictured it with furniture she picked out, just for her. Everything would be perfect.

But it wasn't going to be home.

Part of that would be because it was new. But part of that would be because it would be empty. She wouldn't have anyone to laugh with. Or cuddle up with. But it was more than that. Because the only one she wanted to do those things with was Jack. He was the only person who'd made her laugh so hard she doubled over. And he was the only one with the courage to call her out when she was being ridiculous. Bianca did that for her, too, but she was her sister, and she had her own life. Lexi wanted a life for herself, as well.

"It looks sad and pathetic and terrible."

"Why does it look like that?"

"Because Jack isn't there." Lexi stifled a sob as the emotion welled up inside her. She wanted Jack. She needed him. She couldn't even envision her future without him. The only problem was that she wanted a guarantee, too. She wanted to know that this time, she wouldn't get hurt. That this time, everything would work out. It would be forever. "Oh, God, Bianca. I'm an idiot, aren't I?"

"You aren't, honey. Don't say that about yourself. You have had a very hard road to travel. Anyone would be reluctant to trust after the things that you've been through. But at some point, you're going to have to get up on that horse and try again."

"But when?" Lexi asked. "How do I know when the time is right?"

"You know what? If I were you, I'd stop focusing on the when and start thinking about the who. Jack is the right guy for you, isn't he?"

"I think so," she answered.

"Then forget the timing. You need to go to him before you lose him forever."

"Okay," Lexi said, feeling neither encouraged nor optimistic. "I need to at least try, right? I need to make sure he knows how I feel."

"You can do it, Lex. I'm sure it feels scary, but I promise you that not doing it will feel worse. You don't want to live with the consequences of that."

"You're right. Thank you. I love you."

"See?" Bianca declared. "It's not so hard to say. I love you, too."

Lexi cracked a smile. "I need to go, okay?"

"Yes. Go."

Lexi hung up and immediately called Jack, but she got his voice mail. "Jack. It's Lexi. I'm hoping we can talk. Please call me back." She ended the call and said virtually the same thing in a text, but after ten minutes, she still didn't have a response. Her other option was to call Angie. She didn't relish the idea. Angie and Jack were incredibly close, and she could only imagine what Jack might have said to his sister after last night. But at this point, it seemed like a better choice to risk whatever Angie might say to her than to endure another minute of Jack thinking she didn't care.

"Lexi, hi," Angie said when she answered her phone.

"I need to speak to Jack, and I can't reach him on his phone and he's not replying to my texts."

"He's out on Appaloosa Island. You know how spotty the reception is out there. I texted him an hour ago and I still haven't heard back. If you want, I can tell him to call you when he checks in."

"Why is he out there? The construction is done." It occurred to Lexi that Angie was being remarkably kind to her, not treating her at all like the woman who'd stomped on her brother's heart.

"They're going through the punch list and some final inspections. Plus, honestly, I think he just likes it out there. He could've easily sent Rich to finish up."

"He does love the house." Lexi's memories of her time on Appaloosa with Jack flooded her mind. She had never felt so free as she had when they were there. Jack had opened up her whole world, which was remarkable, since they came from such dissimilar backgrounds. Logic said that Lexi was the one who came from money and sophistication, that it was her place to show him the finer things. But she knew now that it wasn't the nice things she craved. It was everything that was real. How could she have been so dumb as to have not seen that all along?

"Do you think he'll be on the site? It's massive. I could be looking forever."

"You're planning on going out there? Is everything okay?"

"You don't know that he and I broke up, do you?"

Angie audibly gasped. "I don't! He hasn't said a thing about it. But he was in an incredibly bad mood this morning. I figured he was just grumpy because the Soiree on the Bay project was done. He gets like that after a big job."

"Unfortunately, it's all my fault. I have to go talk to him. I need to explain myself before he never speaks to me again."

"Let me call Rich, and I'll find out exactly where he is. I can text it to you?"

"Sounds great. I'll leave right now."

"I'm wondering if you'll make it in time, though. He could be on his way back by the time you drive down there and take the ferry over."

"Oh, I'm not driving. I'm flying." Lexi hung up and realized that Jack was going to have to listen to her apology while she was wearing what was easily her least-cute dress and no makeup. There was no time to change into something sexier or heels, the things that gave her confidence and made her feel feminine. *Jack makes me feel like a woman.* She didn't need the trappings or clothes. She just needed Jack.

She raced to the bank, calling her dad's secretary on the way to make sure the helicopter was available. It was, and Lexi didn't even bother to stop to speak to her father, instead heading straight up to the roof and the helipad. To her great surprise, her dad was waiting for her.

"You're going to see Jack, aren't you?" Winston asked sternly.

"You can't stop me, Dad. I love him and I have to tell him. I've been a certifiable idiot and that ends right now, okay?"

"I wasn't trying to keep you from going, Lexi." Her dad swiped off his sunglasses and looked down at her. "I only wanted to wish you good luck."

"You knew why I needed the helicopter?"

"Your sister and I talk, you know. She tells me everything. She's the one who told me I had to fix things with Jack in the first place."

Lexi should've known it was Bianca who'd set all of that in motion. Lexi would have to thank her, after she chided her for meddling. "My sister is crazy."

"She loves you. Just like your mother and I do. Just like we always will." Her dad pulled her into a hug. "I love you, Alexis. I just want you to be happy. If Jack Bowden makes you happy, I hope you'll have the courage to try to make it work with him."

Lexi smiled and sank into her father's hug. This was all she'd ever wanted from him. Ever. "Thank you, Dad. I'd better go. I don't want to miss him."

"Yes. You go on. I had Vi leave you a surprise on board." Winston shooed her toward the helicopter.

Confounded, Lexi ran over to where the pilot was waiting. He opened the door for her and she climbed inside. There was a small cooler on the seat. She buckled in, then unzipped the container. Inside was a bottle of champagne on ice and two glasses. Her dad had figured it all out. And she was so relieved.

As the rotors gained speed and the helicopter lifted into the air, Lexi looked out the window as Royal became tinier and the details less defined. That was her past, but ahead was her whole future.

It took Jack only a few hours to supervise the items on the punch list. Inspections wouldn't come until tomorrow, so he'd spend the night on Appaloosa and try to straighten out his head. Yes, this had been a bit of a fool's errand to come back to the island, but Jack needed the sea air right now. Everything in Royal felt stifling. Even out on his own property, with stretches of open land at his feet, and no one to bother him, he felt like he couldn't breathe. Life just wasn't going to be right without Lexi, and he was struggling to figure out what his next step was.

Logic said that he needed to give her space. Again. Now that he'd had a little bit of sleep and was out of the pressure cooker of that stupid cocktail party last night, he knew that he could do that. The question was how long he could keep it up. How long until he started to feel that weight again? A month? Two? He wasn't worried about meeting or falling for someone else. What worried him was that Lexi might never be ready. She'd had her heart ground into the dirt twice. That might be as much as she could take. Jack had endured it only once, and it had taken him a decade to fully recover. And honestly, he wasn't sure he had that kind of patience to wait for her to come around. He was staring down his fortieth birthday in a few weeks. It sure would be nice to know that love would be a part of his next decade on the planet. Bottom line? He wanted it all. Marriage. Commitment. Maybe even kids.

But those things seemed like an impossible wish without Lexi. Thus, he was spending his time out on Appaloosa Island, if only to clear his head.

Jack wandered over to the golf cart that belonged to the house he'd rented. He drove along, winding his way down the now-paved pathways, past everything he and his teams had built. After all the hard work they had poured into this project, he was proud of the job they'd all done here and he couldn't wait for the festival. It would be a true spectacle, a real boon for the entire area, and he was pleased that he'd had a chance to play a part in that.

When he crossed over to the western side of the island, he made his way north, up to the house he'd rented. As soon as he pulled into the driveway, his phone started buzzing like crazy with notifications.

"I must've just hit the Wi-Fi for the house," he said, pulling his phone out of his pocket. The first text was from Angie, asking where he was. Jack pinged her his location and replied that he wanted to be left alone for the rest of the day. He didn't bother with the rest of his messages. They could wait. He needed time to just be, which was exactly why he'd headed to Appaloosa in the first place.

He went inside and ran up to the bedroom to grab a clean shirt. It wasn't easy to look at that room and think about the electric nights he and Lexi had spent there. That was when he'd first known he was falling for her. Hopefully he wouldn't be stuck with nothing more than memories when it came to Lexi. It could go either way, and he had to learn to live with that inevitability.

He grabbed a beer from the fridge and headed out to the porch on the front of the house, where the long line of rocking chairs pitched forward and back in the wind. Ahead was the quiet of the private beach and the beautiful blue between Appaloosa and the Texas shore.

He closed his eyes to the rush of salty air as it blew his hair back from his face. If he had to be alone, this was the way to do it. The only trouble was he didn't want to be by himself. Life would mean so much more if he could just find the right person, or in his case, convince the right woman that he was worth the risk.

The door behind him slid open. Jack jumped out of his seat and turned. Lexi was standing there with those same island breezes blowing back her hair, looking like everything he'd ever wanted. For a moment, he wondered if he'd fallen asleep in the chair and this was all a dream. Lexi didn't say a thing. She only looked at him, expectantly. Like she wanted something but couldn't bring herself to utter the words.

"Lexi?" He took a step closer. Her sweet smell hit his nose and that was when he knew that she was real. But he truly knew he wasn't dreaming when she flung herself at him, nearly knocking him from his feet— quite a feat considering he was twice her size.

"Oh, my God, Jack. I made a huge mistake. I was such an idiot. I never should've said that I wanted to take things slow."

He gripped both of her shoulders and peered down into her stunning face. "Lexi, I don't ever want you to apologize for asking for the things you need."

She dropped her head to one side, almost as if she was disappointed. "I need you to stop making excuses for me. I messed up and I'm so sorry. I'm an idiot. Just ask my sister. She'll tell you all about it."

He shook his head. "Thank you for apologizing. I appreciate that, but I also know you didn't mean to hurt me. You were being honest, and that's not easy to do."

"But I did hurt you. It doesn't matter whether it was my intention to do so or not. It only matters that I did."

"I understand where you were coming from. I do. I had a lot more time to go through the healing process after my big breakup, and you had two to get over. I don't want you to be so hard on yourself."

"But that's the thing. If I'm not hard on myself, I'm not going to get what I want."

At the risk of repeating himself, he had to ask the same question he'd asked last night. "And what is it that you want?"

"You, Jack. I just want you."

He felt the corners of his mouth turn up in a smile, his body's instant reaction to her perfect answer. "Really?"

"Yes." She nodded eagerly. "I love you, Jack. I do. I should have had the guts to say it last night. It might sound stupid, but I think I've loved you from that moment out in front of Sheen when you said that you didn't want to talk about any man who didn't have the sense to treat me right."

"Those are just words, Lexi. Any guy can say nice things to a woman. I want you to judge me on my actions."

"And on that count, you've done everything right, too. You're always there for me. You stood up to my dad. You brought me into your life, even when you knew that I might not quite fit."

He could hardly believe what she was saying. He still wasn't sure he wasn't in the middle of a dream. "What do you want to do about this? I think you already know how I feel. I love you. I truly do. And I'm glad that you felt like you could say that to me, too, but you don't have to say something just to be with me." Cradling her face in his hands, he gently stroked her cheek. "If you aren't ready for that leap, I understand."

"I didn't say it just to hold on to you, Jack. I'm saying it because it's what's in my heart. It's what's in my head. I just had to get out of my own way. I'm ready to leap."

Jack's heart was threatening to beat right out of his chest. "What does that mean, exactly?"

She put her hand on his waist and flattened herself against his stomach. "For starters, a few days here on Appaloosa? So we can talk about what we want to do next?"

He pulled her closer and kissed the top of her head, feeling so relieved and overcome with joy that it was difficult to comprehend. He'd hoped for this moment, but he hadn't been sure it would ever happen. "You're going to have to take the lead here, beautiful. Because I want it all with you. I don't want you to buy a house. I want you to move into mine."

She pulled her head back, her bright eyes full of purpose. "We're going to have to have some negotiations about furniture. There are a few things I'd like to change in your living room."

He laughed. "Like what?"

"Do we really need a TV that big?"

"Actually, yes. We do." He leaned lower and kissed her cheek, then her jaw. "But we can talk about furniture. I've been meaning to get a new couch."

"See? This is how negotiations go." She brought her lips to his, delivering one of her incredible kisses. It was soft and tender and everything he'd ever wanted. "I love you, Jack. I will move in with you. I will rearrange your furniture. I will do it all over again in this house if we decide to buy it. And I will stay with you as long as you'll have me."

"Forever, Lexi. That's how long."

"Forever."

Jack's smile was so wide he wasn't sure he'd ever be able to get rid of the expression. He was happier than he'd ever been. Happier than he'd ever thought possible. "Careful, Lexi. It sounds like we're making plans."

"That's exactly what we're doing. Being with you is all I want, and I don't want to wait."

* * * * *

We really hope you enjoyed reading this book.
If you're looking for more romance, be sure to
head to the shops when new books are
available on

Thursday 1st
April

To see which titles are coming soon, please visit

millsandboon.co.uk/nextmonth

LET'S TALK
Romance

For exclusive extracts, competitions
and special offers, find us online:

f facebook.com/millsandboon

🐦 @MillsandBoon

📷 @MillsandBoonUK

Get in touch on 01413 063232

For all the latest titles coming soon, visit
millsandboon.co.uk/nextmonth

A ROMANCE FOR EVERY READER

MODERN

Prepare to be swept off your feet by sophisticated, sexy and seductive heroes, in some of the world's most glamourous and romantic locations, where power and passion collide.

HISTORICAL

Escape with historical heroes from time gone by. Whether your passion i for wicked Regency Rakes, muscled Vikings or rugged Highlanders, awa the romance of the past.

MEDICAL

Set your pulse racing with dedicated, delectable doctors in the high-pres sure world of medicine, where emotions run high and passion, comfort love are the best medicine.

True Love

Celebrate true love with tender stories of heartfelt romance, from the rush of falling in love to the joy a new baby can bring, and a focus on t emotional heart of a relationship.

Desire

Indulge in secrets and scandal, intense drama and plenty of sizzling ho action with powerful and passionate heroes who have it all: wealth, stat good looks…everything but the right woman.

HEROES

Experience all the excitement of a gripping thriller, with an intense ro mance at its heart. Resourceful, true-to-life women and strong, fearless face danger and desire - a killer combination!

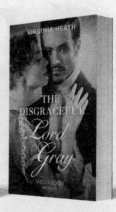

Prepare to be swept off your feet by sophisticated, sexy and seductive heroes, in some of the world's most glamourous and romantic locations, where power and passion collide.

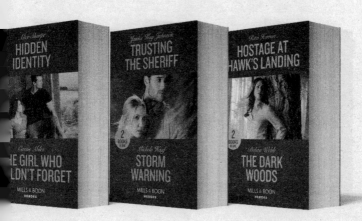

Sensual love stories featuring smart, sassy heroines you'd want as a best friend, and compelling intense heroes who are worthy of them.

MILLS & BOON
True Love
Romance from the Heart

Celebrate true love with tender stories of
heartfelt romance, from the rush of falling
in love to the joy a new baby can bring,
and a focus on the emotional
heart of a relationship.

We Love
Romance
with MILLS & BOON